Catherine Cookson was born in Tyne Dock, the illegitimate daughter of a poverty-stricken woman, Kate, whom she believed to be her older sister. She began work in service but eventually moved south to Hastings where she met and married a local grammar-school master. At the age of forty she began writing about the lives of the working-class people with whom she had grown up, using the place of her birth as the background to many of her novels.

Although originally acclaimed as a regional writer – her novel *The Round Tower* won the Winifred Holtby award for the best regional novel of 1968 – her readership soon began to spread throughout the world. Her novels have been translated into more than a dozen languages and more than 50,000,000 copies of her books have been sold in Corgi alone. Ten of her novels – *The Fifteen Streets*, *The Black Velvet Gown*, *The Black Candle*, *The Man Who Cried*, *The Cinder Path*, *The Dwelling Place*, *The Glass Virgin*, *The Gambling Man*, *The Tide of Life* and *The Girl* – have been made into successful television dramas, and more are planned.

Catherine Cookson's many bestselling novels have established her as one of the most popular of contemporary women novelists. After receiving an OBE in 1985, Catherine Cookson was created a Dame of the British Empire in 1993. She and her husband Tom now live near Newcastle-upon-Tyne.

'Catherine Cookson has an unrivalled capacity to tap sources of human behaviour'
Elizabeth Buchan, *Sunday Times*

OTHER BOOKS BY CATHERINE COOKSON

NOVELS

Kate Hannigan
The Fifteen Streets
Colour Blind
Maggie Rowan
Rooney
The Menagerie
Slinky Jane
Fanny McBride
Fenwick Houses
Heritage of Folly
The Garment
The Fen Tiger
The Blind Miller
House of Men
Hannah Massey
The Long Corridor
The Unbaited Trap
Katie Mulholland
The Round Tower
The Nice Bloke
The Glass Virgin
The Invitation
The Dwelling Place
Feathers in the Fire
Pure as the Lily
The Mallen Streak
The Mallen Girl
The Mallen Litter
The Invisible Cord
The Gambling Man
The Tide of Life
The Slow Awakening
The Iron Façade
The Girl

The Cinder Path
Miss Martha Mary Crawford
The Man Who Cried
Tilly Trotter
Tilly Trotter Wed
Tilly Trotter Widowed
The Whip
Hamilton
The Black Velvet Gown
Goodbye Hamilton
A Dinner of Herbs
Harold
The Moth
Bill Bailey
The Parson's Daughter
Bill Bailey's Lot
The Cultured Handmaiden
Bill Bailey's Daughter
The Harrogate Secret
The Black Candle
The Wingless Bird
The Gillyvors
My Beloved Son
The Rag Nymph
The House of Women
The Maltese Angel
The Year of the Virgins
The Golden Straw
Justice is a Woman
The Tinker's Girl
A Ruthless Need
The Obsession
The Upstart

THE MARY ANN STORIES

A Grand Man
The Lord and Mary Ann
The Devil and Mary Ann
Love and Mary Ann

Life and Mary Ann
Marriage and Mary Ann
Mary Ann's Angels
Mary Ann and Bill

FOR CHILDREN

Matty Doolin
Joe and the Gladiator
The Nipper
Rory's Fortune
Our John Willie
Mrs Flannagan's Trumpet

Go Tell It To Mrs Golightly
Lanky Jones
Nancy Nuttall and the Mongrel
Bill and the Mary Ann Shaughnessy

AUTOBIOGRAPHY

Our Kate
Catherine Cookson Country

Let Me Make Myself Plain
Plainer Still

THE CINDER PATH

Catherine Cookson

CORGI BOOKS

THE CINDER PATH
A CORGI BOOK : 0 552 14260 3

Originally published in Great Britain by
William Heinemann Ltd

PRINTING HISTORY
William Heinemann edition published 1978
Corgi edition published 1979
Corgi edition reissued 1979
Corgi edition reprinted 1979
Corgi edition reprinted 1985
Corgi edition reprinted 1986
Corgi edition reprinted 1988
Corgi edition reprinted 1989 (twice)
Corgi edition reprinted 1991
Corgi edition reprinted 1992
Corgi edition reissued 1993
Corgi edition reissued 1994
Corgi edition reprinted 1996

Set in 11/13$\frac{1}{2}$ pt Compugraphic English Times by
Colset Private Limited, Singapore.

Corgi Books are published by Transworld Publishers Ltd,
61–63 Uxbridge Road, London W5 5SA,
in Australia by Transworld Publishers (Australia) Pty Ltd,
15–25 Helles Avenue, Moorebank, NSW 2170
and in New Zealand by Transworld Publishers (NZ) Ltd,
3 William Pickering Drive, Albany, Auckland.

Printed and bound in Great Britain by
Cox & Wyman Ltd, Reading, Berkshire.

*To the one and only
to whom I owe so much*

Contents

PART ONE

Moor Burn Farm

1

'Bless the food on this table, Lord. Bless my labour that has provided it and give me strength for this day. Amen.'

'Amen. Amen. Amen.'

Before the echo of the last amen faded, Edward MacFell was firmly seated in the big wooden arm-chair at the top of the table, and during the seconds of silence that followed he screwed his heavy but-tocks further into the seat before, with an almost imperceptible motion of his head, giving the three people standing behind their chairs permission to sit, and the elderly woman and young girl on their knees just inside the door of the room permission to rise.

Sitting in silence facing her husband, Mary MacFell wondered, and not for the first time, what would happen if she were suddenly to open her tight-lipped mouth and scream. Yet she knew what would happen; he'd drag her outside and throw her bodily into the horse trough. And if this didn't restore her to his idea of sanity, he'd despatch her to the madhouse and leave her there to rot, whilst he himself would continue here with his daily work as appointed by God.

Her husband and God were on the best of terms; in fact she sometimes thought he handed out orders to God for the day: 'Now today, God, you'll not only clean the byres you will lime wash them; then you will clamp the beet, all of it, mind, and you will do it yourself, don't expect Dawson or Ryton to give you a hand.' He always called people by their surnames, other farmers used Christian names. Over at Brooklands, Hal Chapman always called his men Bob, Ronnie, Jimmy. But not so Edward MacFell. No, if God had a Christian name he would still have addressed Him as God, not Bob, Ronnie, or Jimmy . . . Jimmy God. That was funny, Jimmy God.

Her mind rarely offered her anything to laugh about for her sense of humour which had never been strong was entirely blunted, but now a strange noise erupted from her throat and brought all eyes on her. Her husband's, which seemed to have no white to them but to be made up entirely of a thick, opaque brown substance that toned with his square weather-beaten face and thick shock of dark hair which showed not a streak of grey for all of his forty-eight years, were fastened hard upon her.

Her son's eyes, clear grey, held that constant tenderness that irritated and annoyed her for it expressed his alienation from his surroundings and those of the immediate household, and this included herself.

She sometimes thought that her husband, in spite of all his sly cleverness and his power, was ignorant and blind because he could not see that there was no part of himself in his son, and that the education of which he was insisting his son have the benefit would, in the end, separate them. He thought to make his son a gentleman farmer, utterly ignoring the fact that the boy, although born and bred on the farm, had no leanings whatsoever towards the land. All he thought about was reading, and tramping the countryside, at times like someone in a daze, or not quite right in the head. Moreover, the boy at sixteen was tall and fair and was as unlike his father in looks as he was in character. Yet she knew that her husband was inordinately proud of his son, almost as proud of him as he was of his farm and his fifty acres of freehold land.

Her daughter Betty's eyes, which were fixed tight on her father, were a replica of his own, the only difference being that the brown of the small irises was clear and there was a rim of white to be seen around their edges. Her nose, too, was the same as his, not only long and thin but swelling to a knob at its end; and her mouth, which as yet at fourteen was a thick-lipped pouted rosebud, would undoubtedly widen into sensuousness and become at variance with her other features.

She was startled into awareness by her husband speaking to Fanny Dimple. 'Stop fumbling, woman! And what have I told you about those hands?'

It shattered, too, the waiting silence at the table. It was not a coarse or loud voice, nor did it have a distinctive Northumbrian burr to it, but it was a voice that always arrested its hearers. Those hearing MacFell speak for the first time, in most cases, were unable to hide their surprise, for it was a cultured voice, melodious, belying his lack of education and being completely at variance with the sturdy roughness of his body and features.

Edward MacFell's eyes now travelled from Fanny Dimple's gnarled work-worn hands to her face where the loose skin was drawn upwards by strands of her grey hair knotted tight on the back of her head and hidden under a white starched cap that had the appearance of a bonnet.

'If you can't keep your nails clean cut them off down to the quick, or I'll do them for you!'

'They're already at the quick, master.'

The knife and fork almost bounced off the table, so fiercely did he bang them down. 'Don't dare answer me back, woman!'

His face consumed with rage, he glared at his servant who had been maid of all work in the house for years, and she, as if she had lost her senses, as those at the table thought she had, glared back at him; then turning away, she lifted two bowls of porridge from a tray that young Maggie Benton was holding, and walked to the end of the table where she placed one bowl before her mistress and the other in front of her young master. Returning to the tray, she lifted the last bowl. This she laid, none too gently this time, in front of the only daughter of the house.

Now making no effort to quieten her withdrawal, she went from the room into the long narrow hall lit by two small windows, one at each side of the front door, through a green-baized door and into the kitchen. *And* it was as she turned to close this door that she gave vent to another bout of defiance. Stretching out her arms, she grabbed the handle and thrust the door violently forward.

An ordinary door would have made a resounding crash, so fiercely had she thrust it, but the green-baized door merely fell into place with a muffled thud.

'Him and his gentry doors!'

The green-baized door was a recent acquisition. When they were pulling down the old manor house her master had gone there precisely to buy the door, and afterwards had personally supervised Fred Ryton and Arnold Dawson as they hung it in place of the scarred oak one.

Fanny now came to the table where Maggie Benton was standing gaping at her, and the small girl took in a deep breath before exclaiming, 'Eeh! Mrs Dimple.'

Maggie knew what had upset Mrs Dimple; it was the cinder path; but to answer the master back, and him after only just saying grace. Eeh! she had never known anything like it. Wait till she got home and told them.

'He's a cruel bugger.' Fanny was leaning across the table, her jaw thrust out towards Maggie.

'Aye. Aye, he is, Mrs Dimple.'

'He thinks he's God Almighty and can scare the daylights out of you with just a look. Well, here's one he can't scare. He's a fornicatin' hypocrite, that's what he is. Him and his mornin' prayers and havin' us kneel! Copyin' the gentry again. I had to kneel with the rest of 'em when I was at Lord Cleverley's; but there was twenty-eight of us inside the house and he was a gentleman, his lordship. But him back there, well, he's a sin unto God and takes others with him. An' *you* know what I mean, Maggie Benton, don't you?'

Maggie turned her eyes away from the thrust-out chin. Her head drooped. Yes, she knew what Mrs Dimple meant; no one was supposed to know but everybody on the farm knew. Except, she thought, Master Charles and the missis. Even so she had her doubts about the missis. She never really knew what the missis was thinking, she was so quiet. There was one, though, she wished didn't know, but she knew that he knew all right. Oh aye, he knew, her da knew, you could see it in his face.

Her poor da. He wasn't long for the top. She'd miss him when he went. But not as much as their Polly would. Their Polly would go mad when he died, 'cos their Polly had looked after him for so long now. She had feelin's had their Polly, and that had been proved again this morning 'cos eeh! look how she had got upset about the cinder path and Ginger Slater.

They all knew that Ginger Slater was for the cinder path at nine o'clock, and that was the cruel part of it, Polly said, the waiting to be thrashed. If the master had done it straight off when he had caught him looking at the picture book again, Polly said, she could have understood it, but to make him wait a whole day with his mind on it, it was like a sentence to be hung, she said.

Of course, being a workhouse lad, Ginger expected to be badly treated, and it wasn't the first time he had been on the cinder path, and all because of books. That was funny because, like everybody else who lived on the farm and in the row, he had had the chance to go in the cart to school. He had gone for a time, but then the master, like all the parents, saw no need for so much schooling; in fact they were all dead against it, especially the parents, for it meant the loss of wages, so with one excuse and another they kept them off most of the time. She herself had got off through a bad chest, but when she was there she had learnt her letters and to read a little bit, but Ginger, who wasn't daft in any way, had never picked up reading. The teacher had skelped his backside raw, but still he couldn't read. And yet more than any of them, he wanted to. Oh aye, he did that; that's why he went after books; and that's why he was for the cinder path.

The only one who'd had any real schooling was their Polly. Once when their da was a bit better she had gone to school for over a year at one go, but when he collapsed again and Bob the carrier died about the same time that put an end to it, for she couldn't do the five miles each way for half-a-day's learning. And she, too, wanted to learn; like Ginger, she wanted to learn.

As if Fanny had been picking up her thoughts, she said, 'That lad's bright, he wants to learn; but how in the name of God did he get up to the attic and get that story book!'

'He must have scaled the drainpipe.'

'Aye, that's the only way. But why didn't he ask Master Charlie, he'd have sneaked him a book. I would have meself if I'd known he'd wanted one so badly. But why anybody wants to read I don't know, we learn enough bad things by listenin' and lookin' without pickin' them up off a page.'

'It wasn't a bad book, Mrs Dimple, an' it was an old 'un, it had all the weekly *Chatterboxes* in it for 1895. Master Charlie once lent it to our Polly, an' she read it out to us: all about Mr Dickens an' his little Nell. An' there was wonderful pictures in it. One we laughed at was of pigs pulling a plough. In France that was. I told Ginger about it an' how it said pigs is sensible and could be made to count. You know what, Mrs Dimple?' Maggie now bit on her lip, and became thoughtful. 'Perhaps that's why he picked on that book because I told him about pigs bein' clever.'

'Don't be daft, girl. How could he pick on it if he couldn't read, your readin' hasn't given you sense. That's evident.'

'But he'd seen the book, Mrs Dimple, when our Polly gave it back to Master Charlie, an' he would know 'cos it was big an' in a black cover.'

Fanny stared at Maggie for a moment; then shaking her head impatiently, she said, 'Aw, let's get on ... Listen! there's the bell, and he's knockin' hell out of it. He can't wait to stuff himself now in order to give his right arm strength. God blast him! And He will one of these days, I'm tellin' you.' Fanny now stabbed her finger towards Maggie. 'He won't be mocked, not God, he'll get his desserts, him in there.' Her arm now swung in the direction of the green-baized door. 'An' I hope I'm here to see it. I'll dance on his grave, I will that.'

Eeh! the things Mrs Dimple said. Maggie shook her head as she watched the older woman bang the covered dishes on to the tray, saying as she did so, 'They had their breakfast served up on plates at one time but now it's covered dishes to match the green-baized door. Eeh! the things one lives to see. Get goin'!' She lifted the tray and thrust it into Maggie's hand, and her final words sent the girl scurrying towards the door: 'I hope it chokes him.'

2

It was said that there had been a farm at Moor Burn for the past three hundred years but that the house in those bygone days had been little more than a cottage. The land had been farmed from the earliest times by a family named Morley, and for two hundred and fifty years one Morley had succeeded another, and as each prospered so he added his quota to the house.

The last extension had been in 1840, to accommodate the ever growing family of the then present owner; but the fact that this man sired fifteen children and only two survived to reach thirty, and they both girls, tended to turn his mind, and he became convinced there was a curse on the place for his Bible showed that although there had never been more than two Morleys in any generation, the survivors up till then had been male, so he decided to be gone from the place.

It was about this time on a day in 1858 that William MacFell came riding back from the Scottish side of Carter Bar, accompanied by his wife, after having attended her father's funeral. And he was a happy man at that time, at least as happy as his nature would allow – for his wife had come in to a tidy sum of money.

It should so transpire that the trap they had hired almost lost one of its two wheels just after they had passed Kirkwhelpington, and it was Farmer Morley's younger daughter who came upon them and led them over the fields and along the paths to the farm, the freehold farm that was up for sale. It was then that William MacFell decided to become a farmer . . . on his wife's money. When his wife pointed out to him that it would be an utterly different life from working in a gentlemen's hatters, he had replied briefly that that was precisely the reason why he wanted to farm.

Christine MacFell had not protested against her money being used in this fashion; she had given up protesting years ago when she realised that her people had been right from the beginning and that she had lowered herself in marrying the hatter. Her idea of bringing out the real man she imagined to be hidden beneath the taciturn skin had been a failure, a frightening failure, for what had emerged was an individual given to bouts of ferocious temper, and it was this temper he used as a weapon when thwarted in any way.

So the MacFells took up residence at Moor Burn Farm and although you could walk in the district for hours and not see a soul, and the houses were few and far between, William MacFell soon became well known. Those in the big houses scattered around ignored him, he was of less account to them than one of their dogs; the real farmers laughed at him behind his back; the tradesmen served him but with no respect, to them he was a jumped-up nowt. Only the hands he engaged on the farm feared him, for gone was the security they had felt under Farmer Morley, because the present owner would, they knew, should they displease him, turn them out of their cottages on to the road without giving the matter a second thought.

And then there was the cinder path.

The ashes from the fires in the house and from the piggery boiler had been strewn on the yard to sop up the mud in bad weather, and over the years the remainder had formed a sizeable mound behind the cow byres. Tle byres were almost opposite the kitchen door, and, between them and the barn, was a narrow passage that led out to an open space bordered on two sides by a privet hedge where the cinders were dumped, or at least where they had been dumped, for one of the first things that William MacFell did was to order his men to level the dump. He decided on a path being made from the back of the byres where the ground ran level, to where, thirty yards distant, it sloped down towards the burn, beside which stood the tiny two-roomed dilapidated cottage.

When the mound of cinders was levelled, the path to the burn was only three parts made, but each morning the maid of all work gradually lengthened it by adding to it the huge buckets of cinders taken from the house.

Why, asked the farmhands of each other, did he want a path leading down there? The stone cottage would never be used again; and who wanted to go and look at the burn at that point where it was only a couple of yards wide?

William MacFell didn't give his reasons for taking the path down to the burn, but it soon became evident that he had another use for it, and the first example he gave of this was when he took his eight-year-old son by the collar, threw him on to the cinders, and laid about his back with a birch stick.

That was the beginning.

Jimmy Benton was the next to experience what it was like to be thrown on the cinder path. He was seven years old at the time and scarecrowing on the farm. Jimmy had at an early age developed a taste for raw eggs; he had discovered they would keep him going and would take the gnawing hungry feeling from his stomach.

The morning he stole two eggs from the hen cree William MacFell caught him, and, taking the eggs from him, he had without a word lifted him up bodily by the scruff of the neck and, ignoring the boy's flaying arms and legs . . . and howls, he had thrown him on to the path where the cinders had torn at the palms of his hands and his bare knees. He had thrown one egg after the other on to the back of the boy's head, then kicked him in the buttocks. The action had lifted the child from his hands and knees and sent him sprawling flat out.

The boy's father had been for going and knocking

23

hell out of William MacFell, but the mother reminded him that it was their livelihood, and after all the boy was only scraped on his hands and knees.

With the youngsters on the farm, the cinder path became a fear. The mothers in the cottages no longer threatened the children with the bogey man, but with the cinder path. One thing the farm workers did say in favour of their master, he had no favourites for the path for he treated his own son to an equal share of it.

Such are the quirks of nature that instead of Edward MacFell hating his father, the boy admired him and if he had ever really loved anyone it was his male parent. His mother, to whom one would have expected him to turn, she being of a sympathetic and gentle nature, he almost ignored. Perhaps it was because subconsciously he sensed that she had no love for him, for in character and looks he was the facsimile of her husband.

Edward MacFell was twenty-seven years old when his father had died. William had left no will for the simple reason that he had imagined wills precipitated death, and so according to law Edward was entitled to two-thirds of the estate and his mother to one-third. That almost immediately the legal affairs were settled his mother should take her share and leave the farm to join a cousin in Scotland came as no surprise to him; rather it afforded him a great deal of relief. He was no longer responsible for her; now he could look round for a wife, a wife who was different but, like his mother, someone with a bit of class.

He knew only too well in what esteem his father had been held in the surrounding countryside, and he set out to show them that he himself was different, that he was no ordinary tinpot little farmer, he was as good as they came in the county, and he determined to make the farm an example for others because it contained some of the best pasture land in the county, besides fields that yielded reasonable grains. Even Hal Chapman, over in Brooklands, had had to admit there wasn't another place like it for miles, and he was an authority on land was Chapman.

Edward MacFell was thirty when he married, and like his father before him he, too, aimed high. In his case he went even further than his father for he chose to honour the daughter of a Newcastle surgeon. The surgeon had, the previous year, died, otherwise it was debatable whether he would have countenanced the marriage. But his nineteen-year-old daughter Mary Rye-Davidson was living under the guardianship of an old aunt and uncle, who seemed only too ready to be rid of their frivolous fair-haired, blue-eyed charge, and they congratulated each other on having spent their holiday in Hexham, where their niece had been fortunate enough to meet the sturdy, prosperous farmer.

At what time after the marriage both Edward MacFell and his wife, Mary, realised their joint mistake neither of them could pin-point, but it was well within the first six months.

For MacFell's part, he realised he'd married a

scatter-brain, a woman who, if she had been allowed, would have spent her time reading, playing the harpsichord, and titivating herself up with new clothes. Now these things in their place were all right for it proved that she was of the class, but that she had no intention of using her hands to cook or to help in the dairy, and wasn't even capable of managing the house, infuriated him, and for the first time in his life he began to appreciate his mother and her qualities that had gone unrecognised during all their years together.

As for Mary MacFell, she was brought out of a girlish dream to the realisation that she had married, not a strong, silent lover, but a man with a fiendish temper, and an egotistical ignorant one into the bargain. During the first month of their marriage she playfully opposed him, but these tactics came to an abrupt end when one day, feeling bored, she dared, without asking his leave, to take the trap and drive into Otterburn. On her return he almost dragged her upstairs. What he did was literally to tear the clothes from her back, then, his face red with passion, to thrust it close to hers as he growled at her, 'You take anything on yourself like that again and begod I'll put you on the cinder path.'

When her first child was born Mary MacFell experienced a secret happiness. At his birth her son looked like her, and as he grew he developed more like her. He took on her tall, thin fairness; the only difference in their features being his eyes, which were round, while hers were oval-shaped, and whereas hers were blue, his were grey.

The contrariness of MacFell's nature made itself evident again as he grew fulsomely proud of the son who showed no resemblance to himself, yet when, two years later, his wife gave him a daughter who, as she grew, became a replica of himself, both inside and out, he had little time for her. And again the oddities of nature came into play, for his small dark daughter adored him, while his son secretly feared and hated him.

And never did Charles MacFell hate his father more than at this moment when his eyelids compressed themselves into a deep blink each time the cane came down hard, not only across Ginger Slater's narrow buttocks, but across the backs of his knees, left bare by his breeches being drawn upwards.

As the blows continued to make the small body bounce on the cinders Charlie was unable to witness any more, but as he went to turn away, run away, he was brought to a stiff standstill by the sight of Polly Benton emerging from the further end of the hedge. Polly had one hand held tightly across her mouth while the fingers of the other convulsively gathered up her print skirt until not only did she expose the top of her boots but also her bare shins.

Charlie stood staring at her; and when her hand dropped from her mouth he became aware that the swishing had stopped. He could also hear the crunching of his father's feet on the path and the moaning of the boy he had left behind him.

As he moved towards her, Polly turned and came

towards him, her teeth tightly pressed into her lower lip and her eyes full of tears. When they came abreast neither of them spoke, nor did they move from behind the hedge until the sound of MacFell's voice reached them from the yard; then going quickly on to the path, they bent one on each side of Ginger and pulled him upwards.

'Don't cry, Ginger. Don't cry.'

Ginger's head was deep on his chest and his body was trembling, but once on his feet he tugged his arm away from Charlie's and turned fully towards Polly, and she, putting her arms around him, murmured, 'Come on down to the burn, the water'll cool you.'

Her arm still about him, she led him along the cinder path down the slope, past the cottage that MacFell had had renovated and furnished, supposedly to let to the people who tramped the hills in the summer, and to the bank of the burn.

'Take your knickerbockers off.'

'No, no!' The boy now grabbed at the top of his short trousers.

'Go on, don't be silly. There's three of them back home, I'm used to bare backsides.'

When the boy still kept tight hold of his trousers, she said, 'All right I'll go but Charlie'll stay with you, won't you, Charlie?'

It pointed to a strange relationship that the daughter of the one time cowman could address the master's son in a way other than as young Master MacFell or Mister Charlie, and that she was the only

28

one connected with the farm, besides his parents and sister, who did address him so.

'Yes, yes, Polly.'

'I . . . I don't want to take 'em off.' Ginger sniffed, then wiped his wet face with the back of his hand. 'I'll . . . I'll just put me legs in.'

'All right, have it your own way. But wait a tick till I take me boots off an' I'll give you a hand down the bank.'

With a speed that characterised all her movements, Polly dropped on to the grass and rapidly unlaced her boots, stood up again, shortened her skirt by turning in the waistband several times, then, her arm around Ginger once more, she helped him down the bank; and when their feet touched the ice-cold water the contact forced her into momentary laughter.

Glancing up the bank at Charlie, she cried, 'It would freeze mutton,' and almost in the same breath she went on, 'Come on, a bit further, Ginger, get it over your knees. And here, let me get the grit off your hands.'

As if she were attending to a child, and not to a boy almost two years her senior, she gently flapped the water over his grit-studded palms, saying as she did so, 'They're not bleedin' much, it's your knees that are the worse . . . There, is that better? It gets warm after you've been in a minute. Feel better, eh?' She lowered her head and, turning it to the side, looked into his face, and he nodded at her and said, 'Aye, Polly.'

A few minutes later she helped him up the bank, although he now seemed able to walk unaided, and when he sat down on the grass she sat close beside him; then, her round, plump face straight, her wide full lips pressed tight, she stared up at Charlie for a moment before saying, 'You know what I'd like to do? I'd like to take your da and kick him from here to hell along a road all made of cinders.'

Looking down into the angry green eyes, Charlie was prompted to say, 'And I'd like to help you do it,' but all he did was to turn his gaze away towards the burn, until she said, 'I don't blame you; you know I don't, Charlie . . . Sit down, man.'

As if he, too, were obeying the order from an older person, Charlie, like Ginger, did as she bade him and sat down, and as he watched her dabbing at Ginger's knees with the inside of her print skirt he wished, and in all sincerity, it had been he himself who had suffered the cinder path this morning, just so he could be the recipient of her attentions.

He couldn't remember a time when he hadn't loved Polly Benton. He was three years old when big Polly first brought her into the kitchen and dumped her in a clothes basket to the side of the fire while she got on with the business of helping Fanny Dimple. He had stood fascinated by big Polly's knee as she bared her equally big breast to the infant. He had grown up with young Polly, close yet separated. At times when the master was absent they had played together openly; when he was present they had continued to play, but secretly; and always in their play she had been the leader and he the willing follower.

When, four years ago, his father had taken it into his head to send him to the boarding school in Newcastle, the only one he had really been sorry to leave was young Polly; he hadn't been sorry to leave his mother, although he loved her and pitied her, but her need of him drained him and he was glad to get away from it. As holidays approached it was only the thought that he would see Polly again that compensated him for the irritations that lay ahead in the house.

'You'd better get back if you don't want another dose.'

They all turned and looked upwards and towards Polly's elder brother, Arthur.

Arthur was fifteen years old. He was stockily built with dark hair and a ruddy complexion. He looked strong, dour, aggressive, and he was all three.

'Get up out of that, our Polly, and stop molly-coddlin' him; he'll get worse than that afore he's finished.'

'Aw, you! our Arthur! you want a taste of it to know what it feels like.'

'I've had me share. But not any more' – his chin jerked upwards defiantly – 'he stops when you can look him in the eye.'

It was as if the latter part of his remark had been addressed to Charlie, who had risen to his feet, and again Charlie would like to have endorsed the sentiment by saying, 'You're right there,' for as yet his father had never flayed anyone over fifteen. Instead, he watched Arthur Benton push the small red-headed boy forward with a thrust of his hand, saying, 'Go on, bring some hay down. If you fall it'll be softer on your arse. An' you' – he now turned to Polly – 'get back to the house. You shouldn't be over here anyway.'

'You mind your own interferences, our Arthur. And don't think you'll order me about 'cos you won't.'

Polly was now pulling on her boots, the laces of which passed through only half the holes, and when she rose to her feet the tops of the boots spread out like wings from her shin bones.

'Pull your skirt down.'

'Shut up! An' you go to the devil. I'll leave it up if I want to leave it up. I'll put it round me neck if I feel so inclined.' As she finished she looked at Charlie and laughed; then with a toss of her head she walked away from them, and they both watched her go, not in the direction by which they had come but along by the burn which would bring her out below the cottages.

'Eeh!' Arthur jerked his head to the side. 'She gets cheekier every day.' And there was definite pride in the remark, which caused Charlie to smile at him and say quietly, 'She's Polly.'

'Aye, you've said somethin' there, she's Polly all right.'

They turned together now and walked across the grass and on to the cinder path, and the exchanges between them were again unusual in that they were as between equals.

'You going for a ride s'afternoon?' asked Arthur.

'Yes, I'm to go over to Chapmans'.' Charlie did not say, 'I'm going over to Chapmans' ' but 'I'm to go over to Chapmans'.'

'Is the boss thinkin' of buying the mare?'

'No, no, it isn't about that; I'm to take an invitation for them to come to supper on Saturday night.'

'O . . . h! O . . . h! It's like that, is it? Supper Saturda' night. You'll have to watch yourself.' He jerked his head towards Charlie, and Charlie, looking at him with a blank countenance, said, 'What do you mean, watch yourself?'

'Why, Miss Victoria.'

'Miss Victoria!' Charlie's brows drew together.

'Lor'!' Arthur was grinning. 'If I was lookin' like you at this minute an' somebody said I looked gormless they'd be right. 'Twas as I said, you'd better look out for Miss Victoria. Old Chapman would like nothin' better than to see the lands joined; an' the boss, well, let's face it, the Chapmans are the cream of the milk round here, an' the boss is all for the cream off the milk.'

Charlie brought himself to a sudden stop. He looked at Arthur for a moment; then, his head going back on his shoulders, he let out a laugh. It was a loud laugh, a long rollicking laugh, a sound that was rarely heard around the farm. It even startled Arthur into protest. Casting his glance towards the back of the byres to where the alleyway ran into the yard, he said, 'Stop it, man! What's got into you? There's nowt funny about that. Aw, give over. Stop it!'

Slowly Charlie's laughter subsided, and, taking a

handkerchief from his pocket, he wiped each cheek-bone; then, his face still lit with laughter, he looked at Arthur and said, 'Victoria . . . she's eighteen,' it was as if he were speaking of someone as old as his mother. 'The things you get into your head, Arthur. Anyway, if I was her age what would a high-stepper like Miss Victoria want with me? I'm tongue-tied when I meet her; it's as if we spoke different languages. She goes to balls in Hexham and New-castle, she's been to London; she's left school, and I'm still there, and likely to be for years; and what's more, she's mad on horses and hunting and can talk of nothing else. Now if I was bringing up that subject with her I'd put my foot in it right away by saying her tastes are a contradiction for she's supposed to love horses, yet she takes them over fences that could rip their bellies open. Moreover, I don't think she's read anything but a lady's journal in her life. As for reading poetry, she would laugh herself sick if I mentioned it, even young Nellie is better informed than she is.'

'Well, who wouldn't? Poetry isn't for men.'

'Oh, now who's being gormless, Arthur?' Charlie waved his hand before his face as if shooing away a fly. 'It's men who write the poetry.'

'Aw, no, I don't agree with you there, for they're not what you'd call real men, just those fancy half-buggers.'

'Don't be silly. What about Wordsworth? Is he a . . . ?'

Charlie couldn't bring himself to repeat Arthur's

phrase but substituted the word 'effeminate' which part of his mind told him was hitting Arthur below the belt; he knew Arthur would show no offence at being put down in this way, for he liked to talk, and to get him talking too. And it was odd, but he could talk to Arthur, and Arthur's pet response, 'I don't agree with you,' always pointed to the fact that he was enjoying the talk, having a crack as he called it. He was aware that Arthur was very ignorant and was likely to remain so, for he was too bigoted to learn. Yet he liked Arthur. He liked all the Bentons. Yes, he liked all the Bentons.

Arthur was now saying, 'Wordsworth is different, anybody who lives among the hills is different. I'm talking about the fancy blokes up in Newcastle an' London.'

Charlie blinked rapidly, swallowed, but made no further comment except to repeat to himself, Newcastle and London. They imagined everything bad happened in Newcastle or London and that all the rich people, too, were in these places. They took no account of the vast space all about them which was dotted with manors and huge country houses. To people like Arthur, Newcastle and London were the places where odd people lived and bad things happened; the bad things, the unnatural things that took place among themselves they laid down to nature.

He himself hadn't travelled further than Newcastle but he knew that one day he would break away and see the world, and stop to listen, listen to people talking. He would love to listen to people who could really talk about things besides farming and horses and . . . *the other thing* . . . But then the other thing wasn't very often talked about, it was simply done in the hay field, or behind the barn, or in the copse along by the burn. It hadn't happened much lately, but then the harvest was over. It was at its worst, or at its best – it was how you looked at it – when the hands came over from Chapmans to help out, to beat the weather or to clear a harvest. *The other thing* had been troubling him a lot of late and it was always mixed up in his mind with young Polly.

When they reached the alleyway they parted without further words, or even a nod, Arthur going on towards the piggeries and Charlie cutting through into the main yard, there to be met by his father.

'Who was that laughing?'

'Me, Father.'

Edward MacFell's head moved slightly to the side, his eyes narrowing just a fraction. This son of his was sixteen years old and he couldn't recall ever hearing him laugh out loud before.

'It must have been something very funny.'

It was some seconds before Charlie answered. His gaze fluttering away as if searching for something in the yard, he said, 'Oh, 'twas only something silly that Arthur said.'

Edward MacFell waited to know the substance of what Arthur had said but when it wasn't forthcoming he didn't, as one would have expected of a man of his type, bawl, 'Well, out with it! If it was a joke I would like to share it.' What he said was, 'It was bound to be something silly if a Benton said it.' Then stretching out his arm he placed his hand on his son's shoulder and, turning him about, led him towards the end of the yard and on to a flagged terrace that ran along the front of the house, saying as he did so, 'Come and see what I've got in mind.'

Standing on the edge of the terrace, he now lifted his arm and pointed. 'The burn down there where it widens, I've got the idea to dig out a tidy piece to form a small lake; we'd be able to look down on it from the parlour window . . . What do you think of that?'

Charlie looked over the gently sloping piece of grassland that led down to the burn. The idea surprised him. A lake in front of the house. Immediately his mind linked it with the green-baized door and the morning prayers; but he could see no harm in it, so he said pleasantly, 'I think it would be very nice, Father.'

'An addition to the house you think?'

'Yes, oh yes.' He nodded while still looking down towards the fast flowing narrow rivulet of water.

'And I'll have a stone seat built at the top end where one can sit and look right away through the valley.' MacFell nodded to himself now as he saw in his mind the grandeur of a lake and a stone seat.

When his father's arm came round his shoulders Charlie could not suppress a slight shudder and when, with an unusual show of outward affection, he was pressed to his father's side, he had an upsurging feeling of revulsion.

'Come, there's something I want to talk to you

about.' MacFell now took his arm abruptly away from his son's shoulder and marched ahead off the terrace into the yard and up to the kitchen door.

After scraping his boots on the iron bar that stuck out from the wall, he went into the kitchen, passing Fanny and Maggie as if he wasn't aware of their presence, through the green-baized door, across the hall in the direction of the stairs, then up a narrow passage and into a small room that was almost filled by a heavy ornate desk and a big leather chair, both placed at an angle to the long narrow window. At the near side of the desk was a smaller chair, and the wall close behind this was almost taken up with a break-front bookcase. There was no space for any other furniture in the room.

'Sit down.' MacFell pointed to the chair, and slowly Charlie lowered himself into it. This wasn't the first time his father had had him in his office room to talk to him, but never before had he invited him to be seated. Whatever was about to be said must be of some importance.

When it was said, he was visibly startled.

After taking up a pen from the tray in front of him and wiping the nib clean on a handworked square of stained linen, MacFell jerked his head upwards, looked straight at his son and said, 'Have you had a woman yet?'

As Charlie's lips parted, a valve was released in his stomach sending out a great spurt of colour that not only tinted his pale face a deep red, but heated all the pores of his body.

'Well! answer me, boy.' MacFell was smiling now. 'There's nothing to be ashamed of either way. You needn't go into details, just say yes or no.'

'. . . No, Father.' The heat was intensified, the colour deepened.

Once more MacFell wiped the pen nib, giving it his attention as if it were the important issue of the moment; then again jerking his head upwards, he looked at his son and said, 'Well now, something should be done about it, shouldn't it? This thing can be very irritating and frustrating, and if the mind is continually dwelling on it you won't be able to pay attention to your school work, will you? So the quicker you get release from it the better.'

Laying down the pen, MacFell moved his fingers along the stem of it as if he were stroking fur, before he went on, 'It's of no great importance but it has its place in life . . . mostly as an irritant.' On the last words his tone changed and his jaws visibly tightened. With an impatient movement now he threw the pen on to the brass tray, then drawing in a deep breath, he leant against the back of the chair and asked, 'Is there anyone who has taken your fancy roundabouts?'

Charlie gulped in his throat and his words came out on a stutter as he said, 'I . . . I ha . . . I . . . haven't thought about it, Father.'

MacFell gazed at him under his brows for a moment and a slow smile spread over his face before he said softly, 'Well, it's about time you did, isn't it?'

'. . . Yes, Father.'

'I'd go away now and think about it, and you can leave the rest to me.'

Charlie rose from the chair as if he had been progged with a spoke from underneath, but as he almost scurried from the room he was brought to a standstill by his father saying, 'How do you like Victoria? . . . Oh!' MacFell put his head back and chuckled deeply as he added, 'Don't look like that, I wasn't intending you should start on her. No begod! not yet anyway. All I asked you was, do you like her?'

'Yes . . . yes, she's all right.'

'All right! Is that how you see her, just as, all right? She's a handsome girl, lively, and comes from good stock.' The smile now slid from his face and his eyes took on that look that had frightened Charlie as a boy, and still did, because he wasn't able to fathom what it meant.

MacFell's voice was stiff as, pulling a sheet of paper towards him and picking up the pen again, he began to write, saying abruptly, 'You're going over to Brooklands this afternoon but be back here by five, not later.'

Outside the office door Charlie stood for a moment, his hand pressed tightly over his mouth. He was feeling slightly sick. Whom would his father pick for him? Not Maggie, she was but twelve. Lily Dawson? She was fifteen but she was odd and her nose was always running. He shuddered. There were Nancy and Annie Ryton, they were twins; but they

worked over at Brooklands. That left only Polly . . .
No! No! never Polly.

As he crossed the hall his mother came out of the
sitting-room and, stopping in front of him, asked,
'What did he want you in there for?'

'He . . . he told me I've got to go over to Brooklands this afternoon.'

'You knew that already. Come, what was he on
about?'

'Nothing, nothing.'

'He never takes anyone in there to talk about
nothing. Look, boy, tell me what he wanted you
to do.'

He stared at her for a moment. What did his father
want him to do? Just, he supposed, what he wanted
to do himself, what he had wanted to do for a long
time, have a woman . . . a girl.

Staring into his mother's thin tight-lipped face, he
knew he would have to give her some explanation
and so he said, 'He was asking me what I thought of
Victoria.'

'Oh! oh!' Her head bobbed. 'He's bringing it into
the open now, is he? Now, look, Charlie—' She
grabbed his arm and pulled him backwards into the
sitting-room and there, closing the door, she whispered at him, 'Don't be bullied into doing anything
you don't want to do. Anyway, you're just a bit of
a boy yet and she's two years older than you. And
that's only in years, for she's old in other ways. She's
a fly-by-night if there was ever a one. Now I'm telling
you this, Charlie –' she gripped his hands – 'he'll

push you from this end and Hal Chapman will push her from that end, and they'll join you up without a thought of what your lives together will be, simply because they both want the other's land. And when it's joined they'll spend their time praying for one or other of them to die, and you too, so that they can be lord of all they survey. Oh . . . men! Men!'

As Charlie watched her teeth grinding over each other he released his hands from hers and took hold of her arms, saying softly, 'Don't worry; at least don't worry about Victoria and me. Why, she appears as old as you at times. And what's more' – he smiled wanly – 'she thinks me a numskull; and about some things I suppose I am. But what isn't recognised, Mother, is I have a mind of my own. The few years of education I've had has revealed that much to me and it has shown me I have no taste for land or farming, what I want to do is to travel, to see places, places I've read about. And to meet people . . .' His voice trailed away and his face took on a dreary softness. *The other thing* was forgotten for the moment, and when his mother put her hand up and touched his cheek he placed his hand over hers and pressed it to his face, only to regret the gesture the next moment when he was engulfed in her embrace.

As she sobbed pitifully he patted her head, whispering the while, 'Ssh! ssh! he'll hear you,' yet knowing that if his father did hear her crying he would not come to her for he had ignored the sound for years.

As he stood trying to comfort her he thought that it was strange he should experience such embarrassment by the outward demonstration of affection from his parents. Perhaps it was because it was so rarely shown, or perhaps he sensed it wasn't the result of love on their part, merely a need that had to be filled.

3

The Bentons' cottage was the third along the row. The two end ones to the left, as you approached them from the burn, were empty. The two at the other end were occupied by the cowman Arnold Dawson and his family, and by the shepherd Fred Ryton and his wife. All the cottages were the same in construction, two rooms and a scullery downstairs and a room under the eaves in which it was possible to stand upright only immediately under the ridge.

Peter, aged ten, Mick, eleven, and Arthur slept in comparative comfort in this room because each had a straw pallet to himself. Flo, aged nine, Maggie, twelve, and Polly had the questionable comfort of sleeping together in the three-quarter size iron bed in the front room, while Jim Benton and big Polly occupied the bed set up in the corner of the kitchen.

This bed was wedged between the wall and the end of the fireplace and if Jim Benton was lying on his side he could reach out and move the pan on the hob to stop it from boiling over, or to bring it to the boil, whichever was necessary. This often happened when they were all out in the fields and big Polly had prepared a scrag end of mutton hash or a rabbit stew for their return. But today young Polly was seeing to the meal and talking as she did so.

'Things aren't fair, Da, they aren't right.' With an impatient twist of her hand which indicated her inner feelings, she pulled the skin of the rabbit's body, tugged it from its legs, then, picking up a small chopper, expertly split the carcass in two before looking towards the bed and adding, 'Why has he to do it on the cinder path? Why not in the barn or in the yard?'

Her father gave her no answer, what he did was to raise himself slightly, cough, spit into a piece of paper, then without his eyes following his hand, drop the paper into a chamber under the bed before lying back on the straw pillows. Why? she asked; why did he do it? His Polly was so young in some ways while being as old as the hills in others, but if she lived long enough she'd find out the reason why Edward MacFell did the things he did. The reason was simple, he loved cruelty, he was in love with cruelty; he'd never loved anything or anyone in his life. Oh aye, he thought he loved his son, but that was simply pride because he wanted to be able to show him off to the county folk. That's why he was stuffin' him with education. Edward MacFell loved no one but himself and found no satisfaction in anything but suffering, making others suffer. What had he said? No, that wasn't quite true. There was one avenue that was providing him with satisfaction, for if it wasn't, why did he keep it up? The thought brought him on to his side and, looking towards Polly, he said, 'Where is she?'

'Taken some washin' down to the burn.' Polly had kept her attention on her work as she answered him but when he asked, 'What time is it?' she turned her head towards the mantelpiece and glanced at the little clock that was held in place by a couple of close-linked Staffordshire figures. 'Ten past eleven.'

Jim coughed again and went through the procedure attached to it. Well, she wouldn't be along the burn bank at this time of day. Or would she? He glanced towards the window. At one time he'd had his bed over there from where he could watch her every move, but it had been too much to bear, and so under the pretext of being cold – and that was no lie for he was always cold – he'd had the bed moved into the corner here from where he kept telling himself that what the eye didn't see the heart didn't grieve over. But then he hadn't taken into account his mind's eye.

He lay now looking at his daughter hurrying between the table and the fireplace, and for the countless time he asked himself the question, 'What would I have done without her all these years?' and the same answer came, 'I'd have gone clean mad likely.' She was bonny was his Polly. And then she had that something, a quality that went beyond bonniness. He couldn't put a name to it only to think that it was like the scent that came from some wild flowers and kept you sniffing at them. He looked at her thick mass of hair tied back into a bushy tail with a piece of faded ribbon. The colour was like that of the heather, the dead heather that swept like waves

over the desolate land away towards Ray Fell. Then
again, it wasn't as dark as the dead heather, more like
the bracken when, the summer over, it bent towards
the ground . . . He'd soon be in the ground, and he'd
be glad to go. Oh aye, if it wasn't for her standing
there he'd be glad to go. Not that he would miss her
'cos he wouldn't know nowt about anything, he had
no belief in the hereafter, but he knew she would miss
him.

As he lay looking up at the discoloured ceiling, he
wondered how much longer he had left before they
carried him down the road, past the farm, over the
fields and gentle hills and across the 'new line' road
that now ran from Newcastle far away to the North,
to Carter Bar and over that mighty mound into Scotland. He wished he'd been able to travel that road
just for a few miles. Some said it was a fine road and
a boon to the farmers to get their stuff into the
markets; but others said it was the beginning of the
end, nothing would ever be the same again because of
that road.

Anyway, they would have to carry him across the
road to get to the cemetery in Kirkwhelpington. He
was glad he would lie there for it was a bonny cemetery, perched high on the top of a slice of rock which
his father had once described as being cut out by the
hand of God Almighty to keep off the heathen Scots
from attacking the church and the little village
beyond.

He had been christened in the church of Saint
Bartholomew, and as a lad on his half-day off a

47

fortnight, he had liked to walk that way. He had only once been more than twenty miles from the farm in his life. That was a day long ago when as a young lad he had gone with the drovers into Newcastle.

In his young days they could go all year round and not see a strange soul, but things were different now. In the summer strangers came tramping over the hills with packs on their backs, boots on their feet with soles thicker than clogs, and wearing strange hats, and they sometimes stopped at a cottage door and asked for a drink of water.

Just this summer a young fellow had put his head through the open door there and said quite friendly like, 'Anybody at home?' Polly had given him a cup of buttermilk, which he hadn't liked very much, and it had made her laugh. She and the young fellow had stood talking for a long while and it had worried him somewhat, because it had brought home to him the fact that his Polly was no longer a little lass. She'd soon be a young woman, fourteen in November, she'd be. She had brought him luck because, before her, they had buried five, but after she came there was one each year for the next four years and they all lived. Maggie, Mick, Peter, and Flo, they were all past the danger age now. Flo, the youngest, was nine.

He turned his gaze towards the window. There had been no more bairns since Flo; there had been no more nothing since Flo, for it was at that time that palsy attacked his legs, and as disasters never come singly he took the consumption. He marvelled at times that he had lasted so long, but he wouldn't have if it hadn't been for Polly.

His head jerked and he opened his eyes and stared up into his daughter's face.

'I must have been noddin' off.'

'Aye.' She punched gently at the pillow to the side of his head. 'It does you good to sleep. Would you like a drink?'

'Aye, lass; it does you good to sleep.' He caught hold of her hand now and stared into her eyes as he said, 'I'll soon be takin' a long sleep. You know that, don't you?'

'Aw, Dad, don't. Don't!' She tugged her hand from his and her whole body wriggled in protest. 'Don't talk like that, it upsets me, you could live for years. Looked after proper, you could live for years, an' I'll look after you.'

'All right, all right, don't frash yourself. It's as you say, I could live for years, so it's up to you to keep me goin', eh . . . There, now, there now, don't start bubblin'. Aw, lass' – he again had hold of her hand – 'there's nobody like you in the wide world. By! some fella's gonna get a prize some day.'

'Prize, huh!' She gave a broken laugh now. 'Surprise you mean, when he finds out he's got a quick-tempered bitch on his hands.'

'He'll admire you for your spunk. An' you've got spunk. By! aye!' – he moved her hand up and down as if shaking it – 'you have that. You've got more spunk in your little finger than the other five put together.'

'Oh, our Arthur's got spunk, Da; he'll let nobody tread on him, will our Arthur.'

'Aye.' He released her hand now and his fingers plucked at the patchwork quilt on the bed as he said, 'But there's spunk and spunk, lass. Don't be deceived by those who shout the loudest. It's often the quiet ones who show up the best. It's a funny thing you know, but fear breeds spunk. Aye, it does. I, myself, thought I hadn't much spunk until I was frightened, and then I stood me ground. You're like me' – his eyes lifted to her again – 'you'll always stand your ground. Not' – he nodded at her now smiling – 'that you can be classed as a quiet one, not if me ears tell me aright.'

'Go on with you, our Da! Go on.' She flapped her hands at him, then turned from him, saying, 'If I have any more of your old lip I'll dock your drink.'

As she went to lift the tea caddy from the mantelpiece she was brought abruptly round by the door being thrust open, and she saw Arthur standing there with his arms outspread, one hand gripping the latch and the other on the stanchion of the door. He was gasping as if he had been running. He looked from her to the bed, then back to her again, and on a gasp he said, 'Have . . . have you seen our Mick?'

'No; well, not since he went out this morning. He's . . . he's up in the beet field.' She motioned her hand towards the side wall.

'Oh aye, aye.' His arms dropped to his sides. Then stepping into the room, he asked, 'You makin' tea?'

'Aye, I'm just gona mash it.'

'I'll . . . I'll have a cup.'

'What's wrong?' It was his father speaking.

'Nowt. Nowt.'

'Don't tell me nowt's wrong, you said you were workin' in the bottom fields this mornin', why are you here?'

'I was just passin'.'

'Just passin'!' Jim pulled his useless body upwards in the bed, then said, 'Don't try to stuff me, lad.'

'I'm not tryin' to stuff you, Da. I said I was just passin' and that's what I was doin', just passin', lookin' for our Mick.' Arthur now turned his back on his father and glanced at Polly, where she was standing with the teapot in her hand staring at him, and with a silent grimace and a movement of his eyebrows he indicated he wanted to speak to her; then saying, 'Ah, to the devil!' he went towards the door again and out on to the rough gravel that fronted the cottages.

Thrusting the empty teapot on to the hob, Polly looked towards her father, nodded at him, then hurried from the room and into the open, there to see Arthur standing near the door of the end cottage.

'What is it? What's the matter?' She was close to him whispering as if afraid of being overheard, and he grabbed at her arm, saying, 'I'll tell you what's the matter, come in here,' and pushing the cottage door open he thrust her into the dank room and there, still holding her, he said, 'Brace yourself for the latest.'

'What do you mean? An' leave go of me arm, you're hurtin' me.'

He released his hold on her and she stood rubbing

her arm while she looked into his face. His lips were working tightly one over the other; she saw his cheekbones moving under the skin; there were beads of sweat running between his brows and down the centre of his nose; his Adam's apple was working as if he were swallowing – he had a big Adam's apple for a boy.

'You're for the cottage.'

'*What!*'

'I said you're for the cottage. She's down there now, me ma, an' I heard them. I was at the back near the scullery. I'd set a trap in the thicket. He never comes down there in the mornin's, it's always late afternoon, you know it is, but I saw him coming down the cinder path, and her along the burn bank. She must have got a signal. God knows what it is, I wish I did. And then they went inside, and when I heard him raise his voice straightaway I knew . . . aye well' – he turned his head away – 'I knew they weren't at it, an' that it was something else, so I sneaked up to the scullery window an' I heard me ma keep saying "No! No!" and then she mentioned your name. "Not young Polly!" she said, an' he said "Aye", and she had to send you down atween four and five . . . I was for goin' in there and rippin' them up. You're not goin'! D'you hear? You're not goin'!' He had hold of her shoulders now shaking her; and she allowed him to do so for some seconds for she was feeling dazed by what she had just heard. But of a sudden she wrenched herself from him and cried at him, 'You've no need to tell me I'm not goin', our

Arthur, wild horses won't drag me down there.' She was standing at the far end of the little room now, and he remained where he was, his hands hanging limply by his sides again and his head on his chest, all the aggressiveness seemed to have left his body, and his voice was low and flat as he said, 'That's what me ma said all those years ago when me da could no longer do his stint; but it was either that or the road. It could be the same again, but this time' – his voice took on a stronger, bitter note now – 'it'll be the road we'll take, even if it means pushin' me da on the flat cart.'

'You couldn't take me da from his bed. Anyway, the master wouldn't do that, those roundabout wouldn't stand for it and . . . and he values people's opinion. He . . . he would never turn us out.'

'Well, we'll wait and see, won't we, when you say you're not goin'. But if he doesn't turn us out there's one thing he'll do, he'll make life hell for the lot of us. The cinder path'll be nothin' to it.'

Polly was leaning against the dirty whitewashed wall, her arms folded tightly under her small breasts, and she was shivering inwardly. The master wanted her. He'd . . . he'd had her mother for years, and now he wanted her. Oh no! No! She shook her head in a slow wide sweep. Never! She'd jump in the burn first. But then there were so few places you could drown in the burn unless it was in flood, and she had to think of her da.

'Don't worry; I won't let it happen.' With his arm around her shoulders Arthur pulled her from the wall

53

and led her towards the door. She was in the road again before she said as if coming out of a dream, 'But . . . but what'll I tell our da?'

Arthur gnawed at his lip for a moment, then offered her the solution of his father's one-time weakness by saying, 'Tell him there's a basket of eggs missin' and our Mick an' Flo were gatherin' them first thing, an' the boss is wild.'

She nodded at him, then watched him turn away and walk towards the beet field; but she herself didn't go immediately into the cottage. Again she leant against the wall, and as she did so she saw a figure on horseback riding along the bridle path in the direction of Brooklands Farm, and she knew it was Charlie. Almost instantly she was enveloped in a sweat that clouded her vision and for the first time in her life her feelings touched on ecstasy, and when, some seconds later, her vision cleared she knew that had it been the master's son she had been bidden to meet in the cottage she would have gone gladly.

MacFell had been over to see John Hodgson about a young bull he had for sale. Hodgsons had been tenant farmers of The Manor for generations, yet none had prospered. It was still a poor farm, due mostly to the layout of the land which was fit only for sheep grazing and a few cattle; even so MacFell scorned him for it.

He knew that John Hodgson needed to sell the bull and so he quibbled about the price, and but for the fact that he wanted to be back on his farm before five o'clock, he would have gone on quibbling until he eventually wore Hodgson down. Instead, he told the man that he would leave it for another day and let him think over his offer.

MacFell had no doubt but that Hodgson's curses helped him on his way back over the fields. However, this troubled him not at all, what concerned him at the moment was that his son's needs must be met; then once that was out of the way the boy would apply himself solely to his work, the work of becoming a scholar, an educated man who would be able to converse with the best, be better than the best, the best anyway that lived within the folds of these hills. What were they after all, them in their big houses and their manors, but idle good-for-nothings who had never earned a penny of the money that they were spending, nor yet contributed a stick of furniture to their mighty rooms? Oh, his son would show them. He might not after all decide that he should take over the farm, he could become a barrister, a judge, or even enter Parliament; with education such as he was receiving in the grand school in Newcastle he could go on to a university, and from there he could pick and choose, be whatever he desired, and marry whom he liked, even into the class. Yes, definitely into the class, the top class, from where he could even look down his nose at Chapman's horsy daughter . . . But what about the land? Well, after all it meant more to Chapman than it did to him. Chapman, for all his style, had no freehold land.

He passed the narrow way that led down to the

village of Kirkwhelpington, then a little further on he left the road and mounted the grassy bank and, bringing his horse to a stop for a moment, he glanced at his watch. He had left it late, he must hurry.

When he drove his heels into the horse's side it set off at a gallop and he kept it at its pace for the next three miles until the sweat was running out of the beast. Then when he came to the top of the rise from where, over a rough copse, he could see his farm and its outbuildings lying as if in the palm of a hand, he let the animal drop into a canter before taking the path that ran down through the copse and to the burn.

His intention was not to cross the burn but to remain in the shadow of the trees and watch the Benton chit going to her breaking, if all her mother said was true, and, in his imagination, relish his son's pleasure.

Charlie did not stay long at Brooklands Farm. Mrs Chapman and her husband welcomed him most warmly and said how disappointed Victoria and Nellie would be to have missed him, but Josh Pringle had ridden over from Bellingham way that morning and they had gone back to his place to see a new foal. Mrs Chapman asked after his dear mother, his father, and his sister Betty; then when she received the invitation she said they'd all be delighted to come over on Saturday evening, wouldn't they, Hal?

Hal Chapman endorsed his wife's sentiments; then, his hand on Charlie's shoulder, he once again took him on a tour of his farm, and it was as if he were showing him everything for the first time as he pointed out the value of this horse and that cow, and the fine breed of pigs, and the sheep dotting the hillsides far away.

And so it was with relief that Charlie said his good-byes and made his way hurriedly back home for there were two things he had made up his mind to do.

First, he was going to tell his father that he had no bodily needs that couldn't wait to be satisfied.

When just before setting out for Brooklands his father had told him whom he had chosen to initiate him into manhood, he was so amazed as to be unable to voice any protest. The indecency of it shocked him. That his father could use big Polly and calmly arrange for him to do the same with young Polly was utterly abhorrent to him. In some way, it even sullied the feelings he bore Polly, it ripped from them the secret sweetness of his first love and left it smirched, brought down to the level of 'the other thing' enacted in the hay.

The second thing he must do was to find Polly and ease her mind. How he would go about this he didn't know.

The farm seemed devoid of life; there was no one about the yard except young Peter Benton who, as Charlie unsaddled the horse in the stable, took the saddle from him and with surprising strength and agility for one so young threw it over the saddle stand, then said, 'I can see to him, Mister Charlie,' in reply to which Charlie, smiling at him, said, 'You'll have to stand on something then, Peter.'

'Aye well, I've done it afore an' I like rubbing him down.'

'Where's everybody?'

'Oh, about.' The answer and attitude was that of a man, and for a moment Charlie forgot the weight on his mind and laughed down on the youngster. He was a funny little fellow was young Peter, he'd be a card when he grew up.

Then as if belying this impression, the boy turned a serious face up to Charlie and said, 'What's wrong, Mister Charlie? Is our Arthur in for it? What's he done?'

'Arthur? Done? Nothing that I know of. What makes you ask?'

'He's been goin' around in a tear all day, wouldn't open his mouth. That's not like our Arthur, he's always goin' for me. He was in a while back for a rope and I said what did he want it for, was he thinking of hangin' hissel, an' he clipped me lug, knocked me flyin' he did. Is he in for it, Mister Charlie? What's he done?'

Charlie stared down at the boy before he repeated, 'Nothing that I know of, Peter. Where is he now?'

'He went the copse way.' He thumbed over his shoulder.

'Don't worry' – Charlie grinned now – 'Arthur gets that way, he has fits and starts, you should know that by now.'

'Aye. Aye, Mister Charlie, but . . . but something's up, 'cos me ma didn't come in to her dinner an' our

Polly was sick in the sink. Is the boss gonna do somethin' to us, Mister Charlie?'

Polly sick in the sink . . . 'The boss . . . No, no, don't be silly. Whatever it is, it's got nothing to do with your work, you're all splendid workers.' He absentmindedly ruffled the boy's hair; then looking at the horse, he said quietly, 'You'll give her a good rub, won't you?'

'Aye, Mister Charlie, aye, I'll see to her well,' and taking the bridle, the boy tugged the horse forward into its stall, and Charlie went out into the yard and stood looking about him for a moment.

Polly had been sick in the sink. She had heard what she had to do and was terrified at the prospect. And Arthur knew and he was mad about it, and of course he would be, because in his rough way he was fond of his sister, deeply fond. And the mother, she was keeping out of the way, likely unable to face her husband, a poor sick man.

He turned quickly about. He must find Arthur and tell him, and he could tell Polly and put her mind at rest. He went past the cut that led to the cinder path, through the big barn and out of a side door, then across the field to the rise and the copse.

As he entered the piece of woodland he asked himself what Arthur would be wanting with a rope in here for all the dead trees had been taken down last Christmas and hauled up to the sawing bench; he himself had helped and enjoyed doing so.

It was at this point of his thinking that he saw Arthur. He was crouched down behind a stunted

59

holly growing near the foot of an oak tree. Almost immediately, he heard the approach of a horse from the far end of the copse. It was coming at some speed and although he couldn't see the rider he knew it would be his father.

He remembered afterwards how he had stood rigidly still and wondered what had kept him so, why he hadn't gone straight on down the slope towards Arthur. But no, he had remained stock still until the horse and rider came into view around the curve of the path. The horse was cantering, sending the dried leaves like spray from its hooves. Then he saw his father rise from its back into the air as if he were beginning to fly, except that he was doing so in reverse. His head back, his arms widespread like wings and his legs like a divided tail, he seemed to hover in the air for a moment, then his limbs converging together he fell to the ground, at the same time as the horse's forefeet struck the path and the frightened animal's neighing died away. It was like a scene enacted in the blink of an eyelid.

Dear God! Dear God! Charlie was conscious that his mouth was wide open and that his face muscles were stretched to their fullest extent, but for the life of him he couldn't move from the spot, until he saw Arthur spring up from his hiding place and clutch at the bole of the oak, tearing at something there. It was then he moved. Like a goat leaping down a mountain, he sprang down the hillside and reached the prostrate, huddled form lying amid the leaves just as Arthur stopped in his frantic running, the rope loose in his hand, and stared down at his master.

The two boys now lifted their eyes from the man on the ground and gazed at each other. Then Charlie, dropping on to his knees, went to turn his father from his side on to his back, but no sooner had his hands touched him than they left him again, for as he went to move the body the head lolled drunkenly on to the shoulder.

Again the boys were gazing at each other, Charlie looking upwards, Arthur looking down; and it was Arthur who, on a deep gulp, spluttered, 'God Almighty no! Maim him, break his leg, his arm, aye, that's all I meant, to stop him. You don't know what he was up to. But no, no! Almighty God! no, not kill him. No! Charlie. No.' He was backing away now, the rope dangling from his hand, his words incoherent. 'Just to stop him goin' to the cottage. Our Polly, she's too young for it, for him anyway.'

Of a sudden he stopped his jabbering and, his head drooping forward, he looked at the rope in his right hand. Then as if already experiencing the consequences of his act his left hand came up sharply and gripped his throat. It was this action that brought Charlie out of the dazed, dream-like feeling that was enveloping him. His father was dead. His father was dead. And Arthur would be hanged for it.

The first fact stirred no emotion whatever in him at the moment, but the second alerted him. He stood up, then looked down at the twisted form for a moment longer before turning back to Arthur, whose face was now drained of every vestige of colour and whose whole body was shaking, and so, taking the rope from his hand he ran with it to the other tree, unloosened the end from it, then quickly looping the rope over his hand and his elbow, as he had seen Fanny Dimple do with the clothes line over the years, he thrust it inside his coat. Grabbing the dazed boy now by the arm, he turned him about and ran him through the copse down towards the barn, then along it until they came to the cottages on the rise.

Panting, they both stopped and their eyes lifted upwards towards the end of the row where big Polly and young Polly were standing facing each other evidently arguing. But as Charlie, still hanging on to Arthur, led him up the slope the mother and daughter turned towards them, and big Polly, moving a few steps away from her daughter, cried, 'What's now? What's up?'

When the two boys reached the pathway, big Polly's hands went out towards her son and, taking him by the shoulder, she looked into his face and her voice was low in her throat as she asked, 'What is it? What's happened you?'

Arthur didn't speak but his head drooped on to his chest, and it was Charlie who said, 'Let's . . . let's go in here.' He pointed to the empty house, and one after the other they went into the dank room. It was noticeable that young Polly hadn't opened her mouth, but all the while her eyes were fixed tight on her brother.

'There . . . there's been an accident.' Charlie's

mouth was so dry the words came out gritty as if they'd been dragged over sand.

'An accident? Who?'

Charlie looked at the woman who had caused his mother so much heartache all these years yet who had been as much a victim of his father as his wife had been. Everybody knew why big Polly had to serve the boss; as he had heard Arnold Dawson once laughingly say, 'She paid the rent.'

'My father, he fell from his horse.'

'Fell from his horse!' Big Polly's mouth dropped into a gape, then closed as her son began to gabble, 'I didn't mean it, Ma. I didn't mean it. I just meant to trip 'im. I . . . I thought the rope would catch him round . . . round his chest, but he came at a canter, his head down. I . . . I just wanted to break . . . to break his leg or something to stop him takin' her.' He now jerked his head towards young Polly. Then his mouth agape, he watched his mother gather the front of her blouse into her fist until her breasts looked as if they would burst through the material, and all the while her face seemed to grow larger; her mouth and eyes stretched, her nostrils dilated until it seemed as if the whole face was going to explode in a scream; then her body slumped like a deflated bladder and she whispered, 'You mean . . . you killed him . . . he's dead?'

When in the fear-filled silence the only answer her son gave her was the drooping of his head she sprang on him and, gripping his shoulder, she shook him like a rat while she screamed now, 'You maniac! You bloody maniac you! You interferin' numskull! You'll swing, you'll swing! An' for what? 'Cos he wanted his son broke in. 'Twasn't him. He got what he wanted from me, you all knew that. Aye by God! an' you've let me know it an' all over the years.' She stopped her shaking and thrust him against the wall where he leaned looking at her like a frightened child, all his aggressiveness gone, no vestige of the bumptious youth left.

Big Polly now turned and looked at her daughter. The saliva was dripping from one corner of her mouth, her tongue lolling in the open gap, and she gasped as she said, 'It . . . it was for young master there you had to go down, not the boss. I . . . I didn't tell you 'cos . . . well, oh my God!' She put her hand to her head and rocked herself back and forward. 'What's come upon us this day? As if I hadn't had enough all me life. But now murder. Oh my God!' She turned to Charlie, and as if she were talking about some animal on the farm she said to him simply, 'He wanted you broken in, and he picked on Polly here. I . . . I didn't tell her what she had to go down to the cottage for till the last minute, I . . . I couldn't bring meself to. And now . . . now—' She put her arms under her flagging breasts and, turning from him, began to walk round the small room, her pace quickening to almost a run.

All this time Charlie hadn't once looked at Polly, he had kept his eyes fixed on her mother. Vaguely now, he realised the torment the woman had endured all these years at the hands of his father, for no matter in what capacity anyone was connected with his father they would, in some way, suffer.

His father had been the source of so much suffering, and now he was dead. He clamped down on the feeling of intense relief, even joy, that was straining to escape from some secret cell in his brain and envelop him, and ordered his mind to dwell on the fact that Arthur had killed him and Arthur would undoubtedly be hanged for it, that is if something wasn't done, and soon.

He found himself taking the three steps to bring him face to face with big Polly and which caused her to stop in her pacing. He had never stood so close to her for years, and now he was recalling the peculiar smell that emanated from her, it was a mixture of sour milk and sweat. His voice sounded surprisingly firm, even to himself, as he said, 'It . . . it was an accident.'

'Accident! Huh!'

'It could be looked upon as such . . . he fell from his horse, it . . . it must have stumbled and . . . and the fall broke his neck.'

Her hand was again gathering up the material of her blouse. 'He broke his neck?' The words were a whimper.

For answer he nodded his head just once; then putting his hand inside his coat he handed her the coiled rope, saying, 'There's . . . there's no one knows the facts except us.' His eyes flicked from one to the other; then on an instant recalling his conversation with young Peter earlier, he put in hastily,

'There's . . . there's Peter. It was he who told me that Arthur had taken a rope and gone down to the copse. I . . . I think it would be wise if you talked to him.'

There was silence in the room; then big Polly said quietly, 'Aye, Master Charlie, aye, I'll talk to him. And God bless you this day.' On this she grabbed at his hand and, bringing it up to her breast, she pressed it there for a moment, still keeping her eyes on him.

He was blushing again, the heat was flushing his body like a hot drink. He looked from big Polly to Arthur who was still leaning against the wall as if he were drunk. Then his gaze flicked to young Polly whose face was expressing stark fear, and without a word he turned and left them.

On the gravel outside he stood for a moment, the latch of the door in his hand, and as he stared down towards the farm he straightened his shoulders and jerked his chin to the side. He felt strange, elated; he had gone into that room a boy and he had come out a man. He had managed a dangerous situation on his own. Big Polly had called him Master Charlie and her tone by itself had given him prestige.

He walked slowly along the row of cottages and down the slope towards the farm, and as he did so he saw the cinder path snaking away from the back of the byres down to the cottage, the cinder path on which his father had that morning flayed Ginger Slater. Well, he would flay no more, and one of the first things he himself would do would be to get rid of that path.

He stopped for a moment. Why wasn't he feeling

just the slightest regret at his father's passing? Was he unnatural? Shouldn't he be feeling a little sorrow in spite of everything, for his father had loved him? No. No, his father hadn't loved him, his father had loved no one but himself. What feeling his father had had for him was founded on his desire for power and prestige, and he would have used him to this end. He mustn't feel guilt at his lack of compassion, and he could console himself that he wasn't the only one who would find himself in this state, there was his mother . . . He must break the news to his mother . . . What was he talking about? He wasn't to know his father was dead. If the horse made its way back to the stable, which it would likely do, someone would go out looking. Well, it wouldn't be him. No, no, he couldn't bear to look down on that figure for a second time.

Turning abruptly to the left, he now jumped the dry stone wall and made his way in the direction of the far hills. It was nothing for him to go tramping for miles; he wouldn't be missed, and when he came back the hubbub would be over. But then again – he drew his step to a halt – he'd have to simulate surprise, a kind of grief, could he do it? His step was slow as he moved on. He had never been any good at acting a part. He had found that out at school. One of his masters had said he was of the stuff that made good audiences.

He had walked some miles before he reached the first hill and when he dropped down on to the dead heather he lay stretched out, his face buried in the crook of his arm. He had the desire to cry. All this had come about because his father had wanted to break him into manhood. But he knew now it would be a long, long time before that happened; and then not with Polly, never with Polly. Dear, dear Polly.

The sprigs of dry heather tickled his nose and as he went to rub it he brushed away the tears that were streaming freely from his eyes. And strangely now, he knew he wasn't crying because he had lost Polly but because his father had been deprived of life in that sudden and horrible way. If he had died in bed it wouldn't have mattered so much, perhaps not at all. But the way he had gone it had been equivalent to him being slaughtered. He had never been able to tolerate slaughter, that's why he'd never be any good as a farmer.

His crying broke into sobs and some grazing sheep turned in surprise towards the sound. They had heard nothing like it before.

4

The funeral had been well attended. The privileged mourners who had returned for a meal had packed the dining-room, and the atmosphere had taken on the air of a party, helped no doubt by the lavish spread and the spirits with which most of those present kept washing it down. But as each took his farewell of the bereaved woman, his solemnity returned.

When all but the solicitor had gone, Mary MacFell, Charlie, and Betty went with him into the sitting-room. There the solicitor prepared to read the will, and much to Mary MacFell's chagrin he did not address her but looked directly towards Charlie as he said, 'I didn't draw up this will, your father deposited it with me, but it was signed and witnessed in my presence, so although it is brief and simple, everything is in order; and it reads as follows—'

He now took out his handkerchief, blew his nose and returned the handkerchief to his pocket, then began, ' "I, Edward MacFell, being of sound mind, leave entirely to my son Charles MacFell the real estate, which estate includes the farm and freehold land there attached . . ." '

But he got no further than this for Mary MacFell

almost bounced to her feet crying, '*What!* everything to Charlie? It's scandalous. It isn't right, it's . . .'

'Please, Mrs MacFell. Please wait one moment.' The solicitor held up his hand. 'Your husband didn't forget you; his wishes read as follows—' He waited for her to sit down again and then went on:

' "And to my wife, Mary MacFell, I leave one third of the monies in the bank and of that in bonds, and to be the legal guardian . . ." '

'One third of the money?' Her voice broke in again, high and excited now.

'One third,' the solicitor repeated—' "and the remainder to my son Charles". And that seems almost to conclude the matter. As I said, it is a very brief statement. I wish all were so simple, but nevertheless it will take some little time for the legalities to be taken care of.' He smiled weakly, then looked at the plain, tight-lipped young daughter who was staring fixedly at him, coughed, and rose to his feet . . .

Charlie showed the solicitor to the hired cab which was waiting for him, and when he returned to the sitting-room it was to find that his mother was no longer there; but Betty was, and she was pacing the floor in much the same manner as his father had been wont to do. But when Charlie entered the room she stopped and cried at him, 'He never once mentioned me. None of you cared for him like I did, and he's left me nothing. You hated him. Yes you did; I know, I know.' She stretched her small frame upwards and wagged her finger in his face. 'Like her' – she now jerked her head towards the ceiling – 'you hated him; and you were afraid of him. I was never afraid of him. He knew that, yet' – she now shook her head slowly, bit on her lip and started her pacing again – 'not to mention me, not to leave me anything.'

'He knew you'd be taken care of.' He sat slowly down.

Swinging around, she repeated scornfully, 'Taken care of! I can take care of meself. I can see I'll have to. As for you taking care of anybody, you're too weak-kneed, and he couldn't see it. He was obsessed with the idea of making you what he wanted to be himself, a gentleman. Huh!' She pursed her lips as if about to spit. 'Well, you'll have to forget about that now, won't you, and get down to some real work, a man's work, muck work. Oh' – her lower jaw grated from one side to the other – 'if only I was in your shoes.'

'I wish you were.' Charlie had risen to his feet and he stood looking down at her as he repeated with deep bitterness, 'I wish you were.' And on this he turned from her and walked towards the door. But before reaching it he was brought to a standstill with his head jerking backwards and his eyes cast towards the ceiling, for from above there was coming the sound of high laughter. Swinging round he looked at his sister, and she, as startled as he was, gazed back at him; then they both ran from the room, across the hall, up the stairs and into their mother's bedroom.

Mary MacFell was lying in the middle of the bed; her arms were widespread and she was kicking her

71

heels in a childlike fashion on top of the quilt.

'Mother! Mother! stop it.' Charlie had her by the shoulders. But Mary did not cease her laughing. Her mouth wide, the tip of her tongue curled downwards, her laughter rose to a higher pitch.

'Mother! Mother! give over.'

'Get by!' Charlie found himself thrust aside, and now clutching the brass rail of the bedhead he watched his small sturdy sister lift her hand and bring it in a whacking smack across her mother's face.

In hiccuping gasps the laughter died away, and they stood in deep silence for a moment until the creaking of a floor board told them that Fanny had entered the room. But they did not look towards her where she stood at the bottom of the bed staring at her mistress.

Mary, her body perfectly still now, looked from one face to the other, her expression like that of someone awakening from a deep dream. Slowly she hitched herself upwards in the bed, then leaning her head back against the rail, she looked at her daughter and said, 'It would be you who would do that, wouldn't it, Betty? Don't worry' – she made a small motion with her hand – 'I'm not going mad. Oh no, I've no intention of going mad.' She now raised her body upwards and with a quick movement of her legs, which made her daughter spring aside, she brought herself upright on to the side of the bed. And now looking at her son, she said, 'You heard what he said, Charlie, I'm to have one third. I've a right to one third. Do you know what that means to me, a right to something, something of my own, after all this time? No' – she shook her head – 'not even you, you don't understand, you couldn't understand what it means. Well, you'll see in the future because' – she now looked at her daughter again, then repeated the word, 'because I'm going to spend, spend and spend what is mine. For the first time in years I'm going to handle money . . . And Betty' – she bent her body forward towards the girl – 'I want you to get this into your head. That licence you took a moment ago will be the one and only time you will take the initiative from now on. As long as I'm mistress of this house, and that's what I am, mistress of this house, you will do what you're told, and by me.'

It was as if she had forgotten the presence of her son and Fanny, and strangely it was as if she were addressing a woman of her own age, not a fourteen-year-old girl, but as Charlie looked at them both he knew that his mother was not seeing a child of four-teen, she was seeing her late husband, for, just as he did himself, she realised that as long as Betty remained in this house his father would not really be dead. He also realised that a great change had come over his mother, she was a different person; he couldn't imagine her as the same woman who was continually weeping, who could go for days without uttering a word, who always walked behind her hus-band, never at his side; and he didn't know whether he liked the change or not.

*   *   *

The following morning Charlie knew that he didn't like the change in his mother and that unless he himself changed, unless he asserted himself and showed himself now, young as he was, as master, his father in some strange way had died in vain.

He looked at his mother where she stood dressed for the road in her new black clothes. They were expensive looking clothes: the three-quarter length coat was of alpaca, and the full skirt below it was of a fine woollen material with a deep mud fringe showing round the bottom. On her head she had a large black hat with a feather in it; it looked too gay for a mourning hat, in fact, her whole attire looked out of place for mourning. But then she wasn't acting as if she were in mourning. There was a lightness about her, an air of excitement, both in her attitude and in her voice. But the tone of her voice now was threaded with vindictiveness and the content of her words was amazing him. 'I'm giving them notice,' she was saying. 'The lot, out, they're going out, every single Benton; there's going to be a clean sweep here. Oh yes' – she pulled on a black silk glove, stroking each finger down to the knuckle with such force that the stitching gave way in one of the sockets.

Charlie gazed at her in amazement, his eyes narrowed as if to get a different view of her; and now she cried at him, 'Yes! you can look surprised, but that's only the beginning, there's going to be changes here.'

'You can't do this, Mother.'

'I can't? But oh, I can.'

'No! no! you mustn't.'

74

'Boy!' – she moved a step towards him now – 'do you know what I have suffered at that woman's hands all these years?'

Charlie closed his eyes for a moment, then he looked down towards his feet as he said, 'It wasn't her fault. You know it wasn't her fault.'

'Don't be ridiculous, boy; it takes two to form an alliance like that. She could have said no.'

'And what would have happened then?' His head had jerked up, his words were rushing out, one after the other linked as in a chain. His voice, filling the room, startled her. 'He would have done the same as you're doing now, he would have turned them out; he would have had as much compassion for them as a mad bull. Nobody should know that better than you. You suffered from him all your life, now you're going to act in the same way as he did. Well . . . no, I won't have it. Big Polly's not to blame. And Jim . . . why Jim's on his last legs, you know that and you would talk of putting them out.' He made a swift movement with his hand as if giving someone a back slap. 'Well, you'll not do it, Mother, not as long as I'm here.'

Her body was taut, her face set as if in a mould but her voice had a control about it as she said, 'Do you know who you're talking to?' But his answer nonplussed her as it came back quick and sharp: 'Yes, yes, Mother, I do know whom I'm talking to. And . . . and while we're on the subject, I would remind you—' He faltered now, swallowed deeply in his throat but after a moment went on, 'Whether you like to face it or not, Father left the farm to me. In all respects it . . . it is mine.'

Her gaze was ice cold upon him and he was already beginning to wilt under it, when she said, 'And who, may I ask, is going to run *your* farm for you when you are at school? Who is going to manage the affairs, eh? Tell me that. Mr Big Fellow all of a sudden.'

Up till this present moment he hadn't given the matter a moment's thought, he had taken it for granted he would return to school and finish his education, but in this instant he knew that his school-days were over, and he heard himself saying so. 'I'm going to manage it myself.'

'You're going to *what*?'

'You heard what I said, Mother. I'm going to manage the farm.'

'Huh! Don't be an idiot, boy. You manage the farm! You don't know the first thing about the farm. You might have been born and bred on the place, but you've shown a distaste for it all your days.'

Perhaps it was the scorn in her voice that gave him the courage to come back, in a voice as loud as her own, 'Perhaps the distaste wasn't so much for the farm as for the man who was running it; but . . . but now I mean to manage my farm, Mother. And I don't want to keep repeating it, but it is my farm, and what I don't know I'll learn. Arnold and Fred will help me . . .'

'Arnold and Fred!' Her lip curled upwards. 'They were Dawson and Ryton in your father's time.'

'Well, that being the case, Mother, and knowing that you never approved of anything Father did, I should have thought you would have welcomed the men being called by their Christian names. Anyway, I've always known them as Arnold and Fred; and as I said, I'm sure they'll help me in that part of my education which has been lacking.'

'Oh dear God!' She looked upwards. 'Even your phraseology is wrong, They'll laugh at you, boy, they'll take advantage of you. They'd take much more notice of Betty out there than they would of you.'

The gibe triggered off the distressing feeling of embarrassment and this in turn brought the colour flooding up to his face. She was right, they would take more notice of Betty; he wasn't cut out to be a farmer. He had always known that, yet here he was assuming the position of master, and he'd make a laughing-stock of himself. But what else could he have done, for he knew that, even though his presence in the house might deter her from carrying out her threat, the minute he returned to school she would throw the Bentons out.

Strange, but the Bentons were like the hand of fate directing his life.

'Mother, the trap's ready.' Betty appeared in the doorway. She, too, was dressed for the town.

As she slowly drew on her other glove, Mary MacFell looked towards her daughter and said, 'I'm sure you will be pleased to know, Betty, that your brother is going to run the farm. He feels he must be master in word as well as in deed.'

'Run the . . . run the farm? *You!* . . . You're not going back to school then?'

Charlie looked down on his young sister who, like his father, had always possessed the power to intimidate him, but now he stared straight into her small round dark brown eyes as he said, 'No, I'm not going back to school, Betty; as Mother has said I am going to run the farm, and I am going to start this very day . . . now, and I'd like you to keep it in mind, Betty.'

For once Betty had no ready retort. She looked from her brother, whom she had never made any secret of despising, to her mother, whom she disliked intensely, and there was a note of utter disbelief in her voice when she eventually said, 'And you're going to let him?'

Mary MacFell walked across the room until she was facing her daughter, and then she answered her. 'Apparently I've very little option, but what he forgets is that I'm his legal guardian and I could put spokes in his wheel, but however I'm not going to!' Turning her head on her shoulder, she now glared at her son and she spat her words at him as she said, 'But now I'll point out to you, Charlie, that there are more ways of killing a cat than drowning it, and you'll find this out before you're finished. Let your wretched Bentons stay and we'll see . . . we'll see. Come, Betty.' And on this she went from the room and into the hall. She did not, however, turn and go through the kitchen and so to the yard where the trap stood waiting, but she went out of the front door and on to the gravel drive; and there without turning her head she said to Betty, 'Tell them to bring it round' . . .

A few minutes later Fanny, with Maggie Benton standing behind her, watched from the end of the yard the trap jogging its way down the drive and on to the bridle path, and turning and looking at Maggie, she said. 'God Almighty! would you believe it? I always said I'd dance on his grave when he went but the old sayin's proving truer than ever, 'tis better to work for the devil you know than the devil you don't know! for who would have thought it, the quiet body that she's been all these years turning out to be as snarly as a ferret. The idea! to turn you all out on to the road. My God! she would have done it an' all if it hadn't been for young Charlie. I couldn't believe me ears, I just couldn't, but he stood up to her. Aye, by God! he did that. I never thought he had it in him, soft, I thought he was, with book-learning. The things you live to see.' Fanny shook her head dolefully, then added, 'Ah well, let's get in and get some work done. But if I know owt we're going to see changes here, lass. I only hope he has the gumption to stick to his guns and stand up for himself as he did back there, otherwise . . . well, God knows.'

When they reached the kitchen door they both self-consciously stood aside to allow Charlie to enter the yard, and he turned to Fanny and asked, 'Where would Fred be this morning, Fanny?'

'Fred? Oh well, I saw him go early on with Bett and Floss, so that means he's bringin' the sheep down into the lower pen – there's some for market next week – so about now he should be up at Top Loam. Do you want him?'

'Yes, yes; I'd like to have a word with him, Fanny.'

'Then off you go, Maggie.' She turned to the girl standing wide-eyed to the side of the kitchen door. 'Take to your legs and tell Fred the master wants him. Just say that! the master wants him.' On this she turned and nodded deeply at Charlie, and her words and her action infused strength into him and he smiled at her and said softly, 'Thanks, Fanny.'

'You're welcome.'

He was about to turn away when she put her hand out and lightly touched his sleeve, saying, 'If there's any way I can be of help you've only got to ask; I'm old in me head as well as in me body.'

He said again, 'Thanks, Fanny.' He did not ask himself how she knew about the present situation, she had ears and was soft-footed for all her years.

In the doorway of the byres he looked at Arnold Dawson, who was brushing the muck through the trough that bordered the line of stalls, and he called to him, saying, 'Would you come to the barn in ten minutes, Arnold? I'd . . . I'd like to have a word with you.'

Arnold Dawson leant on the head of his brush for a moment and stared at Charlie, and then he said, 'Yes, aye, yes, Mister Charlie, I'll be there. In ten minutes you say?'

'Yes, Arnold.'

'I'll be there.'

As he crossed the yard towards the barn Ginger

Slater came out from the horse-room. The boy stopped and looked at him. His expression was no longer a frightened one, his hangdog air had gone; in fact there was a cockiness about him. But Charlie did not notice the change in the boy, and he said to him, 'Find Arthur and come to the barn, I . . . I want to have a word with you.'

Ginger didn't say, 'Yes, Master,' or 'Yes, Mister Charlie,' but he turned away and went through the passage that led to the cinder path . . .

It was a quarter of an hour later when the two men and the two boys assembled in the barn. They stood in a rough half-circle and looked at their mistress's son, for in each of their minds it was the mistress who was the boss now. And Charlie, vitally aware of this, asked himself how he was to begin? The idea born of the unusual outburst of anger his mother had evoked had seemed good, easy. He would talk to the hands, to tell them that he was now master and ask for their help. But here they were standing staring at him, two men older than his father had been, and Arthur and Ginger only a year younger than himself yet years older in experience. He'd have to say something, start somewhere. But how?

'You wanted to have a word with us, Mister Charlie?' Fred Ryton's voice was kindly.

'Yes. Yes, Fred.' Thankfully he turned to the shepherd and, his tongue loosened now, he went on hastily, almost gabbling, 'I . . . I just want to say that I'm not returning to school, I . . . I intend to work the farm myself, that is' – his eyes swept the four of them

81

now – 'with your help.' He gave a shaky laugh. 'I know I'll need help for . . . as I said to you, Fred, during my last holiday, at the calving, you remember? I said I didn't think I was cut out for a farmer. And you agreed with me then. But now—' He straightened his slumped shoulders, rubbed his hand tightly over his chin on which the bristles were few and far between, then ended, 'Well, I mean to have a shot at it.'

There was what seemed to Charlie an endless silence before the cowman spoke.

'You'll find it different from book-learning, lad.'

Charlie brought his eyes to those of Arnold Dawson and his reply was surprisingly curt now. 'I'm aware of that, Arnold, but my education, what little I've had, won't, I hope, be a drawback to me managing my own affairs.'

They all stared at him blankly now. This wasn't the gangling young lad they all knew, the lad who couldn't bear to see a cow heaving in labour and didn't appreciate that she would be well recompensed with the first lick of her calf; the lad who had been known to release a rabbit from a trap when it was caught only by the foot; the lad who stood mooning on the hills looking into the distance like some loony, or walked out before dawn to see the sun rise, and came back sodden wet with dew, which landed him in bed for a week. At different times over the years they had had cause to think he was a bit funny in the head the things he did, but the young fellow talking to them now didn't sound like someone funny in the head. It could have been his father speaking, that is if ever his father had spoken civilly to a human being.

Arnold and Fred almost spoke together; then Fred, giving way to the older man, waited while Arnold Dawson said his piece. It was short and to the point. 'Speaking for meself,' he said: 'I'll work as I have always done, fair's fair, I'll earn me wage; apart from that if I can help you you've only got to ask, lad.'

'The same goes for me,' Fred Ryton was nodding at him now. 'But all I can say is you can't learn farmin' from books.'

He should have been satisfied with their response but he felt they still saw him as the boy, the master's son who was destined to be a country gentleman. He now turned his eyes towards Arthur, and Arthur gulped in his throat, jerked his head to the side and what he said was, 'You know me.'

Next, he looked at Ginger Slater and the boy's answer surprised them all, for what he said was, 'Well, me, I never had much choice, had I?'

His answer was understandable yet puzzling, because Ginger had never been known to stand up to anybody in all the years he had been on the farm.

The other three were still looking at him when Charlie said, 'Well, that's settled then. We'll go on from here . . . a day at a time.'

'Aye, a day at a time, you can't take it much slower.' This came from Arnold Dawson as he made for the barn doorway, and the rest followed, leaving him standing alone, and feeling alone, more alone

83

than he had ever been in his life. They weren't for him, not really; they didn't want him as boss.

It was odd – he shook his head and gave a small rueful smile – they would sooner have continued to work under his father, who had paid them barely a living wage, and who, had they asked him for a penny rise, would have thrown them out.

He felt tired, weary, sort of sick in the pit of his stomach. He went to lower himself down on to a bale of hay. His back bent, his buttocks almost touching the hay, he stopped and straightening himself abruptly, muttered aloud, 'I'll have to show them, won't I? I'll just have to show them that I'm me father's son, that they're not going to get away with anything, and that they've got to recognise me as master.' Not one of them had given him the title. Well then, he'd have to earn it, wouldn't he? He'd have to be firm, harden himself; if only outwardly, to make himself a replica of his father. The thought instead of stiffening his fibre, brought his shoulders hunched and his head hanging forward as he walked slowly from the barn . . .

Yet it was less than an hour later when he knew to his great relief that there would be no need to alter himself for the men's attitude towards him changed completely. Both, within a short time of each other, addressed him as sir, and there was in their manner the acceptance of him as their master. It was Fred Ryton who came to him first, 'Can I have a word with you, sir? It's about the sale over at Bellingham come next week. It would be educational like, in a different sort of way' – he gave a hic of a laugh – 'if you come along of me, showed yoursel' like an' got to know the ropes.'

Charlie smiled at the man as he answered, 'Thank you, Fred; I'd be glad to.' And when Fred put his forefinger to his eyebrow that just showed beneath the peak of his cap it was, Charlie recognised, a definite sign of acceptance.

Arnold Dawson approached him next, saying, 'About Hodgson's bull, sir. I don't know if your father clinched the deal or not, but if it's to your likin' I'd go over along of you when you're ready an' look at the beast. Hodgson's a tight man 'cos he needs the money so he'll take you for every penny he can get out of you.'

'Good . . . Good enough, Arnold.' He blinked, gulped in his throat, then added, 'I'll try to make it one day this week.' His shoulders were back again, his head up; his manner was matching theirs.

'Right, sir. Right.' Arnold, too, put his finger to his eyebrow.

Then there was Arthur. They came face to face as Arthur was leading a horse across the yard. His approach was different: he stared at him for a moment before muttering, 'It'll take us all to die afore we get out of your debt.'

So that was it. The change in their manner, it was because he had stopped his mother from evicting the Bentons. They had, he surmised, considered he must have guts of some sort to stand up to his mother, whose silence all these years had been formidable in its own way.

He gave no response whatever to Arthur's words, there was no need to: their lives were bound together by the secret they shared.

He walked on now towards the space between the brick walls that formed the entrance to the farm proper thinking as he did so that there was only Ginger who hadn't approached him. But then in a way Ginger didn't matter, his opinion would carry no weight. Yet he had always been sorry for the work-house boy, and had shown it. There was, he decided, one thing he could do for him now, he could give him books to read. As to his attitude towards himself, well, that was of no account. What did matter was the attitude of the men, and it seemed that they had accepted him wholeheartedly.

Many years later when he was to recall that morning and his summing up of the response of his few workers towards him and of how utterly wrong he had been in his evaluation of Ginger Slater, he was to tell himself he couldn't have known that before noon of that particular day as recognised master of the farm he was to be given evidence of things to come; but even then he wouldn't realise the full conse-quences of the power that lay in the hands of the undersized ginger-headed lad.

He stood now between the walls and looked over the rough road to where the cows were grazing in the long meadow that sloped towards the burn. What should he do?

What had his father done at this time of the day?

He had walked his land . . . with a walking-stick in his hand.

Well, that's what he would do now, he'd walk his land. Tomorrow he'd have the aid of a walking-stick too, but today he'd just walk . . .

He set off, his arms swinging in unison with his long thin legs, and his chin was high as he turned his head from one side to the other and looked over the landscape; and as he walked he told himself that this was his farm, his land, and he was master of it. Yet before he had covered half the perimeter his step had slowed, his shoulders were slumped, his chin was in its usual position, and he was asking himself why it was he could love the hills and the countryside so much, yet could not, even mildly, be stirred by the knowledge that he was walking on his own ground.

He stopped and looked away towards the hills and he had the childish desire to take to his heels and run, run to them, over them, then all the way to Carter Bar and into Scotland. No, not into Scotland. He swung round and faced the other way. If he was going to run he'd run to Newcastle and there board a boat that would take him to Norway, Sweden, Denmark, and on to Germany and Poland, on, on, on . . .

But he couldn't run, he couldn't sail away, for, to use the old phrase, he had burnt his boats. Because of the Bentons he had lost the chance to see the world and, what was more important at the moment, the chance of further education. And further education to him meant literature, reading, travelling, seeing.

Well – he began to walk again – he could still read literature, couldn't he? There was nothing to stop him reading. Only the atmosphere of the house; the farm house wasn't conducive to reading, never had been, there was no restful corner in it.

The sun went in, the sky from being high above the hills seemed now to be settling on them; the mist came from nowhere suddenly. A pale grey curtain, it seemed to rise and fall like a mighty kite. As it enveloped him he shivered and, turning quickly as if he were being pursued, he made his way back to the farm.

It was as he neared the gateway that he caught sight of Polly standing talking to Ginger. He could discern their mist-wreathed faces turned towards him, but before he reached them Ginger Slater had gone through the opening into the yard.

As he came abreast of Polly, he thought that the paleness of her face was caused by the drifting mist, until he saw the look in her eyes. It was the same look that had been there when she had stood speechless in the empty house a little over a week ago.

'Are you all right?'

Polly looked back into his face and, her voice thick as if the very mist were clogging her throat, she said, 'No; no, I'm not, Charlie. Not at this minute I'm not. Do . . . do you know what he's just said?'

'Ginger?'

'Aye, Ginger. He . . . he came on me as I passed, an' he said I've . . . I've got to tell our Arthur to go easy on him. He *knows* . . . he knows, Charlie.'

'Knows what?'

'What Arthur did with the rope.'

'No! *No!* Oh, no!'

'Aye. Aye, he saw it all! you helpin' . . . everything. He said he's not out to cause trouble but our Arthur's got to stop bullyin' him.'

They were standing within a foot of each other; he was looking down at her and she up at him; their breaths were mingling with the mist; then simultaneously, as if both seeking protection, they stepped to the side and close to the wall, and there was no vestige of the young master about him now, for his tone was rather that of a frightened lad as he said, 'Do you think he'll say anything?'

'I don't know.' Her voice was a thin whisper. 'He says he won't. And anyway I can't see what good it'd do him if he did. But you never know with workhouse lads, you don't know where they come from; I mean you've got nothin' to go on when you don't know their mothers or fathers, have you?'

Charlie turned from her and leant his back flat against the wall, and putting his thumb to his mouth he bit hard on his nail. He had been in the habit of biting his nails a lot at one time, but since starting the school in Newcastle the habit had slowly disappeared. More to himself than to her now, he said. 'He could cause trouble, big trouble.'

'Aye . . . aye, he could; we'd . . . we'd better keep on the right side of him.'

'Yes.' He turned and nodded to her; and as she stared up at him she said quietly, 'You shouldn't be in this, you've got yourself mixed up in all ways with us. Now you're up against your mother through us. I . . . I don't know what to say, Charlie, how to thank you.'

He pulled himself from the wall. 'I don't want any thanks.'

Again they were facing each other.

'If . . . if ever I can do anythin' for you, you've only got to ask, Charlie.'

Her eyes were round, mist-filled, and now she gripped his hand and whispered urgently, 'I mean it. You understand? I mean it, anything.'

'Yes, yes, Polly, thank you. Yes, I understand.' He withdrew himself from her hold, then backed two steps away from her. And he was nodding at her again as he said, 'I'll have a word with Arthur; I'll tell him.'

As he went into the yard he knew she hadn't moved away. He also knew what she was offering him by way of thanks. He knew too that he wanted to accept her thanks – Oh yes, he wanted to accept her thanks – but he never would.

Why? Yes, why?

The answer came with the picture of his father taking her mother.

It was ten minutes later when he told Arthur of the new situation that had cropped up, and he watched him as he flopped down on an upturned bucket in the pig-room and thumped one fist against the other as he groaned, 'God Almighty! he's got me in the hollow of his hand. If he opens his mouth I'll go along the line . . . or worse; aye, or worse. The bloody hungry-looking workhouse brat that he is!' Then turning his head to the side, he gazed up at Charlie as he ended, 'An' he's got you there an' all. And that ain't fair. No, that ain't fair.'

Looking back at Arthur, he experienced a feeling of revulsion. Arthur had always appeared to him as fearless, rugged, tough; in a way he had hero-worshipped him for these qualities; but now there was an abjectness about him that was distasteful. His saying 'He's got you there an' all; it ain't fair' didn't ring with true concern, it was more of a statement, 'We're all in this together.' He turned abruptly away, saying, 'Don't worry about me; only go lightly on him for your own good.'

Out in the yard, with the mist almost obliterating the house from his view, he walked towards the kitchen door. He had said 'Don't worry about me' as if he weren't troubled by the fact that young Slater knew of his part in the awful event; but deep inside he was more than worried, he was fearful, for in a way he was as much involved as was Arthur. There was such a thing termed accessory after the fact, and for his part in the affair he would be condemned more so than Arthur, for what had he done but shield the person who had killed his father, whereas as a dutiful son he should have brought him to justice.

The mist bathing his face was mingled with sweat now.

When he opened the kitchen door he actually gulped audibly as he saw young Slater sitting by the table, a mug of tea in one hand and a large shive of bread in the other.

As the boy slithered to his feet Fanny put in quickly, 'Just giving him a bite, Mister Charlie, just a bite.'

Charlie looked from the round penetrating gaze of Sidney Slater to Fanny, then to Maggie who was standing behind her, a toasting fork in her hand and on which was stuck a slice of bread, and he knew that how he reacted now with this boy would set the pattern for future time. Fumbling in his breast pocket, he drew out the watch that his father had given him on his sixteenth birthday, and he made himself stare at it for a moment before taking his eyes from it and fixing them on Slater, then saying, 'It's quarter past eleven in the morning, you have your breakfast at eight and your dinner at one, isn't that so?'

The round eyes looking back into his had a slightly puzzled expression, and Slater's voice faltered slightly as he said, 'Aye . . . aye.'

'Aye what?'

There was a pause in which he heard Fanny's intake of breath.

'Aye, sir . . . Mister Charlie.'

'Well, in future you'll stick to your mealtimes. That understood?'

'Aye, Mister Charlie.'

'Good. Well you may finish that.' He waved his hand towards the mug and the bread on the table; then giving a lift of his shoulders he walked away, up the kitchen and through the green-baized door.

It was actually seconds after the door had closed on him that Fanny spoke. She had one cheek cupped in the palm of her hand as she did so. 'I can't believe it,' she said, 'What's come over him? He was as like the one who's gone as ever I've seen, yet this very mornin' he stood up to the missis and saved the Bentons.' She shook her head. 'I can't believe it. I just can't believe it.'

'I can.' Sidney Slater had lifted the latch of the door, and he turned and looked over his shoulder, adding, 'But don't you worry none about me, Mrs Dimple. Don't you worry none about me.'

Fanny moved towards him now, saying, 'Come back, Sidney, and finish your bite.' She motioned towards the table, but he shook his head, saying, 'No, no. Ta all the same. I tell you what though.' He was actually grinning at her now. 'You give it to him, he'll likely need it long afore I will.'

When the door closed on him Fanny turned and stared at Maggie and, her hand again cupped her cheek, she said, 'I can't believe it. I just can't believe it. There's somethin' here I don't understand: Mister Charlie takin' on the guise of his father, an' Sidney there not frightened any more. Did you see the look on that lad's face? It was strange, it was as if he feared neither God nor man any more. You know somethin' Maggie? An' you might think me barmy for sayin' this, but he looked the same as the master used to after he'd lathered one or t'other on the cinder path, like as if he had satisfied something inside himself. 'Twas an unholy look.'

93

PART TWO

Brooklands Farm

1

'Why you must have your birthday party between Christmas and New Year the Lord only knows.'

'. . . Not forgetting Mother and Father; they should have arranged my coming at a different time, they were very careless about their indulging.'

'Nellie! stop that kind of facetious chatter. If Father were to hear you, he'd skelp your ears for you.'

'Yes, I suppose he would. Yet Mother wouldn't. Strange that, isn't it?'

Nellie Chapman brought her legs up and tucked them under her where she was squatting on the side of the bed, and putting her head on one side, she gazed at her sister who was sitting before the mirror turning the long strands of her hair into a plait, and she said, 'You know you are just like Father, coarse as a pig's back in one way yet finicky refined in another.'

'Don't you dare say I'm as coarse as a pig's back!' Victoria twisted round on the dressing-table stool, her squarish handsome face flushed with irritation, which increased as her sister smiled at her and undauntedly went on, 'Well, you are. You know you are. All you think about is horses. You ride horses, you talk horses, you swear horses. You outdid Father yesterday when you were buggering Phil for not seeing to Laddy right away. It didn't matter about the other two horses, they could sweat themselves to death, but Laddy must be seen to. And your language was such that it even pushed up old Benny's eyebrows.'

'That's a different thing, that's got nothing to do with talk about . . . birth. I mean . . .' Victoria now twisted the end of the plait into a knot and was about to wind it tightly round the back of her head when her sister said, 'What you mean is cohabiting.'

'Nellie Chapman, get off that bed, and get out of my room! Go on, get out this minute!'

'All right, all right, I'll go. But that's what the books call it, and it proves what I said about you and Father. You know what?' She now leant her plump body towards her tall well-proportioned sister as she said, 'I'm always amazed by this stuffy attitude of yours, I really can't understand it. You're a hypocrite, you know that: even the Bible can speak plainly about it, procreation it calls it. And it's going on around us almost twenty-four hours a day. But here you are on the point of collapse because I mention it. But' – she gave an exaggerated sigh – 'it's as I said, you and Father are fakes because underneath you're worse than big Billy for it, and you know you are . . .'

As Victoria swung round to the dressing-table, her hand groping for something to throw, Nellie sprang to the door, opened it and, bent almost double, was scrambling on to the landing when a large china powder bowl, parting from its lid, whizzed over her head and struck the wall opposite and shattered into pieces.

'In the name of God! what's this?' Florence Chapman took the last three stairs at a run. Then stopping dead, she gazed from one to the other of her daughters, then at the broken china bowl that had left a trail of pink powder across the red patterned carpet, and now her angry gaze resting on Victoria, she cried, 'Have you gone mad? You could have knocked her out with that.'

'It's a pity I didn't; I won't miss next time if she dares to put a foot in my room.'

The bedroom door banged and Florence turned her attention to her younger daughter. For a moment she kept her teeth together and her lips spread wide from them while her head moved in small nods; then she said, 'And what did you do to bring this about?'

'Nothing; we were just talking.'

'Talking?' Florence now rushed forward and, grabbing Nellie by the shoulders, she pushed her along the landing and into the end room, and there she demanded, 'Out with it! It must have been something stronger than usual for her to throw a thing like that at you, for if it had hit you it could have split your head open. Come on now, what did you say?'

'Well, nothing really.' Nellie shrugged, then grimaced before she said, 'She was getting at me about my birthday party tomorrow. It was the same last year. She said she didn't see why I couldn't make it one do with the New Year's Eve party. But that wouldn't be my birthday party, would it?'

'No. I can see your point there; but, come on, that isn't what enraged her. What did you really say to her to upset her like that?'

'Aw.' Nellie walked down the length of the large bedroom towards the window; then resting her knee on the padded window-seat she looked out on to the white snow-covered garden and beyond to where the furrowed fields lay, showing crests of straight black earth like ruled lines on children's primers, and she muttered, 'I said she took after Father and they both took after big Billy.'

Florence Chapman's large unlined handsome face remained perfectly blank for a moment; then her eyes seeming to take their direction from her mouth stretched wide, but she spoke no word until, having closed her mouth again and taken in a deep breath through her dilated nostrils, she exclaimed, 'You said what!'

'Aw, Mother!' Nellie turned round and sat down on the window seat. 'Don't look so shocked because you know you're not. And anyway, you know what I say's true. Look how she eggs on Josh Pringle. And she's got Archie Whitaker slobbering. I've seen her and Archie behind . . .'

'Nellie! be quiet! Now you listen to me.' Florence approached her daughter and, sitting down beside her, she wagged her finger in her face as she went on, 'Josh and Archie have merely been friends, and you know it . . .'

'I don't, Mother, I don't know it' – Nellie's face

was straight now, her tone harsh – 'because if I were to get up to some of the things that I've seen her and Archie at and I told you it was all in friendship, by!' – she now turned her head to the side, nodding it as she did so – 'I know what you'd say . . . Lord! don't I!'

Florence Chapman turned her face away from her daughter for a moment and held her brow in the palm of her hand. What was she to do with this girl, this terror of a daughter, this honest individual . . . this her beloved child, for of her two daughters she had love for only one. It was true what Nellie had said, Victoria was very much like her father, talking one way and acting another. Not that she didn't care for Victoria, she did, as she cared for her husband, but she recognised the faults in both of them. Especially did she recognise those in her husband. But going on the premise that no one was perfect, she had for years condoned all his little sharp practices, and the last thing she would have ever thought of doing was to point out his faults to him. But not so Nellie. Nellie was sackcloth on the skin of both her father and her sister, although strangely that wasn't her intention.

Nellie's intention, she knew, was just to present her idea of things and people as they appeared to her. Ever since she had passed the lisping stage she had gone to great pains to express herself fully on all manner of subjects. Having been placed in the most embarrassing situations by their daughter's frankness when in company she and her husband had learned it was wiser to keep their opinions of their neighbours to themselves, at least until they were in the privacy of their bedroom.

That her daughter had of late learned a little discretion, at least with regard to outsiders, was very small comfort, for hardly a day went past but she irritated her father or infuriated her sister, while at the same time, Florence had to admit guiltily, affording herself not a little amusement. And the funny thing about it all was that Nellie's verbal attacks always held more than a smattering of truth, as in her latest statement that her husband and daughter took after the bull, for, as in her father, so there was raging in Victoria deep physical passion, which could only be really assuaged by marriage . . . At least she kept hoping so.

She was in a way worried about Victoria. She wished this business between young Charlie MacFell and her could be settled. Her father was bent on it, had been for years, and Victoria herself didn't seem all that averse. But what about Charlie?

He was an odd fellow was Charlie, not like a farmer at all; took after his mother really . . . Yet no; that woman was a silly bitch if ever there was one, stacking the house wih her fancy furniture and dressing like a girl half her age. That place would soon go to rack and ruin if it wasn't for young Betty. She should have been the man, should Betty. Yes, she should have been the man; there was too much of the woman in Charlie. Not that he wasn't manly. In his own fleshless long-boned way he was an attractive young fellow. But gutless. Aye, that was the word, gutless.

Charlie needed someone strong, someone to guide

him; and Victoria would be the right one in the right place there. It was a pity he was two years younger than her, it made things a little more difficult. But it was a difficulty that must be overcome if she wanted life with Hal to be bearable.

Her husband had a bee in his bonnet about merging the lands. If the positions of the farm had been altered and most of their land had been freehold, like Moor Burn was, then Hal might have taken a different view of the marriage. Oh yes, he undoubtedly would have.

It was funny how land got hold of men. Her husband, almost twenty years her senior, was turned sixty. In the order of things he hadn't all that time to enjoy the acquisition of more land, yet she knew it wasn't only of himself he was thinking but of his grandchildren. He wanted grandchildren, male grandchildren, in whom he could live on, walk in their steps as it were over the land, following the seasons from spring dawns to the mist-shrouded setting suns of winter. Men like her husband wanted to perpetuate themselves for ever. It was when they saw no prospect of this happening they would tend to make life pretty uncomfortable, to say the least, for those around them.

For herself, she didn't like to live uncomfortably: she enjoyed good food, good wine, she liked a soft bed and a warm house; she liked to dress well, according to her station, and have enough spare cash over from the housekeeping and dairy not to have to beg for coppers. She had a good life, an enjoyable life, and she wanted this to go on, so she turned to her daughter now and, her voice low and harsh, she said, 'That was a nasty crude thing to say; but we'll forget about it and we'll talk of tomorrow and your party. Now you want your party to go off well, don't you, Nellie?'

Nellie stared back at her mother but made no reply, and Florence, straightening her broad shoulders, drew in a deep breath and went on, 'Well, it's going to be up to you, because if you get your father's back up – and Victoria's – this will be your final birthday party. Now I mean that, Nellie. There'll be a lot of people here tomorrow, not only your friends but your father's and mine . . . and Victoria's, and I want us all to enjoy ourselves.'

'As it's my party why can't I have just my friends?'

'Well, one reason that should be evident to you is that your friends have all got to be driven here, and you can't leave their parents or their brothers standing on the doorstep . . . now can you?'

They looked at each other for a moment before Nellie said, 'I suppose Betty won't be able to ride over by herself, Charlie will have to bring her?'

'Yes, Nellie.' Florence's words were weighty now. 'Charlie will be bringing Betty . . . and her mother.'

'Oh, that'll be nice, if not for Charlie, for Dad I mean.'

'Nellie!' Florence now ground her teeth. 'There are times when I could skelp you hard.'

'For speaking the truth, Mother? It's under everybody's nose.'

104

Nellie now rose sharply from the window-seat and, making for the door, she said, 'Poor Charlie; she'll eat him alive. He won't know which horse has kicked him by the time she's finished with him. It's like throwing a Christian to the lions.'

Before she had time to turn the knob of the door her mother had her by the shoulders again and, swinging her about, she hissed at her, 'Nellie Chapman! now I'm warning you, you say one word to spoil things for Victoria tomorrow and I'll never forgive you.'

Nellie gazed back at her mother, sighed a deep sigh and said, 'All right. All right, keep your hair on. But you can't stop me feeling sorry for Charlie.'

On the landing Nellie paused a moment and looked towards Polly Benton who was on her knees sweeping up the powder from the carpet and there passed between them an exchange of glances expressing mutual understanding.

2

The birthday party was going with a swing, it had been going with a swing for the past three hours. The guests had sat down at five o'clock to a high tea and it was well past six before they rose from the table. In the sitting-room they chatted and talked for a time and teased Nellie the while; she, as usual, gave back more than she received. Then Florence was persuaded to sit at the piano, and from then the party got under way. They danced the polka; they waltzed; they jigged; there were enough couples to form three sets of lancers, and sufficient of the older ones present to clap and applaud from their seats which had been pushed against the wall in order to clear the floor.

By ten o'clock a deal of wine and spirits had been imbibed and the quantity was beginning to tell on some of the guests, as was evident when the sound of their hoots and laughter reached the kitchen.

Lindy Morton, piling the plates of sandwiches and mince pies on to the tray that Polly was holding, giggled as she said, 'It's like New Year's Eve afore its time in there, isn't it? By! they're goin' at it an' by the look of him the master's nearly blotto, an' the missis isn't far off either. An' your Charlie's knockin' it back an' all.'

'Don't call him my Charlie, Lindy; I've told you that afore.'

'Well, you're always talkin' about him.'

'Not in that way. And if the missis heard you, what do you think she'd say?'

'Aw, she'd just laugh. Well, she would about somebody in your position havin' a shine on someone like Mister Charlie. All right! All right! Look, you'll upset the tray . . . I'm sorry; I was only havin' you on.'

'Well, don't have me on about that.' Polly bounced her head at her work-mate; then swinging abruptly about she went up the kitchen and, turning her back to the door, thrust at it with her buttocks, then edged herself around it and into the broad passage. Using the same procedure with the door at the far end of the passage, she emerged into the hall and although, while crossing it, she kept her eyes averted from where Miss Betty was sitting on the bottom stair by the side of Mr Robin Wetherby, she did note that they both had their heads down and that their shoulders were shaking with laughter, and she remarked to herself that Miss Betty must have had a drop an' all if she was letting herself go on a laugh.

She ignored a second couple standing against the wall in the passage bordering the side of the staircase. They weren't so close together but their shoulders were resting against the panelling as they gazed at each other and this conveyed to her a sense of intimacy, as close as if they had been in each other's arms.

At first she couldn't make her way into the sitting-room because there was a jig in process. Miss Victoria was doing a kind of highland fling opposite Mr Whitaker. They were twirling and hooting to the beat of the clapping, which was almost drowning the music of the piano.

Her arms were breaking with the weight of the tray, but she moved her head back and forward between the shoulders in front of her to get a better view, and as she stared wide-eyed at the two dancing figures, her thoughts ran along the same lines as Nellie's had done the day before: She's like a wild horse, she'll trample him to death.

Her eyes left the dancers now and searched the room, as much as she could see of it; and then she saw him in the corner of her vision. She could see only his head and his hands; he was laughing and was clapping as loudly as the rest.

There was a final great whoop of sound; the dancing stopped and the clapping faded away; but she had to repeat a number of times, 'Excuse me. Excuse me, please,' before those in the doorway parted to allow her through to the table that had been cleared at the end of the room.

As she put the full plates on the table and picked up the empty ones, the laughter and voices beat down on her and she said to herself, 'It isn't fair; it's Miss Nellie's birthday party but they're making it more like a rowdy New Year's do.'

This was the third Christmas she had been here, having taken up the post almost immediately after her father had died, but in all the parties they had had she had never seen so much drink flowing as there was tonight; nor so much – she hesitated on the word – jollification. And anyway, it wasn't like a jollification; well, not a jollification people of the Chapmans' standard were known to indulge in, it was more approaching something she imagined one would see in the Wayfarers' Inn on the high road, where the drovers got together after a big market and things went on, so she had heard, that would sizzle your eyebrows.

As she stretched over to retrieve an empty plate, she glanced to where Mrs MacFell was sitting, and she gave a small shake of her head. She got worse as she got older. Dressed to kill. Her frock would have suited someone half her age. They said she was on the look-out for a man. Well, if nothing else, her get-up would make her fall between two stools, for to a young man she would look like mutton dressed up as lamb, while to a farmer who wanted a working wife she'd look like a giddy-headed goat. Mr Chapman said that she had gone back twenty years to when she first came to the farm as a young scatter-brained lass, and that was what she was acting like now. Her head was back, her mouth was wide open and her arms were flapping at Farmer Kelly.

As she wended her way out of the room, Polly's eyes again searched for Charlie. She must have a word with him, she must; but the only hope she'd have of waylaying him would be when he went to the men's closet outside. And so from now on she'd keep on the watch because surely they'd want nothing more to eat, not for a while anyway; she'd carried four tray-loads of food in there in the past half hour.

She had heard the boss say that you could drink your fill to overflowing as long as you ate with it, and he was certainly seeing that everybody did that the night. The stuff he had hauled up from the cellar was nobody's business; he had even brought up bottles that were twenty years old, the ones he usually bragged about.

She paused for a moment between the doors. It wasn't like a birthday party at all, it was as if he was celebrating something . . . aye, or hoping to celebrate something. She turned about on a gasp as a hand caught her arm.

'Hello there, Polly.'

'Oh!' She now took in a short, sharp breath, smiled, then said again, 'Oh! . . . hello, Charlie.'

'I've been wanting to get a word with you, I've never seen you over the holidays. I wanted to say Happy Christmas.'

'Oh, thanks, thanks, Charlie, an' the same to you.'

In the lamplit passage they smiled at each other. Then her face suddenly becoming straight, she whispered rapidly, 'And I . . . I want to have a word with you, Charlie. Can I see you, I mean outside like, for a minute or so? It's important, Charlie. I'll . . . I'll go over to the dairy in . . . in ten minutes or so, an' I'll wait. It's important.'

There was a burst of laughter beyond the passage door, then it was pushed wide and Nellie entered, accompanied by two laughing girls about her own age. She paused a moment to look at Polly disappearing into the kitchen; then laughing, she came towards Charlie, saying, 'There you are, boyo! And what are you up to, eh? What are you up to?' She lifted her hand and tickled him under the chin, and he caught her wrist and, laughing down at her, answered, 'Looking for you.'

'Liar! Isn't he a liar?' She turned to her companions, and they laughed and said, 'Yes, yes, you are, Charlie MacFell, you're a liar.'

Charlie looked from one to the other of the laughing faces. They were flushed, their eyes were bright. He had the desire to kiss one after the other, just in fun, that was all, just in fun. The wine that was making their faces bloom like roses before his eyes was also making him feel gay enough to sip the dew from them, so he told himself. He had drunk more tonight than he had ever done in his life before; he had never known Chapman to be so generous with his cellar.

'What are you all up to in here?' The voice brought them round to face Victoria standing with the door in her hand, and Charlie stared over the heads of the three girls towards her. She looked beautiful. He had thought so when he had first seen her tonight, but she had grown more so as the evening wore on. Oh yes, he had told himself already that he was seeing her through the fumes of hot rum and old brandy, in fact only a short while ago he had warned himself that he wouldn't be able to see her at all if he indulged himself further.

She was standing in front of him now. She was wearing a green velvet dress, her flesh appearing to pour over the low cut neck like rising cream. Her dark hair was piled high on her head, and two strands had come loose in the dancing and were lying one on each of her cheeks.

'Come on, come on, you're going to dance this one with me.'

'Oh, Victoria! you know I'm no dancer.'

'Leave him alone, our Vic, it's my party.' Nellie's voice was a hiss now, and he looked from one to the other; then stretching his arms wide between them, he laughed with the two young girls who were convulsed with what they took to be a comic situation.

'What's on here?' Hal Chapman had joined them in the passage, and Victoria's voice, still holding laughter, said, 'I want Charlie to dance and she's trying to stop him.'

'Don't be silly, Nellie. Behave yourself!'

The slap that brought Nellie's hand from Charlie's arm was almost in the nature of a blow and she winced and sprang back, and stood against the wall and watched her father pushing her sister and Charlie through the door and into the hall.

'Did he hurt you?' One of the girls had remained behind, and Nellie shook her head vigorously, saying, 'No, no. Go on, go on in; I'll be with you in a minute, I'm just going to the toilet.' On this she ran down the corridor, past the door leading into the hall and up the back stairs and into her bedroom.

Three times during the next hour Polly scurried across the icy yard and into the dairy, but Charlie did not come.

'What you keep going out to the netty for, you got diarrhoea?'

'Yes, a bit.' Polly nodded at Lindy.

'What's given it you, you been drainin' the glasses?'

Polly smiled weakly as she answered, 'Aye, a few,' thinking as she did so, I'd be hard put for a drink to drain glasses, I would that.

'Well, you missed a few 'cos I've had a lick at some. Eeh! the stuff that's been swilled in there the night, you could launch a boat on it. The boss must be in a generous mood. It's some party.'

'Aye; but it isn't like a birthday party, it's not as Miss Nellie wanted it, I'm sure of that.'

'No, you're right there; 'tis more like a wake or a weddin' . . . You off again?'

'Yes.' Polly pressed her hand against her stomach and, grabbing a cape from the back of the door, she put it over her head, and ran out into the yard once more; and as she did so she saw the side door open and a dark figure show up against the snow and make its way unsteadily towards the dairy.

'That you, Charlie?'

'Yes, Polly. S . . . sorry I couldn't get here before. Goin' mad in there.' He laughed.

They were inside the dairy now. The cold seemed more striking than outside, and the clean bareness of the place could be sensed even through the darkness.

'Wait a minute,' Polly whispered now; 'I'll light the candle. It won't be seen if we keep it this end.'

As the flame of the candle flickered upwards, Polly looked into his face. It wasn't the face she knew so well, the face that was deeply etched in her mind burnt there by the trammels of young love. His thoughtful, even sombre, look was replaced by a large inane grin; the grey eyes, whose kindness and concern was usually covered by blinking lids, were half closed as if he were about to fall asleep where he stood.

'Charlie.'

'Yes, Polly.' He had hold of her hand.

'It's Ginger.'

'Ginger? What about him?'

'He . . . he wants me to marry him.'

'What!' For a moment he seemed to sober up completely, his eyes widened, and his lids blinked rapidly. 'Ginger . . . you marry Ginger? You'll not! Wait till I see him. The bloody insolence!'

Funny, it was the first time she had ever heard him use a swear word, but then she hadn't been with him much since they had grown up and she had come over here to work. She took him by the arm and shook him slightly and, reaching her face up to his, she whispered as if they might be overheard, 'There's . . . there's nothing else for it, Charlie, is there?' Her last two words seemed to pierce the fug of his brain and he repeated to himself, 'Is there? Is there?'

'Do . . . do you want to marry him?'

'No. *No!*'

'Well then.' He knew as he said it it was a stupid answer to give her and that was why she was actually shaking him.

'But don't you see, Charlie? If I don't he could . . . he could split.'

He looked down into her face and for a moment he forgot about Sidney Slater as he thought, She's bonny; not beautiful, but bonny, warmly bonny. That's what he wanted, warmth. He had always wanted Polly, the warmth of her. He had continually dreamed of her until recently, when he had realised the stupidity of it. But what was she saying? That Slater! that ginger-headed weasel wanted to marry her! It was strange but he had never imagined that he could really hate anybody, yet as he had watched the undersized skinny lad sprout inches and his shoulders broaden until now at eighteen he was a presentable young fellow, he knew that his mere dislike of the boy had grown into hate, for never once had Slater looked at him over the years but his eyes had said, 'Don't come the master with me; we know who's got the upper hand, don't we?' As for the fellow's effect on Arthur, at times he wouldn't have been surprised if Arthur hadn't tried his hand at a second murder.

He said now, 'Arthur, does Arthur know?'

'Yes.'

'What did he say?'

'Well—' She turned her head away and looked

towards a bench on which stood a gleaming row of copper pans, the candlelight bringing out gold from their depths, and her voice was low in her throat as she said, 'When me mother told him, she said he banged his head against the wall, then went out and got drunk.'

Again there was silence between them, and now he stuttered, 'You . . . you're too young to be married.'

'Don't be silly' – her tone was astringent – 'me ma was married at sixteen.'

'Do . . . do you like him?'

Again she turned her head to the side, right on to her shoulders now, and out of the corner of her eyes her gaze rested on the wooden churn, the handle of which had hardened the muscles of her arms since she had come on the farm, and she looked at it for a full minute before saying, 'I don't dislike him; he's . . . he's always been decent towards me, not like he's acted with Arthur . . . an' you. He hates you both.'

'I'm well aware of that. Anyway—' He made an attempt to straighten his shoulders and his lips worked one over the other before he said, 'Leave it to me, I'll see to him. I'll bring it into the open . . . Should have done it years ago. Who's going to believe him, eh? Who's going to believe him? Think he's mad, that's what they'll think, think he's mad. Don't worry, Polly' – he put his hand on her shoulder and his face hung over hers for a moment – 'you'll not marry him, I'll see to that. Leave it to me, eh? Leave it to me.'

She gazed back into his eyes before she whispered, 'Yes, Charlie. All right, Charlie.'

Their faces were close, their noses almost touching, he felt himself swaying. Once she had offered to pay him for what he had done for them. He would like to take the payment now. Oh aye, he would like to take the payment now, to hold her in his arms, to kiss her, to hug her, to roll with her on the floor . . . to love her. Oh, to love Polly. The old dream was returning. Their noses touched; his arms were moving upwards when she sprang back from him, 'I've . . . I've got to go; I've been comin' back an' forward for the last hour, an' Lindy's been wonderin'.'

He didn't speak. His arms were still extended in front of him as he watched her nip out the candle, then walk through the open door into the whiteness of the yard. There went his love, his buried love. He knew he'd never have Polly. Yet he had said 'Leave it to me.' What did he mean? Aye, what did he mean? . . .

Polly didn't run across the yard, she walked, her head deep down on her chest until it was brought abruptly up, when a cry bordering on a scream came from her open mouth as she felt her arm being gripped. She was pulled into the side doorway, then into the light of the passage and the sound of merriment.

'What've you been up to?'

It was almost with relief that she looked down into Nellie's face.

'Oh . . . Miss Nellie . . . Miss Nellie . . . I've just been to the dairy.'

'Yes, I know you've just been to the dairy, and I know who's been in the dairy with you. What I'm asking you is what you are up to.'

'Nothin', Miss Nellie, honest, nothin'. Well . . . there's trouble at home' – there was always trouble at home so that was no lie – 'an' I asked Mister Charlie to give me a minute of his time 'cos I wanted him to take a message . . . a message to me mother.'

'And you had to go into the dark dairy to do it?'

'It wasn't dark, Miss Nellie, I lit a candle.'

'Oh, you lit the candle . . . the better to see him with. Well' – Nellie was now stabbing her anger into Polly's chest – 'you know I've always been decent to you, don't you?'

'Aye, Miss Nellie. Oh, aye.'

'Well, I'm going to give you some advice; get Mister Charlie out of your mind.'

'What?'

'You heard what I said. Oh, I haven't been blind all these years, I've seen you watching him every time he comes to the place. I'm not blaming you, mind, I'm not blaming you, but I'm just telling you there's no future in it for you. And you're sensible enough to know that, so why do you carry on?'

Polly's mouth opened and closed, then her hands working agitatedly on her apron smoothed the bands around her waist, then the wide bib before she ran her fingers down the broad side hems as far as her hands could reach, and when she stopped pressing and plucking she said in a tone that definitely held dignity, 'I think you're barking up the wrong tree, Miss Nellie, never such a thought crossed me mind. I . . . I'm . . . well . . . I'm about to give me word to Sidney Slater at the farm.'

There was silence between them for a moment; then in a soft voice now, Nellie said, 'Honest?'

'Yes, honest.'

'Oh well . . . well I'm sorry, but you must admit it looked fishy. And just think Polly, if Mother had caught you or . . . or her ladyship.' She grinned now. 'If you had told her you were going to marry ten Sidney Slaters it wouldn't have convinced her but that you were up to something.'

Again they looked at each other; then with a slight toss of her head Polly turned and walked away, and as she disappeared through the doorway into the kitchen Nellie turned and ran into the yard again, and it was just as she reached the door of the dairy that Charlie came out.

'Ah-ha! Master MacFell, what have you been up to? Come on, come on, I want to know.'

She had him by the arm now leading him across the yard, not in the direction of the house but towards the barn, and as they skipped and staggered on the ice she talked at him, saying, 'Romeo, Casanova, and Benny Blackett the drover, you're all of them rolled into one. Do you know that, Charlie MacFell? Heart breaker, that's what you are.'

She had pushed open the door of the big barn and their joined laughter was smothered by the padding of the bales of hay.

'You're a naughty girl, do you know that?'

'Yes, I know that, Charlie. And you're a daft lad, do you know that?'

119

He paused before saying solemnly, 'Yes, I know that, Nellie.'

'Well, naughty and daft, let's join forces and enjoy ourselves, eh? Come on . . . here, light the lantern, I've got something to show you.'

'But wait . . . wait' – he pulled at her arm – 'we'd better get back, they'll be missing us.'

'You didn't think that when you took Polly into the dairy, did you?'

'Oh now, now Nellie, wait.'

She was laughing loudly at him as she said, 'I'm not waiting. Here! hold it.' She thrust the lantern into his hand. 'And keep yourself steady else you'll set the place on fire. You're tipsy, you know that?'

'What about you?'

'I'm only half tipsy yet, but the night's young. Come on.'

'Where you going?'

'Up on to the floor,' she said, making for the ladder.

'Now, now, Nellie.'

'Now, now, Charlie.' She turned her head over her shoulder and scoffed at him, 'Come on, be a brave boy, follow little Nellie.'

He followed her, but slowly, having to feel his way up the ladder. She was a caution was Nellie, lovable in a way. You couldn't help liking Nellie, but she was a terror for all that. By! yes. To them back there in the house she had brought some blushes in her time with her tongue. She had a sharp wit, had Nellie, like a rapier, and he had no doubt that she was also cruel

120

at times, but she had never used the sharp edge of her tongue on him. No, funny that, she'd always been kind and sympathetic towards him. He liked Nellie. Oh aye, he liked Nellie. And he loved Polly, and he admired Victoria . . . Was that all the feeling he had for Victoria? Victoria was beautiful; in a heavy sort of way, but she was beautiful. They wanted him to marry Victoria and he'd be a fool if he didn't because it was someone like Victoria who was needed to cope with his mother, he himself was no match for her. There were times when she irritated him so much he felt like striking her. And that was strange because he couldn't even watch a beast being goaded without feeling the nail piercing himself. Yet how near he had come to hitting her. Oh yes, he'd had the desire more than once to lift his hand and skelp his mother across the mouth. Nature was a funny thing.

'Look where you're goin', you'll fall over the edge, you fool!'

Nellie grabbed him and pulled him down on to the hay. She had hung the lantern on a nail in the stay post that reached from beneath the floor in the middle of the barn right up to the apex of the roof. They said that piece of wood had been carved out of a single tree three hundred years ago and she didn't disbelieve them. It was still unmarred by beetle rot, strong, sturdy, oozing strength.

She wished she could draw some of the strength from it and inject it into this lovable, soft, long individual by her side. She turned from him and began to grope among the straw close under the roof, and when she found what she was looking for she brought it out with a flourish and dangled it before his face, crying, 'One of the best, eighteen ninety. He never dipped that far down tonight, but nevertheless he'll have fits when he sobers up tomorrow an' finds out just how far he did dip down among his precious bottles . . . An' you know why he did it Charlie? You know why he's made such a splash?'

As she dangled the bottle before his face dull purple and and green lights swam before his eyes, and as she widened the arc the lantern light added shots of gold reflected from the straw.

Grabbing at the bottle now, he peered closely at it as he said thickly, 'That's brandy. Oh, Nellie, you shouldn't.'

'Well, oh Charlie, I did. And it's not the first time neither.'

'You don't mean . . . you don't mean you drink the lot?'

'No, no, not the lot, I share it with old Benny. I . . . I get it for him. He loves a drop of good stuff does Benny, and when would he ever be able to afford stuff like that? And I'm telling you this, dear papa wouldn't afford it either if he didn't get it on the cheap. It's all customs fiddled stuff, like Mother's expensive scent . . . and Vic's and mine. Do you know he's got a secret place upstairs for it? Well, he has, he has. So what chance has anybody like old Benny to taste a drop of the real stuff?' She slapped the bottle with her hand. 'Things are badly distributed, don't you think, Charlie?'

'Yes, yes.' He nodded at her. 'Oh yes, Nellie, things are badly distributed, I agree with you. Yes, I agree with you there.' His head was bouncing on his neck as if on wires. 'But all the same this is real old stuff, priceless really. Couldn't you have taken a younger brand, sort of?'

'Yes' – she sat back on her heels – 'I suppose I could, but I heard somebody coming. It was his nibs himself and Lord! There was only just time to get out, and as I made my escape I took the first thing that came to hand, and it was this.' She laughed now, adding, 'My hands have very good taste; what do you say, Charlie?'

'I say you're a rip, Nellie. That's what you are, a rip, an', an' I think you'd better put it back an' get old Benny a younger bottle.'

'Not on your life! And anyway, there won't be very much left for Benny when we're finished with it.'

'Now, now, Nellie.' As he made to rise from the straw she pushed him back, saying, 'Be brave, Charlie, be brave. For once in your life be brave.'

'Nellie.' His face became straight and his tone took on an offended note. 'That isn't nice, Nellie; you are talking as if I'd sometime acted as a coward. I'm not a coward, Nellie, I'm . . . I'm simply sen . . . sensitive to people's feelings.'

'I know that, Charlie, but everybody doesn't look at it that way. The way they see it is you're short on guts.'

'Now Nellie.'

'Stop sayin', now Nellie. Here, drink that.' She handed him a battered tin mug, which he pushed away, saying, 'No, I don't think . . .'

'Well, don't think, just drink.'

'Oh, Nellie.' He shook his head over the tin mug; then he put it to his lips, swallowed, screwed his eyes up tightly, turned his face towards his shoulder as if to bury it there, then coughed and spluttered as he said, 'By! you swa . . . swallow the d . . . date all right with this stuff, eighteen ninety . . . eighteen ninety.'

Nellie had just taken a drink from her mug and now she, too, was coughing, and as she thumped her chest she gasped, 'Oh boy! giant's blood.'

'What?'

'I . . . I said it's like giant's blood. Stuff like this's not supposed to be gulped. Sip it. Go on, sip it.' She pushed the mug towards his lips, and he, laughing now, sipped at the brandy again, while she, twisting about, pressed herself closely to his side, then followed suit.

There must have been the equivalent of two double brandies in each of the mugs and when she poured the third draught out for him he made no objection. He was sitting with his back to a bale of straw, his knees up, his wrists dangling between them, the mug held loosely in his hands, and she sat in much the same position, her knees up, the mug held between her hands.

There was a quietness all around them and in them; they were suffused with a great but gentle mellowness; they had no desire to laugh any more, they were content just to sit on this hazy planet and to talk at intervals. They touched on subjects that had no relation to each other such as the day when Big Billy had taken the prize for the best bull at the fair, how well her mother played the piano, and from that to the difference the new road had made. Their remarks on each subject were disjointed, terse, but lucid enough to evoke some sort of reasonable answer. And then she said, 'You know all this is for your benefit tonight, Charlie.'

'What . . . what do you say, Nellie?'

'I said, over at the house, the big do, me birthday party, they don't give a damn if I'm seventeen or se . . . seventy, it's all been done to bring you up to . . . to scratch.'

'Scratch?'

'Yes, scratch.'

'What scratch?'

'Oh, don't be so damn dim, Charlie. Vicky, Victoria the great, the she stallion, that's the scratch, *Victoria*!'

'Vic . . . Victoria?'

'Aye, yes, an' you. You were meant to pop the . . . the question the night.'

'No.'

'Fact. Fact.'

' 'Magination, Nellie.'

' 'Magination the bull's backside!'

At this they fell against each other hooting. When their laughter eased away they were still sitting but now their arms were about each other, and when they hiccuped loudly together they laughed again.

'She'll swallow you alive, Charlie.'

'Never get the chance.'

'Oo-oh! but she will. It's like when . . . when she gets her legs over a horse, she digs her knees in an' . . . an' the poor old beast goes where she wills; you're her latest poor old beast, Charlie.'

'Oh no! Nellie, not me.'

'Yes, you, Charlie, you're next in line for breakin' in. They've got it arranged 'tween 'em, Father'n her. Not a word spoken, but I know. Oh I know. I know the lot of 'em . . . aw!' She turned on to her hip and laid her face in his neck and now she whispered, 'Tell you somethin', Charlie, tell you somethin'. I'd hate to see you marry her, Charlie; you're too nice for her. You're too nice for me an' all, but me, I wouldn't treat you like she treats you, Charlie. An' you're older'n me, which's as it should be, isn't it? . . . Would you marry me, Charlie?'

He was shaking with laughter inside. It bubbled up to his lips and spilled over as, easing her face from his shoulders, he held it between his hands. And now he pushed out his lips and wagged his head and said, 'Marry you, Nellie? Course I'll marry you. Nothin' better to do come New Year but marry you, Nellie. An' we'll bring our bed up here an' live in the barn happy ever after. Oh! . . . The lantern's gone out.'

'You would, Charlie, you'd marry me?' She groped at him.

'Any . . . day . . . in the week . . . Nellie. Any . . . day . . . day . . . in the week . . .'cept the month's got an R in it.'

'Oh Charlie!' She had her arms around his neck. 'That's a promise?'

'A promise, Nellie.'

He held her tightly for a moment; then they both overbalanced and fell into the straw. And there they lay for the next hour or more oblivious of the voices calling in the yard; oblivious of the lanterns swinging on the ground floor of the barn; oblivious of everything until she was brought from the comfort of his arms and her drunken sleep by a mighty hand which held her swaying body upright as the voice thundered over her, 'What in hell's flames are you up to now! You slut you! You slut you! God! for two pins I'd thrash . . .'

'Don't! Don't! Leave her alone!'

Charlie staggered to his feet but had to put his hands behind him to support himself from falling again, and with his mind so fogged that he imagined himself to be in some sort of nightmarish dream where all the figures were swaying he tried to sort out the faces coming and going before him.

His gaze swung from Hal Chapman to Nellie, then from her to where Victoria was climbing on to the platform, and beyond her to where figures were milling about in the straw below, their faces all turned upwards.

'You! you little bitch you!' Victoria made a lunge towards her sister, but her father's arm swinging backwards thrust her aside and she, losing her footing, fell plump on to a bale of hay.

Charlie now had to subdue a strong desire to laugh: it was all so funny. What were they making the fuss about; it was a party, wasn't it? But what was he doing up here? He must have fallen asleep. Was he still asleep?

The next minute he knew he wasn't asleep as Nellie's voice startled him with its loudness and the content of her words as she screamed and strained towards her sister. 'It's not what you think, you mucky-minded horse-mad harlot you! Yes, harlot you! We didn't do anything, nothing. We don't jump at it like you, we can wait 'cos . . .'cos we're going to be married, Charlie'n me, we're going to be married. He asked me. You did, didn't you, Charlie?'

He was standing straight now. Marry Nellie? He had asked Nellie to marry him? Nonsense! Oh God! his head was thumping. Somewhere in the dream, right back, he could recall somebody talking about marrying Nellie; but he wasn't going to marry Nellie; he didn't want to marry Nellie.

'Is . . . is this true?' Hal Chapman, his body swaying, thrust his beer-red face gleaming with sweat in front of Charlie's. 'D'you hear me? Is it true?'

'What . . . what's true?'

'You silly bugger!' Hal Chapman now let loose of his younger daughter and, gripping Charlie by the shoulders, shook him, saying, 'You're so bloody drunk you don't know if you asked her to marry you or not, an' likely put a seal on the bargain?'

'Yes, I suppose I am bloody drunk.' Charlie laughed weakly now.

'Did you or did you not, lad?' Another shake.

'What?' Oh Lord! Lord! his head.

'Ask Nellie here to marry you?'

Charlie turned his hammer-beating head and looked towards Nellie. Her face swam away from her body; it moved round in a circle until it merged into Victoria's. The comedy of the situation became too much for him, and he laughed, a great bellow of a laugh, the way he hadn't laughed for years, perhaps not since the morning of the day when his father had died. Then he heard someone who wasn't at all like himself shouting, 'Yes, yes; is anything wrong in that?'

Hal Chapman allowed a silence of seconds to elapse before enveloping Charlie in his embrace. What did it matter which one of them he had chosen. After all it made no difference did it? The land would be joined and that was all that mattered. He now stepped back from Charlie and slapped him heartily in the chest with the back of his hand, then let out another roar of laughter as the tall figure tumbled once again into the straw. But that over, he turned to where his elder daughter was pulling herself upwards from the hay and, taking her arm, he gripped it and, keeping his eyes averted from her distorted features, led her to the top of the ladder, and there he growled at her, 'Put a face on it. Put a face on it.'

As she wrenched herself from her father's hold, Victoria looked to where Charlie was leaning on his elbows in the straw, his head back and his mouth still emitting laughter; and from him her gaze swept to her sister and their eyes shot hate of each other with the deadliness of bullets.

Hal Chapman, following his daughter down the ladder, shouted the news to the waiting guests below, who were all men, and who, after a moment of surprised silence, cheered and waved their hands up towards the loft where Nellie, now kneeling by Charlie's side, was looking woefully at him and repeating, 'I'm sorry, Charlie, I'm sorry,' while he comforted her by saying, 'It's all right, Nellie. It's all right.'

But what was all right, he wasn't quite sure; he wasn't sure of anything except that he was still tickled to death about something; what he didn't know, because he was so tired he wanted to sleep. Oh, he just wanted to sleep . . . and not wake up again . . . Was that so . . . not wanting to wake up again? There must be something wrong. He turned on to his side and laid his head on his hand and actually dropped off to sleep again.

3

He was brought up from the depths of sleep to the awareness of an ear-splitting voice calling his name. 'Charlie! Charlie!'

He groaned, went to shake his head, then swiftly put his hands up to it to still the agonising pain.

'Charlie! Charlie! wake up.'

The light sent arrows of agony through his eyeballs.

'Come on, sit up and drink this.'

Two hands helped to drag him into a sitting position. The cup pressed against his lips burned them, and he jerked his hand backwards and the hot liquid spilt over his chin, bringing him fully awake.

'Oh God! God Almighty! where am I?' He squinted into Nellie's face. 'What's up?'

'Drink that coffee. Go on, drink it.'

He gulped at the liquid, and when the cup was emptied and she went to pour another from the pewter jug he stopped her with a quivering, tentative motion of his hand; then shutting his eyes, he lowered his head as he asked quietly, 'What happened?'

'You got drunk. We both got drunk.'

'Both of us?' He squinted at her again.

'Yes; don't you remember?'

He went to shake his head, then hunched his shoulders against the movement as he answered, 'Can't remember a thing. God! I'm cold.'

He looked about him. The winter sun was streaking through the cracks in the barn timbers, watery yet painful to his eyes. He tried to recall what he should remember, but his mind took him no further than the dairy and Polly's face. Polly was going to marry Ginger. Or was she? No, she wasn't; he was going to put a stop to it.

. . . 'We're engaged to be married.'

He consciously stopped his head from jerking around. He did not even turn his face towards her when he said, 'What did you say, Nellie?'

'I said we're engaged to be married.'

Now he did look at her, but slowly, and he repeated, 'We're engaged to be married? Huh!' Even his smile increased the agony in his head. 'What do you mean, Nellie, engaged to be married? Huh!'

'Apparently we plighted our troth.' Her tongue came well past her teeth and lips as she dragged out the last word.

Again he said 'Huh!' but now he laughed. With his two hands holding his head he laughed as he said 'We must have been stinking.'

'We were.'

'How did we get like that?'

She twisted round on the straw now and picked up the empty brandy bottle and held it out towards him, and when he took it from her and read the label he whistled, then said, 'We went through that, a full bottle?'

'Apparently.' Her voice held a slightly sad note now.

'And the best brandy . . . my! my! that must have cost something.'

'Not as much as you think. It's all smuggled stuff, Father's got friends. I think somehow I told you. Anyway, if he'd had to pay the real price for it I suppose he'd have considered it worth while, as it got us engaged.'

'Your—' He turned on to his knees now and steadied himself by gripping at a bale of straw and his mouth opened twice before he muttered, 'Your . . . your father knows?'

'Yes; they all know.'

'Aw, Nellie, no! No!' Now he actually did shake his head, and vigorously.

'Is it so terrible?'

She was kneeling opposite him and he raised his head and stared at her. No . . . no, he supposed, looked at calmly, it wasn't so terrible 'cos she was a very appealing girl was Nellie. But he had no feeling for her, not in that way. Good Lord! no, never in that way, not Nellie. She had just left school, she was still a young girl somehow. If he had thought about marrying into the Chapmans', and he had thought about it, it was Victoria his mind had dwelt on; in fact he could tell himself he had been coached over the years to think of Victoria as a wife. And now her name escaped from him, 'Vicky!' he said.

'Yes, what about Vicky?'

'Nellie . . . well, you know.'

'What do I know?' Her words came clipped, cold.

'Aw, don't be silly, Nellie. What happened last night must have been a prank, we . . . we were drunk. You said yourself.'

She stared hard at him for a number of seconds before rising to her feet and saying in the same tone as before, 'I'd better go and tell them then, her in particular . . . put her out of her misery. Then they'll have to send the bellman round all the villages, telling people they got the name wrong.'

He was standing now, and he repeated, 'All the villages?'

'Yes, all the villages, where the Hodgsons, the Pringles, the Fosters, the Charltons, the Whitakers, and Uncle Tom Cobley an' all live.'

'Oh my God!' He held his brow with his hand, and now his voice low, almost a whisper, he said to her, 'Don't be mad at me, Nellie; it would never have happened if we hadn't got drunk, you know that.'

'No, it wouldn't.' She was thrusting her face up to his now. 'You're right there, Charlie. But I'll tell you this much, there'll come a time when you'll wish you'd stuck to your drunken proposal. I'm no prophet but I know that much.'

'Nellie! Nellie!' He watched her going down the steep ladder, and again he called, 'Nellie! Nellie!'

When she reached the bottom she stopped and looked up at him and when he said, 'I'm sorry, I'm so sorry, Nellie,' she answered back, her voice soft now, 'Yes, I know, Charlie; but it's nothing to what you will be, and I'll be sorry for you then.'

She had reached the open doors when he called again, 'Nellie!'

When she turned to face him he asked, 'My mother and Betty, are they still here?'

'No; the Pringles dropped them off on their way back.' Now the old tart note was in her voice again as she ended, 'Your mother couldn't get away quick enough, Betty an' all. I think they wanted to lock the doors so I wouldn't get in. Whoever you take back there, Charlie, you're going to have a fight on your hands.' She shook her head slowly, then jerked her chin upwards before turning and disappearing into the yard.

God Almighty! He lowered himself down on to the scattered straw. Trust him to make a hash of things. Proposing to Nellie! How in the name of God had that come about? And she had wanted to keep him to it. Yes – he nodded quietly to himself – she had. And now he had Hal Chapman to face. But worse than that, there was Victoria. What must she have felt when she heard the news. Perhaps she, too, was too drunk to take it in; but no, it would take a lot of the hard stuff to deprive Victoria of her senses. More than once he had noticed that she was like her father in that way, she could carry her liquor, it only made her jolly. He must go down, tidy himself up, try to explain away the whole silly affair, and then he must get home and face his mother, and her wrath. Nellie was right in what she had said: whoever he took back to the house he'd have a fight on his hands because his mother was certainly mistress in that house and she intended to go on being so. He had given into her over the years because not having done so would have made his life sheer hell on earth. While he played the master during those first months after his father had died she countermanded every order he gave, and the confusion in the house had been chaotic.

Why did things never go smoothly for him? What was it in his nature that made him the object of ridicule? After three years of managing the farm he still, to put it plainly, had no bloody horse sense. If left to himself he would have bought animals out of pity for their leanness. When in company with other farmers he didn't talk farming; he didn't slosh himself with drink on market days; nor did he inveigle himself with the right people who would drop a case of brandy along with the fodder every now and again. In a way, he knew he was still considered as his father's son, an outsider. That the farm had not gone downhill since his father died wasn't any credit to himself, it was Arnold and Fred who kept the standard high, and kept Sidney Slater up to scratch. Yes, and Arthur too, for Arthur's fear had undermined his promising ability.

And now this latest farce. He'd be a laughing stock; they'd say he'd had to get blind drunk in order to propose marriage to a lass and then when he was sobered up he couldn't go through with it.

What was wrong with him anyway? Was he a weakling?

No, no. He denied this strongly inside himself. He was just a square peg in a round hole, and he had been rammed into it by sympathy for the Bentons.

Polly! There was Polly. He became alert. She couldn't marry Slater; he couldn't let that happen. He must get home and talk to Arthur. Something must be done.

He went down the ladder, but not as steadily as Nellie had done, and when he was on the floor of the barn he dusted himself down, picking the straw from his suit and out of his hair. And he was busy with this when a shadow filled the opening. He turned to see Victoria standing there.

Victoria, looking silently at Charlie, wondered, and not for the first time, what it was she saw in him that attracted her. It wasn't his long, lean thinness, nor his grey passionless eyes, nor his mop of fair hair that he wore over-long. So what was it? Was it his weakness that challenged her strength? Yet it was a strange weakness, for it wasn't gutless. There was a time when she had imagined he was gutless; that was until the day she had glimpsed a fighting light in his eyes when he witnessed Josh flogging his horse for having thrown him and so causing him to lose a race. The winning of the race would have meant little to Josh, for what was a race at a fair but an opportunity to enter everything from a donkey to a stallion, and to have a good laugh at the assortment; but the losing of it on a thoroughbred meant a lot, and this she'd had to point out rather forcibly to Charlie to prevent him from going for Josh.

But did she really want him? Yes, yes, she wanted him; and she was going to have him, for she saw him as her last chance of becoming independent and getting away from this house. No one would believe her if she said that her main aim in life was to depart this place where her mother ruled supreme. And she herself would not believe anyone who told her that she was jealous of her mother, jealous of her looks, of her popularity, of her capabilities, and, most of all, of her power over her husband.

She had always admitted to herself that her home was divided in affection. She had her father's love while Nellie had her mother's; but her mother also had her husband's love and herein lay the core of her jealousy. But she had made herself blind to it. What she wanted she told herself was a home of her own, a place in which she would be called mistress; and, it definitely had to be a house with stabling attached, and Moor Burn had the best facilities in that line for miles around. Of course there was Madam MacFell, but she would deal with her when the time came.

Over the past months she had decided that Charlie must be brought up to scratch. It had become imperative that she should have him. Archie Whitaker had dropped from her horizon, he had even got himself engaged, and Josh . . . Josh had made it plain he was in no position to marry for years. Being the youngest of four sons was the excuse he put forward. She had been openly careless where Josh Pringle was concerned and had got herself talked about. She knew that her name now was such that she could not hope to find a husband in her own class for miles around. She admitted to herself that she had been foolish, too free, but there was that craving inside her that demanded release. All during her teens her body had burned for this release, so much so that at times it frightened her. Were all women like this, she wondered. Archie Whitaker had told her they weren't, and that she was out of this world. She marvelled now why she hadn't fallen pregnant in those first two months; after that she had made sure she wouldn't.

Now Archie Whitaker was gone, and Josh Pringle was becoming less available. She stilled the voice inside herself which said she had been too much for him. Now there was only Charlie to fall back on, and up till a few minutes ago she thought she had lost this chance too. That little bitch! She shuddered as she thought of her sister and of what she might have done to her last night if her father hadn't pulled her hands away from the plump throat. Afterwards she had managed to control her rage until the last guest had gone, but then she had allowed the storm to break, and by God! it had been a storm. Six ornaments she had smashed, a piece of Worcester, two pieces of Doulton, and her mother's treasured group of Dresden figures; that was before she pounced on Nellie.

And this morning she'd sworn to her father that

she'd never rest until she'd done her sister a serious mischief. Then five minutes ago the little bitch had walked jauntily into the dining-room and proclaimed it had all been a joke. They had both been drunk, she said, and she had no more intention of marrying Charlie than she had of marrying Josh Pringle.

She had made a small motion with her head as she mentioned Josh's name, and the motion had indicated the extent of the little bitch's knowledge as much as if she had shouted it aloud.

Well, now things had come to a head, and she must slacken the bit. She must alter her tactics.

She started by walking slowly towards him and putting out her hand and picking a piece of straw from the side of his coat collar.

'They always say you should take more water with it.'

He looked at her in slight amazement for a moment. She wasn't furious, in fact she was looking amused, kindly amused.

He dropped his head and, grinning, said, 'You're right there, Victoria; I'd better get some practice in at holding me drink.'

'Well, don't start on Father's special, a couple of glasses of that would knock a prize-fighter over . . . That little monkey, she wants her ears boxed.'

He looked at her from under his lids. 'You heard about the result of it, I suppose?' He now gave his head a shake. 'Of course you have.'

'The proposal?' She made herself laugh. 'Oh yes,

I heard about the proposal. It's a good job it wasn't one of the Stacey girls you were drinking with.'

Now they both laughed together, for the title 'girls' was a jocular courtesy given to the forty-five year old spinster twins, who were as hefty as their father, the blacksmith. Then their laughter dying away, Victoria turned to the side and, her voice low and flat now, she said, 'I . . . I have to confess though I was a little startled last night when they all came in babbling about it.' She turned her head on her shoulder and looked at him. 'I couldn't believe my ears. I . . . I didn't want to believe my ears.'

'I'm sorry, Victoria.'

'You . . . you don't care for Nellie, do you?'

'Oh no, no' – his words came rapidly now – 'not that way. Why, she's still a little girl. Somehow, I couldn't think of her in that way.'

'You're sure?' She still had her head turned towards him.

'Of course. Well, you should know that.'

'I . . . I thought I did.' She walked away from him now to the distant corner of the barn to where some stacks of grain stood in a row against the timbers, and she kicked against one with the toe of her shoe; her head was down, her hands hanging limply by her sides.

He watched her for a few seconds before moving towards her. Putting his hand lightly on her arm, he turned her towards him and, looking into her face, he said, 'You believe me, don't you?'

She paused a moment, then nodded at him and said, 'Yes; yes, Charlie, I believe you.'

'But it's true, I mean when I said I'd never thought of her in that way.'

Their heads were almost on a level. She stared into his eyes before she asked quietly, 'Have you thought of me in that way, Charlie?'

His lids blinked rapidly, he swallowed, stretched his chin out of his collar, then said, 'Yes . . . yes, I have, Victoria.'

She now lowered her gaze and directed it towards the sacks of grain as she asked, 'Would you have proposed to me if there hadn't been two years between us?'

Dear God! His head was aching, splitting, his mouth tasted like a midden. What must he say? What could he say? He said, 'Yes, yes, I suppose I would, Victoria.'

She turned to him, smiling quietly, and, putting out her hand, she gripped his. 'You'll be twenty in a few months' time and I'll be still twenty-one, at least for a few days; the difference won't seem so much then, will it?'

He smiled back at her, made a small motion with his head and said, 'No; no, it won't, Victoria.'

'Will you ask me then?'

'Yes; I'll ask you then.' As he spoke he had a great desire to laugh, to let forth that bellow that he so rarely gave vent to. Here he was, the quiet, shy, retiring fellow, because that was how he was looked upon by those who thought well of him; anyway, here he was proposing to two sisters within a matter of hours.

'What are you finding so funny?' She was smiling at him.

He bit tightly on his lip, wagging his head from side to side and screwed up his eyes for a moment. When he opened them they were glistening as if with tears and he said, 'I . . . I was just imagining what would happen if I went into the house and said . . . well, if I said I'd proposed to you . . . to two of you in a matter of hours.'

She put her hand over her mouth now as if to still her own laughter, and with the other hand she gripped his as she whispered, 'Well, now that would really cause a sensation, wouldn't it? The gay Lothario would have nothing on you. Charlie—' She checked her laughter, and he checked his, too, as she looked at him and said softly, 'This must be a secret between us for the next few months, eh?'

'Yes, Victoria; just as you say.'

'What about your twentieth birthday?'

'That'll be fine.'

She went to take his arm; then withdrew her hand, saying, 'We . . . we must be careful, mustn't we? Circumspect.' She pushed him playfully now. 'Go into the house and get cleaned up and have something to eat, and look contrite.' She tapped his cheek. 'You're a very bad boy. You know that, Charlie? You got drunk on father's best brandy, you were almost accused of seducing his younger daughter, and you've started a rumour around the

143

countryside that's got to be denied. Go on, do your penance, you're a very bad boy.'

He went from her laughing, but the laughter faded away before he had crossed the yard.

You're a very bad boy, a very bad boy. She had talked to him as if he were ten years younger than her, not two. You're a very bad boy. Would he ever be a man, man enough to manage her?

PART THREE

The War 1914

1

The bloody Kaiser, he was a maniac, him and his
little Willie. What had the British ever done to him?
Nowt, nowt, said the ordinary man, but be too soft
with the buggers, let them live in this country, feed on
the fat of the land, make money out of the poor with
their fancy pork shops all over the place. We were too
soft, that's what we were, live and let live we always
said. But we'd show them now. By God! we would.
We'd teach them a lesson they'd never forget. Join
up we will in our thousands. England must be saved
from hooligans like that, maniacs, barbarians. We
were a civilised people: couldn't you remain at school
beyond the age of thirteen? didn't the old receive a
pension when they were no longer able to do their bit
at seventy? The Liberals were spending money like
water in making things better for the sick and needy,
and now that bloody maniac goes and starts a war!
Well, the Geordies would soon settle his hash. By
God! they would. Just let them get at him; they'd give
him some stick for what he was doing to the poor
Belgians.

And they did get at him. Those who weren't
already in the Territorials or Special Reservists

volunteered to go across there and 'wipe the buggers off the map'.

The Northerner is not just patriotic, he is enthusiastic with it, especially when he's got drink in him, and it must be said that a number of volunteers woke up with thick heads and asked themselves what the hell they were doing lying on the floor among this mob, and when a voice bellowed over them they told the owner of it where he could go to, only to be brought to their feet with boots in their backsides. Didn't they know where they was? Well, Corporal Smith, Jones or Robinson was here to tell them where they was, they was in the flaming army, that's where they was. And they could take their choice of the Third, Fourth, Fifth, Sixth, Seventh, Eighth, or Ninth Battalion of the Durham Light Infantry. They could have the pick of any battalion they wanted to join and Colonel Cardiff would be entertaining them all together the night . . . Move! Move! Get a move on! Look slippy!

Most of the first batch of volunteers from the North-East were pit lads, and they didn't take kindly to orders. As for discipline, there was no need for that kind of thing that they could see; all they wanted to do was to get across the water and fight those bloody Germans.

'You'll meet 'em soon enough, but in the meantime get that bloody shovel in yer hand and dig that trench.'

'What here, in South Shields, Corporal?'

'Yes. Ever heard of coastal defences?'

148

'An' you! you're for the cookhouse.'

'An' you the latrines.'

'An' you! it's guard for you.'

'. . . Bugger me!'

'I will when I get time . . . Move!'

Arthur Benton was about the only one in his platoon who didn't question an order in those first days. He had been used to taking orders all his life, different kinds of orders, orders that old MacFell had kicked into him, and the polite orders that Charlie had given him; and perhaps he was the only one in his particular section who had been sober when he enlisted.

To Arthur the war had come as a godsend, a means of escape from the farm and that red-headed bastard who had been his brother-in-law now for the past year. At times he would question why their Polly had done it, yet he knew why their Polly had done it, it was to save his neck.

It was some weeks before Arthur, among others, was given a rifle, and it was as well, so scoffed the sergeant at the time, that they would never be called upon to use them. It was a good job Kitchener had sent the Fifth Division of the British Expeditionary Force over to France, because if the winning of the war depended on this lot they'd all give up the ghost.

Arthur didn't mind if he never saw France but the first instant he held the rifle he had a vivid picture of Ginger Slater standing in front of him, and his mind went bang! bang! bang! and he saw Ginger lying with the blood pouring out of him, not only from three places but from his head, his chest, his arms, his legs, his feet. By God! if he ever came across him.

The war became a puzzle to Arthur as it did to many another. Where were all the uniforms? Where were all the big guns? It would appear you only got a uniform if you were going to the front. And the officers, why some of them had been dug up from the Boer War. He wished he had never joined the bloody army. At least, so he wished until the day his unit was sent to Ravensworth Park. From that day Arthur had an aim in life.

2

By the middle of 1915 the war was settled in, in trenches so to speak. It was said in high places that it would have been over by the end of 1914 had it not been for the Germans discovering the value of a trench. It was when the fleeing Germans reached the Aisne and were too weary to run further from the pursuing British Expeditionary Force that they dug trenches, and from then checked the Allied advance. So began trench warfare; bloody, soul-destroying gut-exposing trench warfare.

There was at this time dissension among the generals: Kitchener was going for Sir John French; and General Joffre, the French Commander-in-Chief, came under Kitchener's instructions to command the British Army. As one general was heard to say, 'You haven't to die before you shed tears of blood.'

There were commanders who didn't speak French and, therefore, had to take their orders through interpreters. There was confusion, there was massacre; but as the propaganda said there was also glory for those who gave their lives for their country.

But as thoughtful people dared to say, who can prove that the dead can enjoy what their passing has evoked?

And the fact now that men dying in their thousands brought forth from English women the hysterical desire that more should join them, was not a phenomenon but merely, in the main, the outpouring of frustration. Why should their man be out there, up to the waist in mud and water and crawling with lice, while even one man went about the streets in a civilian suit?

Charlie had been the target of this frustration more than once as he had passed through Newcastle and Gateshead.

'Somebody drained your liver, lad?'

'Don't tell me you're in a reserved occupation, not a big fellow like you!'

'Flat feet have you? Weak eyes? . . . weak-kneed more bloody like.'

Sometimes he wondered if he was the only one who had been subjected to this, but no, Tom Skelly was suspected of falling accidentally on purpose down a scree hill. The result was a broken leg. No France for him.

Meeting up with khaki-clad men was the worst experience. There were three coming along the street now, walking abreast. He lowered his eyes and went to step into the gutter when he was startled by a hand coming out and grabbing him, and he brought his head up sharply as a voice said, 'Charlie! Why, Charlie!'

'Arthur! My goodness!' They were shaking hands and smiling into each other's face.

'It's good to see you, Charlie.'

'And you, Arthur.'

Arthur now turned to his two companions standing to the side and said, 'Oh, this is Mr MacFell, he's me old boss. Wish he was still.' He jerked his head and laughed. 'Look, I'll see you later on. All right, eh?'

They both smiled and nodded and said, 'Aye, all right. So long.'

'So long,' Arthur said, then turned again to Charlie, asking now, 'Have you got a minute?'

'All the minutes you want, Arthur. Are you on leave?'

'Aye, you could say I was. We think we're for over the water any time now . . . Come an' have a drink.'

'Better still, you come along to the house with me and have a bite.'

'The house? What house?'

'Oh' – they were walking side by side now – 'you wouldn't know about it but Victoria's aunt died just after the war started and left her and Nellie a house each. Victoria's is in Newcastle here and Nellie's is in Gateshead.'

'You don't say!'

'Yes.'

'And you live here now? What about the farm?'

'Oh, the farm is still going strong, and always will as long as Betty's about. But I'm there most of the time. I pop over here for an occasional week-end.'

'Aye. How things change.'

'Yes, they do, Arthur, they do indeed.'

'Where's your house?'

'In Jesmond.'

'Posh. Oh posh, eh?'

Charlie smiled and said, 'I hope you don't mind, it's a good ten minutes' walk further on.'

'You jokin', Charlie? You're talkin' to the feller with leather feet.'

'How are you finding the army, Arthur?'

'Oh—' The grin slid from Arthur's face and he said soberly, 'So-so.' Then turning his head fully towards Charlie, he said, 'I'm glad I met you, Charlie, I've a lot to tell you. I sometimes thought of takin' a trip out to the farm to have a natter with you, but then I didn't know whether I'd be welcome as there's no one of ours left there now, an' old Arnold and Fred didn't think much of me for goin' off like that, I know. But I just had to get away. You understand?'

'Yes, yes, I understand, Arthur.'

'I knew you would. But you know somethin', Charlie? There's an old saying, if the devil's got you marked out there's no escaping him, and it's true, by God! I've found out it's true. I met up with him again, Charlie . . . Slater.'

They both paused in their walking now, and Charlie, shaking his head slowly, said, 'No!'

'Aye. Aye, Charlie. He's a bloody sergeant instructor, would you believe that? That skinny undersized bastard that he was, who could neither read nor write, he's a bloody sergeant, an' by God! didn't he let me know it. Do you know something, Charlie? I nearly added a second notch to me totem pole, I did that. It was the lads, those two I left back there, who saved me skin more than once. Pit lads they are . . . or were, sensible, stubborn, good mates. They fought me battle for me, but in a backhand kind of way; they waylaid him one night and they did him up. By God! they did that; he was in hospital for a week. The whole camp was afire with it, but he couldn't lay the blame on me 'cos the bastard had put me on guard duty just afore he went out and I was still on it when they carried him in'.

'Who goes there?' Arthur stopped in the middle of the pavement and took up the pose of holding a rifle at the ready.

'One Sergeant Sidney Slater who's been done up.'

'Pass friends and God be with you.'

Charlie put his head back now and indulged in his rare deep roar of laughter and Arthur, himself shaking with his mirth, flapped his hand against Charlie's chest as he spluttered, 'And the best of it was those two that did it carried him in, found him in the lane they reported.' Again he struck a pose, saluted and said, 'Yes, sir; we, me and Private Blackett, were returnin' to camp, sir. It was Private Blackett, sir, who tripped over his foot in the dark. We thought it was the . . . leg . . . of . . . a couple, sir, who were at it . . . pardon me, sir, you know what I mean, sir, but when the foot didn't move, sir, we investigated an' found Sergeant Slater, sir, in a bloody . . . in a right mess, sir. Yes, sir. Thank you, sir . . . About turn! Quick march!'

To the amusement of some passers-by, Arthur now did a quick turn a few steps away from Charlie and again they were roaring their heads off, but they hadn't traversed another street before Arthur said solemnly, 'But it was no laughing matter, Charlie, not really, not then. God! he put me through it. And you know what?' He turned his head slowly and met Charlie's gaze. 'We're going to meet up again – it would only be a big injustice if we didn't – an' over there they say a lot of funny things happen. I've heard tell of officers being shot in the back but I won't shoot him in the back, Charlie. No, right atween his two bloody eyes. An' I'll have to be quick, because if he can get me first he will. I know that. Oh, I know he will.'

After a pause while they tramped in step up a broad avenue lined with trees, Charlie said quietly, 'I hope you never meet up, Arthur; and it isn't likely if he's an instructor.'

'Oh.' Arthur's tone was light again, 'Oh, you can never tell with this set-up; they're shakin' you around all the time. In the past year I've been in Durham, Jarrow, Shields, Boldon Colliery, Roker; you're shuffled about like a bloody pack of cards. Them up there, begod! I doubt if any of them know what they're doin'. They've got to make a show to fill up their forms, so they say, you, you and you, pack up your troubles in your old kit-bag and get the hell out of this, and there you land up in some field or some bloody great house. Not that we ever get billeted in the houses; no, that's for the top brass. And some of them officers, nowt but kids with fancy voices, you can't understand a bloody word they say. An' mind' – he now pushed Charlie in the side – 'the poor young

156

buggers look all at sea when the Geordies get crackin'. As one young bloke said, "I can understand German but damned if I can make out a word these fellows say."

'There were these lads from Shields' – Arthur was laughing again – 'they were pit lads into the bargain and when you add the pitmatic to the Geordie twang, well believe me, I can't undentand half what they say meself . . . Oh, we're here then.' Arthur stopped at the gate and looked up the short drive to the detached house. It was built of red brick and the paintwork was black.

'Eeh, by! it's a fine looking place, big an' all. Any stables?' They were walking towards the front door now.

'No, no stables, Arthur, just a coach-house.'

'Miss Victoria won't like that; she'll miss her stables.'

Charlie inserted a key in the front door and opened it, then stood aside, saying to Arthur who was hesitating on the step, 'Come on, come in.'

Slowly Arthur entered the hall. His cap in his hand, he gazed about him. Like the outside, the woodwork in the hall was black and the walls in between white. There was a red carpet in the middle of the polished floor and red carpet also padded the stout looking stairs; the newel post, shining with the dark hue of polished oak, looked as if it had been rooted there.

'Come into the kitchen, there's generally something in the pantry. We have a woman, an old lady,

Mrs Crawford, she comes in every morning and sees to the place. But I think her main passion is cooking, and she always finds something to cook with here, we're not short of an egg or two.' He turned and grinned at Arthur, and Arthur added, 'Nor butter, nor cheese, I bet me life.'

'Ah yes, here we are.' Charlie came out of the pantry carrying a pie. 'Ham and egg.' He nodded at Arthur; then putting the plate on the table, he said, 'Coffee or tea? Or something hard?'

'Both if you don't mind, Charlie, I never say no to a cup of tea but I'd like a drop of hard this minute.'

'Well, come on.'

Arthur now followed Charlie back into the hall and through a heavy oak door and into what could only be described as a drawing-room, and the sight of it silenced Arthur for a moment while he stood gaping about him. There was a touch of awe in his tone now as he said. 'By! I've never seen such furniture, lovely. Aren't they lovely pieces! What you call antiques, Charlie?'

'Yes.' Charlie had turned from the cabinet in the corner of the room and he, too, stood for a moment looking about him, and his eyelids were blinking rapidly as he said, 'Yes, Arthur, antiques.'

'Eeh! by! she was lucky.'

'Yes, she was lucky.'

The drinks in their hands, they returned to the kitchen, and presently they sat down at the table which was now spread with pickles, bread, butter, cheese, and the ham and egg pie.

'Help yourself, Arthur.' Charlie nodded across to the khaki-clad figure, and Arthur, grinning widely now, answered, 'I don't need to be told twice, Charlie.'

It wasn't until he had finished a large shive of the pie and was wiping his mouth by the simple procedure of flicking a finger against one corner and then the other that he said, 'Everything goin' all right with you, Charlie?'

Charlie reached out and took a slice of bread, then a piece of cheese from the wooden platter, and finally he cut off a pat of butter and put it on to the side of his plate; then he stared down at the food before he said, 'You wouldn't have had to ask that question if you had visited us over the past year or so.'

'Sorry.'

'Oh, don't be sorry for me, Arthur; I got what I asked for. Young fools should be made to pay for their foolishness; the only hope for them is that they don't grow into old fools.'

'What's the trouble? The missis . . . I mean your mother?'

'Yes and no. But even without her there would still have been trouble. We're the trouble, Vicky and I, we're a trouble to each other. It should never have happened. I'm a lazy fellow, Arthur.'

'. . . Lazy? Not you! You can do a day's work with the rest of 'em.'

'Yes, physically I suppose I can, but in my mind . . . well, I never use it, Arthur, I let other people use it for me. I follow where others lead.'

An embarrassed silence enveloped them both now until Arthur, in a high jocular tone, said, 'Did you ever think of joinin' up, Charlie?'

'No, never, Arthur. Can you imagine me with a bayonet.'

'Well, you never can tell. They say snakes are harmless until you stand on 'em. No offence meant, but you know what I mean. And did you see that advert in the paper yesterday?'

'What advert?'

'Why, they're advertising for officers; going round beating the drum didn't do much good, so there's this advert in all the big papers for officers. Why don't you have a shot? You wouldn't have to use a bayonet; by all accounts the top brass stay well behind the lines.'

'Thanks, Arthur, but I'm a good distance behind the lines now and that's where I intend to stay.'

'Aye, well, I suppose you're wise.'

'How's . . . how's Polly? You haven't mentioned her.'

'Well, that's 'cos I know so little about her now. I can't go there an' see her, can I? I only hear of her through me ma; she's up the flue again.'

'Up the . . . ?'

'Aw' – Arthur tossed his head to the side – 'gona have another bairn. I don't think of her much, at least I try not to; the very thought of her with him nearly drives me mad. An' she's putting up with it all because of us . . . aw' – he lowered his head and wagged it – 'I mean me.'

'Where is she living?'

'Somewhere in Hebburn, me ma says, she doesn't tell me exactly. Just as well I suppose. Two bairns in two years! She'll have a squad afore she's thirty, an' she'll be old an' worn out by then. You know something?' He again wiped his mouth, but on the back of his hand this time. 'You should have married her, Charlie.'

'That would have been impossible, Arthur. You know it.'

'It might have been then, back on the farm, but not now, this war's turned everybody and everything topsy-turvy. There was a lass in our canteen over at Durham, she's just got herself married to a second-lieutenant.'

Charlie gave a small laugh. 'He might have been a waiter before the war.'

'Aw no, not second-lieutenants, not the officers. No, they're all educated fellows. Some of them now are comin' straight from the universities, all lah-di-dah . . . You were gone on our Polly, weren't you, Charlie?'

'Yes, I suppose you could say I was, Arthur.' Charlie smiled wanly. 'But we were young then, children really. Things have changed as you said, times have changed.'

And how they had changed. How old was he now? Twenty-three. Was that all he was, twenty-three? And had he been married only two years, not twenty? It was hard to believe that the hysterical scenes, the physical body struggling, and his introduction into the emotions of rage, frenzy and desire had all taken place in less than two years, less than a year, in less than six months.

'What did you say, Arthur?'

'I said I enjoyed that, Charlie, a good home-made pie. But now . . . well, I'm afraid I'll have to be off.'

'Oh yes; your friends will be waiting.'

'Oh, it doesn't matter about them, we'll meet up at the bus, it goes at four. Fancy having to go back to camp on a Saturday night. Any other night in the week I wouldn't mind, but a Saturday! No, the reason for me hurry is I . . . I want to look in on me ma. She's mostly on her own now, she's only got Flo at home. She's sixteen now an' a handful; working in munitions she is; me ma can't get her in at nights. Mick and Peter are in the Navy. Peter gave a wrong age. Isn't it funny how we've all left the land; except you of course.'

'There's still time, Arthur.'

'Aye, by the looks of it, this bloody war could go on for the next ten years. It would be funny, wouldn't it, Charlie, if you an' me met up over there . . . Colonel Charles MacFell, top brass.' He again struck a pose, of a bullying sergeant this time. 'Spit on those boots! I want them to dazzle me eyes. And Brasso your buttons, 'cos you know who we've got comin' the day? Colonel Charles MacFell.'

This time Charlie wasn't amused, but he patted Arthur on the shoulder, saying quietly, 'After this business is over you must go on the stage; you'd do well, you know.'

'There's truer things been said in a joke, Charlie.

They had me in a concert party last Christmas. I did a fresh farm lad milking a cow; I had 'em rollin'.'

'I bet you did.'

They were at the door now. 'Well, good-bye, Charlie.'

'Good-bye, Arthur.'

'Here! there's no call for that.' Arthur opened his palm and exposed the crumpled notes.

'Go on; you'll do more good with them than I will.'

'Thanks, Charlie, thanks. It's good of you; I'll be thinkin' of you.'

'And me of you, Arthur.'

They looked at each other for a moment longer, their hands gripping; then Arthur went hurriedly down the drive. Charlie didn't wait to see him go through the gate but he turned and closed the door abruptly behind him, then stood rigidly still, staring in front of him. He had a longing to be with Arthur, and to be going . . . over there, in fact anywhere that would take him away from the owner of this house, and from his mother and sister . . . But it was because of his mother that he was here.

He walked slowly across the hall and up the stairs. The landing was square, with six doors going off from it. He went to the second one on his left and thrust it open. He didn't enter. It was as he always remembered it, the bed unmade, the clothes strewn about the room, the whole seeming in a way to represent his wife. It had her body spread all over it, her mad, thrashing, ravenous body, that was governed by seemingly superhuman urges that were a torment to herself for they could never be satisfied.

He was about to close the door when his eye was attracted to the dressing-table mirror. It lay to the left of him. He paused a moment, then crossed the room and, bending down, peered at the mirror. Three words were written across the bottom corner of it in lipstick. They read 'That's me girl!'

He straightened his back, stared at the writing for a moment longer, then walked out of the room and down the stairs again and into a small room at the end of the hall. This room was lined with bookcases and the only pieces of furniture in it were two easy chairs and a small round table. He sat down and, resting his elbows on the table, lowered his head into his hands.

Well, he knew, didn't he? Why should he feel so surprised, so ashamed, so humiliated? That's me girl! He could see her prancing naked about the room like a demented witch; but the man who wrote 'That's me girl!' wouldn't, as he himself had done, have rushed from the room as if from a witch. No, the one who had written those words would have applauded and said 'That's me girl!'

He had never ceased to be amazed at the fires that burned in Victoria, weird, primeval fires. To live at all, he knew one must wear a façade for there were depths in all human beings that were better not probed, that is if you wanted to live what was termed a normal life; and he also knew that the wedding ceremony was a licence which allowed some of the lava to erupt from the murky depths where the

sediment of human nature lay. And he had con-
formed, he had gone along with it. Natural sex had its
place in life, and at its best, he felt, could be a beautiful
experience. But what had happened? She had behaved
like a stallion at stud, any time of the day or night, the
hour didn't seem to matter . . . and without love; yes,
that was the worst part of it, without love. He had once
said to her, 'You don't act like a woman, you're more
like a wild beast,' and she had come back with, 'And
you're no man, you're a runt, and you know what they
do with runts on the farm!'

He rose from the chair and walked to the window
and looked out on the back garden. It was a nice
garden; it was a lovely house; in ordinary circumstances they could have been so happy here. He would
have gladly left the farm to Betty and his mother and
got a job in the town.

And there were books here, hundreds of them. Her
aunt had been a cultured woman; if only she had taken
after her in some way; and if only her aunt hadn't died
and left her this house and enough money to live on,
for then she would have had to stay on the farm. But
would she? And would life have been any better? No,
no; a thousand times worse, for his mother and Betty
hated her as much as she hated them.

And now he had come here to ask her to return to the
farm, at least for a short while until his mother was on
her feet again . . . or died. He must have been mad even
to think she would comply. But what was he going to
do? Things couldn't go on back there as they were.

As he turned from the window he heard the front

door open, and when he entered the hall he saw her standing in front of the mirror about to take her hat off.

She turned towards him, her arms upraised, her face stretched in surprise, but no trace of fear or shame on it, he noted.

'Well! Well! What wind's blown you in?'

She turned to the mirror again and, withdrawing the pins from her hat, she placed them on the hall table; then lifting the hat carefully upwards from her high piled hair, she placed it on top of the pins. Bending towards the mirror, she pursed her lips, then stroked them at each corner with her middle finger. It reminded him of the action a man might make in smoothing his moustache, and it linked with previous thoughts that she was a man under her female skin; yet not enough of a man to want a woman. How much easier things would have been if the balance had swung in that way.

She walked before him now into the drawing-room. She looked big, full-blown was the word to describe her, yet she was handsome, like one of those seventeenth-century Rembrandt women. Her dress was of a blue material and straight, with an overskirt that was parted in the middle. The belt of the dress was loose about her waist, the collar was of a self material – she never wore lace trimmings.

He watched her go to a side table and, opening a silver box, take out a cigarette. When she had lit it and drawn deep on it she looked at him over her shoulder and said, 'Have you lost another of your faculties? Have you gone dumb?'

He closed his eyes for a moment, then said, 'I've come to ask you something.'

'No! No!' She turned with an exaggerated flounce now. 'You're going to beg me to go to bed with you? Oh, Charlie!' When she dropped her head coyly to the side he had the conflicting desire to turn and flee from her while at the same time some part of him sprang across the room and gripped her by the throat.

He walked to the empty fireplace and stared down into the bare iron basket as he said, 'Mother is very ill, young Sarah has left, Arnold has hurt his back and is of no use any more. Betty . . . Betty can't manage on her own.'

'Well! Well!' The words dribbled out of her mouth on a laugh, and she put her head back and drew again on her cigarette before continuing, 'You know, Charlie, you're funny. You are, you're the funniest fellow in the world. You're a weak-kneed gutless sod, but you're still funny because you're so naïve, so gullible, so . . .' She tossed her head as she tried to find further words with which to express her opinion of him; then her manner suddenly changing, she stubbed the cigarette out on the first thing that came to her hand, which was an old beautifully painted Worcester plate, and as she ground the ash over the enamel, her voice, having now lost all its jocularity, bawled at him, 'You have the gall to stand there and ask me to go back and look after your mother! You must be flaming mad! Do you remember how we parted? I could have throttled her, the old bitch! As for dear Betty, if I had to come in contact with her again I just might.' She screwed up her eyes and peered at him, then in a lower tone she said, 'You must be barmy, you must, to come all this way to ask me that!'

'My mother is dying. That's putting it plainly. As for Betty, well, you wouldn't have to put up with her much longer, she's engaged to Robin Wetherby, and if they get married she'll go straight over to his place.'

'Really! And so you'll be left on your own. Poor, poor Charlie. Well, say your mother dies and Betty goes, what then? I come back and play the dutiful wife, which would help you no doubt to lift your head up again in the markets; that's if a conchie will ever be able to lift his head up again anywhere . . . Can you see the picture, Charlie?' She waited a moment while they stared at each other across the room; then she flung her arms wide as she cried, 'If your mother was dying ten times over, and you along with her, you'd never get me back in that house again. I felt tied at home, but it was a home . . . Your place! What is it but a bloody prison, an uncomfortable, cold, bloody prison. I hadn't even anyone to keep me warm in bed, had I? Eh! Had I?'

'That was your fault.'

'My fault? Aw, don't make me sick. You know what you are, Charlie MacFell; you know what you are, you're a nincompoop, nothing more or less, a nincompoop. You'll never have an experience in your life that's worthwhile, you'll never touch the depths, and you'll never touch the heights; you'll live on that same plane of niceness.' Her lip curled on the last word, and she went on, 'Nice fellow, nice and easy going; nice and polite, *nice, nice, nice* . . . Get out of me sight!'

He didn't move. 'You had a man here last night.'

Her eyes widened slightly as she pressed her lips together; then she moved her head slowly up and down and said, 'Really! how do you make that out?'

'He left his approbation on the mirror.'

'Oh dear, dear! that was a mistake, wasn't it? I should have rubbed it off. But then I didn't expect to see you today.'

'I can divorce you.'

'You can what!'

'I'll repeat it for you, I can divorce you.'

'Aw no, Charlie, no, don't come that with me. You cannot divorce me, but I can divorce you . . . for non-consummation.'

'That's a lie!' His voice came suddenly loud and sharp, and he repeated, 'That's a damn lie and you know it!'

She took three slow steps towards him; then she stopped and said, 'You try, you try and divorce me, you blacken my name and I'll stand up in the highest court and tell them how I tried every way to make you love me as a man should. And you didn't . . . or couldn't.'

His face was ablaze; he felt the sweat in his oxters. It was he who moved forward now as he growled at her, 'Then I'll contest it. Yes, I'll contest it; with my last breath I'll contest it.'

They glared at each other for a moment. Then lifting her hand she patted her cheek as if in perplexity, saying to herself, 'My! my! Victoria, have you made a mistake and there's a man hidden somewhere in there?'

'Be careful!'

They were glaring at each other again.

'Good-bye, Charlie.'

He looked at her for a moment longer; then swinging round, he went from the room; and she went hastily after him and watched him grab up his coat and hat, but when he opened the door she cried at him, 'Why don't you try Nellie? She might help you out; that's if you can get her sobered up.'

When he opened the gate into the avenue he wanted to run. The anger inside him was acting like a fire stoking an engine; he wanted to use his limbs, to flay his arms, to toss his head. God! was there ever anybody in this world like her? But he had only himself to blame; surely he had known what to expect. Hadn't he gone through it all before? What in the name of God had made him think she would come back to the farm and help him out? Desperation, he supposed.

His walk was on the point of a run when he emerged into the main thoroughfare and there was forced to slow his pace, so that he was near the station when he recalled her words: 'Why don't you try Nellie? That's if you can get her sobered up.' Had she taken to drink that bad?

It was almost a year since he had seen Nellie; he

had been to her house in Gateshead when she had first gone to live there. Her place, being in a terrace and three-storey high with a basement, wasn't anything like the one Victoria had, but it was a substantial house nevertheless. The basement and the upper two floors were let off, and Nellie had taken up her abode in the ground floor. The property brought in a small income, and Nellie, who had taken a course in short-hand and typing, had got a job in the office of one of the hospitals. That being so, he now thought, it wasn't likely she would leave it to help him out. Anyway, with the war restrictions, perhaps she wouldn't be allowed.

Should he go and see her? He had only to cross the bridge over the river; he could be there in ten minutes if he took a bus . . .

The street looked dingy; the tall terraced houses looked like old ladies who had seen better days. He went up the four steps and into the hall that smelt dank and was thick with the aroma of cooking.

Before he knocked on the door he stood listening for a moment to the sound of laughter coming from within, and when the door opened, Nellie stood there, her mouth wide, a glass in her hand, saying, 'Come in. Come—' Her voice trailed away and she leaned forward, and then in a whisper said, 'Charlie!'

'Yes, Nellie; it's me.'

He watched her swallow, glance over her shoulder, then smile brightly as she said, 'Well! well, what are we standing here for? Come in. Come . . . on . . . in. Come . . . on . . . in.'

He walked into the room and looked at the two

171

soldiers sitting on the couch, and they looked back at him, while Nellie, going towards them, swung her head from one side to the other, saying, 'This is an old friend of mine, this is Charlie. And this is Andy, and Phil.'

'How-do!' The two soldiers spoke together and their heads bobbed together.

And Charlie answered, 'How-do-you-do?'

'Sit down. Sit down.' Nellie was pointing to a chair. 'Let me get you a drink. You're in clover, I can tell you; Andy brought this.' She laughed towards the shorter of the two men sitting on the couch. 'You can't get Scotch for love nor money, but Andy's got ways and means. Haven't you, Andy?'

'Aye, aye, I have that, Nellie; I've got shares in a Newcastle brewery.' His voice was thick with the Tyneside twang.

'Well, you should have, you've bought enough of their beer over the years.' The other man nudged his friend with his shoulder and they both laughed together.

When Nellie handed Charlie a glass with a good measure of whisky in it, he said 'Thanks', then raised it to her and afterwards to the men before he sipped at it.

'Its good stuff.' He nodded to them now, and the man called Andy laughed and said, 'Nowt but the best for the British Tommy.' The silence that followed was broken by Nellie in a loud voice exclaiming, 'What's brought you into town, Charlie?'

'I . . . I had a bit of business.'

'Oh . . . Everything all right on the farm?'

He paused. 'Well, not quite, Mother's pretty bad and Arnold's off with severe back trouble.'

'Oh, I'm sorry to hear that. You got help?'

'No, that's the problem. Young Sarah . . . you remember young Sarah? Well, she left an' all.'

'Aw goodness me!' Nellie put down her glass and, leaning towards Charlie, said, 'You must be in a pickle then.'

'Yes. Well' – he gave a shaky laugh – 'everybody's in a pickle these days.' Of a sudden he gulped at the whisky and drained the glass, shuddered, then rose to his feet, saying, 'I'll have to be off; I have a train to catch.'

'But you've just got here!' She was standing in front of him, one hand gripping the lapel of his coat. 'Look, stay and have a bite; I'm . . . I'm not at work, I've been off with a cold. Come on, stay and have a bite.'

'I'm sorry, Nellie' – he smiled weakly down at her – 'they'll be waiting for me and, as I said, we're short-handed; I'll have to get back.' He turned his head now and looked at the men and said, 'Good-bye.'

One of them answered, 'So long, chum,' while the other said, 'Ta-rah. Ta-rah.'

She went with him into the hall, closing the door after her, and there, gazing up into his face, she said softly, 'You look awful, Charlie. Aren't you well?'

'Yes, yes, I'm all right, Nellie.' But he could have returned the compliment by saying, 'And you look awful too.' How old was she, twenty-one? She

173

looked thirty-one at this moment; her face was puffed, there were bags under her eyes.

'Have you been to see Vick?'

'Yes.'

'Any progress?'

'Just downwards.'

'Well, you're not missing anything there, Charlie.'

'Do . . . do you ever meet?'

'What! her and me? Only when we can't help it. She's doing a stint at present in a canteen. I went in there with the lads one night and there she was . . . Huh!'

'There she was, what?'

'Oh, nothing.' She shrugged her shoulders, then said harshly, 'What am I covering up? You know how things are as well as I do. Yes, there she was, and aiming to serve in more ways than one.'

'Don't, Nellie.' He turned abruptly from her.

'I can't help it, Charlie.' She was again holding him by the lapels, with both hands now. 'You're a bloody fool.' Her voice was a thin whisper. 'You should never have married her, you know that. She's a maniac . . . Do you still love her?'

He turned his head sharply from the side and looked at her. 'Love her! love Victoria! Still love her did you say? I can't remember ever having done so in the first place. You said she was a maniac; but no, you are wrong there, Nellie, it was me who was the maniac.'

After a moment of silence she slapped him with the flat of her hand in the middle of his chest and she grinned at him as she said, 'You'd have made a better bargain with me, wouldn't you?'

'Oh, Nellie!' He returned her smile and shook his head, and she went on, 'You would, I know you would.'

He put up his hand and stroked her cheek. There was something endearing about Nellie, and always had been; she was so frank, so open, so adult, yet at the same time so child-like. He leaned forward and put his lips to her cheek. 'Take care of yourself and . . . go easy on the Newcastle brewery, it's bad for the complexion.' He opened the door and went down the steps, and when he turned she was standing just as he had left her, and she did not answer the salute of his hand, nor as he walked away did he hear the door close.

You would have made a better bargain with me, Charlie.

He had no doubt of it, no doubt at all.

Mary MacFell was dying and she was dying hard. She didn't want to go. She was resentful that she was being forced to go; she hadn't got her money's worth out of the place; she hadn't been repaid for what she had suffered at the hands of Edward MacFell, and later from the tongue of her daughter-in-law. And when she was gone who would control the place? Betty? Yes, Betty. That gangling son of hers was no match for his sister.

She gasped at the air as she looked up into the face of her son, the son she had once loved. For sixteen years she had loved that face, but over the past eight years she had come to hate it. Her son was soft; and yet not soft enough to give her control of the farm, not easy-going enough to let her write out cheques. He had stopped her buying furniture and finery. In a way she had suffered as much from his hands as she had from her husband's . . . But if only she could get her breath.

'Take it easy, Mother. There, there!' He smoothed the pillows; then taking a cup from the side table, he put one hand under her head as he said, 'Try to sip this. Come on, it will ease your throat. Try to sip this.'

She thrust his hand and the cup away from her and the linctus spilled over the bedcover.

He turned from the bed and went to the washhand stand. After dipping a flannel into the basin of water, he went back to the bed and rubbed at the collar of her night-gown and the sheet and the eiderdown; and while he did this she lay gasping, her glazed gaze fixed tight on him. And he was aware of it; as also he was aware of the antipathy emanating from it.

Betty came into the room and, coming to the bed, demanded, 'What happened?'

'I spilt the linctus.'

'Trust you!'

His glance flashed upwards towards her, but she took no notice of it; then as if her mother was past hearing she said, 'Come downstairs a minute, I want a word with you.'

After she had left the room he straightened the

bedclothes and said, 'I won't be long.'

When he reached the kitchen Betty was taking a pan of broth from the stove, and after she had placed its sooty bottom on an iron stand on the table she said, 'Robin just called in. He tells me they've got German prisoners working over at Threadgill's place. You want to go and see if we can have some.'

'How can I go and leave her now?'

'She'll last out; Doctor Adams said it could be days or even weeks.'

'I don't agree with him; she's in a pretty low state.'

Betty stopped stirring the broth and, lifting the long steel ladle out of the pot, she banged it down on the table, saying, 'Well, we're all in a low state if you ask me. I'm at the end of me tether. And I'm telling you, Charlie, here and now we've got to talk about things.'

He rested both hands on the end of the table and, bowing his head, said, 'All right, all right, we've got to talk about it. But with me it's the same as before. You may marry Wetherby tomorrow if you like but I'm not having him living in here; if he marries you he's got to make a home for you.'

'Well' – she leant towards him now, her hands flat on the table – 'if I go, who's going to look after the place, inside and out?'

'That wouldn't be your worry. I'd get along some-how.'

'Oh yes, you would. Look' – she moved round the table now until she was within touching distance of him – 'what you hoping for, that when the house is empty she'll come back?'

He lifted his head and stared at her and said, 'No, that isn't my hope, Betty. She'll never come back here; nor do I want her here, but at the same time I don't want Wetherby either.' His voice had risen now.

'What have you got against him?'

'I'll tell you what I've got against him. He's never kept down a job in years. He lives on his old people, and they haven't got much, and if he came here you would find yourself doing the work for both of you.'

Her small body stiffened. 'I couldn't be expected to do more than I do now. I know . . . I know' – her head bobbed on her shoulders – 'you don't want me to get married, you're afraid of losing me. I'm worth two men outside and a couple of women inside to you, and what for? What do I get out of it?' Her tone sounded weary now.

'I've told you, marry him tomorrow or any time you like, and when you do I won't let you go empty-handed. But now we'll say no more about it.'

As he turned from her and went up the kitchen again she called after him, 'I will marry him! I will! I'm not going to die in this god-forsaken place looking after you, you with a face like a melancholy owl!'

The green-baized door cut off her voice and he walked across the hall and up the stairs. The whole house seemed silent, empty, as if there were no life in it. A face like a melancholy owl. Yes, he supposed that's how he looked to people, like a melancholy owl. He stopped on the landing. Why didn't he let her bring Wetherby here? If anybody could make him work she could. And anyway, he himself didn't have to live with them, he could go away. He could join up.

What! and stick bayonets into German bellies, blind men, blow off their legs, their arms, disfigure them for life? Join up? Him? Never!

3

It was in March 1916 that conscription for single men came into force, the married men being given two months' respite. Then, on June 5th to be exact, Kitchener went down with the *Hampshire* – the ship struck a mine off Scapa Flow – and so the man whose portrait and pointing finger had admonished every Britisher that his king and country needed him was no more; that he had been a great strategist only to the unknowledgeable, the ordinary man, was an accepted fact by those in high places.

Power is a disease, the only disease that man hugs to himself and bandages with strategy. And so Lloyd George had made himself Secretary for War. Those who, for the last year, had been crying out for conscription waved their banners while their opponents verbally lambasted them as fools, for were there not more than enough men already recruited to fill the gaps in Flanders? And where was the money coming from to equip the new intake? What was wanted was guns and more guns; machine-guns, not merely rifles, machine-guns that went rat-rat-tat-tat, taking a life with every beat.

And what was more, leaders were wanted, young

imaginative men, not old dodderers who couldn't see their noses before their faces. This wasn't a war of 'Up men and at 'em!', the Charge of the Light Brigade all over again, but a war that was to be fought out in the ground as it were. Men had to become like moles, looking only to the earth for their habitation, and while being moles they had to develop minds like foxes.

Of course, as it always had been said, all young generations thought they knew better than the older ones, but in this case a lot of the younger commanders did know better, for they were stressing it was motorised vehicles that were wanted, not horses and waggons. There were twice as many horses in France as there were motor-buses, motor-cycles, and lorries put together, and horses had to be fed, and undoubtedly there would come a time when their straw and chaff would be needed to supplement the bread back home.

It wasn't until July 1st 1916 that the romance went completely out of the war. On that day nineteen thousand men never lived to see another, for the Germans mowed them down as if they had been insects, and, added to the list, fifty thousand crippled in one way or another.

The Somme changed the Britishers' attitude towards the war. The slaughter went on until November, when both sides were brought to a halt. Choked with mud, their senses dulled against death, they dug in for the winter.

Yet poets still wrote poetry – although the tang had

181

become bitter – and officers still behaved like gentlemen. Whenever possible officers' uniforms were immaculate, and to ensure this should be so a batman was as necessary to an officer as was the port in the mess.

There was trouble in Ireland – there was always trouble in Ireland – there was trouble in Russia, there was trouble in Roumania, there was trouble at sea, but Lloyd George still kept giving out his messages of hope to the people. Weren't they pushing the enemy back? Weren't they taking German prisoners? Hadn't they scared off the German Fleet? No mention that the Germans had scared off the British Fleet too.

Such is war. It can be lost on despair, or won on morale.

Charlie stood before a wooden table which was the top one of six in the long, narrow room. He looked down on the head of the soldier who was writing, and like a prisoner up before a judge, he answered the questions thrown at him. Age? Name? Occupation? Eventually a card was handed to him. The arm lifted, the finger pointed: 'Go along the corridor.' But he never saw the speaker's face.

He had no need to ask what he was to do along the corridor. He stood in a queue and eventually he was told to take his clothes off. He was sounded and prodded, his knees were tapped, he was told to put his clothes on again.

'Bloody conscripts!'

'And had to be pulled in.'

'And what a bloody lot! all but the deaf, blind and lame.'

'But you, mate . . . they'll use you for a trench board over there, you're long enough. Go on, get the hell out of it!'

He didn't get angry, it was no use; anyway, he was feeling too numbed to arouse himself and the whole procedure was as he had been led to expect. The ignorant were always bullies; and he told himself he wouldn't find them only in the ranks.

This last assumption was proved when after four hours and twenty minutes of sitting, standing, waiting, he found himself outside being ordered to get into line with another twenty or more men.

'Officer is goin' to inspect you, an' my God! if he doesn't pass out it's 'cos he's got a strong stomach . . . Get Charlie off yer back, you!'

As the fist hitting him between his shoulders knocked him out of line, Charlie coughed, and when he turned swiftly about and faced the corporal, that individual cocked his chin up in the air, narrowed his eyes and from his jutted lips he said, 'You would like to, wouldn't you, lanky? Well, me advice is, watch it! watch it! If you weren't short on spunk you wouldn't be here now, so you'd better keep the little bit you have till you meet up with Jerry.'

Charlie stood in line again, his shoulders straight now, his face red, his teeth clenched.

He was a fool. Once again he had been a fool. He could have got out of it, he was a farmer, but in a moment of madness he had decided he must get

183

away, away from the farm and Betty and her constant nagging to have Wetherby there. Well, he had potched her on that. Anyway, he had left Fred Ryton in charge and Fred got on well with the German prisoners. Funny that, the German prisoners. He had liked them, and had learned to speak a bit of German from them. One of them had spoken fluent French and he had polished his own French on him. Yes, he had liked the Germans; and now he was going to learn to kill them. But by the time they had taught him to use a rifle the war would likely be over. Pray God it would anyway. If not . . . well a German might get in first and that would solve all his problems.

'Divn't let him rile you, mate.' The voice came to him in a whisper.

Charlie didn't move his head but he cast his eyes sideways, then looked to the front again to where the corporal was walking across the square towards a row of buildings on the opposite side.

'He's a nowt!'

'I agree with you there.'

The head was turned slightly towards him, and again Charlie cast his eyes sidewards.

'How did you get here, you're not from these parts?'

'Yes . . . yes, I am.'

'Well' – there came a smothered laugh – 'you divn't sound like it.'

'I come from over near Otterburn.'

'Aw, I'm from Gateshead. Me name's Johnny Tullett.'

'Mine's Charlie MacFell.'

There came the sound of the laugh again. ' "Charlie." And he called you Charlie. "Get Charlie off yer back," he said; that's what made you turn on him likely. Me mother always used to be sayin' that to me when I sat humped up . . . Look out! Look out! here comes Nancy-Pan.'

The corporal was once more standing in front of the line.

'This 'ere's the new batch, sir.'

'Ye-rs. Ye-rs.'

The young second-lieutenant with a chin that looked as if it had never given birth to a hair walked slowly along the line of men.

'I can see what you mean, Corporal. Ye-rs. Ye-rs.'

At the end of the line he turned and walked slowly back, eyeing each man as if he were viewing something that had been dragged out of a cesspool. Then as if the sight of the men had made him slightly sick and he couldn't bear to address them, he looked at the corporal and nodded to him as he said, 'Carry on, Corporal.'

The corporal carried on. And he carried on, too, in the hut when he never ceased to shout as he instructed them into what they had to do with their bedding and their kit, and what would happen to them if they didn't do what he told them to do with their bedding and their kit. He was in the middle of telling them what life was going to be like for them during the next few weeks when the door of the hut opened and a sergeant came in. The sergeant stood just within the door and the corporal was shouting so loudly that he didn't hear him until the sergeant spoke his name.

'*Corporal!*'

The voice startled every man in the room, even those who were looking at the sergeant, and the corporal sprang round and said, 'Yes, Sergeant. Yes, Sergeant,' and scurried like a scalded cat to his side.

It brought a feeling of pleasure to Charlie when he realised that here was someone who could out-shout the obnoxious individual. He likely could out-bully him too. In any case he evidently had the power to make the fellow jump. He noticed, too, that the sergeant didn't even condescend to look at the corporal as he said, 'Get down to the office, there's another batch there.'

'Yes, Sergeant. Yes, Sergeant.' The corporal almost left the hut at the double, and now all the men watched the sergeant walk slowly into their midst. They watched him turn around slowly and survey one after the other of them; and then, his voice quite normal sounding, he said, 'Been putting you through it, has he?' His tone, Charlie noticed, wasn't unlike that of his talkative companion in the line.

When no one answered the sergeant said, 'Well, you'll get a lot of that in the next few weeks. And you'll have to take it whence it comes; but you and me'll get along all right so long as you don't pull any tricks, 'cos they won't come off, I'll tell you that for a start. And another thing I'll tell you, I can't abear tricksters. You know the kind? Wife's goin' to have a bairn, poppin' out any minute, browned off with being in the oven.' There was a snigger at this.

'Mother on her death-bed . . . Likely with the lodger!'

There was actual laughter now, but immediately the sergeant stopped his pirouetting. His face grim and his tone to match, he said, 'Now! now! we'll have no laughin'! No; no laughin'. I'm a funny man, I know that, but I cannot stand being laughed at.'

His features slowly melted and there could have been a twinkle in the back of his eye, but it didn't bring forth a murmur now, and he turned and walked slowly back up between the row of beds, saying as he did so, 'Now we've been introduced, I'll give you one word of advice. Whenever you're told to do anything, jump to it! Believe me, it'll save you a lot of trouble in the end.'

At the door he turned and once again his eyes moved over them all, and then he said in that ordinary tone that was in itself so disarming, 'There's grub over in number three block, an' if you're not there within fifteen minutes you won't eat till the morrow mornin'. And now this is your first lesson in learnin' to jump to it; it'll take you all of fifteen minutes – that's if you go at it – to get your kit put straight, to get your bed made, and this hut left tidy. But of course if you learn to jump to it, well, you might be able to manage it in less.'

He gave three nods of his head then turned and walked out, leaving behind him a blank silence that lasted for about three seconds. Then the silence was exploded by a mad scramble, during which Charlie actually laughed one of his rare laughs.

And Charlie's mood remained light for the next week in spite of skinned heels, aching limbs and indigestible food, and ears that were becoming numbed with the shouting, the bawling and the cursing. That was until the shuffle round started. It happened, he learned from one of the old hands, every so often. The numskulls at the top found a lot of empty forms that had to be filled in. But what did they fill them in with? A shuffleabout: postings, here, there and every God damn where.

The postings, of course, didn't concern the new batch of conscripts, it merely concerned one man, their sergeant who everybody conceded was as decent a bloke as you'd ever get in a sergeant. Mind, that wasn't saying much, but still they could have worse.

And they got worse. The rest of the platoon was only affected by the new sergeant being, what they termed, true to bloody-minded form; but in Charlie's case he was an old acquaintance.

The first time Charlie came face to face with the replacement he stared unbelieving at Slater, and when his mind groaned, Christ Almighty! not this an' all, the words carried no trace of blasphemy. It was as if he were addressing the Almighty and asking Him as man to man why He was leading him into these situations.

True, he had walked stubbornly into managing the farm, telling himself that in time experience would sit on his shoulders and make him appear as if he were cut out for the job. Then blindly, weakly like a lamb, no, like an ass to the slaughter, he had allowed himself to be led into marriage.

But this latest situation wasn't of his choosing, either through purpose or weakness; he had been dragged into this. No, that wasn't right; he could have got out of it, he was a farmer. But since finding himself here, strangely, he was beginning to enjoy it; it was the companionship, the rough and tumble among men, ordinary, everyday men like Johnny, raw, blunt, kindly, humorous men. Only yesterday he was regretting not having joined up before conscription; that was until he made himself remember why he was here, merely to learn how to kill. However, that was in the future, at least it had been until this very minute when he looked down the room and saw the new sergeant.

At first Slater didn't recognise him. Using the trick of all sergeants he looked silently round at the men who were standing in different parts of the room waiting for him to speak, but his eyes hadn't traversed the full circle before his gaze stopped its roving and his eyes narrowed, then widened, while his head moved just the slightest bit forward like a bull weighing up the obstacle before it, the human obstacle.

After a moment he allowed his eyes to finish their inspection. Then unlike his predecessor had done on first viewing his new charges, he made no prolonged speech to them, all he said to the assembled men was, 'Well! well! well!' Then marching smartly up the end of the room he stopped before the tall figure, and

again he said, 'Well! well! well!' And after a pause
headed, 'So they raked you in at last.'

Charlie made no answer, he just stared into the
thin face that, unlike the body, hadn't seemed to
have grown with the years but still retained the
pinched look about it. The only thing that was missing was the look of fear that the eyes had carried
until the day he had been given food for blackmail.

'Strange world, isn't it, MacFell?'

Still Charlie didn't answer.

'I was speaking to you.'

There was a short silence before Charlie answered;
then in tones that the men might have expected to be
used by an officer he said, 'I endorse what you say, it
is a strange world.'

Slater's hair was cropped close yet it still showed
red, and now the colour seemed to be seeping down
into his pale skin and his features went into contor-
tion, his mouth opened wide, his nostrils expanded,
his eyes became slits; it was as if he were on the
parade ground and about to issue an order, but what
he barked was, 'Say sergeant when you speak to me.'

In the heavy silence that followed Charlie pro-
nounced the word sergeant in the same tone he had
previously used and it sounded like an insult.

Again there was silence before Slater spoke; and
when he did his voice was scarcely audible except to
Charlie and those standing quite near to him, for
what he said was, 'It's gona be a hard cinder path for
you, MacFell. If it lies with me I'll see that there are
fresh ashes put on it everyday.' On this he turned

about and walked smartly from the room, and no eyes were turned to watch him go because they were all directed on the fellow most of them were thinking was barmy to have got the new sergeant's back up like that.

'You know 'im?' They gathered round him now.

'He's got it in for you.'

'What was that he was sayin' about cinders?'

'He'll put you on fatigues . . . Still it isn't a bad job; keep your hands warm.'

'You must have known him afore.'

'What've you ever done to him?'

'I heard about 'im, he's nicknamed the Red Sod. Take the guts out of a gate-post, they say, he would. I'd go careful, mate, if I was you.'

As yet Charlie had answered none of the questions, but now he looked from one to the other and said simply, 'He worked on my farm.'

'You had a farm?'

Johnny nudged the speaker and said in an aside, 'Aye. Aye, he's a farmer, up Otterburn way.'

'I thought they were exempt?'

'It seems he didn't want to be.'

'He must have been a bugger,' the voice muttered again. 'He doesn't look like one, anything but, yet you never know. Anyway, the new un's got it in for him for something.'

The voices faded away and Charlie sat on the side of the bed and applied himself meticulously to rolling up his putties, and Johnny Tullett, sitting on the opposite bed, slipped in the button shoe under the top brass button of his tunic and rubbed vigorously at it until it showed a high polish; then holding it from his gaze, he surveyed it, after which he brought it to his mouth, breathed on it hard and began polishing again. And now as he rubbed he said under his breath, 'What did you ever do to him, Charlie, to make him feel like that?'

'Nothing, nothing personally.'

'Funny.'

After a while Johnny spoke again, still under his breath. 'What did he mean by hintin' that your time here was gona be like a long cinder path?'

'He was referring to a cinder path on the farm.'

'Oh . . . Has it got to do with how he feels?'

'Yes.'

'A cinder path?' The words were like a large question mark, and Charlie looked up and met Johnny's gaze and he said simply, 'My father took pleasure in whipping the lads for any misdemeanour. He did it on the cinder path; it hurt more there when they fell on their hands and knees.'

'Good God!'

'Yes, Johnny, good God!'

They both lowered their heads to their work again until Johnny said, 'I can understand how he feels. Bugger me, aye, I can that, it's enough to colour your resentment for life. Still' – he leant towards Charlie now – 'you didn't do owt like that to him, did you?'

'No.'

'Well, what's he got it in for you for?'

'I'm my father's son.'

'Oh! Oh aye, I see. Has he been long left the farm?'

'Some three years. He left when he was twenty.'

'Is that all he is, twenty-three? God! he looks years older. Is he married do you know?'

'Yes, he left to get married.'

'Did she . . . did his wife work on the farm?'

'Not on ours, the next one.'

Johnny was now staring at Charlie and he asked quietly, 'Do you know her?'

'Oh yes, yes.' Charlie nodded his head emphatically as he said this, and again he said, 'Oh yes, we were all brought up together.'

'Fancy that.' There was speculation in the statement.

'Yes, fancy that.'

Charlie now took his tunic off and started on his buttons, and as he gazed down at the dials of shining brass he saw Polly's face the day she had come to say good-bye to him. She said she had been up to the cottages to have a last look round the old place. There were tears in her eyes, and when he said to her, 'You shouldn't do it, Polly,' she had answered, 'What else is there for me?' and he had turned his head away from her gaze and said, 'Life dictates to us.' Her only answer to this was, 'Aye, I suppose it does.' Then when he had begun to say 'Should you ever need me, Polly . . .' she had stopped him abruptly, asking, 'Why should I need you now? Why should I ever need you, I'm gona be married? Oh' – her head had wagged – 'don't worry that he'll ever be tough on me. You needn't worry about that,

Charlie, for there's one thing I'm sure of, an' that is he cares for me. He always has, right from the beginnin', and although, well, I don't love him. I like him, and that's not a bad start.' Her tone was aggressive.

'No,' he had agreed with her; 'that's not a bad start.'

When she had offered him her hand he had held it while they gazed at each other, seeing a life that might have been. And then she had turned and was gone from him.

He had stood watching her until she disappeared from view, and when he turned it was to see Slater standing in the middle of the yard.

'Sayin' your good-byes then?' He had ignored the fellow's tone and said, 'Yes, we were saying our good-byes.'

Then Slater's eyes narrowed and his lips squared away from his teeth as he said, 'You're a loser, you know that. You've wanted her, haven't you? All these years you've wanted her, but you haven't had the guts to face the neighhours and take her. Your father offered her to you on a plate, didn't he? Oh. Oh, she's told me; there had to be a reason why bully-boy Arthur throttled your old man. An' you know, something I'll tell you that'll surprise you, in a way I've admired him for doing it, but you, who watched your father bein' murdered then covered it up, why, I've despised you all these years. You know, I used to envy you having a mother and father, and as big an old sod as yours was, I'd have given me sight, aye, I'd have given me sight just to have been able to call somebody father, to know who he was, or who she was. But there was you, you watched him being lynched and you covered it up, but not to save Arthur's neck, oh no, it was because of Polly you did it, wasn't it? 'Cos you wanted to shine in Polly's eyes, be the big hero. Now fancy that, you a hero! Well, you've lost again, an' you always will.'

How had he stood there and taken all that and not struck out? He had wanted to. In fact, part of him had jumped for the birch stick that was still hanging behind the door in the harness-room, and he had seen himself lashing the fellow across the yard and out of the gate; no, not out of the gate, through the alleyway and on to the cinder path; but all he had done was to raise his arm and point towards the gate, saying, 'Get out! And now, not tomorrow, now! You thankless scum.'

'Fancy that!' It was Johnny speaking his amazement aloud again.

4

Had he been in the army only five months? Wasn't it five years, five lifetimes, five aeons?

He was in what they called the new army, the training section of the reserve battalion. Battalions were shuffled and re-shuffled. The sixteenth and seventeenth battalions of the Durham Light Infantry became the First and Second Reserve Battalions. There were young soldier battalions, graduated battalions; a soldier was passed from one to the other, allotted to a company, and every three months or so the young men were spilled from the battalion on to a ship, and thus into the mud of France. There was always mud in France; seasons weren't long enough to dry it off.

It was usually the nineteen-year-olds that filled these drafts, but there had been a rumour flying around for the last few days that their own lot were ready for a move, and it wasn't for Durham or Shields, or Seaham Harbour, or Barnard Castle, or Ravensworth, but France.

Some of the men had the jitters and had to reassure themselves by continually saying they were in a reserved company and were simply a basis for reserve battalions, and that it was just the young 'uns who were drafted to the main battalion; they had been given to understand at the beginning that their unit wouldn't be required to serve abroad.

Who had given them to understand this?

Nobody knew.

Charlie thought he was the only one, at least in his platoon, of thirty men who longed to be one of the chosen to be sent overseas – it must be overseas – because wherever they went here Slater would inevitably go with them.

He had he knew become a different being during the past five months. And the change wasn't due to the army; the army could never have made him hate. He could never have opened his mouth wide enough to let out that piercing scream as he stuck his bayonet into a bag of straw if it hadn't been for Slater. It had been terrifying when it first happened, it had even caused him to vomit. Afterwards he had to get up in the middle of the night and go outside because he couldn't get the picture out of his mind that the bag of straw was Slater. Perhaps if it hadn't been for Johnny he might have tried, but Johnny, the escaped pitman, as he called himself because he had left the pits before the war started, only later to find himself conscripted because he wasn't in a reserved occupation, talked to him like a brother, a comforting older brother. How many times and in how many different ways had he said, 'Hold your hand, lad. Just remember that's what he wants you to do, hit out at him. An' then you'd be for it, the glasshouse. An' likely he's got mates there. What he can do to you now'll be nothin' to what they'll find to fill your days with. I've heard about some of them bastards. It can't go on for ever. I only know one thing, Charlie, I wouldn't be sayin' this to you if we were out there, 'cos there'd be no more need. I've heard of fellows like him dyin' suddenly, shot in the back while they're facin' the enemy. Hang on, Charlie. Hang on, mate.'

But how much longer he could hang on, he didn't know; the situation was becoming desperate because Slater's latest tactic was to talk at him. Only yesterday, addressing some of the other men in the billet he had said, 'You know some fellows are unfortunate, they never drop into the right occupation, they're put in a position where they have to kill animals, you know, like slittin' a pig's throat, an' God! you should see 'em, yellow they turn, yes, yellow, real nancy-pans! They should have picked a job like servin' in a shop, ladies particularly, camisoles 'n knickers 'n things like that, that's just about what they could handle.'

Some had laughed, being of the opinion that the sergeant was decent enough on the whole; it was how you took him.

Yes, the sergeant was wily enough to be decent enough on the whole. He spoke civilly to others, he gave some small privileges, he joked with others, and so not a few were in sympathy with him.

It was open knowledge now that he had been flogged on the cinder path; in fact some had been given further to understand that the treatment hadn't ceased when he had grown out of boyhood.

Charlie knew that the whole thing had been blown up out of all perspective and it would be no use him trying to alter the picture, even if he felt so inclined, which he didn't.

They had all been given forty-eight hours' leave. Was this the sign? Rumours were flying hither and thither.

'What do you make of it?' Johnny asked.

'It could be. Hope to God it is.'

'Well, I'm not as eager as you, Charlie, but I wouldn't mind gettin' out of this. Anyroad, I'd better go home and see wor lass, and prepare her. She's likely to go mad, she thought I was sittin' cushy for the duration. You wouldn't like to come along of us and meet her, would you, Charlie?'

'I'm sorry, Johnny. If I get another chance I will, but if this is our last leave then I've got a lot of things to do.'

A voice from down the room shouted, 'Can't mean we're goin' across, they give you embarkation leave, an' they tell you you're for it.'

Another answered in a tone deceptively soft at first, 'Who does, the colonel? Does he send for you and tell you to go and enjoy yourself, lad, 'cos this is your last chance?' The tone rose almost to a bellow now. 'Don't be so bloody soft, they keep these things secret. Five minutes after we come back Sunday night we could be skited like diarrhoea into trucks an' off we'll go hell for leather to the bloody south, an' them Southerners will be lining the streets and shoutin'

"Here come some bloody Geordie aborigines!" And you know what? They'll get the shock of their lives 'cos they think we still carry spears up here and paint worsels from the eyebrows right down over the waterfall to the toe nails. The Scots, they think they're civilised compared with us 'cos their fellows wear skirts.'

The hut rocked with laughter and Johnny, his mouth wide, looked at Charlie and said, 'Isn't Bill a star turn? I hope he comes along of us wherever we're goin'.' Then his face sober, he said, 'I hope I go along of you, Charlie, wherever you're bound for.'

'I hope you do, Johnny. Oh yes, I hope you do.'

The sincerity in his voice came from his heart, for of all the men he had met in his life he had never known companionship like that which existed now between this rough looking, rough talking man and himself.

'What you goin' to do with yourself?' Johnny asked now.

'First of all, go straight home and leave things in order there as much as I can; then I've one or two visits to make.'

Johnny, now pulling on his greatcoat, muffled his words in his collar as he said, 'You won't do a skip, will you, Charlie?'

'Do a skip? You mean?' He paused before giving a slight laugh and, shaking his head, he said, 'No, no, Johnny; don't worry about that, I won't do a skip.'

'Good. Good.'

He had caught a train to Newcastle, swallowed three

mugs of hot, scalding tea and two sandwiches, then made his way to the Otterburn road to see if he could pick up any army transport. Within half an hour he was lucky and got a lift in an army truck which dropped him just before one o'clock near Kirkwhelpington.

He did not immediately walk from the main road and into the lane but stood looking about him. The late November sky was hanging low over the land. It had cut off the tops of the distant hills and its leaden shadow was lying on the fields, which were still stiff from the overnight frost. There was snow in the air; he could smell it. He put his head back and sniffed and listened to the silence. But was this silence? The very air vibrated with different sounds. The old stones gripping each other for foothold on the walls sang; the road under his feet trembled with the distant echo of marching feet; the cattle standing silhouetted in the field below him murmured with the knowledge of instinct, 'We're going to die. We're going to die.'

His lids blinked rapidly, and he hunched the collar of his greatcoat further up round his neck. These were the kind of thoughts he used to think when he stood on the hills alone, wisps of imagination, words linking themselves together in an effort to explain his emotions. Funny, for a moment he had felt a boy again, young, alone, lost, yet one with all this, this aloneness, this wildness, this closeness that gave off the feeling of never ending, eternity past and eternity to come.

He walked from the road now and on to the bridle

path, on and on, leaping gates, tramping over fields, going through narrow gaps in stone walls; and then he was in the copse. He never passed through the copse but he remembered the day his father died. Yet today when the thought touched his mind it brought no regret, no feeling of guilt. Those feelings had been washed clean away over the past five months by Sergeant Sidney Slater.

The farmyard looked clean, in fact cleaner than he had ever seen it. As he made his way across it to the kitchen door a voice from the corner of the yard called, *'Bon jour, monsieur,'* and he turned and answered brightly, *'Bon jour,'* then walking towards the man who instinctively stood to attention, he said in English, 'How are you getting on?' and the man replied slowly, 'Oh, very . . . well, sir. Very well.'

'I'm glad.'

'You . . . on leave, sir?'

'Yes; a very short one.'

'Oh.' They smiled at each other and Charlie said, 'I'll see you again before I go. The others all right?'

'Pardon. Pardon.'

Now Charlie answered him in French, saying, *'Les autres; sontils heureux?'*

'Oui, monsieur.'

There was no one in the kitchen when he entered and he went through into the hall, calling, 'Hello! Hello there!' Instantly the sitting-room door opened and he smiled sadly to himself when Betty, disappointment on her face and in her voice, said, 'Oh, it's you!'

'Yes, it's me.'

'You cold?' She stood aside and let him into the room where a big fire was blazing in the open hearth.

'Frozen; there'll be snow soon.'

'We had some last week.'

'Yes.'

'What's brought you here today?'

He took off his greatcoat and stood with his back to the fire, his hands on his buttocks, before he replied, 'I've a forty-eight hours' leave. It could be embarkation; I don't know.'

'Overseas!' She stared up into his face. 'I thought you would be in clerical or something like that.'

'Well, they seem to think differently.'

'Are you hungry?'

'Yes, a bit; I haven't had anything since early on.'

'There's only cold stuff, chicken and a bit of lamb.'

'Only!' He laughed down on her now. 'I never realised how lucky we were with regards to food; the eggs they dish up there could never have been laid by hens.'

She smiled up at him, a tight, prim smile; then turning from him, she said, 'You'll have a lot to see to before you go then?'

'Yes, quite a bit.'

She looked at him over her shoulder, saying, 'I'll get you something.'

Left alone, he sat down in a chair to the side of the fireplace and let his gaze wander slowly around the room, the room that had been changed from a comfortable workaday parlour into the imitation of a drawing-room, a French one at that. There was a spidery-legged French Louis suite taking up one corner of the room and next to it and standing underneath a large ornate gold-framed mirror was what his mother always referred to as her *bonheur du jour*, never the writing-desk. Then there was the small nest of tables and the chaise-longue; the only piece left of the old furniture was the suite, and this was covered with a chintz, of which the pattern sported gold garlands and bows. There wasn't a room in the house which hadn't escaped her change, except the kitchen and his bedroom.

When her own money was exhausted she still defiantly went on buying; and the bills had come to him until he was forced to put a notice in the newspaper stating that he would no longer be responsible for her debts. The rows, the recriminations this brought forth rang in his ears even yet. Wasn't it *his* house she was furnishing? He'd bring a wife here some day, wouldn't he?

But not until the day he broke the news that he was in fact bringing a wife to the house did the hurricane of her temper sweep through the place, when she threatened to make a bonfire of every stick in it.

Now she was gone, and he'd soon be gone and he might never come back again. What then? The place would go to Betty; he had made a will to that effect and it was about that he must talk to her. If anything happened to him Victoria would likely put a claim in, as was her right. But under the circumstances she might not. Anyway they could fight that out between them.

She brought him a meal on a tray and while he ate they exchanged hardly a word. He did ask how she was getting on with the men; and her answer was, all right, but she kept them in their place, for after all they were Germans, weren't they, and she was a woman alone here.

After he had finished his meal and she had poured him out a second cup of tea she repeated those words by saying, 'Have you ever considered my situation now that I'm alone here among these prisoners?'

'You'll not be alone as long as Arnold's there. Where is he, by the way? I thought he would have popped over.'

'It's his time off. Anyway he's gone into the town. And what use would he be if any of them attacked me? He can't straighten that back of his.'

'I don't think you need worry about that.'

'Huh!' – she screwed her small tight buttocks down into the couch – 'I'm as attractive as the next; true I'm not like a full blown horse' – he took it that she was referring to Victoria – 'but when it comes down to the needs and seeds, looks won't bother men.'

He closed his eyes for a moment, then turned and looked into the fire before saying heavily, 'I wasn't underrating your looks in any way, you know that, but Heinrich is a gentleman, what he says seems to go with the others, Moreover . . .'

'Moreover, nothing!' She spat the words at him. 'Will you never grow up, Charlie? He's a gentleman!' She mimicked his voice. 'So is the bull; he's the

205

best of his breed but if he thinks at all there's only one thing on his mind. And it's the same with them, more so 'cos they're frustrated.'

'All right, all right, Betty.' He was shouting now. 'You can have it your own way; Wetherby may come, that's if you get married, but the stipulation still stands that when I return you'll have to find a place of your own. You won't have to do it empty-handed, I can assure you, you've worked hard here, no one harder, so you're entitled to half the profits that are standing when I come back . . . if I come back. If I don't' – he shrugged his shoulders – 'well, then you'll have it all your own way. I've already put that in writing, and also the business of you drawing cheques on the bank while I'm away.'

She stared at him for a moment, then bit on her lip. 'You'll come back,' she said.

He rose from the chair and walked across the room to the window and stood looking out for a moment before he spoke again. 'At the present moment I don't much care, the only thing I want is to be posted, anywhere, Land's End, John o' Groats, overseas.' He swung round and looked down the room towards her. 'Ginger Slater is my sergeant. He's been giving me merry hell.'

'Ginger!'

'Yes, Ginger.'

'Good God! How did he become a sergeant?'

'Because he's smart and he's got a head on his shoulders and he's wily.'

'But why should he want to take it out on you? I

knew he didn't like you very much, in fact at times I thought . . . well—' She turned away and put her hand on the mantelshelf and looked down into the fire, and he came towards her now, repeating, 'Well what?' and she turned to him and ended, 'Well, at times the way he used to speak to you and you stood it, well, I thought he had something on you.'

'What could he have on me?' He stared down at her as she bent and lifted a log from the side of the hearth and pressed it into the red glow of the fire, and she was dusting her hands as she said, 'Oh well, it was just a thought.'

'What was?'

'Well, that he had you where he wanted you 'cos you were over pally with Arthur.'

'What! You mean . . . ?'

The look on his face told her how wrong she had been, and she repeated, 'Well, it was just a thought.'

'Just a thought. My God!'

He turned from her. She must have been thinking all these years that he and Arthur . . . No wonder she had treated him like muck. He had the strong desire to tell her the truth, but common sense prevailed for he knew she was her father's daughter and nothing but vengeance would satisfy her.

'Well, what is he getting at you for?'

He turned and faced her. 'He can't forget that he was flogged on the cinder path.'

Her face stretched in amazement. 'You mean he's borne that grudge all this time and now he's holding it against you?'

207

'What else?'

'You must be mistaken. Father flogged all the lads.'

'He flogged this one too often.'

'It's unbelievable, he must be crackers.'

'No, he's not crackers, he's just got a long memory.'

She was nodding, about to speak again, when the sound of the front door bell clanged through the house and she looked at him slightly surprised, saying, 'The front door, who can that be?'

He watched her hurry from the room; he heard her go across the hall and open the door; he heard the murmur of voices; and then she was coming back into the room, followed by Florence Chapman.

He felt a slight flush creeping over his face. It was almost two years since he had last met his mother-in-law. He had got on well with her. She had done her best to try and smooth the situation that had arisen so soon after his marriage.

He went towards her holding out his hand and she took it, saying, 'Hello, Charlie.'

'Hello, Florence.' It had been her suggestion that he call her by her Christian name. 'Come and sit down.' He led her towards the fire.

'Will you have a drink?' Betty was addressing her now. 'Tea? The kettle's boiling.'

It was evident that Betty was ill at ease yet at the same time curious why this woman who had never set foot in the house since a week after her daughter's wedding should be here now.

208

'I wouldn't mind a cup of tea, Betty, thank you.'

The request didn't urge Betty to run to the kitchen, but looking directly at Florence she asked, 'Is anything wrong?'

Florence looked from her to Charlie, then back to her, and she said slowly, 'Hal's ill, very ill. The doctor doesn't hold out much hope. I . . . I was going to get word to Victoria and Nellie, I was about to send one of the boys in this afternoon, when Archie said he saw you.' She turned to Charlie. 'He was up on the hill, and he guessed it was you, because as he said, he knew your walk.' She smiled weakly. 'And so I thought, if you wouldn't mind telling them when you get back . . . that's if you're going back tonight?'

He'd had no intention of going back tonight for where would he stay? But he nodded his head now, saying, 'Yes, I was going back. I can go right away; there's nothing to stop me. I'm sorry to hear about Hal . . . What is it?'

'His kidneys, and he's just been out of hospital a month.'

'Oh!'

He couldn't prevent a sardonic thought crossing his mind. It didn't look as if his father-in-law was going to live long enough to gain any benefit from their joined lands. It had been a bad bargain all round.

She stared at him sadly for a moment, then turned her gaze back to Betty, saying, 'You need never have anything on your conscience, Betty, for you did your duty by your mother, and I think I can say that at times it mustn't have been easy for you, yet here I am

209

with two daughters, who had everything they ever wanted, and what did they do? Under one pretext or another they faded out of our lives.' She now looked at Charlie and, her voice breaking and her eyes filling with tears, she said, 'We haven't seen either of them for six months. In a way I could understand Victoria's attitude but not Nellie's. I . . . I don't know what's come over that girl. I'm afraid for her, Charlie.'

'Oh, Nellie's all right, Florence. It's a long way out here you know, and she's got a job, and nobody's their own boss these days.'

Florence now shook her head and sighed, while Betty, having heard all she needed to know, got up to go out and make the tea.

Florence looked at Charlie where he was sitting opposite her, and she smiled at him as she said, 'You look well, Charlie, very fit.'

'Well, they either make you or break you.'

'Yes, I've . . . I've heard it's pretty tough, especially for the—' She paused in slight embarrassment, and he finished for her on a laugh, 'The conscripts? Yes, they make it tough for the conscripts, Florence. But now my only regret is I didn't join up before.'

'Really!'

'Yes, it's an eye-opener, you think you know people, men. But after all, our circle out here is very small, isn't it, Florence?'

'Yes, I suppose so, Charlie. But . . . but I'm surprised you're liking it.'

'Ah, I wouldn't say I was liking it, Florence, just let's say I'm learning from it.'

Charlie watched her now look down towards her gloved hands, thinking that it wasn't only the men who were different out here, the women, too, seemed to belong to another generation. Florence's coat rested on the toes of her buttoned boots, her felt hat was set straight on the top of her grey hair. How old was she? In her mid-forties yet somehow she looked elderly. Back there in the town the women were wearing skirts up to their calves; he'd actually seen one marching along wearing a coat that came just below her knees. But these, of course, were exceptions. Yet, as Johnny kept prophesying with his rough wisdom, what Newcastle did the day, Shields, Gateshead and likewise towns did the morrow. Hang silk bloomers on the line and there'd come a time when you wouldn't be able to buy a pair of woolly ones for love or money.

'How is Victoria?'

He now looked towards the fire before admitting, 'I . . . I haven't seen her for a while.'

'How long is a while, Charlie?'

'Some months.'

'Oh, Charlie!'

'It's no good saying Oh, Charlie, like that, Florence, you know yourself it should never have happened, we're poles apart. I'm not blaming her. I blame myself, I'm so blooming easily led it's a wonder they don't shear me twice a year.'

'Oh, Charlie!' Florence smiled sadly at him. 'You

know what your trouble is, you're too nice. And I'm as much to blame for this mess as anyone. Hal wanted you to marry her. I needn't go into that, you know why, and I wanted everything for Hal that he wanted for himself, but . . . but I also wanted you in the family. I thought somehow you would soften her, change her; I should have known that you can't change people, at least not people like Victoria.' She gave a wry smile now. 'She was christened after the old Queen and it's strange but she has a lot of her traits, she'll have her way or die . . . Anyway, Charlie, go and tell them how things are with Hal, that he's very, very ill, and that they must come and see him. He'd not asked for them until last night, and because of that I somehow deluded myself into thinking that he wasn't as bad as he is, but I know now that his time is running out . . . Look'– she got quickly to her feet, her eyes full of tears – 'I . . . I won't wait for the tea, I'd better be getting back, he misses me.'

'I'm sorry, Florence.' He was holding her hand tightly. 'If there was only something I could do for you.'

'You can do that for me, Charlie' – her voice was breaking – 'go and see them both, tell them that they must come. If they don't they'll have it on their conscience for the rest of their lives.'

They were already in the hall when Betty pushed open the green-baized door and came through carrying a tea tray, and she stopped and looked at Florence in surprise and said, 'You're not going?'

'Yes, yes, Betty, I . . . I feel I must get back; Hal

212

worries when I'm not there. Good-bye.' She didn't wait for Betty to approach her but went out of the front door, and Charlie followed. He helped her up into the trap, then he stood aside while she turned the horse around; and he remained standing on the drive until she disappeared from his view.

Betty was waiting for him in the hall and he said flatly, 'I'd better get a move on.' He looked at his watch. 'What time is it? I can't hope to get another lift, I'll have to get up to Knowesgate Station and catch a train. I expect it'll be quicker in the end.'

As he spoke she turned and looked at the hall clock. 'Three o'clock.'

'I'd better be off then, Betty.' He turned towards a chair and picked up his greatcoat; then pulling his cap on he stood looking down on her for a moment, saying, 'I'll just have a look in on the fellows before I go.'

'Yes, all right.'

'Good-bye, Betty.' He bent down to kiss her cheek, and when her arms came round his neck and she kissed him on the mouth he held her tightly to him for a moment, then turned from her and went quickly out.

He was lucky and managed to get a ride on a farm cart, which at least kept him off his feet for about two miles but took longer to cover the journey to Knowesgate than if he had walked.

He was nearing the station when he saw a car emerging from the quarry road. When he noticed the direction it was to take he sprinted forward and flagged down the driver and when the car stopped he bent his length down and said, 'Pardon me, but may I ask where you're bound for?'

'Aye, you may. Newcastle, if it's anything to you. Want a lift?'

'That's about it.'

'Well, what are you waitin' for?'

It seemed too good to be true.

Sitting beside the driver he expressed his admiration of the car which was a Daimler, and the driver agreed with him. 'Aye,' he said; 'it's a nice piece of work.'

Listening to the rough Northern twang and having taken in the equally rough appearance of the man, Charlie couldn't be blamed for probing by asking, 'Are you in a firm?'

'Aye, you could say I'm in a firm, lad.'

'Chauffeur?'

The head was turned sharply to him. 'Chauffeur! Do I look like a bloody chauffeur? Not in uniform, am I?'

'I'm sorry, I just thought.'

'Aye, I know what you thought, lad, you thought a fellow like me shouldn't have a car like this. That's what you thought, isn't it? Like all the rest of the ignorant buggers you'll say I got it through profiteering. But let me tell you, son, this here was got through damned hard work. I was a taggerine man for years, scrap merchants they call us now and I'm one of the fellows that's supplying the wherewithal to see that blokes like you don't get your bloody heads knocked off, afore your number's called that is.'

'Yes, yes, I see.'

'You don't see.'

'I'm sorry if I've offended you.'

'Everybody offends me, but what do I care! You can stand being offended when your belly's full and your arse is sitting soft. What are you, anyway?'

'I'm a private in the . . .'

'I can see that, I'm not blind, lad. What were you afore you were a private?'

'A farmer.'

'A farmhand?'

'No, not a farmhand, I have my own farm.'

'Begod! I thought farmers like pitmen were exempt.'

'I didn't want to be exempt.'

'You must be bloody well barmy!'

'Yes, I think I am.'

The man now turned his head and gave a faint grin. 'Well, it's something when we know what we are, I'll give you that. I'm a successful man an' I mean to go on bein' successful; I can swim through the sneers. It's funny you know' – he cast his glance in Charlie's direction again – 'it's funny you know, you were no exception back there, 'cos everybody takes me for a numskull, for somebody's bloody chauffeur without the uniform. When I open me mouth I can hear them thinkin', Dear, dear! What have we come to, chauffeur talkin' like that! And I can tell you, lad, I mean to go on talkin' like this. I've changed me hoose but

I'm not changin' me tongue for the simple reason I couldn't if I tried.' He let out a bellow of a laugh now, and Charlie laughed with him. He was a character and a likeable one at that.

'I was born into a taggerine family and I'll die in the taggerine family, even if they've given us the title of scrap merchants. But I'll tell you something, lad' – he leant sidewards towards Charlie while keeping his eyes to the front – 'it's a comfortin' feelin' to know you're goin' to die in the lap of luxury, and not with your da's working coat over your feet on the bed.'

Again they were laughing.

As they entered Newcastle the man asked, 'Where you billeted, son?'

'Oh, down the river, Shields way, but . . . but I've got some business to do in the city and in Gateshead first.'

'Oh aye, well you wouldn't like to give it a miss an' come along for a bite to our place would you?'

'Thank you very much indeed. And I mean that.' Charlie nodded at the man. 'I would like nothing better, but my father-in-law is seriously ill and one of the things I have to do before I go back to camp is to let my wife know.'

'Your wife? Isn't she back on your farm?'

'No, no; she lives in Newcastle.'

'Oh well, some other time then. Look, here's me card.' He took a hand off the wheel and pushed it into an inner pocket, and when he handed the card to Charlie he said, 'Gosforth. See that, Gosforth. That's where I live. John Cramp's the name. You're welcome any time. Lots of the lads pop in, they're always sure of a bite and a drop of the hard, two or three if they want it, I'm never short. See to number one and let two, three, and four look after themselves. That's the only way you'll get on in this world, lad, and I'm tellin' you from one who knows.'

When he stopped the car he turned fully round to Charlie now and said, 'It's a pity you can't come along, I've got a fancy I'd like havin' a natter with you, not that you've said anything edifyin' like up till now, it's just that I've got a fancy.'

Charlie was laughing again.

'Well, don't look surprised if I take you at your word and drop in on you some night.'

'My pleasure.' The man held out his hand, and Charlie took it and said, 'And thanks for the ride; I don't know when I've enjoyed one more, and I hope it's a long, long time before you find yourself dying in comfort.'

The man seemed reluctant to let go of his hand and what he said now was something that Charlie was to remember later on. 'If I'd had a son like you I would've seen he didn't spend his time in the bloody ranks. I've got all the money in the world, lad, but I've neither chick nor child, it's only the missis an' me an' about three thousand bloody in-laws and relations, all waitin' for me poppin' off.'

They parted on laughter, through which on both sides was streaked a thread of sadness, and while Charlie waited for the bus to take him to the house his thoughts were still with the man. Poor devil; he was rotten with money, the making of which was apparently his only happiness. Life was strange and there were so many unhappy people in it, unhappy people who could still laugh.

He got off the bus and walked up the dark avenue towards the house, thinking as he did so that he would ring. He still had his key but it wasn't his intention to surprise her. He didn't dissect the reasoning for his consideration but he told himself that if she wasn't at home he would use the key and leave her a note. In fact, he hoped she wasn't in for he had no desire to confront her; all their meetings seemed to end in anger.

The house appeared to be in darkness, yet it wasn't completely for there was a slight glow coming through the curtains of the sitting-room. He approached the window and through a small chink in the end curtain he could see the glow was from the fire; and it was a fresh glow implying that she hadn't been long gone from the room.

Perhaps she was in the kitchen. No, she liked plenty of light, she always left lights blazing all over the house.

He inserted his key in the lock and when the door was opened he switched on the hall light, turned down the collar of his coat, looked about him for a moment, then opened the door of the sitting-room and switched on the light there.

As he started towards the fireplace he imagined that his whole frame was swelling, the long intake of breath was wafting into every part of his body, down to his feet, into his finger ends, and up to the strands of his hair.

Before him, standing behind the couch that bordered a long sheepskin rug which lay before the fire stood his wife and a man. They stood at each side of the fireplace and the flickering rosy light from the glowing fire illuminated them as would flashes of sheet lightning. His wife's nakedness was partly covered by the crumpled dress she was holding to her chest and her hair that was hanging loose about her. She hadn't been as quick as her companion to dress for he had managed to get into his breeches, apparently between the time he had heard the key in the front door and the light of the sitting-room being switched on.

Having fastened the top button the man now stood still. They all stood still, their eyes in a triangle of amazement, anger and embarrassment. It was Charlie who was amazed, and yet at the same time he was asking himself why should he be. It was the man who was showing embarrassment; but Victoria, as usual, was expressing her feelings through anger.

Yet did he detect a trace of fear in his wife's emotion? He watched her drop down behind the couch, then emerge again pulling the dress over her head. The man, his head bowed now, reached to the corner of the couch for his shirt and coat. In silence Charlie watched him. There was something familiar about the man's face; they had met somewhere, but where? As the man pulled on his uniform coat and Charlie recognised the insignia, an exclamation of

'Good God!' almost escaped Charlie's lips. Major . . . Major Smith!

His body was being deflated now, the air was rushing from it and taking its place was heat made up of embarrassment, shame and anger, a fierce anger that was urging him to take a run at this man who had been cohabiting with his wife, to leave the imprint of his fist right between his eyes. No one would blame him, even a court martial would surely find extenuating circumstances in the situation; in any case it would be the end of Major Smith's career.

Victoria was standing in front of him now, hissing through her clenched teeth, 'What do you want?'

He saw her through a red mist. She looked very like a witch, her black hair, her blazing eyes. 'Just a word with *my wife*,' he said.

It sounded silly, theatrical, like lines delivered by a ham actor.

'You've no right here!' Her hair danced as she tossed her head. He could imagine the hair to be snakes and she Medusa, but her look could not turn him to stone, and he proved this for now his voice carried no trace either of the ham actor or of any actor at all, but that of an angry man, for it was so surprisingly near a roar that it startled her, and she stepped back from him as he cried, 'I have every right here! Until I divorce you I have every right here!'

For the first time in their acquaintance he saw that he had frightened her. He saw her glance towards the man who was sitting now, putting on a pair of shining leggings, and he, too, looked towards him as he ended on a yell, 'And divorce it will be!' Then turning to her again, he finished, 'And that's without any stipulations from you. Now I'll tell you why I came here tonight. Your father happens to be dying and would like to see you . . . if you can spare the time.' He watched her open her mouth, then put her fingers across her lips before going towards the door. But there she turned and said, 'I've got to talk to you. Wait, don't go. I'll . . . I'll be down in a minute.' There was almost a plea in her voice.

The man and he were alone now; the man was on his feet straightening his tunic, putting his belt to rights, pulling at the large flap pockets of his tunic, smoothing his hair back, adjusting his tie, anything apparently to keep his hands busy.

Charlie walked up the room until he reached the back of the couch, and now the man's hands became still, hanging stiffly by his sides while they stared at each other.

'I . . . I suppose I should know you, shouldn't I?' The voice was cultured yet had the suggestion of the Northumberland burr in it.

'You happen to be the officer commanding my company.' There was no addition of sir to the statement.

'Oh my God!' The man now turned his head to the side, dragged his lower lip in between his teeth, then said, 'I . . . I fear I owe you an apology.'

'Huh!'

The head was snapped to the front again and for a moment it was the senior officer viewing a private who had dared to speak in his presence without first having been given permission. Then after a tense moment during which their gazes were locked, the slightly greying head was turned to the side again, and now the words coming tight from between his lips, the major said, 'I . . . I understood you were separated, officially.'

'You understood wrong then.'

The major again drew on his lip, so tightly now that the skin of his chin was drained of blood; then once more he was facing Charlie. 'I . . . I understand that she can get a divorce, there are certain circumstances that would provide her . . .'

The major's voice trailed away, and Charlie, his jaw bones working hard against the skin, snapped, 'That's a concoction on her part. I've told her I'll take the matter to court, a high court, if she attempts to make that plea because it's a lie.'

Again they were staring at each other. Then Charlie dared to look his superior from top to toe and back to the top again before saying slowly, 'But this isn't a lie, is it?' and turning abruptly, he marched down the room.

'Wait, please. Wait.'

Charlie turned his head to look over his shoulder and the answer he gave to the major was, 'Tell her she'll be hearing from my solicitor.'

He had closed the front door when he heard her calling his name, and he was out and going through the gate when the front door opened again and she cried, 'Charlie! Charlie! Wait.' But he walked on, taking no heed.

It was strange, he was burning with anger and humiliation yet he was experiencing a sort of elation. For the first time since he had known her, he felt on top. Had she ever run after him before calling him back with a plea in her voice, 'Charlie! Charlie! Wait!'? She was scared, and so was her major. My God! the major. And they said he was a decent bloke an' all, well liked. In a way he could feel sorry for him, but he wasn't going to let pity baulk him in this case; oh no, no, he had a handle, and by God! he was going to use it.

She had been naked, stark naked . . . both of them. She had no shame. But then he must remember she liked being naked. How many men had she sported with before the major, and in the romantic glow of the fire in the sitting-room?

He jumped on a bus that took him over the bridge into Gateshead and as he walked towards Nellie's house he was asking himself who would get the first move in? In a matter of hours, in fact as soon as he returned to camp, he could probably find himself singled out from the platoon and packed off to France, no uncertainty, no hanging about . . .

Nellie was definitely at home. Her voice came to him as he knocked on the door. She was singing 'If You Were the Only Girl in the World', and as she opened the door she flung one arm wide and, her head back, she sang at him, 'If you were the only boy in the world and I were the only girl'. Her voice trailed away, her chin lowered, and she exclaimed, 'Charlie! Charlie! Oh Charlie!' Putting out her hand, she grabbed his arm and pulled him into the room. 'I . . . I thought you were some friends; I'm expecting some friends. Come and sit down, come and sit down. Where've you been all this time?'

He allowed himself to he pulled towards the fire and for a moment the sight she presented blotted out for him the last hour; Nellie was drunk.

'Sit, down, sit down. T . . . take your coat off. Here, s'let me help you.'

Her speech was slurred, and as she reached up to his shoulders and went to tug at his coat he took hold of her hands, and with a slight push caused her to sit down with a plop on the couch. The effect on her was almost the same as if he had douched her face with cold water for she lay back, opened her mouth wide, gasped, and then said, 'I . . . I know what you're thinkin', and you're right, I'm drunk. Well, everybody's got to have something. What did you come for anyway? You never show your face for weeks on end, then you turn up uninvited, yes, uninvited.' She brought herself up from the back of the couch. 'An' I'm expectin' friends.' Suddenly she was yelling at him, 'Don't look at me like that, Charlie MacFell! Keep those looks for your wife; she earns them, I don't. The only thing I do is drink. I know what you think. I know what you think.' She hitched herself to the edge of the couch now.

When he shouted at her, 'Be quiet! Nellie. For God's sake be quiet!' she cried back at him, 'Why should I be quiet? This is my own house an' I can do what I like in it. But . . . but let me tell you something,

Charlie MacFell!' She was now wagging her finger up at him. 'I don't do what you think I do in it. No, I don't. I'm not like me sister, I'm no whore.'

'Nellie!'

'Oh, you can say *Nellie* like that, but I know I'm speaking the truth, and you know I'm speakin' the truth. An' . . . an' you know something, Charlie?' Her voice dropped now. 'I'm speaking the truth when I tell you I'm . . . I'm not that kind. You know what I mean. You know what I mean. I'm a fool, I'm a bloody fool, Charlie. Pals, I say to them; that's all I want to be, pals. They can come whenever they like, have a drink, somethin' to eat an' a laugh, an' they respect me. Yes, they do. But they think I'm odd. An' . . . an' it's all your fault.' Her body bending now almost double, she began to cry.

God, what a night! What a day! What a life! What a bloody life!

'Nellie! stop it. Sit up and listen to me.' His tone was quiet now.

She sat up and he put his arm around her shoulders, and like a child now she turned to him and lay against his chest, and her body shook with her sobbing and the more he tried to console her the worse it seemed to get.

'Nellie! give over. Come on now, no more.'

When her crying subsided she pulled herself away from him. Her body was still shaking and she was muttering something when there came a ring on the bell, and now she looked over the top of the couch towards the door and groaned, 'Oh no!'

He got to his feet and went to the door, but having opened it kept fast hold of it as he faced the two visitors.

'Miss Chapman isn't well; she's sorry, she'll see you another time.'

'What?'

'I said Miss Chapman isn't well; she'll see you another time.' He addressed the man who had spoken.

'She invited us around for eight.'

'She may have done, but she can't see you tonight.'

'Who the hell are you?'

'I'm . . . I'm her brother.'

'Ger out of me way!' They both advanced on him at once and he was knocked from the door.

'What's your game, anyway, she's got no brother?'

Still eyeing him, they hurried up the room to where Nellie sat on the couch with her face turned from them.

'What's he done to you, lass?'

'Nothing, Roy, nothing.'

'He's not your brother, is he?'

'He's . . . he's my brother-in-law, the one I told you about, the farmer.'

'Well, what's he done to upset you like this?'

The two men were staring hard at Charlie now, and he, staring as hard back at them, said, 'I came to tell her her father is ill, dying, and that if she wants to see him alive she'd better go as soon as possible.'

He turned his gaze down to Nellie. She was staring

up at him, her lips apart, her eyes wide.

'Oh, I'm sorry, I'm sorry, Nellie, we didn't know. Only you did ask us round.'

Nellie now looked up into the face of the young fellow who was bending over her and she said, 'Yes, Alec; I . . . I know I did. I'm sorry. Another time.'

'Aye, another time.'

'Sorry, chum' – one after other they nodded at Charlie – 'our mistake. Be seein' you, Nellie. Ta-rah.'

It wasn't until Charlie closed the door on them that he realised they were both sergeants and the rueful thought crossed his mind that he was certainly combating the higher ranks tonight all right.

When he returned to the fire, Nellie, her hands joined between her knees now and looking like a schoolgirl who had been caught out in some misdemeanour, said, 'Was that true?'

'Yes.'

'How d'you know?'

'I had to go over to the farm today to settle things with Betty because there's a rumour we may be off soon, and your mother got word that I was there and she came across. She was about to send someone in to you but she asked if I would bring the message.'

'Does . . . does Victoria know?'

He wetted his lips and swallowed deeply before answering, 'Yes, yes, she knows.'

'Is . . . is she going straight across?'

He turned from her as he answered, 'I doubt it tonight.'

'Did . . . did you row?'

227

'I wouldn't say we rowed. Look . . . shall I make you some coffee?'

'Yes. Yes, please.'

He went into the little kitchen and lit the gas and put the kettle on and looked around until he found some coffee. Everything, he noticed, was scrupulously clean and tidy; she might have slipped in some ways, but she still kept her place spotless.

He took some time to make the coffee and when he carried it into the sitting-room she was coming out of the bedroom. He noticed that she had combed her hair and powdered her face.

They sat side by side on the couch silently sipping at the coffee, and it wasn't until she had almost finished the cupful that the spoke. 'If anything happens to Father, Mother'll crumble away.'

'I shouldn't think so; your mother's strong.'

'Not strong enough to live on her own. She'll want me back there, but I couldn't go, Charlie, I couldn't live there again.'

'You'd be better off there than you are here.'

'How do you make that out? There's nothing there for anybody, except for those who've got a man by their side and . . . and children. And what men are there left there? A woman needs a man. Yes, she does, Charlie, she needs a man, not men, just one man.' Her voice now was throaty and tired sounding.

He turned and glanced at her for a moment before looking back into the fire and saying, 'Very few women, from what I can gather, are satisfied with one man.'

'She's made you bitter.'

He gave her no answer, and again there was silence between them until she asked, 'Is it true what you said about being posted?'

'Yes, as far as rumours go, it's true.'

'Will you let me know where you are?'

'Yes' – he smiled at her now – 'I'll let you know.'

'If the rumours are just rumours, will . . . will you come and see me again, Charlie?'

'Yes, yes, of course, Nellie, yes.'

'Promise?'

'I promise.'

'And . . . and if you're going to be sent over there, is there some way you'll let me know?'

'Yes, yes, of course. I'll drop you a line.' And now he looked at his watch and said, 'I'll have to be off.'

'Must you, Charlie? Couldn't you stay a bit longer?' She was gripping both his hands now, and he found that he had to look at them because he dared not look into her face.

'We've . . . we've got to be in by ten.'

'Yes, yes.' She released his hands quickly and got to her feet. He too rose and got into his coat, and with his cap in his hand he walked slowly towards the door, she by his side.

'Bye-bye, Nellie.'

'I might never see you again, Charlie.'

'Aw, you'll see me again, Nellie, never fear.'

As he bent down to kiss her, her arms came round his neck and her lips were pressed fiercely to his mouth. For an instant he returned the pressure of the

229

kiss and held her tightly to him; then he opened the door and was gone.

In the street once again, he walked rapidly, his mind in a whirl now, but one question that had pushed itself to the forefront he was answering loudly: No, no! that couldn't be, he didn't think of Nellie that way.

But she thought that way of him.

She was still tipsy.

No, she had sobered up; and anyway he had known all along how she felt. But that hadn't mattered as long as he knew how he felt. And now he didn't know how he felt. God! what a situation.

And where was he going to spend the night? He couldn't go back to the camp because they would think he was barmy . . . The Y.M.C.A. Huh! it was funny. A house in the country, a house in Newcastle, his sister-in-law's place, and he had to go and spend perhaps one of the last nights before he went overseas in the Y.M.C.A.

He could go back and stay with Nellie.

Don't be such a bloody fool! What did he think would happen if he went back there tonight? Wasn't he in enough trouble? In any case, he had already lied to her he was to be in by ten. The best thing he could do was to get settled down somewhere and think over what he meant to do about his wife and her top brass friend.

He got on a bus, walked to a front seat, paid his fare, and was staring out of the window into the dark night when he felt a gentle tap on his shoulder. He turned to look at a young woman who was saying to him, 'It's you, Charlie, isn't it?'

As he twisted further round in his seat and said, 'Why, Polly!' his thoughts gabbled at him. It only needed his mother to rise from the grave and they'd be all here, all the women in his life, not one of whom had brought him pleasure. But to come across Polly of all people tonight! And she wasn't the Polly he remembered. She was so much older, fatter, settled. She looked just like a thousand and one other women that could be encountered on the streets of Gateshead or Newcastle.

'How are you, Charlie?'

'Oh . . . oh not so bad, Polly. And you?'

'Oh, I'm fine. I'm fine.'

As she spoke he repeated to himself, fine, fine. Funny, she could say she was fine and she was Slater's wife. Yet there was no evidence in her face that she was anything other than fine. Her skin was as clear as ever, her eyes were bright, she was still bonny, yet she looked different, ordinary. It was funny, even fantastic, but if he had met her yesterday he would have told himself he was still a little in love with her. But everything had changed since yesterday, and the main thing was, not that he had found his wife with another man, but that he had suddenly felt a deep, exciting warmth seep through him when Nellie had kissed him. But could a moment like that wipe out years of love? And he had loved Polly. Oh yes, he had loved her. But how had he loved her? That was the question.

'Charlie.'

'Yes, Polly?'

'Do . . . do you think we could get off and have a cup of tea?'

He hesitated a moment while he stared at her; then said, 'Of course. Why not?'

They rose together and left the bus at the next stop and they were half-way up Northumberland Street before she said, 'I'll . . . I'll leave you to pick a place. Somewhere quiet, Charlie, but not posh, please.'

'Posh!' He laughed at her now. 'They don't allow privates in posh places, Polly.'

'Well, you know what I mean, it doesn't matter where it is as long as it's quiet. You see it's funny, but I've been sort of prayin' I'd come across you, Charlie, 'cos I wanted to have a talk with you.'

'Oh! anything wrong?' Even although his mind had accepted the burial of his boyhood love, he was hoping to hear that her feelings hadn't altered, that she was unhappy. And who wouldn't be unhappy with a man like Slater? Now if it had been anybody else he would have accepted the fact that she had transferred her affections.

'Will this café do?' She was pointing to a dimly lit window.

'I've been in there before, it's usually quiet.'

'Fine. Fine.'

A few minutes later they were seated at a corner table and, looking across at her, he said, 'Just tea? Anything to eat?'

'No; no thank you, Charlie. It's not long since I

had a meal. I've just come from me mother's.'

'How is she?'

'Oh, she's fine, fine.'

He smiled at her before turning and threading his way to the counter.

'Yes, lad?'

'Two teas, please.'

'I was here afore 'im.'

The elderly waitress behind the counter looked at the man in civilian clothes and said, 'And likely you'll be here after 'im an' all, 'cos there's no chance of you being shot, not in those clothes, is there?'

As the young fellow turned his head away muttering 'God!' Charlie wanted to put his hand out and reassure him, saying, 'It's all right, it's all right, I know just how you feel, I've been through it,' but he took the two teas from the smiling waitress and returned to the table.

As he handed Polly a cup she looked around her and said, 'It's packed; I've never seen it as full as this. But then I've never been here at night afore.'

There followed some moments of uneasy silence while they sat drinking their tea. Then in the impulsive way that he remembered she thrust her cup on to the saucer, leant towards him and in a low tone began to talk rapidly. 'I just wanted to say I'm sorry, Charlie, 'cos I know what you've been goin' through these past weeks. He must have led you hell. He . . . he says as much. He's bent on gettin' his own back. In a way I understand him, Charlie. You can't blame him 'cos, you know, your father put him through it, then—' Her eyes fell away from his now. 'And he knows that I was fond of you an' he thought you were likewise. It's all mixed up in his mind. And then there was the business of our Arthur. But as I said to him, why take it all out on you? It worries me, it's the only thing . . .'

'All right, all right, Polly.' He checked her gabbling and smiled at her as he said, 'It's all right, don't worry. Anyway, I think I'm on embarkation leave so we'll soon be parting, at least I hope so.'

'Yes, I know, I know; but he might go along of you.'

'I sincerely hope not.'

'So do I. Oh so do I, Charlie, for your sake.'

'What about you? How . . . how does he treat you?'

'Oh me! Treat me?' Her eyes widened. 'Oh, I've got nothin' to complain of, Charlie, not there. He's as good as gold to me. I couldn't have a better husband, an' I'd be . . . well—' She turned her face from him as she finished, 'I'd be as happy as Larry if it wasn't that I had you on me mind and how he's treatin' you.'

It was unbelievable that Slater could treat anyone well, the mean little swine that he was, yet here was Polly, his Polly as he used to think of her, almost glowing with affection for him. The longer he lived the more puzzling he was finding people.

'I've got two bairns now, you know.'

'Yes, yes, so I understand, Polly.'

'And I'll have a third come spring.'

She was bragging about his bairns. Could he himself have given her any bairns? He hadn't given Victoria any. But then Victoria was like a species from another planet, a wild Amazon; and she had stated openly that she hadn't wanted children.

'Oh, I'm so glad I met you, Charlie; me mind'll be at peace now.'

He stared at her. He had always thought she was a bright girl, an intelligent girl. And she was, yes, she was, but as in everything else there were levels. Because she had seen him and talked to him she imagined that he could now accept her husband's treatment as the natural, and even right, outcome of the rejection, frustration and humiliation he had suffered when young. She could never understand that what Slater was doing was taking it out of him not only because he had been flayed on the cinder path, but also because he had been born in the workhouse. It all stemmed from there. He recalled his expressed need for a father and his inability to understand anyone covering up the murder of his own father.

The past was all too complicated, but what was evident here in the present was the fact that Slater could be making a woman happy while at the same time finding new ways each day to torture someone else.

He was surprised when again in her impetuous way she rose to her feet and, looking down at him, said, 'Don't bother to come with me, Charlie, I'd rather you didn't.' She didn't add, 'Just in case we are seen,' but went on, 'There's only one thing. If . . . if you should both go out there together be careful, Charlie, I mean' – she shook her head – 'go carefully with him. Try to understand.'

He was on his feet now shaking her hand. 'Don't worry, Polly, everything will work out. I'm glad you're happy.'

'Thanks, Charlie. But . . . but I must say it, I'm sorry you're not, I am from the bottom of me heart.'

He sat down again and watched her threading her way towards the door. Her back view was broad and dumpy, so ordinary. But what had she said? 'Be careful, Charlie.' That had been a warning. Oh yes, that had been a warning; although she had altered it to 'Be careful with him,' she really had meant, 'Be careful of him, Charlie.'

What a day! Embarkation leave; his sister ravenous for sole control of the farm, for let him face it that's what Betty wanted, sole control; his wife, a brazen whore; his sister-in-law a drunk; and lastly his old sweetheart, for in his mind Polly had always been his sweetheart, telling him in so many words he'd better look out if he wanted to survive.

Well, what better way to end a day like this than to get drunk . . . But if he did they wouldn't let him into the Y.M.C.A., nor any other place except a common lodging-house.

He had a longing to be with Johnny, to talk to him, to be tickled by his humour and to be soothed by his rough understanding, but most of all to be warmed by his affection.

Women caused nothing but trouble. Wherever

236

there were women there was trouble. The only thing that was worth while in life was the companionship, the comradeship of another man; in that you could rest and be refreshed . . .

He left the café, went to the Y.M.C.A., spent a restless night, and had returned to the camp before twelve the next day.

5

The rumours were still running rife; they were going to France, they were going to Gallipoli; they were going to Aldershot; but one thing was sure, their company was going some place because the officers were on their toes and the N.C.O.s were running round like scalded cats, so said Johnny. He also said he'd go round the bend if he wasn't soon put out of his misery.

It was twenty-three hours now since he had returned to camp and they knew nothing more than they had done before they had been given leave. For the past hour they had been on the square listening to Slater's voice mingling with those of other sergeants bellowing, 'Left! right! left! right! Lift 'em up! At the double! Move! move!'

Although the day was grey and raw each man was sweating when at last they were told to stand easy. Charlie was at the end of the line, his eyes directed straight ahead, his stomach muscles tight as he waited for Slater to walk past him, then round behind him. Sometimes he did it without a word, at others it was with a skin-searing remark. He was coming from the other end of the line but when he was halfway he was stopped by a corporal who had come to his side and was apparently giving him some message. Whatever the message was, Charlie noted that Slater pondered on it before continuing on. And now the dreaded moment had arrived again, he was about to pass. But no, this apparently was going to be one of the mornings when he intended to indulge himself in a frontal attack.

'MacFell!'

'Sergeant.'

'What have you been up to now?'

Charlie made no answer.

'I asked you a question.'

'I don't know to what you are referring, Sergeant.'

There was a long pause before Slater said, 'You are to report to Lieutenant Swaine. Two paces forward, march!'

Charlie marched forward.

'Accompany the corporal. Right turn; quick march!'

He quick marched down the line to the waiting corporal, who turned and fell into step with him. Across the square they went through a passage between two buildings and into another square, this one sporting a lawn which they circled before mounting a set of wide stone steps and going into the building that had once been a college.

The hall was large and men were coming out of and going into different doors; some had either one, two, or three stripes on their arms, others one, two, or three pips.

They crossed the hall now still in step and came to a stop opposite a door marked Four. For the first time the corporal spoke. 'Wait here,' he said, the words coming out of the corner of his mouth. Then he bent stiffly forward, knocked on the door, opened it, and after entering the room he closed the door again.

Two minutes passed, the door was pulled open. The corporal gave a slight jerk of his head. Charlie stepped smartly forward and into the room.

The officer sitting at the desk looked at the corporal and said, 'That will be all,' to which the corporal answered, 'Yes, sir,' came smartly to attention, saluted, turned about and went out.

Also standing stiffly to attention, Charlie looked across the desk and over the head of Lieutenant Swaine.

Lieutenant Swaine was dubbed as a decent bloke amongst the men. He was a Southerner, at least from well south of this area, but compared with some of the others he wasn't bad at all.

'MacFell?' He looked up at Charlie.

'Yes, sir.'

'Stand easy.'

'Well now.' The officer eased himself back in his chair, twisted his body slightly, put his elbow on one arm of the chair and capped the other arm with the flat of his hand as he repeated, 'Well now.' Then went on, 'Let me first ask you a question. Have you ever thought about a commission?'

There was a pause before Charlie said, 'Sir!'

'Don't look so surprised; I said have you ever

thought about putting in for a commission?'

'No, sir.'

'Why?'

Charlie considered a moment. 'I suppose it's because I couldn't see myself in command of men, sir.'

'But' – Now Lieutenant Swaine leant forward and gently spread out some papers on his desk and scanned them as he murmured, 'You were a farmer?' He raised his eyes up to Charlie.

'Yes, sir.'

'Then you would have had men under you?'

'Four at most, sir.'

'Nevertheless' – the officer lay back in the chair again – 'you have handled men; you had to give them orders.' He stared at Charlie now before adding, 'I'm surprised you didn't put in for one right away. You went to a good school.'

'Yes, sir; but I had to leave before I was seventeen.'

'Oh well, that's really neither here nor there. Well now, as you know, we're looking for officer material and I've been through your papers and you seem, well –' the face stretched into a smile – 'pretty suitable material.'

Charlie supposed he should have said, 'Thank you, sir,' but he remained silent; he was experiencing a sort of pleasant shock. That was until he was attacked by a thought. Why were they choosing him all of a sudden? This business of recruiting officers had been going on for weeks. Was Major Smith putting him on the spot where he wouldn't be able to do anything about Victoria, at least put him in a position where he would find it very difficult? His jaws were tight, his face straight, his words clipped, as he asked, 'May I enquire, sir, when my name was first put forward?'

'What? . . . Oh! . . . Oh! let me see.' He again thumbed through the papers, then said, 'It isn't here, it's likely in the files.'

The lieutenant stood up, then in a leisurely fashion strolled towards a cabinet in the corner of the room. He pulled open the top drawer, flicked through some files, closed it, opened the second drawer and after some more thumbing picked out a single sheet of paper, glanced at it, then as he replaced it in the drawer he turned and looked at Charlie. 'Ten days ago, but, of course, we have to go into things, you understand?'

'Yes, sir.' The excited feeling was flooding him again and at the moment he could think of only one thing, one person, Slater, and the ecstatic satisfaction of breaking the news to the red-headed swine.

'You . . . you haven't any children?' Again the papers were being flicked through.

'No, sir.'

'Your wife runs the farm?'

'No, sir, my sister; my wife lives in Newcastle.'

'Oh!' The head was back on the shoulders. 'You have a house there?'

'Yes, sir.'

'How nice, how nice; and convenient; nice to slip home at times.'

'Yes, sir.'

'I myself am from Dorset, it's quite a way.'

'Yes, sir, it is quite a way.'

'Well now, you know everything doesn't happen overnight. Well, that is, not quite.' He gave a little laugh here, then said, 'You'll have to do a little training, and so although, as you know, a great many of us here are, well, just on the point of making a move, I'm afraid we'll be going one way and you another. Pity, but that's the way of things. But we may meet up again, who knows. Let me see. Ah yes, you can report within the next hour to Second-Lieutenant Harbridge. I'll get in touch with him and he'll put you wise to everything. Now all I can say is—' He rose to his feet, extended his hand, and ended, 'Welcome.'

'Thank you, sir.'

The grip of Lieutenant Swaine's hand was firm, in contrast to his lazy-sounding voice.

'The best of luck.'

'And to you, sir.'

The movement of the lieutenant's head was a signal that the interview was at an end. Charlie came smartly to attention, saluted, turned about and marched out of the room.

The corporal standing outside stared at him but said no word, but with a narrow-eyed, quizzical look he watched him leave the building and would no doubt have followed his progress from the window had not he been beckoned back into the room by the sound of the lieutenant's voice.

As Charlie went through the gap between the

buildings part of him seemed to be afloat. He was going to be an officer, *an officer* !

How would he break the news to Slater? Stick it into him like a bayonet or let it be seemingly slowly dragged out of himself by taunts?

Bayonets. He wouldn't be required now to stick a bayonet into somebody's belly, twist it and pull it out, and all the while screaming at his victim. No, he'd be able to finish him off cleanly with a pistol shot. But then again he might never be called upon to use a pistol.

He was going to be an officer.

He was really going to be an officer. He had lied when he said that he didn't think he was officer material. He had often wished to be in that position, if only for twenty-four hours. And now he had been given the chance, not only for twenty-four hours but for as long as the war lasted. No, that was wrong, for just as long as he managed to survive in it. But all he wanted at present was to savour the next half-hour.

As he crossed the main square he saw Slater standing in the far corner talking to an officer, and he hurried towards the hut. It wasn't his intention to break the news to him when he was alone, no, he wanted the same audience around him that Slater had felt he was entitled to.

He found the hut in a bustle of activity.

'It's come! We're moving,' someone called to him.

And another voice cried, 'What did they want you for, Lofty? Did you get it in the neck?'

Before Charlie had time to answer, some joker called out.

'Why, no! man; they're short of generals and they asked him to step in.'

'Stranger things have been known to happen.'

There was a pause in the bustling for a moment as all eyes were turned in his direction; then when he went to his bed and, instead of grabbing at his kit, sat down on the edge of it, some of them gazed steadily towards him.

'Come on! you'd better put a move on.' It was Johnny speaking to him now. 'We're due outside in ten minutes . . . Oh this bloody cap!'

'I shan't be coming with you, Johnny.'

'Either me bloody head's swollen or it's shrunk . . . What did you say, Charlie?'

'I said I'll not be coming with you.'

'What's he done to you now, put you in clink?'

'No.'

'Well, what, man?' He was bending down to Charlie now, whispering, and Charlie, putting up his hand and gripping his friend's tunic, whispered back, 'Say nothing yet, I want to hit him with it, I'm getting a commission.'

'Bugger me! No!'

'Yes.'

'God Almighty! of all the things I expected to hear. Eeh! Charlie lad! Charlie!'

When Johnny's two hands came out, Charlie said quietly, 'Not yet! let him come in first.'

'Aye, aye!' Johnny backed from him and flopped down on to his bed and he shook his head slowly now as he said, 'By! I'm glad for you, I am that. And yet

245

what am I talkin' about? That's the finish of us, isn't it? Officers an' men from now on. Aw, I'm sorry about that, yet at the same time, eeh! I can hardly believe it.'

'What can't you believe?'

One of the men hugging a pack up the aisle stopped for a moment and glanced at them, and Johnny, looking towards him, grinned as he said, 'Charlie here's tellin' me his great-granny's gone on the streets, an' he's given me her number. Would you like it?'

'To hell with you!'

'And you an' all, mate.'

'Come on! Come on! Jump to it!'

Slater had entered the hut. He was throwing his orders from left to right as he walked briskly forward; then he came to a dead halt when he saw Charlie sitting on the side of his bed. Johnny, having now got to his feet, was busy gathering his kit together.

'Well! well! what have we here? A sick man no doubt.'

Charlie remained seated. A momentary stillness crept over the room as the men looked towards the tall figure sitting upright on the bed, all their eyes expressing the same thought: Silly bugger! he was asking for it now all right.

'You're goin' to report sick, eh?'

'No, Sergeant.'

'No! Yet here you are reclinin' on your bed. Surely you've been told' – he moved his hand in a slow, wide motion to encompass all in the room – 'that we're off for foreign parts!'

'Yes, Sergeant.'

'Well then, you've decided that you don't want to go 'cos . . . well you're more than likely to see a lot of nasty blood an' there'll be bang-bangs?'

This pleasantry was received without the sound of one titter, there was something going on here that the men didn't understand, except that some of them thought that Lofty must have gone mad and had decided to do for the sergeant and stand the consequences. And who could blame him?

'On your feet!'

There was the slightest pause before Charlie unfolded his long length and stood upright, but not too straight, certainly not to attention.

'Now, Mis-ter MacFell, you either get *fell* in' – Slater stressed the pun – 'or I'll assist you with me boot in your arse.'

'Sergeant, I'd advise you to be careful!'

The tone had the effect on the men in the room of an electric shock. Their eyes stretched to their fullest as they listened to the long-suffering and easy-going fellow they knew as Lofty saying, 'As at this moment I am not in a position to put you on a charge but nevertheless I can report you. For your information, Sergeant Slater, I would inform you that I have been recommended for a commission.' Whether the promotion would be starting at this precise hour he didn't know, and neither would Slater or anyone else in the room, but what he did know, and what he was experiencing at this moment, was an amazing feeling of triumph as he watched the effect his words were having on Slater. For the moment the man seemed dumbfounded and there was on his face, not the same look of fear that had been on it, as Charlie remembered when a child, but the look of a defeated man. But it remained only a matter of seconds, and then Slater had turned from him and was bawling at his platoon, 'Out! Out the lot of you! Get goin'!'

He was marching up and down the room now hustling and bustling while Charlie remained standing perfectly still by the side of his bed; that was until Johnny gripped his hand and said, 'Well, so long, lad.'

'So long, Johnny.'

'Think we'll ever see each other again?'

'Yes; yes, I do, Johnny. I'm sure we shall, somewhere some time, and if not now, after the war. I'll never forget how you've helped me over the stickiest patch of my life. I think I would have done murder if it hadn't have been for you.'

They stared at each other for a moment, until Slater's voice, almost screaming now, filled the hut crying, 'Come on! Come on!'

'Bye, lad.'

'Bye, Johnny.'

After bustling the last man out of the hut, Slater didn't follow him, he banged the door closed behind the man, then walked slowly back up the room until he was once again confronting Charlie. But he seemed to find it difficult to speak now; when he did he said, 'So you wangled it somehow, did you? 'cos you couldn't have got it any other way. Oh' – he looked about him – 'as you said yourself, you don't know when exactly you're comin' into your glory so to all intents and purposes you're still muck to me, and there's nobody here to hear me say it.'

'No, for once you haven't got an audience, Slater. And it may surprise you that I didn't wangle it, it was offered to me.'

Their eyes were locked in mutual hate; then Slater, his mouth twisting, said, 'There's something fishy here 'cos I've blacklisted you all the way through, I haven't said a good word for you.'

'Well, all I can say to that, Slater, is that the officers are not the fools you take them for, and when they have been summing up my capabilities most likely at the same time they have been summing up the lack of yours; otherwise, surely, if for nothing else but your raucous voice you should have been a sergeant-major by now.'

'Be careful!'

'Oh, as you said, there's no one to hear us.'

Slater swallowed deeply, took one step back, went to move away, then turned and faced Charlie again; and now he said, 'This is a flash in the pan; you're a loser; you were born a loser; you couldn't even keep a wife. I managed that, and I've got two bairns to show for it.'

The quick steps died away, the door banged, he was alone in the hut. Again he sat down on the edge of the bed. Slater's last words were rankling; you couldn't even keep a wife . . . you're a loser; you were born a loser.

For a moment he was overcome by a fear of the future when he'd be entering the company, not of men, but . . . of officers. Would he lose out there an' all?

It would be up to him, wouldn't it?

Yes; yes, it would.

He did not spring from the bed, determined now to start as he meant to go on, definite, full of purpose and patriotic enthusiasm. Instead, he took time gathering up his belongings before walking with them towards the door. But he did not go out on to the square, for it was packed with men, the men of 'A', 'B' and 'C' companies, almost the whole battalion. He watched the R.S.M. strutting about like a stuffed peacock, and the company sergeant-majors following suit, for all the world like dominating cocks shooing their families together. The lance-corporals acting as markers, the corporals and sergeants were outdoing themselves in throat-tearing commands.

. . . And the officers, the second-lieutenants, the lieutenants, the captains, all batmen – spit and polished; and standing apart, yet commanding the whole, was the major.

Charlie's eyes were fixed tight on him. Although he couldn't make out his face from this distance he told himself he didn't look any different in his clothes.

In his clothes!

Would anybody believe him if he were to tell them that that dominating figure was the man who was to be the means of getting him his freedom . . . But wait! what had he let himself in for? Could he do it now?

Orders were ringing out: 'By the right quick march! Left! right. Left! right.' A band was playing, the mass was moving, feet were stamping, arms swinging: rank after rank disappeared, until, just as if a wave had washed over the place, the square was empty.

In the strange silence, he again asked himself the question, Could he do it now? Could he name the major? If he did his promotion would likely be squashed; these things could be fixed. But say he were still allowed to get his commission, life would become unbearable when the story got around. He was wise enough to know you got no medals for disgracing a major, and under such circumstances.

And then there was Slater.

You're a loser; you were born a loser.

No, if it meant being tied to Victoria for life, well, that would have to be. Anything was preferable to being the butt of Slater's maliciousness which, were he to return to the platoon now as a private, would mean one or the other of them ending the conflict.

He straightened his shoulders, picked up his gear, and walked out of the hut, across the square, through the alleyway, around the circle of lawn and up the steps and into the wartime life of an officer.

PART FOUR

Mud

1

The second-lieutenant looked extremely smart. He was unusually tall but he was straight with it. When he was saluted in the street he answered the gesture almost as smartly as it was given. But he'd have to get out of that; Radlett had hinted as much.

He liked Radlett, at least he didn't dislike him; but he wasn't at all keen on Lieutenant Calthorpe; very old school, Calthorpe, without the good manners one would expect from that kind of upbringing. He spoke to some of the men as if they were serfs.

The captain was as different again, a very understandable fellow Captain Blackett; but the major, oh, the major, he talked as if he were still in the Boer War. Radlett said openly he was a fumbling old duffer.

It was funny, Charlie thought, how some people were able to voice their opinions of others and get off with it. For instance now if he had called the major a fumbling old duffer ten to one he would have been up on the carpet before his breath had cooled. Radlett acted and talked like an old hand but he was almost as new to the game as he himself was.

As he left the Central Station to board a bus that

would take him across the water to Nellie's, the glow that had been with him since early morning began to fade. Another man in his position would be making for home. He had two homes but he was going to neither: the home among the hills was too far away to get there and back comfortably in a forty-eight. Moreover, you had to chance getting transport. And the home where his wife resided was barred to him now for good and all. So there remained only Nellie's; and even about this visit he was feeling a little trepidation, for he hadn't done as he promised and written to her.

It had been understandable in the first two or three weeks because everything had moved so fast. He had been kept at it all waking hours. They called it a crash course in pips, and it was certainly that all right, for as Radlett so grotesquely illustrated in his garrulous way, the only thing they didn't ram into you was how to die with your guts hanging out. Did you yell, 'Carry on, men!' before you pushed them back, or let them drip as you waved your fellows on crying, 'Good luck! chaps.'

Anyway, he had forty-eight hours and he was going to enjoy it. Why not? He would take Nellie out. Knowing Nellie, she'd get quite a kick out of his change in fortune. But then it might not come as a surprise to her after all, because if she had visited home and run into Betty, Betty would surely have told her. Yet again it had been a good three weeks before he had informed Betty of his change in position. Still, he was looking forward to seeing Nellie.

A passenger walking down the aisle happened to catch the end of the cane that lay across Charlie's knees, and when he had retrieved it from the floor and handed it back to him, saying 'I'm sorry, sir,' Charlie smiled at him and said, 'That's all right,' and the man jerked his chin and smiled back, saying, 'Good-day to you.'

'And to you.'

Amazing the difference a pip made and, of course, the style of the uniform, the leather belt and the rakish cap, not forgetting the trench coat. Oh yes, the trench coat finished the ensemble off.

But let him be honest with himself. He liked the difference it made and the deference it commanded. He had felt a different being since first donning this uniform; it had magical properties, it enabled one to issue orders, although until now he had been mostly on the receiving end. Even so, when he'd had to deal with the men in the platoon to which he had been assigned, he had carried it off all right.

He felt that in a way he had an advantage over the other officer trainees for he was the only one of his bunch who had served in the ranks, so he prided himself that he knew how the men would view him, and above all things at this period he wanted their opinion to be, 'Oh, he's a decent enough bloke, Mister MacFell.'

Second-Lieutenant. How long would it be before he was fully fledged? Was it as Radlett said, you only stepped up when the other chap above you fell down dead? Radlett had the uncanny knack of putting his finger on the realities; it was a known fact that there was rapid promotion on the battlefield. Well, he didn't want his promotion that way, so he'd better make up his mind to be satisfied to stay as he was . . .

The twilight was deepening as he neared Nellie's house and it had begun to drizzle.

Before going up the steps he adjusted his cap, then his collar, and finally tucked his cane under his arm.

On entering the hall he was assailed by the usual smell of stale cooking, and he thought for a moment, Why does she stay here, there's no need? She could let her flat and get a better place.

He rapped smartly on the door! Rat-a-tat-tat! Rat-a-tat-tat! drew himself up to his full height and waited.

Again he knocked, louder this time, and when there was no reply his shoulders took on a slight droop.

He was knocking for the third time when a voice came from the stairway to his right, saying, 'It's no use knocking there.'

He walked to the foot of the stairs and looked upwards. A woman was leaning over the banisters and as he stared up at her she said, 'I'm sick of telling 'em, one after the other, it's no use knocking there. They should put a notice up.'

Slowly he mounted the stairs until his face was directly below that of the woman's, and now he said, 'She's left?'

'Left! I don't know so much about leaving, I'll say this much for her, she tried to. No, she didn't leave, they carried her out.'

'What do you mean, she's not . . . ?'

'Well, it isn't her fault. She tried hard enough, and she might be even yet for all I know.'

He now ran up the remainder of the stairs and round on to the landing until he faced the woman and, his tone brisk now, appealed, 'Please explain; she . . . she was a dear friend of mine.'

'She was a dear friend of everybody's if you ask me.'

'She's my sister-in-law.'

'Is she? Oh, well, you got the gist didn't you? She tried to do away with herself, gassed herself. They all use gas, it must be the easiest way . . .'

'When did this happen?'

'Oh, four days ago. And it was someone like you knocking on the door that saved her, one of her pals.' The woman now peered up at Charlie and demanded, 'Why wasn't she taken in hand? A bit of a lass like that on her own. And then them there every night. I tackled her about it once and she invited me in with them. Mind, I didn't go, but she said it was tea and buns and a bit of a sing-song, that was all. Well, I ask you. Anyway, she was off work for a week, cold or something, and it was likely being on her own got her down. One of her pals came up and asked me to look in on her. Well, I did; but I couldn't keep it up for I'm out all day you see, munitions, and I've got two bairns and I've got to pick them up from me mother's every night. Anyway, I came in this night and there were these two sergeants hammering on the door. They were the same ones that asked me to go in and see to her. And then they said they could smell gas. Well, that's about it. They did smell gas. Then there was the divil's fagarties: the doctor, the polis, the ambulance.'

'Where is she now?'

'Still in hospital, I should say.'

'Do you know which one?'

'Not really; it'll be the infirmary likely.'

He turned from her without saying, 'Thank you', but the look that he left with her caused her to lean over the banisters and yell after him. 'Don't take it out on me, mister! Anyway she brought it on herself, drink and men. Can't tell me it was all tea and buns and . . .'

Her voice faded away as he banged the door closed behind him.

Neighbours! Someone lying alone ill in a room and nobody bothering, except the soldiers. Even back on the hills, even as dour as some of them were, they would travel miles in all weathers to give a helping hand to each other in times of trouble; and in the poorer quarters of the town, in the back-to-backs, he'd like to bet no-one would have lain for a day without someone coming in.

It was in the third hospital he visited that he found her. He could have found out immediately by going to the police station, but somehow he baulked at this for it would be admitting that she had by her action touched on something criminal.

Yes, a stiff-faced nurse said, they had a Miss

Chapman here, but it was long past visiting hours; and moreover, she was under surveillance and rather ill. Was he a relation?

'Yes,' he said; 'I'm her brother-in-law and I'm on a short leave. I'd appreciate it if I could see her for a moment or so.'

He had to pass the staff-nurse, then the night sister before he was admitted to the small side ward, and then he was told briefly, 'Ten minutes at the most.'

The nurse stood aside and allowed him to enter; the door closed behind him; and then he was standing in the small, naked room, where the green-painted walls lent a hue to everything, even to the face on the pillow.

He walked slowly to the bedside. On closer inspection he saw that the face wasn't green, but white, a dull, pasty white, and so much had it altered since he had last seen it that he thought for a moment there had been a mistake and he had been shown the wrong patient. That was until the eyes opened, and then there was Nellie looking up at him. The expression in her eyes remained slightly vacant for a moment or so; then he watched her lids slowly widen and her lips part three times before she whispered, 'Charlie.'

He did not speak for he was finding it impossible at the moment to utter a word, but he bent over her and clasped her hands between his own.

'Charlie.'

He nodded at her now.

'Thought . . . thought you'd gone.' Her voice was like a croak.

He shook his head slowly.

'Forgotten me.'

'No . . . held up . . . one thing and another.'

They continued to stare at each other; then without letting go of one hand he turned and pulled a chair to the side of the bed and sat down, and as he leant towards her she muttered hoarsely, 'Know what I did?'

For answer he said softly, 'Forget about it; you're going to be all right.'

He now took his handkerchief and wiped the gleaming blobs of sweat from her brow, then he tucked the bedclothes closer around her chin, and as he did so he felt the steam from her body on his hand. She was ill, very ill and so changed. Of a sudden he wanted to gather her into his arms and comfort her, soothe her, saying, 'It's all right, Nellie. It's going to be all right, I'll look after you. From now on I'll look after you.'

'What's that, my dear?' He put his head closer to her mouth.

'I . . . I was lonely . . . nothing to live for.'

'Oh Nellie. Nellie.' He now stroked the clammy hand lying limply within his own. 'You've got everything to live for; you're so young, Nellie, and so, so bonny . . . lovely.' He spaced the words and inclined his head downwards with each one, then ended, 'And you have friends who care for you.'

When her head began to move agitatedly on the pillow he said hastily, 'Now, now, Nellie; don't distress yourself, please.'

She became still. Her eyes were closed and now from under the compressed lids there appeared droplets of water that weren't sweat.

'Oh, Nellie, Nellie, don't! Look.' He shook her hand gently and, his tone aiming to be light, he said, 'They'll throw me out; they told me you had to be kept quiet and I hadn't to distress you.'

Her tear-filled eyes opened and she looked at him a moment before she said, 'You always distress me, Charlie.'

'Oh! Nellie.'

'Oh! Charlie.' She smiled faintly now, but even as she did so her face became awash with tears.

He sat gripping her hands now unable to pour out the words speeding from his mind because he was suddenly and vitally aware that their meaning would express emotions that would go far beyond words of comfort, and he couldn't . . . he mustn't allow this complication to come about.

'I'm . . . I'm sorry, Charlie.'

'Oh, Nellie; I'm . . . I'm the one who should be saying that. I . . . I was utterly thoughtless; I should have written.'

'Yes, you should.' In the two admonitory small movements made by her head he glimpsed for a moment the old Nellie and he smiled at her as he said, 'It won't happen again.'

'That a promise?'

'Definitely.'

'Where are you now?'

'Outside Durham.'

'For long?'

He paused before he said, 'I'm not sure; you can be sure of nothing in this war.'

He was about to ask if her mother had been when the door opened and the nurse standing there said simply, 'Please.'

'Oh, not yet . . . oh, Charlie.'

He was standing on his feet now but still holding her hands and he bent over her, whispering, 'I'll be back, Nellie.'

When the look in her eyes told him that she didn't believe him, he bent further forward and placed his lips on hers; then looking into her eyes again, he said, 'I'll be back.'

She said no more and he went from the room.

In the corridor he said to the night nurse, 'She's very ill, isn't she?'

'Oh' – the voice was airy – 'she's not as bad as when they brought her in. She's lucky to be alive. You know she tried suicide, don't you?'

He stared at the nurse. They said some of them were as hard as nails and they were, especially when dealing with their own sex.

'Good-night.'

'Good-night.' The nurse's opinion of him was expressed in her farewell. It was a certainty she wasn't one of those who were impressed by an officer's uniform.

He paused in the corridor. Nellie hadn't noticed that he was no longer a private; but then she was too ill, and anyway Nellie was the kind of person who would lay little stock on rank.

What would he do if she died?

He didn't know except that her going would set the seal on his ineffectiveness, the ineffectiveness that stamped his whole make-up. Not one thing had he done off his own bat. He had allowed himself to be led up to or pushed into every situation in his life. There was that one time he could have taken the initiative by sticking to the gun that Nellie had fired. Had he done so he knew now that his life from then would have been different. But what in effect had he done? Walked backwards out of the situation and, as he deserved, fallen into a trap.

He was, he knew, one of those people who are dubbed nice fellows, men who are never strong enough to alter circumstances, men who surfed as it were on the waves of other people's personalities, until finally being dragged into self-oblivion by the undertow.

'Can I help you, sir?'

He looked at the night porter, and after a moment's hesitation, he said, 'Yes; when are the visiting hours?'

'Saturday, sir, is the next one between two and four; and Sunday the same time. But I think they make allowances for uniform.' He smiled.

'Thank you.'

'Thank you, sir. Good-night.'

'Good-night.'

As he went down the hospital steps and walked

into the starlit night he thought in normal life men are kinder than women, less hard. He'd had evidence of it with his mother and Betty . . . and Victoria. Yes, and even Polly. But people would call Polly sensible, not hard. And then those nurses back there, tough individuals. He should hate women, yet the only person he hated was Slater.

What about Major Smith?

Yes, what about Major Smith? Truth to tell he didn't know how he felt about the man. He thought he despised him rather than hated him. Strangely, he saw him as a weaker man than Slater. Yet he would have to be a strong type both physically and mentally to hold his own with Victoria.

He had heard nothing from Victoria since that particular night; she was likely waiting for a move from him and sitting on hot bricks wondering what he was going to do about her dear major.

He stood outside the iron gates and looked up into the sky. Somewhere Zeppelins were dropping bombs out of it; somewhere else the stars were being outshone by the flashes of artillery, and all over Flanders' fields men were lying staring sightless up into the heavens. Yet momentarily all this was being obliterated by a flood of personal feeling, an all-consuming feeling.

He walked on, boarded a bus, afterwards walked on again. Then he entered the Officers' Club in the centre of the city for the first time, and he did so without a feeling of embarrassment. He was not merely Second-Lieutenant Charles MacFell, the grouts of the officers' hierarchy, he was Charlie MacFell, who was vitally aware that he was loving someone, really loving someone for the first time in his life, and that because of it he imagined he would never again be ineffectual.

2

'There you are, sir, shining like Friday night's brasses.'

'What was that, Miller?' Charlie turned to his batman who was brushing him down . . . He'd have to make himself get used to this and not take the brush from the man and do the job himself.

'It's what me mother used to say, sir. Everything in wor house was cleaned on a Friday, and we'd lots of brasses on the mantelpiece. They used to shine like silver, and me mother used to say to wor lads, "Now scrub your faces till they shine like Friday night brasses." '

Charlie smiled at the man. He was a nice fellow was Miller, always cheery. He had been assigned to him when he finished training and he felt that he had struck lucky for he had been so helpful. He was a real morale booster was Miller.

'There you are, sir.' The batman took two paces backwards and surveyed his handiwork. 'You know, sir, I think you're the tallest officer in the camp. What is your height, sir?'

'Six foot three and a half.'

'Aw, good. Good.'

'What do you mean, good?'

'Well, sir, Private Thompson is betting on Captain Blackett, and . . . and he said he could top you, sir. But you've done 'im by half an inch.'

Charlie laughed. 'I hope the half-inch proves worth your while.'

'Well, a dollar's not to be sneezed at, is it, sir?'

'No, it isn't.'

As the batman handed Charlie his hat and stick and Charlie responded by saying, 'Thank you,' a habit he found he couldn't get out of, there came a knock on the door, and when Miller opened it, a corporal stood there. Stepping smartly into the room, he saluted Charlie, saying, 'Lieutenant Calthorpe's compliments, sir, and would you meet him in number two room?'

Charlie hesitated a moment before saying, 'Yes, thank you. I'll be there.' Then he looked at his watch; the bus went in twenty minutes.

As he crossed the square some of the men in his own platoon were walking towards the gates; their faces bright, they were laughing and joking among themselves. Many of them, he knew, would be making for home, others would have a blow-out in the first pub they came to.

Lieutenant Calthorpe was standing before a mirror adjusting his tie. He didn't turn when Charlie entered the room but, putting his face closer to the mirror, he said, 'Ah, MacFell, I'm sorry an' all that but there's been a change in the time-table. I should've seen you earlier but I was held up. It's just this, I'd like you to change with Radlett; he's coming

269

into town with me. He's got a little business to see to.' He turned round now, straining his neck out of his collar as he ended, 'Rather important. Be a good fellow and take over for him. Make it up to you tomorrow, the whole day off if you like.'

There was a significant pause, then he turned so smartly about that he almost overbalanced Calthorpe's batman.

Standing outside the block, he looked towards the far gate where Radlett was standing beside his car, but before taking a step in his direction he warned himself, Be careful.

Radlett's unblinking round blue eyes looked straight into his as he said, in that drawling twang that was so like Calthorpe's, 'I'm sorry. It's rotten luck, but what could I do? He wanted a lift into town and transport that would get him back . . . well, latish. He said he'd make it up to you tomorrow. Of course I know, old fellow, that leave on a Sunday around here is equal to being drafted into the cemetery.'

Charlie made no reply, and Radlett added, 'You won't hold it against me, old chap, will you?'

'Oh no, certainly not.' The tone was the same as that used by Radlett, and the second-lieutenant stared at him for a moment, then said, 'Good. Good.' But then he added. 'Of course, if I were in your shoes I'd be flaming mad.'

'Perhaps I am.' He stared pointedly at Radlett before turning abruptly away.

In rank he was the same as Radlett, yet he knew

that in the eyes of the lieutenant, the captain, and the major, he was an outsider; not only had he come up from the ranks but he was a conscript. To be placed in only one of these situations would have been enough to stamp him as an outsider, but the double infamy was, he had been given to understand, if albeit silently, an insult to the regiment. Though it was likely this company wouldn't see Flanders, still it was hard lines if it had to be the recipient of the dregs of the army.

Oh, he knew the feeling that his presence created in the mess all right, yet he had played it down till now, but he'd had enough and he'd make this plain, at least with Radlett, when doubtless his attitude would be passed on to the lieutenant.

All morning he had felt in a state of excitement about seeing Nellie again. Three days ago he had written to her and told her he'd be with her some time over the week-end. It was a good job, he thought now, that he hadn't stated an exact time.

He made for his room again and when he opened the door it was to find Miller sitting in his chair with his feet on the camp table and a mug in his hand.

So abruptly did the man get to his feet that the tea splashed in all directions and Charlie stepped quickly back, putting out his hand to ward off the splashes.

'I'm sorry, sir, I . . . I thought you had gone, sir.'

Charlie threw his hat on to the bed, and as he took off his trench coat he said, 'So did I.'

'Something gone wrong, sir?'

Charlie looked at the batman. He was a man old

enough to be his father, and he smiled wryly at him as he said, 'The lieutenant wanted the use of a car. I don't happen to possess one.'

'Aw, rotten luck, sir. He changed you over with Lieutenant Radlett then, sir?'

'Yes, Miller, yes, that's what he did . . . Is any tea going?'

'Yes, sir. Oh yes, sir; I'll brew you up one immediately.' The man went to move away, then stopped and stared at Charlie and moved from one foot to the other before saying, 'Sir, can I speak me mind?'

Charlie's eyes widened slightly before he nodded, saying, 'Yes, yes, of course.'

'Well, sir, it's like this. A man can be too easy-goin', too soft, kind that is, and some folks don't understand. You've . . . you've got to throw your weight about, not too much, you know, sir, but just enough to let them know you can't be sat on. And . . . and I'm not talkin' about the men, sir, the platoon, no, your platoon's all right, they understand and appreciate things, but there's t'others if you get me meanin', sir. I'm sorry if you think I've spoken out of turn, sir.'

Charlie nipped on his lower lip for a moment; then his voice coming from deep in his throat, he said, 'Thank you. Thank you, Miller. I may as well tell you that I've been thinking along similar lines myself, but it's heartening to know that one has a little backing.'

'Good. Good for you, sir. One last thing I'd like you to know, sir. You're . . . you're well liked among the men.'

Charlie smiled broadly now as he said, 'Well, if that's the case it's because I remember, as I gather you all know, that not so long ago I was one of them, and in a way I suppose' – he shook his head – 'I still am. That's the trouble, if trouble it is . . . Anyway, what about that tea?'

'On the double, sir, on the double.'

As the man went out of the room Charlie sat down on the chair Miller had vacated and he thought, That's the only piece of ordinary conversation I've had with a man for months.

He fingered the pip on his shoulder. Was it worth it? It was questionable. What was he talking about, remember Slater!

He had made use of the first half of his full day's leave by paying a quick visit to the farm. He had not intended to do this but he had heard of a transport lorry having to make a delivery to a camp up on the fells. It only took a little back-hander to the driver to persuade him to pick him up again an hour later.

Betty greeted his unexpected arrival with her usual lack of enthusiasm. Her only comment about his commission was, 'Well, you look tidier in that than you did in the other rig-out.'

Everything on the farm seemed to be working well, except she voiced her usual tirade against the prisoners; they didn't like a woman over them, she said, but she let them know what was what. His reaction had been, poor devils, but, of course, merely as a thought. When he had enquired if she had heard anything about Nellie, she had answered, 'How do you expect me to get news here except what I can gather from out-of-date papers? She doesn't bother to come over here' – meaning Florence Chapman – 'and I can assure you I have no time to trail over there. So what has she done now, the smart Miss Nellie?'

But he didn't inform her what Nellie had done, only to say she was in hospital with pneumonia, and when he had bidden her good-bye and left the farm and was walking through the fields – his fields – he had asked himself which was preferable, to be living alone back there with Betty, or to be in the army? And without hesitation he plumped for the latter. What it would be like after the war he dreaded to think; but then again there mightn't be any after the war for him if he was sent over there. And that was a journey that could quite easily come about in the near future, for although the battalion wouldn't move as a whole, it was being broken up and sections sent hither and thither almost every week.

It was a quarter to three when he arrived at the hospital. He hurried along the corridor, past the wards where every bed had its visitors, to the small side ward. He didn't stop to ask the nurse for permission to enter but went straight in, then came to a stop at the sight of the soldier sitting by the bedside holding Nellie's hand. He noted immediately that Nellie looked much better for she was sitting propped up against the pillows; he also noted that the fellow sitting by her side had a possessive look about him.

The soldier was quickly on his feet, he was a sergeant, and although he didn't stand to attention he stood slightly away from the bed.

It was Nellie who spoke first. 'Hello, Charlie,' she said.

'Hello, Nellie.' He moved to the bottom of the bed.

'Don't you remember Alec? You know, he and his pal were together that night you called.'

'Oh yes, yes.' He smiled towards the sergeant now, and the man, relaxing somewhat, smiled back at him, before turning to Nellie and saying, 'I'll wait outside a bit, dear, eh?'

'Yes, Alec.' He went to take her hand, then changed his mind, but he smiled widely down on her before turning to go out of the room.

'Come and sit down, Charlie.'

He took the chair by the bed. 'How are you? You look better.'

'I'm feeling fine now. You did remember him, didn't you?'

'Yes, yes, of course, Nellie, I remembered him.'

She looked at him for a moment in silence. 'He's . . . he's been a very good friend to me, Charlie.'

'Yes, I'm sure he has, Nellie.'

'He . . . he was a bit embarrassed to see you, I mean being an officer.'

'He needn't be.'

'I got your letter.'

'Good.'

'I . . . I couldn't write back, I felt so tired.'

275

'I didn't expect you to. I'm so glad though to see you looking so much better.'

She nodded at him, then turned her gaze from him and looked down towards her hands as she said, 'Mother'll be here today. She's going to make arrangements to take me home for convalescence' – now she slanted her eyes towards him – 'and to see that I don't try anything funny again.'

'You won't. And I'm glad you're going home.'

'I don't mean to stay there, Charlie, I couldn't, but I'll be glad to rest for a time. It isn't that I'm physically tired, it's . . . it's more in my mind.'

'I know.'

'Charlie.'

'Yes, dear?'

'Alec wants to marry me.'

As he stared into her eyes there rushed through his mind a voice as if coming from a deep well, shouting, 'Charlie! Charlie! will you marry me?'

'Do . . . do you care for him?'

'I like him.'

Who else had said that? Polly.

'Enough to marry him?'

'It all depends, Charlie. I'm lost, I'm lonely.'

'But I thought . . .'

'Don't say you thought I had lots of friends, Charlie, please don't. They were soldiers, young fellows who hadn't a fireside to sit beside, and I wanted to laugh and dance and sing; I wanted all kinds of things, Charlie, to make up for what I lost. You know what I'm saying, Charlie?'

He was silent, lost in the depths of the revelation in her eyes.

When his gaze dropped from hers and he bowed his head and she said, 'I didn't mean to embarrass you, Charlie,' his chin snapped upwards and his voice was loud as he cried, 'You're not embarrassing me.' Then he closed his eyes and covered the lower part of his face with his hand, saying, 'I'm sorry, I'm sorry, Nellie.'

She gave a small laugh now as she said, 'Don't apologise, it's nice to hear someone shout; they've been going round here for days whispering as if they were just waiting to lay me out, which I suppose they were, at first anyway.'

'Nellie' – he gripped hold of her hands now – 'I'm married, I'm still married to Victoria and she's your sister, but I've never wished for freedom more than I do at this moment. Now do you understand me?'

He watched the colour spread over her face; then, her voice a whisper, she said, 'That's all I wanted to hear.' But now her head gave an impatient shake and her face twisted for a moment as she said, 'No, it isn't. No, it isn't . . . Charlie—'

'Yes, dear.'

'Will . . . will you put it into plain words?'

Bringing her hands to his breast now, he pressed them tightly there, and he stared at her and gulped in his throat before he said, 'I . . . I love you, Nellie. I think I must have always loved you.'

She lay now looking at him for a full minute before she spoke, and then she said, 'You're not just saying it, Charlie, because I'm down? You see I know you, you'd swear black was white if it meant pleasing somebody. That's true, isn't it?'

'I suppose so.' He nodded at her. 'It could have been once, but not any more; the easy-going, good old Charlie was shot dead some months ago. I'll tell you about it some time.'

'Victoria?'

'Victoria.'

'Will you divorce her, Charlie?'

'Yes, as soon as this business is over.'

'Kiss me, Charlie.'

He kissed her. His arms about her, he lifted her up from the pillow and with her arms around his neck they clung to each other. When he laid her back they laughed into each other's face and, his hands on each side of her head, he pressed it into the pillow, then he kissed her again.

Following this, they were silent for some little time. Their fingers interlocked, they remained looking down at their hands until she said, 'I'd like you to know something, Charlie.' When he waited she went on, 'The lads, the soldiers, I haven't been with one, I mean I haven't let any of them sleep with me.'

He looked away from her for a moment before he said, 'Playing the big fellow, I should say it wouldn't matter to me if you had, but . . . but I'd be lying.'

She stared straight into his face now as she asked, 'We won't be able to be married for some long time, will we, Charlie?'

'No, I suppose not. Some months ago I was about

278

to go to a solicitor, I'd all the proof I needed, but then almost overnight this happened' – he touched his shoulder – 'and . . . and I was in a fix because the proof was in the army, high up. But the minute I'm discharged the proceedings will start. I can assure you of that, dear.'

'But that could be a long time, Charlie, or never.'

'Don't say that, Nellie. Don't say that.'

'But it could, Charlie, so listen to me. Once I am home back . . . back in my own place, I want to come to you.'

He made no response to this for some seconds; then taking her joined hands, he brought them to his lips, and as he held them there the door opened and her mother came in . . .

Florence Chapman, taking in the situation, stared at them fixedly for a moment; then walking towards the bed, she said, 'Well! Well now!'

Charlie had risen to his feet and was holding the chair for her and as she sat down he said, 'Nice to see you, Florence.'

Her face was straight as she turned it up towards him, saying, 'I don't think I can return the compliment, not at the moment, Charlie.'

'I can understand that, Florence.'

Florence stared at him. It was only a matter of months since she had last seen him, but he didn't appear the same Charlie. The flatness had gone out of both his manner and voice, even his stance was different, but perhaps that could be put down to his uniform. It was hard to believe that this was the same young fellow who had caused havoc in her family. But of course he wasn't really to blame for that, that had been Hal's doing, God rest his soul, Victoria had merely been a tool.

And what a tool her daughter had turned out to be, for she was now man mad. But hadn't she always been man mad. And of all the men she had to marry it had to be poor Charlie MacFell. But why was she thinking poor Charlie? That adjective could no longer be applied to him for here he was chancing his arm again, and of all people with Nellie, while he was still tied to Victoria. Well, she'd put a stop to that. What next? she wondered. She looked now at her daughter and, forcing a smile to her face, she said, 'You're better?'

'Yes, Mother, much better.'

'I've just had a word with the sister. She says if you keep up this progress I can take you home next week.'

'Aw, that'll be good.'

'And it'll be for good, I hope? I was talking to Ratcliffe in Hexham the other day. He could sell your house and . . .'

'No, Mother.' Nellie had pulled herself up from the pillows as she said again, 'No, Mother, I won't sell the house and . . . and I must tell you now, far better be above-board, Mother, but I mean to return to the flat once I get on my feet. And another thing . . . I can say this, Charlie, can't I?' She looked up at Charlie now and when he nodded to her she went on, 'Charlie and I love each other. It's no news to you that I've always loved him, and . . . and if he hadn't been forced . . .'

'That's enough, Nellie! Nobody forced him.

280

Nobody forced you, Charlie, did they?' She now turned her heated face up towards Charlie, and he, looking down at her, said quietly, 'No, you're right there, Florence, no one forced me. Coerced would have been a better word, quietly coerced.'

'Charlie!' Florence Chapman stared up into the long face. He had changed, changed completely, indeed he had; the old Charlie would never have come out with a thing like that. That's what an officer's uniform did to one, she supposed. Yet she had always known that he wasn't as soft as he made out to be; there was a depth there and a sly depth if she knew anything about it. But he was right, he had been quietly coerced, and she, as much as Hal, had had a hand in it, and when things had gone wrong almost from the start she had known periods of remorse and guilt. But remorse or guilt wasn't going to let her countenance this new situation. And what did they think Victoria's attitude would be when she knew that her sister was aiming to get the better of her in the end? Because that was how she would view it. And although she herself had no use for Charlie, and had made that very, very plain, she would, if she knew anything about her daughter, put every spoke possible in the way of Nellie getting him, even maybe to depriving herself of the freedom she so definitely wanted . . . But wait. She must remember that that had seemingly been her daughter's intention up to a few months ago. Then of a sudden she had stopped discussing the matter. She again looked up at Charlie, a deep frown between her brows now. There was something fishy going on and she couldn't get to the bottom of it.

She now watched her son-in-law take her daughter's hand and say, 'I'll leave you for a while, dear; I'll be back before the time's up.' And when he did not excuse himself to her she stared at his back as he left the room and when the door had closed on him she looked at Nellie and said, 'We're acting the big fellow these days, aren't we?'

'He's always been a big fellow, Mother, but none of you could see it.'

'Dear, dear!' Florence shook her head. 'What infatuation can do! The old saying that love is blind is surely true . . .'

'Mother!' Nellie was leaning forward now, her breath coming in short gasps, and she pressed her hand tightly against her breast bone as she said, 'Don't run Charlie down to me. And I'm not blind with love; I began by liking Charlie MacFell when I was a little girl, because you were always laughing at his father, making fun of him. You laughed at the ideas he had for his son, and then you all laughed at Charlie as he grew up because he didn't farm like the rest of you, or drink like the rest of you, or whore like the rest of you . . .'

'Nellie! that's enough.' Her mother's voice held deep indignation. 'I'll say this, that if he didn't do any whoring, his father made up for it. And who's to know what he did anyway?'

'Mother, you know as well as I do that everybody knew what everybody else did in our community, but

282

I think Charlie was the only one who didn't know that your eldest daughter was at it from she was fifteen and she never stopped, and now she's almost a licensed prostitute, her name's a byword in some quarters.'

Florence Chapman was standing on her feet now. Her lips were working one over the other as she pulled on her black gloves; then she adjusted the fur collar of her black mourning coat before she said, 'I can see you're well enough to fight again, Nellie, so I'll leave you and hope to find you in a better mood on my next visit.'

'Mother! please.' Nellie put out her hand. 'I'm sorry, I'm sorry; but you know what I say is true. You know it, you do.'

'She's my daughter the same as you are.'

'Then face up to the fact that if you can condone the life she leads, then you've got to let me have my way of life, and my way of life from now on is with Charlie and he with me; and I'm telling you something, Mother, and this is true, if I don't have Charlie I'll take no-one. The reason why I tried to finish it—' she now drooped her head and paused before going on, 'I didn't think he even thought of me as a friend any longer, because he hadn't shown up, and hadn't written – he could have been dead, there was no word of any kind – and . . . and I knew that without him life would be totally empty. You could say I'm young and I would get over it, but I knew I'd never get over Charlie. I don't know why, I can't explain the feeling, but without him there is nothing. As you know I

283

tried drink, but that didn't do any good.' She lifted her head sharply now as she said, 'But I never tried men, only as pals. I thought of it more than once. Oh yes, yes I did, but I knew I couldn't bring myself to it. Funny' – she slowly shook her head – 'the difference between us, our Vic and me, both from the same parents, same blood, yet we're as opposite as the poles, and you know, Mother, you won't believe me when I say I'm sorry about this because we're irrevocably divided and you need comfort from us both, you need us as a family now more than ever and we'll never be a family again.'

Florence stared at her daughter. How was it that everything, everybody had changed? Was it the war? Would things have been different if there hadn't been a war? No, not with her daughters. It was as Nellie said, they were irrevocably divided. She had always loved Nellie better than Victoria, but in this moment she felt she loved neither of them, they had gone from her, life had taken them as the grave had taken her Hal. Oh, how she missed Hal. What were children after all compared to a husband? Children were mere offshoots of a moment's passion, they were of your body yet they didn't belong to you, whereas a husband who was no kin, no blood tie, a stranger in fact, became your all, your life merged with his and when he left you all that was vital in you went with him. She turned away from the bed and walked out of the room.

In the corridor she looked first one way then the other. A sergeant was standing at one end, and at the other end stood Charlie. They were both looking towards the door behind her. She turned her back on Charlie and walked in the direction of the sergeant and she passed him without apparently seeing him, yet he stared hard at her.

When Florence had gone Charlie and the sergeant looked at each other over the distance and when Charlie made a motion with his head the sergeant grinned, gave a salute, and went hastily into the side ward.

Knowing it wouldn't be long before the sergeant came out again, and not wanting to witness the look on the man's face, he went into the main hall and stood to the side.

He hadn't long to wait, not more than five minutes, then he saw the man marching towards the door. He didn't look to right or left but went straight through the main doors and disappeared from view.

As he hurried back to the ward he felt a spasm of pity for the fellow, who was likely thinking, Bloody officers, they get in because of their uniform.

When he entered the room again, he made no comment on either the sergeant's or Florence's visit; he didn't speak at all, all he did was to gather Nellie tightly into his arms and hold her there.

3

It was a conspiracy. Why him? Why his platoon? Radlett was older than him. As for Lieutenant Calthorpe, he had been in this depot for over a year now . . . yes and would likely remain here until the end of the war, if he knew anything about it. In any case, if he had to go why wasn't Radlett going along with him and not the new young fellow who was so raw he still thought it all a merry game?

But why was he asking such damn silly questions?

He wouldn't have minded in the least being sent over there if it wasn't for leaving Nellie. She was still at the farm and he'd seen her only twice since she had come out of hospital, and now with this lightning move there'd be no chance of seeing her again.

If he could only be with her for just five minutes, just five minutes. He'd a damned good mind to walk out and take the consequences . . . And what would be the consequences? Absent without leave. But what could you expect from someone who in the first place had to be dragged into the army. The result would be worse than the white feather, the colour would be yellow.

Things would have been simpler, he thought, if he

hadn't discovered how he felt about Nellie; much simpler, yet he wouldn't wish his feelings to be other than they were at this moment.

He had been told to stand by, and he was standing by, but in the hope that all those for embarkation would be given at least twelve hours' leave. Wasn't there a rule about this? But then who considered rules when chits were flying about? You did what you were told, or else.

'I'm glad I'm goin' with you, sir.'

'Thanks, Miller. I'm glad you are too.'

'Where do you think we're bound for, sir?'

'I'm not exactly sure at the moment, Miller.'

'Could it be across the water?'

'It could be.'

'Well, if that's the case I'm afraid I won't be looking forward to it, sir.'

'Only a fool would, Miller.'

'They were breakin' their necks to get across there this time last year, sir, but they've changed their tune now I think. The Somme did that for 'em.'

'Yes, the Somme did that for them.'

'Do you think there's any chance for any of us gettin' a bit of leave, sir?'

'I don't know, Miller; quite candidly I'm as much in the dark as you with regard to that, but I certainly hope we get a few hours.'

'Yes, so do I, sir. There's the missis, she's likely as not to go and raise hell . . . I mean play up, sir, if I don't say her ta-rah.'

They smiled at each other; then Miller proffered

his usual comforter, 'Will I brew up, sir?'

'No, thanks, Miller; I'm going to the mess and there's a meeting after.' Hastily he looked round the room. 'Everything ready?'

'Yes, sir. An' I did as you said, I just packed two of the books. What's goin' to happen to the rest, sir?'

'Oh.' He glanced towards the bed, then laughed and said, 'My replacement will likely use them to heighten the bed, it's too near the floor.' They exchanged smiles again before he went out.

When the door had closed on his officer, Miller looked towards the small pile of books in the corner of the room and nodded, Aye, that's likely what the next one would do. Poetry books, and books in French, and others that were as understandable as that one written by a fellow called Platt-o. Funny fellow his officer, nice, kind, a decent bloke, but somehow he still didn't seem to fit in. It was a pity. He was glad he was going with him; he felt sort of protective towards him somehow.

4

The dock had the appearance of a madhouse. There were two ships lying alongside, both discharging wounded; ambulance men were running hither and thither with stretchers; nurses were assisting limping men, leading blind ones; Salvation Army lasses were handing out mugs of tea; non-commissioned officers were issuing orders; the only people who seemingly weren't joining in the mad frenzy were the lines of soldiers, who stood at ease, their kit-bags by their sides.

Charlie's platoon was at the end of the jetty. He and his men had been assigned to 1/6th Durham Light Infantry. The 1/6th, 1/8th and 1/9th were battalions that had been made up of remnants from other companies. As Charlie's new lieutenant had laughingly said, 'The stroke apparently indicates we are not all there, but let's get across and we'll show 'em. What do you say?'

Charlie could do nothing but confirm his superior's words for he was still both angry and worried inside by the fact that there had been no embarkation leave. And now here he was in the midst of this madness. Yet it was an ordered madness and strangely in parts a jocular madness for the wounded men were throwing jokes at the waiting platoons. That their cheerfulness was in most part the outcome of hysterical release at being back in Blighty didn't matter, it had a cheering effect on those waiting to take their places in the mud.

For the men knew they were going into mud. It was strange but they didn't talk of killing, or of being killed, but of how to combat mud. One joker had cut out a pair of cardboard snowshoes, and Charlie's new captain by the name of Lee-Farrow had encouraged the joker and all those with him by saying, 'That's the spirit, boys. That's the spirit.'

It was funny, Charlie thought, the little things that bought loyalty. All the men would now consider the captain a decent bloke, whereas back in camp his platoon had considered Captain Blackett a bloody stinker because he rarely addressed them; and yet he was a very good fellow. His lieutenant came up to him now, saying, 'Everything all right at your end?'

'Yes, sir.'

'Taking their bleeding time to unload.'

'They must have been heavily packed, sir.'

'I'll say . . . God! I wish we were across and settled in.'

A sardonic smile rippled somewhere in Charlie . . . I wish we were across and settled in. It sounded as if they were off on a holiday trip with an hotel at the end of it.

They both moved aside now as a line of stretcher-bearers came towards them. There were five stretch-ers; on the first two the men were conscious and were looking about them; on the third stretcher a man's whole face was bandaged up except for a slit where the mouth was; on the fourth stretcher the man looked asleep; and on the fifth one the man looked already dead.

Charlie was turning his gaze away when he almost flung himself round again and towards the last stretcher; then addressing the lieutenant, he said, 'Could I be excused for a moment, a friend?'

'Carry on.'

He now hurried after the line of stretchers, and when he reached the end one he looked across at the nurse on the other side and started, 'Is he?'

'No, no.' She shook her head. 'But he's in a bad way.'

When the stretchers were lowered to the ground to await their turn for transport, he bent down and whispered, 'Arthur! Arthur!'

There was a flicker of the eyelids, the head turned just the slightest.

Again he said, 'Arthur! it's me, Charlie.'

The lids were raised slowly, the jaw dropped, the lips moved, they said Charlie but without making a sound.

'Oh, Arthur.'

'Excuse me, sir; we must get him in.' The stretcher was lifted again, the jaw moved, the lips moved, Charlie put his hand out and cupped the ashen face. 'Oh, Arthur.'

'Excuse me.' He was pushed gently aside; the stretcher was lifted up into the ambulance; he turned and looked at the man who was giving some kind of instruction to the nurse. She climbed up into the ambulance, the doors were closed, and it drove away.

The man spoke now. 'You knew him?'

He gulped in his throat; there was an avalanche of tears pouring down inside him.

'He . . . he was a friend.'

'I'm afraid he's in a bad way.'

'What's . . . what's wrong with him?'

'Almost everything I should say; he's lost both legs and an arm.'

God Almighty!

He was closing his eyes against the picture when a voice acting like an injection in his own arm yelled, 'Fall in! Come on now! Come on now! Look slippy! Fall in!'

Without further words he and the doctor parted.

Now he was at the head of his platoon, looking along them, seeing them all without legs and minus an arm each.

'Quick march!'

The quick march developed into a mark time, then into a scramble up the gangway, and they were aboard.

The quay had seemed crowded and it was a long quay and the boat seemed very small compared with it, yet everyone who had been on that quay seemed to have boarded the boat. They stood packed like up-ended sardines, one against the other, and as the ship left the quay and a cheer went up, he thought, We're mad. Everybody's mad. Life had become so cheap that they were cheering for death.

Poor Arthur. Poor Arthur.

Good-bye, Nellie.

5

He was seasoned; he had been pickled in mud, blood, and slime. The anatomy of man had been laid bare for him to examine in the first week in the trenches when his sergeant's belly was split open. It was in that moment when he had viewed the squirming mass of intestines that a strange, almost lunatic thought struck him. It was the first time his whirling mind told him that the sergeant's innards had seen daylight. It was in that moment too that he lost his fear. What was death after all? A mere blowing from existence into oblivion, you wouldn't know anything about it. In a way it was better than being maimed, burned, gassed, or blinded. If he had to go, well, that was the way he wanted to go, like his sergeant had gone.

Yet there was another side to this business of dying, the side that was still alive . . . over there, his sergeant's wife and her four children. But one tried not to dwell on this. Such things were docketed in the corner of the mind where Nellie dwelt and from where she was apt to escape and occupy the narrow camp bed with him.

He was sharing this particular dug-out with

Lieutenant Bradshaw. He liked Bradshaw, he had come to respect him. Beyond his ah-lah fashion of talking he was a nice fellow. Three of his brothers in a Kent battalion had been killed near Arras last year; another had gone on the Somme; an uncle had been killed near Hebuterne early in this year. He seemed to have relatives in all the regiments; a cousin who had died in the 20th Wearsiders and another brother who was severely wounded in the Pioneers.

Bit by bit, Charlie was able to gauge his companion's family history. They were army people on his mother's side but not on his father's. His father was a judge. He, Bradshaw, was one of six brothers, and all four who had been killed had been going in for law. There was only himself and his elder brother left.

He had come close to Bradshaw in the last few months. He was flattered that Bradshaw thought him so well-read, even admitting that he was no reader himself, not of literature at any rate, mathematics was his subject. He felt he would have got a first at Oxford if he'd had time to finish, but he had wanted to get into this business.

The weather had been stinking. It was April but there had been snow; there was mud everywhere, and when going over the top should you slip and fall you swallowed it, and you hadn't to be surprised if as you groped and pulled yourself to your feet there was a hand outstretched to help you.

The first time he had gripped such a hand he had sprung back as if he had been shot, and he had felt he wanted to vomit as he stared down at the stiff wide-spread fingers appealingly held out to him.

There were days when the mud was the sole enemy, when it bogged down horses, guns, lorries and even the new monsters, the tanks, and at times like this the spirits of all those concerned would sink into it, only to be dragged upwards by their lieutenant's voice.

Bradshaw was popular with the men. Charlie himself was popular too, he knew that, but in a different way from Bradshaw. The men would talk to him, ask him questions, try to pump him; they never took that liberty with Lieutenant Bradshaw. Of course Bradshaw was a pip up, that might be the answer; but no, there was a subtle difference between them, it was in the tone of the voice, the tilt of the chin, the look in the eye. Bradshaw always remembered that he was in command, that was the difference.

But at the particular moment spirits were high and they had right to be. They had heard that the 10th had broken through the Hindenburg Line from the West and then within a few days had been relieved by the 6th and 8th, and the 5th and 9th. And as news of further advances by other divisions came through so morale soared, from the still spruce top brass behind the line down to the lice-ridden Tommy in the thick of it.

There was rejoicing too that the casualties had been light compared with other battles for only seven officers and around three hundred and fifty N.C.O.s and men had been killed and wounded – that was all. Cheap payment for the Wancourt line.

At times Charlie likened the whole affair to a game of chess played with the Mad Hatter and Alice; that the divisions, brigades and battalions, even platoons ever got themselves sorted out was a miracle to him. In some cases they overlapped so much, with the result that chaos followed and with chaos unnecessary death. But that was war as played out by the generals.

It was the middle of May and both Charlie and Lieutenant Bradshaw had decided long before this that their Blighty leave was overdue. They had been relieved and had had a few days behind the lines twice within the past months; but what was that? As Bradshaw said, they'd never had a real bath. He would, he said, be quite content to drown in steaming hot water. Of course, he had added with a laugh, it would be an added comfort if he had a companion by his side at the time.

'What are you going to do when you get back, Charlie?' They had come to using Christian names by now.

'The same as you, first go off, although I won't let the water up to my eyebrows, there's no outlet beyond; then I'll have the biggest meal that's ever been cooked, roast lamb, six veg. I'll have the veg on a separate plate because there won't be room for them on the main one, and then I'll have three Yorkshire puddings, two with gravy and one with milk and sugar.'

'Oh my God!' John Bradshaw screwed up his face in disgust.

'Well, what would be your choice?'

'Salmon, a whole salmon, fresh, straight out of the river, lightly boiled and floating in butter and nothing else, nothing . . . no vegetables, just the whole salmon to myself, and wine . . . wine, of course. Then a whole bottle of port, thick, sliding, tongue-coating port. And then I'd be ready to meet the ladies. Of course, you won't want any ladies, you'll have your wife, and by the number of letters you get from her I imagine she'll be as eager to see you as you are to see her.'

'Yes, yes, I hope so.'

Nellie . . . his wife. Well, she'd be as good as when he got back.

When he got back? The thought caused him to say, 'Do you think they'll clip us and we'll be in the next push?'

John Bradshaw remained silent for a moment. Then he moved his tongue around the inside of his lower lip before pushing it into his cheek and saying, 'I hope the hell not; but there's something in the wind. The pressure must be off the Germans now on the Russian front, and the French are no more bleeding use, and so it would appear it's solely up to us. One good sign is the stuff they're bringing up looks enough to blow the bleedy world to bits. Anyway, we'll see, Charlie boy; we'll see.'

Second-Lieutenant Charles MacFell and Lieutenant John Bradshaw didn't get their leave, but like thousands of others their senses had become dulled with the continuous bombardment of the past fortnight.

In the early morning of June 7th Charlie, walking along the duck-boards, stopped here and there and, when he could make himself heard, spoke to the men leaning against the parapet, their guns by their side. 'Good luck!' he said, and the answer always came back, 'An' you, sir.'

When he stopped near his sergeant he checked his watch, and the sergeant, without speaking, looked at his.

'Three minutes.'

'Yes, sir, three minutes. Good cover, isn't it, sir?'

'Excellent.'

At a curve in the trench John Bradshaw was standing and next to him Captain Lee-Farrow. It was the captain who asked, 'Everything set?'

'Yes, sir.'

'Good cover?'

'Excellent, sir.'

The captain now looked up into the sky, to the stars twinkling between the flashes from the guns. 'Nice night,' he said.

Both John Bradshaw and Charlie, following the captain's gaze, answered together, 'Yes, sir, nice night.' Then in the darkness they smiled at each other without being aware of it.

'Good luck.'

'And you, sir.'

'Better take your positions.'

Charlie and John Bradshaw moved away, and when they parted a few steps further up the trench,

Bradshaw said quietly, 'All the best, Charlie,' and Charlie answered, 'And a whole salmon done in butter.'

Another deafening explosion smothered the chuckle, then Charlie was standing in place.

'Thirty seconds.'

'Twenty.'

'Ten.'

'Over. Over. Over.' The word ran along the trench like the echo of a song that was cut off here and there by the noise of the band.

How far did he run across the open space before he started to yell? How many of his pistol shots found their target? He didn't know, he heard screams and groans between the deafening blast of the artillery. A shell exploded near him and he was thrown off his feet, but surprisingly as soon as he was down he was up again. He remembered being worried for a flashing second in case his pistol had been blocked with mud. He couldn't remember reloading.

When he fell flat over a body and heard a broad North Country voice, saying, 'Bloody hell!' he shouted 'All right?' and the face close to his bawled, 'Is that you, Mister MacFell?'

'Yes!' He was screaming, and he was answered by a scream. 'Thought it was Jerry. I've copped it in the knee. In the knee, sir.'

'Well, stay put! I'll be back.'

'You will?' There was the slightest trace of fear in the question and he yelled firmly, 'Yes, definitely, I'll be back,' while thinking the man would likely be blown to smithereens in a few minutes, if not by the enemy by his own artillery.

He was going through a maze of blasted barbed wire; it tore at his hands, then he was in a mêlée again, but now he could make out the whirling, prancing figures. 'Thrust it in! Turn. Pull. Thrust it in! Turn. Pull.'

The steel blade was coming at him. He pulled on the trigger of his pistol but nothing happened; the blade within inches of his chest was knocked sidewards, and in the flare of the bursting shells he gave a lightning glance towards the man who had saved his skin. But there was no recognition; as far as he could remember he wasn't one of theirs. But this often happened, companies got mixed up.

It was as they came under a hail of fire from the further German lines that he came across John Bradshaw. In the illumination of a Very light he saw him lying against the side of a trench, his fingers gripping the wooden support that led to a dug-out. He turned him round and saw in the flashes that he was still alive; one arm was hugging his chest and his sleeve was already stained. He grabbed up the pistol that was lying by his side and glanced swiftly around. There were bodies strewn here and there and a few men were still milling about along at the far end of the trench where it turned a corner. As a shell burst overhead he ducked and covered the lieutenant; then shouting at him, 'It's all right! It's all right!' he put his hands underneath his oxters and pulled him into the shelter of the dug-out. Then for the second time in a matter of minutes he yelled, 'I'll be back! I'll be back, John.'

The men at the end of the trench were pinned down now by a barrage of bursting shells.

There was a sudden explosion at the opposite end of the trench and timbers and clay were thrown high in the air.

'We're cornered, sir,' a voice was bawling in his ear, and he nodded at the crouching speaker and, pointing backwards, he gesticulated wildly; then waved his arm in a 'Come on!' movement and the huddle of men followed him, stumbling over the bodies strewn on the duck-boards.

Within a few minutes the dug-out was full with fifteen privates, a corporal, a sergeant, and Lieutenant Bradshaw.

It had been an officers' dug-out, as the light of a torch showed, and Charlie saw that it was well equipped, better far than theirs had been, in fact it appeared luxurious. What caught his eye immediately were three towels hanging on a bench near an enamelled bowl with water. Gathering up the towels, he went to John Bradshaw and said quickly, 'Let's see the trouble, John?' But he had to force his arm away from his ribs before he could open his jacket. When he ripped down the blood-sodden shirt it was to disclose a bullet wound at the top of his chest.

'I know what to do, sir, I've done first aid.' The voice was to his side and Charlie said, 'Good.'

'We'll tear the towels, sir.'

With the help of other hands the towels were

quickly torn into strips, and when the rough bandaging was done, they carried the lieutenant to the bed in the corner of the dug-out and laid him down, and for the first time John Bradshaw spoke. 'Thanks, Charlie,' he said.

'It won't be long before we get you back.'

They looked at each other steadily for a moment; then John Brasdhaw merely nodded.

The barrage had lessened somewhat but was still strong, and Charlie issued orders to the sergeant, who relayed them to the corporal to post men at intervals along the trench, and for others to remove the bodies to the far end; but not to go beyond the bend. The trench was long and although there was no sound of fighting activity coming from further along it, it was not known who could be lurking there. They would investigate later. Then he went out, the sergeant going with him.

Cautiously now he raised his head above the parapet. The early morning light showed a sea of barbed wire. What was he to do? He couldn't think of advancing with this handful on his own; but if they stayed here they'd likely all be blown to smithereens.

He turned now and went down the trench and looked over the other parapet in the direction where he imagined lay their own lines, but as far as he could see there was merely barren land pitted with craters, except where two small hills lay to the right . . . Or were they hills? That was the direction from where the bombardment had been coming, likely they were camouflaged fortifications. He hadn't any idea at the moment where he was. He couldn't remember seeing those two mounds on the map.

What he did see now were two figures slowly emerging from a crater. From this distance he couldn't make out whether they were Germans or his own fellows. He called quietly, 'Sergeant, take a look.'

The sergeant raised his head slowly upwards, then said, 'Blokes crawling this way, sir.'

'Yes; but who are they?'

'Bareheaded, no helmets on.'

'I think there's one of them injured, one's pulling the other . . . Yes, and they're ours. Come on.'

Without hesitation they both jumped the parapet and, bent double, made for the crawling men. They had just reached them when the barrage of fire was intensified, and it was definitely coming now from the direction of the mounds.

Grabbing one man by the collar, Charlie pulled him unceremoniously forward, and they had almost reached the trench when a shell burst just behind them and the force of the explosion lifted them all and threw them in a bunch back into the trench.

When they had sorted themselves out, they lay panting for a moment and took stock of each other. One of the men Charlie recognised straightaway, it was the man he had stumbled over, one of his own men; and now the man actually laughed at him as he spluttered almost hysterically, 'You said you'd come back an' get me, an' you did.'

The other soldier was covered with wet slush from

head to foot, and as he watched the man take his hand round his face, then through his mud-matted hair, his heart actually missed a beat.

No, no! not here; not under these circumstances; not Slater.

But it was Slater, and Slater had recognized him.

As another shell burst near the parapet Charlie yelled at his sergeant, 'Get them into the dug-out.'

No sign of recognition had passed between them but immediately he entered the dug-out he felt an almost desperate urge to speak to Slater, in order to make their stations clear once and for all, yet he had to force the question through his lips.

'What battalion?' he asked. His voice was cool, the words clipped.

Slater stared at him, and his hesitation in answering was put down by those present to shock; fellows did act like that at times, didn't jump to it, they got past it.

'12th . . . sir.'

The sergeant looked sharply at the mud-covered figure, the fellow was acting queer; the way he had said 'sir'; shellshock likely.

Charlie stared into Slater's face for a moment before turning away; then he looked around the dug-out, saying, 'Seemingly they didn't go in for tea, but there's a few bottles of wine there. Open them, Sergeant.'

'Yes, sir.'

'And those tins of beef; you'd better make a meal of it for I think we might be here a little while longer.'

He now went to the corner of the dug-out where John Bradshaw lay, and the lieutenant, looking up at him, said, 'They didn't take all that sector then?'

Charlie shook his head. 'No.'

'They will.'

'Yes, yes, they will. Don't worry.'

'The shelling, where's it coming from?'

'One of the hills on our flank, it's still very much alive.'

'What do you aim to do?' Suddenly Bradshaw bit on his lip and his right arm went across his chest and covered the one that was strapped to his body with the towels.

'Look,' Charlie bent over him: 'don't worry. If our lot don't send reinforcements over we can hold out till dark. Just lie still.' He nodded down into the pain-twisted face, then went outside again.

The sergeant was standing along near where the last man was posted and where the dead lay conspicuously piled on both sides of the parapet, and he turned to Charlie, saying below his breath as he pointed to the bend in the trench, 'There's movement along there, sir, I went a little way round and I'm sure I spotted a head peering out of a dug-out.'

Charlie remained still for a moment; then drawing John Bradshaw's pistol from his holster and looking first at the sergeant, then at the sentry, he said, 'Come on,' and slowly the three went forward. First pausing before a dug-out, their guns at the ready, they would then jump almost as one man into it. Each was well constructed but not so comfortable,

Charlie noticed, as the one they had claimed as their temporary headquarters.

They had almost reached the last dug-out before the trench made yet another sharp bend when Charlie held up his hand and they stood perfectly still.

The minutes ticked away, almost five of them before, signalling to the sergeant to follow him, they both sprang forward and through the opening.

His finger was wavering on the trigger. Instinctively he was about to pull it when 'Kamarad! Kamarad!' The word emerged from three throats at once; two of the men were lying on the floor, the third was leaning on his elbow, one arm thrust high above his head; his trouser knee was soaked red; the second man on the floor hadn't raised his hands because they were holding the side of his head; the first man now stood up, his hands well above his head.

'Come on!' Charlie signalled to the standing man to move forward, then called to the private: 'Stay with them! We'll send someone forward for them.' He went out and followed the sergeant who was now thrusting the German along the trench at the point of his bayonet.

In the passage along the trench Charlie detailed two men to go and bring the wounded Germans down. Back in their own dug-out the man who was acting as orderly exclaimed on sight of the prisoner, 'Blimey! a live one.'

Slater, sitting hunched up in the corner of the dug-out, said nothing, and as Charlie's eyes swept over him, as if unseeing, he noticed, with surprise, for the first time that his sleeve now bore no stripes. Slater had been deprived of the power to bully and blast. Why?

After a moment be said in an aside to his sergeant and with a backward lift of his head in the direction of Slater, 'Put him on guard.'

'I . . . I think he's in shock, sir, shellshock, he won't open his mouth.'

He wanted to say, 'Yes, he's in shock all right, but it isn't shellshock, it's hate that's tying his tongue.'

And as the thought came to him, he swung round to stare into the eyes of Slater. It was as if their steel-hard gaze had willed him to turn, and he experienced a fear that all the guns and slaughter hadn't so far evoked in him.

'You'd better watch out.' It was as if someone had spoken aloud, for he answered the voice, saying, 'Yes, by God, yes, I'd better watch out.' . . .

It was around midday when he was almost about to give the order to make it back to their own lines that the bombardment from the mounds started in earnest and two men on sentry duty at the farthest end of the trench were killed outright. To add further to the confusion, their own batteries took up the challenge.

He didn't know how far their line had advanced, or if they had advanced at all, but he gauged that as long as there was the crossfire there would be no surprise attack from the German flank to retake this particular section of the line, and so he ordered the remaining men into the dug-out, only almost immediately to feel he had made a mistake and they would all be buried alive, for a shell bursting near up above cracked the timbers in the roof and brought the clay spattering amongst them.

The German prisoners showed little emotion, they sat huddled together staring before them; even the one who wasn't wounded looked dazed.

As the afternoon wore on, the shelling became intermittent from both sides, and then as dusk was about to set in there fell over the whole land a silence. It was a weird silence. Back home Charlie would have thought of it as the silence of evening falling into night; here, he knew, it was the calm before the storm.

John Bradshaw who was doubtless in great pain and who looked pretty sick muttered, 'What are you thinking of doing?' and Charlie replied, 'Once it's dark, make a break for our lines again, go back the way we came. I've been looking at the map. We'll have to move north-west. Battle Wood I think lies to the north, and to tell you the truth I don't know if we've come through two sets of lines or not.'

'I shouldn't think so; our artillery seems too near for that.'

'I hope you're right.'

'I . . . I know they are dead beat but I think you'd be wise to put some of them on guard before it gets too dark, you don't know but what we may be surprised.'

'Yes, I'll do that.'

He turned away now and issued orders to the sergeant to place his men again at intervals along the trench leaving only three men behind. Then beckoning these three men to the opening of the dug-out he said in an undertone, 'You know what to do when I give the signal. Get him on to the stretcher. Don't take any notice of his protests, just get him on to it. Then put the able-bodied prisoner at the front and one of you take the back. When you go out of here turn left.' He pointed. 'The three wounded men' – he jerked his head backwards – 'well, two of you get in between them, you know the drill, and follow the stretcher. We'll be around you. The main thing is to make as little noise as possible. And if they start lighting up, well, drop where you stand. Good luck.'

They made no answer, they merely nodded, and he went out and walked slowly along the trench, first to the right speaking to each man as he came to him, then he retraced his steps and walked to the left.

The last man in the trench was Slater. He was alone in the section where the trench curved slightly. Charlie did not stop but walked past him for some yards to a point where he intended they should climb out and make their way back, or at least join up with another unit, and as he stood peering over the parapet into the dusk he tried to still the churning inside him. The menace of the man had been weighing on him all day and it was never heavier than at this moment. It was with an effort that he made himself turn slowly about and walk back in his direction.

Slater was bending forward against the wall of the

trench, his gun at the ready. His eyes were directed towards the top of the parapet and it was to this he seemingly spoke as he said clearly and distinctly, 'I've heard of blokes buyin' commissions in the old days but never one payin' for it with his wife's whoring.'

He was directly behind him, and now Slater turned his head, but not his body, and looked at him.

'What did you say?'

'You heard, you're not deaf. You heard . . . sir.' He put emphasis on the drawn-out sir. 'You didn't think you got it off your own bat, did you, you who hadn't the guts to kill a pig? . . . I wouldn't do that if I was you.'

Unconsciously, but driven by an inner desire to stop this devil's mouth in some way, Charlie's hand had moved towards his holster.

'That would be the finish of you if you did that . . . sir, too many witnesses about. Anyway, you wouldn't have the gut. You never had any guts, had you . . . sir?'

The most terrible thing Charlie was finding about this moment was that Slater's tone was conversational. He was now saying, 'They were all doin' it in their pants in case you named the major, so what was the best thing to do? Well, as Corporal Packer said – he was Lieutenant Swaine's corporal you remember – put you where you couldn't talk. He said he'd never seen such a flap as was on, or a promotion got so bloody quick . . . Didn't you know that? . . . Oh you must have; you never thought you could get a pip on your own, now did you? As I've always said, you're a born loser, you lost the lass you loved, you married a whore, and now you've even lost yourself and your bloody platoon. A cuckold, that's the name I think the gentry have for a fellow like you, but to me you're just a loser, a pipsqueak loser.' . . .

He was never to fathom out correctly if it was the shell suddenly bursting near or the fact that Slater brought his body swiftly round with his gun at the ready, he was only aware that he was firing his pistol and straight into the man in front of him. The blast of another shell bursting flung him against the opposite parapet and he was lying there, the gun still in his hand, still pointing when the sergeant came running into view. Taking in the truth of the situation straight away, he shouted, 'What happened, sir? He tried to do for you?'

Another shell burst, and then both he and the sergeant were flung down to the bottom of the trench and his face was hanging over Slater's, staring into the mouth and eyes which were wide as if he had died in a moment of surprise.

'Let's get out of this, sir.' The sergeant had hold of his arm and, bent double, they were running, but before they reached the dug-out another shell burst and the trench caved in behind them.

Then they were inside the dug-out and he was standing upright and shouting orders, yelling them. 'No use waiting any longer . . . Have to make a break for it. They've got us pin-pointed. Get the lieutenant up. Come on! Look slippy! Look slippy there!'

He had killed Slater. He had killed Slater.

What was the matter with him, why was he yelling like this? It was only sergeants who did the yelling.

'You can't go right now, go left outside. Direct the prisoner.'

He had killed Slater. He had killed Slater.

'Come on! Come on, move!'

He was outside now hustling them along the trench whilst making his way to the front of them. It was at the point where they had picked up the German prisoners that he ordered them to push the stretcher on to the parapet, and when Bradshaw protested he shouted him down, bawling, 'Shut up!' then 'Get him up and over! All of you, over!'

Amid the scrambling there were curses and so, forgetting now that he himself had been bawling, he ordered, 'Quiet! Quiet! Keep together in twos, follow the stretcher.' He did not issue orders for the two men and the wounded, for they would of necessity trail behind.

Quietly now he called, 'Sergeant!' and when the man came to his side he said, 'I'll go ahead of the stretcher. Keep them together, keep them coming.'

'Yes, sir.'

It was dark now, except for the moments when the sky was illuminated by the flashes of gunfire coming from both the north and the south-west of them; there was no shellfire at the moment from the mound. He couldn't imagine that the hill had been taken; for if that had been so a patrol would surely have investigated the trench.

313

In the illumination of a Very light he got a momentary impression of their position. He was on the right track, the hill lay behind them to the north, their lines were due west, in fact they couldn't be much more than a few hundred yards away.

Another Very light burst now but almost directly over them, and almost at the same moment the cross-fire began.

'Keep going!' he was yelling again, and the sergeant repeated his order, almost on a scream. 'Come on! Keep going!' but before he uttered the last word a shell burst to the right of them and they were all lying flat, hugging the earth.

The sergeant came crawling to his side. His face was near his own and his voice was loud in his ear. 'It's . . . it's our lot, sir; they're aiming at the hill.'

For a moment he didn't answer, the noise about them was deafening. Then there came a slight lull, at least from the artillery to the front of them, and the sergeant's voice came again, saying, 'They're knockin' bloody hell out of the trench, we did it only just in time, sir.'

There were Very lights bursting here and there about them, and now Charlie, twisting round on his elbow, shouted down the straggling line of cowering bodies, 'When the next Very bursts anywhere near, jump to your feet and yell, shout, bawl anything, let them see it's us.'

'We . . . we could be blown to smithereens, sir, the artillery's well behind, they couldn't get in touch in time.'

'That's a chance we'll have to take, Sergeant.'

'As you say, sir.'

Why was it, even in this moment when he was on the border of death, he asked himself, would the sergeant have questioned the lieutenant if he had given that order?

'Up! Up!' He had jumped to his feet, the sergeant beside him, but only a few of the men followed suit immediately.

'Wave your arms! Shout! Do you hear? Shout!'

Did he hear someone near bawl, 'What's the bloody good of that? He's up the pole. They'll never hear us in this?'

'Forward! Forward!'

Naturally it seemed to the men that they were being ordered to walk directly into the midst of the bursting shells, but they followed. An officer had given an order and it was their duty to carry it out, come hell, high water, or being blown to smithereens; and that was the fate every man thought awaited him.

Yet as they made straight across the tortured land being aided by the flashes of artillery that momentarily pin-pointed the potholes, some as big as craters half full of water in which many of them would have drowned, so weary were they, it was as if they were following a known path.

When a shell burst near and they were all spattered with earth the sergeant's voice now almost drowned the echo of it as he yelled, 'Keep going! Keep going!'

Then of a sudden the barrage in front of them stopped, and although the German battery behind them still kept peppering away, it was as if a deep silence had fallen all around them.

Charlie paused, bringing the rest to a halt as there arose from out of the ground in the distance dark shadows, darker than the night. He felt rather than saw them spreading out and he called wildly, 'Hello there! Hello there! I'm Lieutenant MacFell, we are the . . .'

'Well! what the hell you all playing at standing there! Come on! Come on! Did you ever see the likes of it?'

It was as if they had been bidden to come in out of the rain. They came on, the utterly weary men at a run now, laughing as they dropped over the parapet. The canvas stretcher was eased gently down into the trench, and lastly the two soldiers with the three wounded men between them . . .

Ten minutes later he was sitting in the very dug-out he had left only that morning, occupied now not only by a new lieutenant and his second, but also at this moment by a captain and a major.

'Have another.' They refilled his glass, and the major for the second time in a few minutes said, 'How you got your fellows through that lot I'll never know, but there's one thing sure, you would have had it by now if you had stayed in that line. Those batteries are cut off but they're going down fighting. They must have had the idea that the whole line was occupied. Well, their number'll be up soon; the cavalry are going over in half an hour. Then we are moving on . . . Show's going well. You look all in, old chap.'

316

'It's been a busy day,' he found himself answering in the same vein.

'I'll say . . . Pity about the lieutenant. But they'll soon dig that out of him back at base. He's lucky, it must have just missed his heart. Well now, we'll have to be about our father's business, won't we?' He turned to his officers and they laughed with him and repeated, 'Yes, sir, about our father's business.'

Turning to Charlie again the major now said, 'I'd have a nap until daylight, then you can go back to base with the wounded and have a wash an' brush up before you return to your unit. Only God knows where they are now.' He shook his head. Then in the same airy tone he ended, 'Very good night's work. Not only did you bring your men back safely and the lieutenant, but three prisoners. They might prove to be helpful, and they don't seem averse to being captured. Strange fellows . . . Well, goodbye.'

'Goodbye, sir.' Charlie was on his feet. He had managed to salute smartly. The major had reached the opening of the dug-out when he turned and said, 'You'll be mentioned. I think it was a very good effort. Foolhardy, of course, to walk into a battery but nevertheless a very good effort.'

He sat down on the edge of the camp-bed and lowered his head into his hands. God above! Was he dreaming? You'll be mentioned. Good effort. And for what? For coming backwards instead of going forward. But what else could he have done, he couldn't have left John? Couldn't he? Well, anyway, he seemingly had done the right thing according to the major, whose tone had also implied it was just what would be expected of an English officer and a gentleman.

An officer and a gentleman, not a conscript, and certainly not a man who had been made a cuckold and been paid for it by being given a pip on his shoulder.

God Almighty! He mustn't think about it, he must sleep, sleep. But when he slept he would still think about it, he would never be able to stop thinking about it, not till the day he died. And pray God that would be soon, because he couldn't live with the pictures in his mind.

Against his closed lids he now saw illuminated as if by a battery flash, the office and the lieutenant sitting behind the desk. He heard his own voice, saying, 'May I enquire, sir, when my name was first put forward?' He saw the hand thumbing through pages on the desk; then the man sauntering to the cabinet in the corner of the room; he saw the face turn towards him and the lips mouthing, 'Ten days ago; of course, we go into these things.'

Now the lips were moving again. 'Your wife runs the farm?'

God! how they must have laughed! They had treated him like a country bumpkin, a yokel, a fool. Charlie MacFell the fool. The idiot, and that's what he had been, otherwise he would have pursued the thought that made him enquire as to when his name was first put forward. Hadn't it struck him as being too much of a coincidence that the very day after finding his wife sporting with the major he would have been offered a commission? Hadn't he known in that moment that his hands were being tied? Yes, he had; but he thought he had tied them himself, and all he could really think of was that he had got one over on Slater.

But Slater had had the last word.

'Good effort. You'll be mentioned.'

And would he himself mention that he had shot a private, shot him dead? He'd have to, because there was the sergeant, and men talked, and tales got distorted. But the sergeant could vouch that this particular soldier had acted oddly since first coming into the trench.

Slater could win again; even dead Slater could win. No! No! He mustn't win now, not now, not after that effort, not the effort the major had referred to but the effort it had taken him to draw his revolver and shoot. He must go and report it, report it to the major.

He made to rise from the bed but instead he flopped flat on to it, rolled on to his side, buried his face in the crook of his elbow, and as sleep overtook him he muttered thickly, 'Don't cry. For God's sake, don't cry.'

He was standing to the side of a long white scrubbed table. Sitting behind the table was a colonel, a major, and a lieutenant. He had met this particular lieutenant and major yesterday for the first time, and he'd asked the major for a hearing on a matter that was troubling him; and now he was getting that hearing.

The sergeant was speaking. Standing stiffly before the table he was saying, 'As I said, 'twas pretty rough there, sir. Under crossfire we were, and had been for some time, when this Private Slater came crawling out of a mud-hole with a wounded man. They were both in a pretty bad shape. The man Slater I think was under shock, sir. He acted funny from the start, aggressive like, jumpy. Later in the day I made him relieve a sentry. It was just on dark, sir. Second-Lieutenant MacFell had told us what he intended to do to get us out of there. The barrage had eased off; I saw him making an inspection, talking to each man as he went along the trench. I . . . I had just given orders about the strappin' up of Lieutenant Bradshaw when I heard the shell burst. It was along towards the end of the trench where the lieutenant had just gone. I ran in that direction and when I rounded the bend I saw the lieutenant lying against one parapet and Private Slater against the other. Private Slater had his rifle in his hands. He had been shot through the chest. I said to the lieutenant, ''Are you all right, sir?'' He seemed dazed. He looked down at his pistol and said, ''Yes. Yes, I'm all right.'' I said, ''Did he go for you, sir?'' and he said, ''Yes; it . . . it must have been the reaction to the blast.'' . . .'

Had he said that? He couldn't remember. No, no, he hadn't said that.

'He was a man who seemed to resent authority, sir; he had turned on me earlier on when I asked his name and number but I let it pass as I thought he was under shock, sir.'

'No doubt he was. Thank you, Sergeant. You have been very explicit.'

'Sir.' The sergeant saluted smartly, turned about and went out of the room.

Now he was standing in front of the table and the colonel was speaking to him. 'Sorry about this business, MacFell. We all understand how you must feel, and it was very commendable of you to bring it to our notice. Under the circumstances we don't see what else you could have done.' The colonel now cast his glance towards the major and then towards the lieutenant, and they nodded in agreement; then he slowly fingered some papers that were lying in front of him before lifting his eyes upwards again and saying, 'A very good report here from Major Deverell. You got most of your platoon back. Good work. Good work. Well, I think that will be all, gentlemen.'

'Sir.'

'Yes, MacFell?'

'May I ask how Private Slater's dependants will be informed of his death?'

'Oh . . . oh the usual, died in battle . . . bravely, you know. The man was definitely under shock. It happens. Yes, died in battle. One can't do anything else, can one?'

'No, sir. Thank you.'

'Hope to see you at dinner then.' The colonel now got to his feet, smiling as he said, 'You look a little more presentable than you did this time yesterday.'

'I would need to, sir.'

They all smiled at him as if he had come out with

some witticism. He stood straight, he looked cool, self-possessed, the kind of officer that men would follow into and out of tight corners. And hadn't he proved he was that type of man? Slater hadn't won. Conscript, cuckold, fool, loser, not any more, not any more. Cover up, lie, play the officer and gentleman, anything to show him, and keep on showing him for he was still alive, in his mind he was still alive.

PART FIVE

The End of War and The Beginning of the Battle

1

'It's over! It's over! Can you believe it? It's over!' The nurses were running round the ward; they were kissing everybody in sight. Two of them took the crutches from Captain Pollock and, their arms about him, made him hop into a dance. One of the nurses slid along the polished floor, then fell on to her bottom amid roars of laughter.

Six of the ten men in the ward beds were sitting up shouting and joining in the fun, but the other four lay still. Charlie was one of the four, but he laughed when Nurse Bannister, her big moon-face hanging above him, said, 'I'm going to do it, Major, I'm going to do it. There!' She kissed him full on the lips, a long, hard, tight kiss, and when she had finished he laughed at her and said, 'I won't want any sweet today, Nurse.'

'Go on with you. But isn't it wonderful! It's over. Can you believe it? I can't, it'll take time for it to sink in.'

Another nurse came running to the foot of the bed and, amid laughter, she chanted:

'I do love you, Major MacFell,
But why, oh why, I cannot tell;

325

But this I know, and know full well,
I do love you, Major MacFell.'

Nurse Bannister picked up an apple from a bowl
standing on the bedside locker and threw it at her
tormentor, who caught it and then threw it to
Charlie, but when he caught it he flinched visibly and
Nurse Bannister, all laughter disappearing from her
face, said, 'That was a damn silly thing to do.'

'Sorry. Sorry, Major.' Nurse Roper was bending
above him now, and he grinned at her and said,
'Well, if you're sorry, show it.'

'O.K.' Her eyes lifted to the nurse standing on the
other side of the bed before she bent and kissed him
on the lips.

'You've got a nice mouth.' She patted his cheek,
then hissed, 'Oh Lord! look out, here she comes!'
and proceeded to straighten the sheet under Charlie's
chin, all the while talking down to him in a quiet
conversational tone, saying, 'Armistice or no armistice, Major, we must remember who we are, where
we are, and with whom we are dealing. Ti-tiddly-aye-
ti . . . ti-ti!'

Charlie wanted to laugh, but laughter expanded
the chest and that was painful.

As Sister Layton walked up the ward, the hilarity
died down somewhat, but the men sitting up in bed
called to her in various ways yet all asking much the
same question: 'When are we celebrating, Sister? . . .
How are we celebrating? . . . Having a dance?'

The last might have been said with bitter irony for

most of those in bed had lost at least one leg and the sister, showing that she wasn't without a sense of humour below her stiff ladylike exterior, said, 'Why not! And the first of you to get out of bed within the next week can have the honour of accompanying me.'

There was a pretended scramble which caused the muscles of her face to relax into a prim smile before her usual manner took over, and she was issuing orders to her staff as if this were an ordinary hour in an ordinary day.

When she stopped at Charlie's bed she looked down on him and asked, 'Comfortable, Major?'

'Yes, Sister.'

'Doctor Morgan is very pleased with you.'

'How many did he unearth this time?'

'Oh, quite a few.'

'Did he get the main one?'

She bent over him and smoothed the already smoothed sheet.

'Main one? They are all main ones. Now lie quiet; that's all you're called upon to do for the next few days.'

As she went to move away he asked, 'When will it be possible for me to be moved, Sister?'

'Don't you like it here?' She turned her haughty gaze down on him.

'Yes, yes, I like it, and would be prepared to stay for ever if it was three hundred miles nearer home.'

'We'll have to talk to Doctor Morgan about that.'

He watched her continuing up the ward. You were

in their hands, you were helpless. He had already talked countless times to Doctor Morgan who had promised that after the next do he would see about having him moved up North. He wouldn't have minded staying here, not in the least, if it hadn't been for Nellie. It was only a week since her last visit, but it seemed like years; it was a long way for her to come, first to London, then another hour's train journey. It meant her taking three days altogether for a few hours spent sitting by his bed. Yet it was all he seemed to live for, all he wanted to live for. But would he live if they didn't get that last bit of shrapnel out?

How many times had he been down to the theatre? How many pieces had they taken out of him? Peppered they said he was. He didn't remember being brought over from France but the last words he recalled as he awoke in a clean bed in the middle of the night with a nurse wiping his mouth with something wet was a voice saying, 'He'll never make it, he's like a sieve.'

And that is what the doctor had said to him. 'You're very lucky you know, Major; when you came in you were just like a sieve.'

It was odd when he came to think of it, he had gone through battle after battle without a scratch, right up till two months ago; then one day he had walked right into it. It was just after returning from leave, his second leave, one as disappointing as the other. On his first leave shortly after the Messines do, he had found Nellie still at the farm with her mother. She had once again just returned from hospital, after having an appendicitis operation this time, and Florence Chapman had guarded her against him as if he were bent on rape. He experienced the strong feeling that she hoped he would be killed for he knew that she wanted her daughter to herself. She was lonely and prematurely ageing.

He knew before his second leave that Nellie had long since left the farm and gone in for nursing training, and when he returned to the North it was to find that she had been transferred to a hospital in Dorset. Four days of the seven he stayed down there, but spent hardly any time with her; her off-duty hours were limited. Even when they met in his room in the hotel they were strangely both constrained. Although she was warm and loving and he wanted above all things, above all things to love her, there was a barrier between them. The barrier was Victoria. They both knew it, although her name was never mentioned. She loomed up between them as his wife and Nellie's sister.

It was just before they parted that he said to her, 'I've written to my solicitor today, I've asked him to go ahead with divorce proceedings,' and her only answer to this was to put her arms around his neck and press her mouth to his.

Now she was back in the North and he was here, and all he seemed to be living for was to be moved nearer to her, for he knew that once he was on his feet, divorce or no divorce, they would come together.

And there was another thing he didn't like to think

about that happened on that leave; he had made it his business to look up Johnny only to be told that Johnny was dead. He had been kicked by a horse while on some kind of a manoeuvre up on the fells. Johnny who didn't want to go to France in case he caught one had died by a kick from a horse. Life was crazy. The whole world was crazy.

'Ah, that's it. Nice to see you sitting up, Major.'

'I'll feel better when I'm standing up, Doctor.'

'All in good time . . . Well, while I'm here I might as well have a look at my handiwork.'

There was some gentle shuffling, the curtains were drawn round the bed, the bedclothes were drawn, pads removed, then began the jokes.

'Nearly a complete board for noughts and crosses here. Whose move is it next?'

'Mine I hope.' There was no amusement in Charlie's tone.

'All in good time. All in good time. Healing nicely, Sister, don't you think?'

'Yes, Doctor, beautifully.'

'When can I be moved?'

'That will do for now, Sister. Put the pads on temporarily, leave the dressing, I want a word.'

The nurse now pushed a chair to the side of the bed, then departed.

The doctor sat down, gave a special nod to the sister, and she too departed; then he looked at Charlie, and he said slowly, 'You may go back North once you are on your feet.'

'You mean it?'

'Yes.'

'You got them all out then? I thought . . .'

'Not quite.'

He pressed himself back against the pillows now and stared at the doctor, 'It's still there then?' he said.

'That's about it.'

'But you said . . .'

'Yes, I know what I said, but when we got in we thought it was a bit tricky. You're a lucky man you know to be alive.'

'. . . And I mayn't be alive much longer?'

'Oh, nonsense! Nonsense! You could go on for years and years until you become a doddery old farmer.'

'That's if it stays put?'

'No, no, of course not; we're hoping it moves. They do you know.'

'But in the right direction.'

'As you say' – the doctor lowered his head now – 'in the right direction.'

'The other direction would be short and swift?' There was a pause before the answer came: 'Yes, short and swift.'

Charlie rubbed one lip over the other before he asked, 'And if it went in the right direction would you try again?'

'Like a shot.' The doctor put his hands over his eyes. 'Sorry, like a surgeon.'

They both smiled now, then the doctor said, 'Of

course when I say you may go North it will be into hospital. You know that, don't you?'

'Yes, I suppose so.'

'Well, we can't let you go in the condition you're in at present; it'll be a little time yet. I don't think you realise how badly shattered you were and we've dug into you seven times in the last three months, but if you'd had any flesh on your body you know the shrapnel wouldn't have got so far. You've got to be built up, and it's got to be done before you get back to your farm and pick up everyday responsibilities, you understand?'

Yes, he understood, and also the meaning behind all the doctor's kindly chat. They wanted him in hospital for observation in case the piece of shrapnel inside him decided to move. If it moved in the right direction they could get it out, or given time he understood it could settle in and make a home for itself where it was at present near his heart.

It was three weeks later when he went North, but before that time he'd had a visitor. It was on the day after he'd had the conversation with the doctor when the nurse, waking him from a doze, said, 'There's someone to see you.' His heart had leapt at the thought that Nellie had made it after all. He'd had a letter from her only that morning to say that the dragon of a sister wouldn't even allow her to put her two weeks' leave together in order to make the journey South, but she had put in for her discharge offering as an excuse her mother needed her to run the farm. And her mother had willingly gone along with her on this, hoping that she would eventually return home.

But when his visitor turned out to be Betty, he was really visibly startled and not a little touched by the thought that she must have some affection for him to have undertaken the journey to this out of the way place.

It was only a matter of nine months since he had last seen her and he was shocked at the change in her. She looked haggard, old, and her expression was even tighter than usual, so much so that it was hard to believe she was only twenty-four years old.

Then in a matter of minutes after the usual greetings had been exchanged he thought he had found the explanation for her visit when, looking him straight in the face, she asked bluntly, 'Is it true what I hear about you and Nellie Chapman?'

He considered her for a moment before replying, 'Well, Betty, if what you have heard is that I intend to marry Nellie once the divorce is through, it's true.'

'You're mad.'

'That's as may be, but that's what I intend to do. And this time I know what I'm about.'

'And what about me?'

'Well, we've been over this a number of times, Betty, haven't we? We agreed that when you left to marry Wetherby I would see that you didn't go to him empty-handed.'

'And what if I don't marry Wetherby?'

'What do you mean, has something happened?'

'I'm not marrying Wetherby.' Her lips scarcely moved as she brought out the words and he stared at her for a moment before putting out his hand and placing it over hers. But it hadn't rested there a second before she jerked her own away from his hold and demanded, 'So where does that leave me now?'

'There'll always be a home for you there, Betty, you know that.' But even as he said the words he was thinking in agitation, Oh no, not this now! Betty's tongue, he knew, could impregnate a house with so much acid that it would turn everything sour. Yet what could he do?

'A home?' she repeated. 'Where? In the corner of the kitchen? I've run that place since my father died, yes, since he died because Mother wasn't any good, and you weren't much better. It would have gone to rack and ruin if it hadn't been for me and now you say I'll always have a home.'

He was feeling very tired and he was becoming increasingly agitated inside. He lay back on his pillows, and a nurse passing up the ward came to his side and said, 'You all right, Major?'

He nodded at her, saying, 'Yes. Yes, I'm all right.' Then the nurse, looking across at his visitor, said, 'Please don't stay long, he's easily tired.'

Although Charlie closed his eyes for a moment he felt rather than saw Betty's impatient shrug and lift of the head.

When he again looked at her she was searching in her handbag for something, and she brought out a sheet of paper, saying, 'Will you sign this? I want to sell some cattle.'

'But you have my authority to sell the cattle; it was all arranged before I left.'

He watched her press her lips together and turn her head to the side, saying, 'Well, I wish you'd tell the authorities that. The laws are changing all the time, men coming round to examine this, that, and the other, and because it's your farm and you're back in England they want your signature.'

She handed him a pen, and he obediently wrote his name on the bottom of the folded sheet of paper.

As she replaced the paper in her bag she brought her short body straight up in the chair and asked, 'When are you likely to be home?'

'Oh' – he shook his head – 'not for some time yet I should think, they're going to transfer me North, but I'll still be in hospital. I don't suppose they'll let me out, for good that is, until I'm fit, but as soon as ever I can I'll take a trip out and see you.'

She was on her feet now – she had pushed the chair back – and she stood looking at him for a moment before she said, 'Good-bye, Charlie.' There was something about the emphasis she laid on the words that made him sit up and lean towards her, saying, 'Now, you're not to worry, Betty. I'll see you're all right, I promise.'

'I'll be all right, never you fear.' She pulled at the belt of her coat, and he noticed that it was one she had worn long before the war. She had never spent money on herself, not like their mother.

'Good-bye, Charlie.' Again it sounded like a definite farewell.

'Good-bye, Betty. Take care of yourself. I'll . . . I'll be with you soon.'

She had walked to the bottom of the bed by now, and she stood there for some seconds and stared at him before she turned and went down the ward, a small, shabby, dowdy figure.

He felt an urge to jump up and run after her and to take her in his arms and comfort her. She must be taking the business of Wetherby very hard. He had always known the fellow was no good, but if Betty had liked . . . loved . . . and was capable of adoring anyone it had been Robin Wetherby. It was odd that this small sister of his who was so accurate in her appraisal of others had not been able to see through Wetherby. Indeed love could be blind. Anyway, he decided he would talk to Nellie about her, and Nellie would agree with him that he must be generous towards her.

He closed his eyes. He had become upset by her visit; he felt very tired, he wanted to sink through the bed and down into the earth, down, down. He'd had this experience a number of times of late. He couldn't understand it. Why hadn't he felt like this during all the battles? But he had, that time on the Menin road just outside Ypres. That was when he had been transferred to the Third. They were making for the Blue Line and were being peppered most of the way by machine-gun fire from the ruined houses, and he had become so tired that he felt his legs were giving out.

But it was on that road he realised that in the last extreme officers and men became as one: there were officers who gave their lives for their men and men who gave their lives for their officers. Never again after this did the ah-lah twang of some of his fellow officers irritate him. Whether the breed of officer he had encountered back home was of a different species he didn't know. Perhaps the simple answer was that when a man was confronted with death his spirit rose and faced it. Death had a way of levelling rank.

It was after the Menin road and the battles that followed in October '17 when they fought through rain and gale, mud and slush, when men from colonels downwards died like flies, and when the subaltern often found himself in command, that the pips began to descend on to his own shoulders . . .

But he was going down again, down, down, he was sinking into the mud. He grabbed at a leg and it came away in his hand. The top was all raw flesh but there was no blood coming from it because it was frozen. Now he was crawling into a hole. It was a big hole, it widened even as he looked at it; there had been water in the bottom which had been soaked up by the bodies heaped there, but those pressed tight against the sides were live. The hole began to spin and he opened his mouth and shouted, yelled, bawled, and all the men scrambled out of the hole, but as they stood up so they toppled back one after the other as an aeroplane came diving towards them, the pilot hanging head down, his face on fire. When he fell among the men he landed on his feet, and he looked young and unscathed and he flung his arms wide and he laughed as he shouted, 'They only gave me days but I've been alive for six weeks and now I've got all eternity!' All eternity. All eternity. All eternity. The heap of men in the middle of the hole got higher, the whirling became faster. A face was pressed close to his; it was the adjutant's. How had he got there? He should have been back at base. He was smiling quietly at him. He liked the adjutant: he had the funniest sense of humour; it was odd though to see him smiling because he never smiled, not when he was being funny. When he came to think of it he had never seen the adjutant smile. But now he was lying on his back smiling.

He was yelling again. His mouth was wide and there was mud pouring into it, it was going down his throat.

'Take it easy. Take it easy.' The curtains were drawn round the bed, the sister was holding him, she had her arms about him, holding him, pressing him to her. He liked that, he liked the feel of her, she was his mother . . . Oh, not his mother, she was Nellie . . . *Nellie. Nellie*.

'It's all right, it's all right, let go now. That's it, that's it, relax, relax. You're quite all right.'

Funny, he thought that it was she who had been holding him. He opened his eyes, then gasped, drawing in a great long draft of clean ward air. There was no mud in his mouth, he was in bed.

'I . . . I . . . I'm sor . . . ry.'

'It's all right, it's all right. There now, go to sleep. There now. There now.'

As something sharp went into his arm he muttered again, 'I'm sorry . . . I'm sorry.'

'Bring two hot water bottles, he's cold.'

God! he was going to cry. No! no! he mustn't cry, not that again. Oh no! no! What was making him want to cry now? Was it because she was being so kind to him? She was usually so correct, so stiff and starchy. Camisole Kate they called her because she had a high bust and the nurses said she wore an old-fashioned camisole. How old was she? Forty? Forty-five? She was being very kind to him. What had happened? He was going down again, but there was no mud now. Thank God! there was no mud now . . . And something else, something else. As a thought struck him he tried to rise and tell her . . . he had been down into the mud again and hadn't seen Slater there. Now that was strange: for the first time he had been in the crater – and Slater hadn't been there.

2

He didn't feel at home in his new surroundings; he was missing Pritchard and Johnson and Thurkel. They had only three legs between them but they had seemed so glad to be alive. The night before he left the three of them had done a form of tap dance in the ward, and even Riley who could only move his head because he had very little else to move, had raised it from the pillow and laughed for the first time since coming into the ward.

And they'd all seemed sorry that he was going. That had given him a nice feeling, a warmth inside. Sister Layton arranged to be the last to say good-bye to him as he entered the ambulance. Putting her head down to him she had said softly, 'Give a thought to Camisole Kate now and again.'

He had looked up into the tight smile and murmured back, 'Oh, Sister! Sister!'

They had been a great bunch, more like a family.

He didn't think he'd ever look upon the crowd here as a family, there were so many of them, both staff and patients.

The hospital was situated in grounds. He hadn't been allowed out in them yet but from what he could see from the window of his cubicle they were full of shambling figures.

His companions on each side of him were captains, one called Fraser, the other Bartlett. They had been in and introduced themselves. Bartlett, besides having lost an arm, was still suffering from the remnants of shellshock; and Fraser, he supposed, was in the same boat, and he never stopped making jokes about his artificial foot. As far as he could gather most of those he had seen were suffering from some kind of war shock. Was that why he had been sent here?

No! no! he hadn't been shellshocked. He felt he had become immune to bursting shells, and until the very last had got the idea in his head that in some odd way he was protected, and he couldn't be blamed for that, he told himself, when men not feet away from him had been blown to smithereens.

The contrast between the patients and the staff was striking. Whereas all the patients seemed to amble, the staff were brisk in step, voice, and manner; another term for it would be hearty. They were mostly nuns and it was likely their usual approach to illness, but it could be wearing. He hankered for the administrations of Bannister, Roper, and Sister Layton.

He was startled when the door was thrust open and a small thickset nun entered.

'Ah! there you are, Major. Waiting patiently for your breakfast, are you? Well now, what about swinging those feet out of bed, putting on your dressing-gown and having it at the window? Look, it's a lovely morning, beautiful. Look at that sun, you can believe that God's in His heaven and all's right with the world. My name's Sister Bernard.'

'. . . Oh my God!'

'What did you say? I heard you, yes I did. Come on.' The sheets were pulled back from him. 'Oh my God!' you said.

He didn't move from the bed. Who did she think she was talking to, a child?

'Now come on, come on. You know what the Chinese say: A journey of a thousand miles begins but with one little step. So come on, make it . . . There you are, that wasn't hard, was it? . . . By! you're a length.' She looked up at him, her peasant-looking face beaming out of the white starched frill encasing it. 'And you know, you get longer lying in bed. Oh yes, you do, it stretches you. I bet they called you Lofty . . . or was it Tich? Some go to other extremes . . . There you are, sit yourself down. Now that wasn't too bad, was it? And don't look at me like that, Major.' Her face now on a level with his poked towards him. 'We're going to see a lot of each other within the next few weeks and I can prophesy one thing here and now, and that is at the end of it you won't have fallen for me.'

Her head now went back on to her shoulders and she let out a high gurgle that might have come from the throat of a young girl, and at this moment the door opened again and another nun entered, and the first turned towards her and said, 'Oh there you are,

Sister Monica. Well, we'll get on with this bed. He insisted on getting up, didn't you, didn't you, Major?' She stuck her finger into his arm and all he could do was to look from one to the other in amazement.

Sister Monica could have been the younger of the two but they were both women in their forties, and he now watched them tackling the bed with such precision and swiftness as he had never seen before.

That done, they both stood before him and Sister Bernard did the talking – the other one hadn't opened her mouth – and now she said, 'When I'm not at you, Sister here will take me place. Don't be deceived by her looks, she's worse than me, we're known as the Toughies. At night you'll have Sister Bridget. But don't think you'll get anywhere with her either, she's worse than us. Well now, your breakfast will be here in a minute, and eat it up, every last crumb.'

Simultaneously, as if they were controlled by one mind, they both nodded at him; then Sister Bernard, bending slightly towards him, poked her face out again and said, 'And don't go complaining to Matron about our manners and treatment because if you do we'll only get worse and give you hell.'

He sat looking towards the closed door for a moment; then his head going back, he laughed, the deep-sounding laughter that on rare occasions in his life released the tension of his body. But he hadn't been indulging in it for more than seconds when the door burst open again and the two black figures rushed in once more.

'Now! now! now!' Sister Bernard had hold of him

by the shoulders, and he put up his hands and caught her arm and patted it even while he was still shaking with laughter, and slowly she released her hold on him. And now as they stood watching him wiping his eyes they began to smile, and then to laugh, and Sister Bernard turned to Sister Monica and said, 'He was just laughing . . . just laughing.'

His face screwed up, his shoulders still shaking, Charlie nodded at them, and Sister Monica, throwing out her arm as if she were about to address a company, exclaimed, 'God's good, we're on our way,' and once again they bounced their heads towards him, then turned and went out while still laughing.

Charlie sat looking out of the window. It had been like a pantomime. How long was it since he laughed like that? Years, years . . . Those two, the Toughies . . . God's good . . . He was in His heaven and all was right with the world, their world.

The smile slid from his face, the laughter lines smoothed out from around his eyes. Was His heaven full of the dead? Had He directed them into His many mansions? How did He manage about housing the officers and the men? Surely after dying together they wouldn't be separated up there?

But he felt better for having laughed, his rare explosive laugh; yet he knew it was going to take some time before he settled down in this place, for it wasn't like a hospital at all, more like an asylum, a place not only for broken bodies but for broken minds . . .

It was the following afternoon. He was sitting in a chair near the window. Captain Bartlett had just gone, and he was feeling exhausted with his constant prattling bonhomie. He understood that Bartlett had been here three months and Fraser four, and while listening to them both he had wondered what they were like when they had first come.

He wasn't like them, was he? Mentally he was all right, except for, well, sort of nightmares; but he only went into those when he felt exhausted.

He'd had a letter from Nellie this morning. She was coming as soon as possible. If only he could see her now, this very minute.

He closed his eyes, then opened them swiftly again and blinked rapidly as Sister Bernard came towards him, saying, 'Let me see, are you tidy and fit to be seen?'

Oh, he wished she wouldn't treat him as a child. He sighed as she tucked the rug around his knees and she came at him quickly, saying, 'Stop your sighing else I won't let her in.'

'Who?' He pulled himself up from the back of the armchair.

'Your visitor.'

'A visitor?'

'Her name's Chapman. She's young, and pretty. And I'm warning you, behave yourself, no hanky-panky.'

He bit on his lip and closed his eyes again and when he opened them Nellie was coming in through the door, and the door had been closed only a second before they put their arms around each other.

'Oh, Nellie! Nellie! Oh, am I glad to see you! Oh, my dearest, my dearest.' He held her away from him for a moment, then pulled her swiftly to him, and when the kiss was ended she laughed and said, 'Look! I've got the cramp bending over like this.'

'Oh! Oh! I'm sorry. Come on, sit down.' He went to rise from the chair, and she stopped him, saying, 'I'm quite able to get a chair for myself, sir.'

Seated close by his side now, she looked into his face as she said, 'You're looking fine, so much better than when I last saw you. Do . . . do you feel better?'

'Oh yes, yes, much better, except' – he gave his head an impatient shake – 'I still get so tired. I can't understand it.'

'Well, you should, you above all people, it's battle fatigue.'

'I suppose so . . . Oh! Nellie. Oh! it's wonderful to see you.' His arms went out again and pulled her close, and as her head rested against his neck he whispered, 'I dream of this all the time, you and me like this, close, closer, never parting. And . . . and we never will, will we?' Again he pressed her from him and looked into her face, and her lips trembled slightly as she said, 'Never, Charlie. If it lies with me, never. You know that.'

'Oh! Nellie, Nellie, I wish I could put into words how I feel about you. And you know, recently I've thought more and more about the wasted years of our youth, I mean my youth. There you were just a few miles from me and I never realised what I was missing. All I want to do now is to get out of here and back there and start all over again, just you and me . . . and oh, I told you in the letter, didn't I, there'll be Betty. But I'll fix her up in some place of her own soon. In the meantime, you won't mind . . . What is it? Why are you looking away? I promise you, dear, it won't be a case of Victoria over again, you won't have to put up . . .'

'It isn't that, Charlie. It isn't that.'

'Then what is it?'

'Oh, nothing, nothing really.'

'It's something about Betty, isn't it?'

He watched her swallow; then she said, 'Well, I . . . I know how she must be feeling, for Wetherby to drop her like that, it must have come as a bombshell.'

'Has he got someone else?'

'Yes, oh yes, and definitely, he went off with Katie Nelson. You remember the Nelsons. They have a farm over Bellingham way. She must be all of ten years older than him. She was the only daughter and her parents are pretty old. You can see the picture, can't you? Apparently Betty didn't know a thing about it until it was all done. Then he wrote to her. It was enough to send any girl round the bend; you can't blame her . . .'

'Oh my God!' Charlie held his brow with his hand. 'It's my fault really. I should have let her have him there during the war. But I knew once he was in I wouldn't get him out, and I couldn't stand him.' He now looked at Nellie and asked, 'How is she taking it? I mean, she wouldn't do anything silly.'

She smiled gently at him as she said, 'Not Betty, not like me, no, no, Charlie, you needn't worry on that score, she's too practical.'

'Oh, I wish I were home.'

She rose from the chair now and, going to the side of the window and looking out, she said, 'They're lovely grounds here.' Then turning to him again, she added, 'You mustn't rush; you'd be no good at all back on the farm the way you are now, you know that. You've got to get your strength up and get some flesh on your bones, and get . . .' She couldn't finish by adding, 'Get your nerves steadied', for one thing he didn't seem to understand was that it wasn't only his body that had been shattered.

'Get what?'

'Well, I meant get yourself well enough to fork hay.'

'I'll be well enough to fork hay, never you worry. It's odd how I longed to get away from that place and now I long to be back. How's the farm looking?'

She blinked, pressed her lips together for a moment while she swallowed, then said, 'Fine, fine, as usual, and I've brought you the evidence of it in there.' She pointed towards a case at the foot of the bed, then added hastily, 'Oh, I forgot. You'll never guess who I saw, and in this very place, today.'

He shook his head and caught at her hand as she sat beside him again.

'Polly.'

'Polly, here?'

'Yes; just as I was going out of the gate. There's a

big new wing over there' – she turned her head towards the window – 'at the far side, and Arthur's there.'

He opened his mouth twice before he could say the name 'Arthur? Why! I thought Arthur was gone.'

'No, no, he's still alive, what's left of him.'

'But . . . but when I saw him on the quay, I think I told you, his legs were gone and his arm; they didn't expect him to last.'

'Well, he has.'

'Good Lord!' He shook his head. 'And . . . and I've never given him a thought all this time except to think, Poor Arthur. Well! well!' He smiled. 'I'll have to go and see him.'

'Yes, he'd like that, I'm sure. I told Polly.'

'Was she surprised that I was here?'

'Yes, very surprised . . . Of course you know Slater's dead, don't you?'

He leant back in the chair. The tiredness was assailing him again. He opened his mouth and gasped for breath; then he said quietly, 'Yes, yes, I heard about it.'

'Polly looked well, quite bonny in fact. But then she was always bonny. You were gone on her at one time, weren't you?' She pushed her face playfully towards him, and he said absent-mindedly, 'Was I?'

She tapped his cheek and brought his gaze on to her as she said, 'You know you were.'

'Yes,' he smiled faintly. 'Yes, I suppose I was. The madness of youth.'

'I was mad in my youth too. I fell in love with a tall,

lanky lad, and my madness didn't fade away, it developed into a mania.' She took his face between her hands now and said softly, 'If you and I, Charlie, were to have nothing more than we've got at this moment I'd still thank God that I've loved you . . . Oh! Charlie, don't cry. Oh my dear, my dearest, please, please don't cry.'

The door opened and Sister Bernard entered carrying a tray laden with tea things and she did not exclaim loudly at the scene before her but, putting the tray down on a side table, she went to the other side of the chair and, lifting Charlie's drooping head, she said briskly, 'Do you the world of good, we don't cry enough. Englishmen are fools, they keep it bottled up.' Now nodding across at Nellie, whose eyes, too, were full of tears, she went on, 'The French and Italians and suchlike, they howl like banshees on the slightest provocation, and they're better for it. Now what you both want is a good cup of tea; I've made it nice and strong.' She indicated the tray with a jerk of her thumb over her shoulder; then looking towards the case at the bottom of the bed, she said, 'I understand he's got a farm, I hope you've brought something worthwhile from it, for in the main it's bread and scrape and so-called jam in here. I suppose we should thank God for that but somehow I can't give praise unless it's due. Well, I'll leave you to pour out the tea.' She nodded her head towards Nellie, and almost without seeming to change its motion she jerked it in Charlie's direction while still speaking to Nellie and said, 'He hates me guts but I don't care,

I'm here for his punishment and I'm going to see that he gets it.' Her lips pressed tight together now, a twinkle deep in her eye, she nodded from one to the other, then marched out.

The door closed, their glances held for a moment before they fell about each other trying to smother their tear-mixed laughter.

3

After the first week which had seemed long and endless the days slipped by unnoticed. He woke up one morning to see the window sill banked with snow; it was winter, he hadn't seemed to take it in before. His time was filled with eating and sleeping and sitting by the window.

As Christmas approached the activity in the hospital heightened and an excitement ran through the place. It was the first Christmas of peace, and on Christmas Day he went for the first time from the narrow confines of the ward to the main dining-room and the Christmas tea party, and he found to his surprise that he enjoyed the change and the company. He also discovered that the two toughies were universally beloved clowns, and that in a way he was lucky to be under their care.

He did not see Nellie over the holidays for she was on duty, and when he did see her he was troubled for during her last two visits he had sensed there was something wrong with her. The only comfort he had was the knowledge that it had nothing to do with her feeling for him. He had probed but to no avail; all he could get out of her was that everything was all right and he hadn't to worry, he had just to get well.

He had made himself ask if she had seen Victoria and she had answered no, but she had heard quite a lot about her and did he want to hear it? When he had replied, 'Is it necessary?' her answer had been, 'That all depends on how you feel about her. If you are still bitter you're bound to think that she's the last one who deserves any happiness. I . . . I understand she is going to marry her one-time Major Smith.'

'Really!' He hadn't been able to cover his surprise and added somewhat cynically, 'He's still going, then?'

'As far as I understand he's a lieutenant-colonel now and he's never been out of England.'

'No? Well there's greater merit due to him that he has survived with her.'

'Oh Charlie!' she had said; 'it isn't like you to be bitter.' And he had answered and truthfully, 'I'm not the same Charlie you once knew, Nellie.'

But there was something wrong with Nellie, something troubling her. Was it her mother? He doubted it; she had said that Florence seemed willing now to countenance their association; the fact that she would eventually be living only a few miles away seemed to have modified her attitude . . .

It wasn't until a day towards the end of January that he found out what was troubling Nellie. Then the earth was ripped from under him once again and he felt that Slater's curse was really on him . . . he was a loser, he had been born a loser and he would die a loser.

It was a bright clear morning; there had been snow but it was almost all gone except for that which lay on high ground. Sister Bernard and Sister Monica were busily making the bed when he said, 'I feel like a walk outside today.'

'Good. Good. Now you're talking.' It was Sister Bernard who answered him. When they were together Sister Monica never opened her mouth. It was, he understood, some part of a rule that was enforced upon them that only one should talk.

'Wrap up well, put a scarf on 'cos that sun is deceptive. Don't think if you go and get pneumonia we're going to look after you because we're not; are we, Sister?'

She nodded across the bed, then answered for Sister Monica who simply smiled at her, saying, 'No, we're not.'

He went to the wardrobe and, taking down his greatcoat, he put it on, and as he buttoned it up he looked towards the two black-robed, furiously working figures, and he addressed Sister Bernard, saying, 'Do you know, Sister, you would have made a splendid sergeant-major. The army lost something in you.'

'Sergeant-major indeed!' She pulled herself up to her small height and, bristling now, she said, 'Who you insulting? I passed the sergeant-major stage years ago; I'd have you know me rank is equal to that of a general. I'm surprised that you haven't noticed it!'

He laughed aloud now, saying, 'I'm surprised too. What do you say, Sister?' He was looking at Sister

Monica now, and Sister Bernard, leaning across the bed again as if waiting for Sister Monica to repeat something, said, 'Cook-general, she says. Well! when your own let you down what do you expect from others? Have you put that scarf on?'

'Yes, I've got it on. Look.' He turned the collar of his coat back, then asked, 'Do you think it would be possible for me to pay a visit to the annexe?'

'I don't see why not. You know someone there?'

'Yes, someone I knew well at one time.'

'You've never mentioned him before . . . why?'

'I . . . I hadn't thought about it.'

'Well' – she turned from him – 'better late than never. Do you know how to get there?'

'I'll find my way.'

'You needn't go out into the grounds at all, you can keep to the corridors all the way. If you get lost ask a policeman.'

As they both giggled at him, he went out.

They were a pair, they were really as good as a music-hall turn. The stage had lost something in them, especially Sister Bernard.

He had to ask his way several times, and when at last he was walking along what seemed an endless corridor, he could feel the change in the atmosphere. The nurses he passed were young. There were young nurses on his block but they seemed of a different type. There were male nurses here too, but they weren't young, at least they weren't under thirty like many of the male staff back on the block.

He came to the end of the corridor and into a large

comfortably furnished hall, with several smaller corridors leading from it. At the far side he saw what he thought to be a notice on the wall, but before he reached half-way across he recognised it was a plaque. On nearing it, he looked at it casually and read: This stone was laid on January 19th, 1914, by John Cramp Esquire whose benevolence has made possible the building of this annexe.

Cramp. Cramp. John Cramp. Yes, the man in the Daimler; the taggerine man, the scrap merchant. Well! Well! And he had done this before he'd made his pile out of the war. Odd that he should have come across the name again. And he remembered the man himself vividly. He was a character.

'Can I help you, sir?' A nurse was smiling up at him.

'I'm . . . I'm wondering if it would be possible to see a Private Benton? . . . I think he's a private.'

'Oh yes, sir, yes, Private Benton. Will you come this way, sir, he's in the day-room.' He was being led along another corridor now. Here wide doorless rooms went off at each side, and he had glimpses of men or what was left of them being lifted from the beds and into wheel-chairs. In one room he saw a patient being laid on a flat trolley face downwards.

Now they were in a large room with a great expanse of polished floor, one wall being made up entirely of huge windows, and everywhere he looked there were men sitting in wheel-chairs; some he saw had legs but no arms. Others arms and legs but their bodies remained motionless. There were faces so scarred that he found he had to turn his gaze away quickly from them. And then he was being led in the direction of a small group of men in the corner of the room near the window.

He knew that heads were turning in his direction, and as he neared the group the chairs spread out.

The nurse said, 'Arthur! you've got a visitor.'

'Oh aye!' The last chair was swung round by one hand, and there he was looking at Arthur, what was left of him, a stump of a body and one arm.

'Charlie!'

Arthur's voice was a mere whisper at first, and then it exploded into almost a yell as he now shouted, *'Charlie!* Why *Charlie*! Polly said you were here. Aw, man!' The hand was thrust out towards him and he was gripping it; then before he could speak Arthur was addressing the half-dozen men who had made up the group and was crying at them, 'This is Charlie, the fellow I told you about on the farm, he was me boss but we were like mates . . . Eeh! what am I sayin'?' Arthur now pulled his hand away and flapped it towards Charlie. 'You'll have me court-martialled for talkin' like this, forgettin' meself.' His voice dropped now and he stared up into Charlie's face for a moment in silence before he said, 'Sit down, won't you, Charlie?'

Charlie sat down and, speaking for the first time and with a tremor in his voice, he said, 'It's good to see you, Arthur.'

'And you. Charlie. Ech! and a major. Who would have believed it!'

'Yes, who would have believed it.'

'Oh, no offence, man. You remember me sayin' to you that day, why didn't you put in for an officer. Did you take me advice?'

'No, I'm afraid I didn't, Arthur; they . . . they just sprung it on me.'

'They knew good stuff when they saw it.'

'Huh!' Charlie turned his head to the side; then casting his eyes about him and noticing that the men were still looking at him, he said, 'Nice ward this . . . the whole annexe.'

'Oh aye. Aye, they do us proud. Well' – Arthur now leant towards him – 'they owe us somethin', don't they, and they're payin' us in the only way they can.'

'Yes, yes, I suppose so.'

'How are things with you, Charlie? I heard you were badly knocked up, but I see they've left you your limbs, and that's something.'

Yes, it was certainly something. Having been riddled with shrapnel, he thought he had come off badly, but these poor devils in here, God! why did they go on? Yet the atmosphere was cheerful, bright, you could even say happy. But, of course, this was the stiff upper lip attitude, putting a face on things. He wouldn't like to be inside one of their minds at night.

He answered Arthur now saying, 'Oh, I got some shrapnel here and there.'

'Oh aye . . . Have they got it all out?'

'Well, not quite, so I understand; they've had a few goes but it roams you know.'

'Aye, shrapnel has a habit of doing that . . . Nurse!' Arthur hailed a young nurse who was passing and as she came towards him he said, 'Bet you didn't know I had a major for a friend?'

'How do you do, Major?' She inclined her head towards him, smiling widely.

He had risen to his feet and he answered, 'How do you do?'

'We were brought up together, would you believe that?'

'I believe everything you tell me, Arthur.'

'Then do you believe I love you?' He had now placed his only hand on his heart and with his face poked towards her and in what he imagined to be dramatic tones he said, 'An' the morrow I go to Sir Humphrey to ask him for your hand.'

'And you'll get mine across your ear-hole if you don't behave.' She had come close to his side now and she caught hold of his hand and, looking across at Charlie, she said, 'He's impossible, this friend of yours, Major; he's a philanderer, no girl is safe where he is.' She now patted Arthur's cheek, and as she made to go away he said, still in a bantering tone, 'Don't leave me, love.'

She was about to make a jocular rejoinder when a strange sound came from the other side of the room and she said quickly, 'Oh dear me! I've got to go. I can see you'll be needed later on, Arthur.' She nodded at him, and he nodded back at her now in an ordinary fashion, and when she had left them he muttered below his breath, 'One of the chaps, he gets depressed like, howls like a banshee. I make him laugh.' He grinned at Charlie now. 'I make 'em all laugh. Funny, isn't it?'

Yes, yes, it was funny. This wasn't the Arthur he remembered. Less than half of him remained, yet in that half he had grown another personality. He remembered the dour, ignorant boy that used to irritate him, he remembered the youth who became a bundle of nerves through fear instilled by Slater. But those people were no more, the war had cut him into bits, yet had left him with a new character, a different character, a strong character. It was a fantastic thought but nevertheless true, he was sure, that Arthur was happier now than he had been in his life before. He had no responsibility, he was being cared for by pretty nurses; he was sure of good food and warmth, and he hadn't to worry about the wherewithal to provide them; what was more, this Arthur was liked as the other Arthur, the young Arthur, never was.

He was now leaning towards him whispering, 'You heard Slater got it?'

He felt the old desire to open his mouth and gasp for air, but he pressed his lips together tightly before saying, 'Yes, yes, I heard.'

'Died bravely on the field of battle. By God! that wouldn't have happened if I'd come across him. An' I mean that, Charlie, I do. That was one thing I prayed for, to come across him. God! he led me hell. An' you had a taste of him an' all, hadn't you?'

'Yes, yes, I had a taste of him.'

'Couldn't understand our Polly; she was so upset. She got to like him, man, and when he lost his stripes through her she wanted to pin medals on him herself.'

'Lost the stripes through her, how do you mean?'

'Oh well, she was about to have the third bairn and things went a bit wrong and he thought she was a gonner and he wouldn't leave her. He told the doctor he was on leave and he stayed by her for three days, four I think, before they came and took him. I wish I'd been there when they stripped him down. Of course you can't say that to her. She talks about him as if he were a bloody hero.' He paused now, then ended, 'Funny, what the war's done to us lot, isn't it, Charlie?'

'Yes, indeed, Arthur.'

'How's things with you, Charlie, I mean you happy like?'

'Well, you could say yes and no, Arthur. Victoria and I are getting divorced.'

'No! No, man! Is . . . is that why you've sold up the farm?'

'What!'

'I said is that why you've sold up the farm and things?'

'Sold the farm? I haven't sold the farm.'

Arthur blinked his eyes, then looked down towards the blanket sagging from his waist, and he said now, 'Well, Polly must have got it wrong. She heard a rumour, likely it was only a rumour, but she heard that you were selling up and likely going to Australia or some such place as that. She thought it was because you were in a bad way and wouldn't be able to manage any more.'

His mouth was open, he was drawing in great draughts of air. *No! No!* He yelled at himself he had to keep steady; there was something afoot that he must see into, and now, right now.

He wasn't aware that he had risen from the chair but he was bending over Arthur now, saying, 'Look, Arthur, I'll be back, but there's something I've got to see to.'

'Have I said something wrong, Charlie, I mean startled you in some way?'

'Yes, I suppose so, Arthur. There's something not right over there. I . . . I have no intention of selling the farm.'

'No!'

'No, none whatever. I'll be back, Arthur. I'll be back.' He squeezed the hand held out to him, then turned and hurried down the ward.

'You're in no fit state to drive a car, Major.'

'Then I can take a taxi.'

Doctor Arlet looked across his desk at the tall, solemn-faced figure before him and he closed his eyes for a moment and shook his head as he said, 'I think you know the position as well as I do, Major, any extra physical activity, over-excitement at least for the present . . .'

'I am aware of all that, Doctor.'

'Then why take unnecessary risks?'

'Doctor, I am being given to understand that my farm is being sold up, I want to know what it is all about. I left my sister in charge. The farm is my only means of livelihood, that is if I'm given the opportunity to work it.'

'Why don't you get your solicitor, or better still your friend, Miss . . . Miss—' He looked about him as if searching for a name, until Charlie said, 'Chapman.'

'Yes, Miss Chapman. Now she could go out there . . .'

'She lives out there and I'm now under the impression that she knows more about it than she said, her intention being not to worry me. Now, doctor, whatever way I get out there I'm going, and the frustration of being kept here is going to be more detrimental than my driving a car or sitting in a taxi.'

'I'm . . . I'm not worried about the journey out there, Major.' The doctor's voice was tight now. 'What I am worried about is your reaction to whatever situation you find out there. Doctor Morgan's report said . . .'

Charlie now put his hand to the side of his head as if he were shutting off his hearing and he said, 'I know, doctor, only too well Doctor Morgan's opinion, and I respect it, and also from where I'm standing if this thing inside here moves to the right then I won't need to worry any more about the farm or anything else. But there's a fifty-fifty chance it will give me a break and move to the left, or even north or south, and if that should happen then I'd be pleased to let you all get at it and hoick it out.'

The use of the dialect word brought a twisted smile to Doctor Arlet's mouth, and he said on a sigh, 'Well I won't say I'll wash my hands of you, but I'll say, for your own sake, go careful, both physically and mentally. Now'– he rose from his seat – 'a taxi I think would be the best bet, although it's going to cost you a pretty penny to get out there.'

'I think I'll just about manage it.'

'All right. I suppose you'll have to stay overnight but I'll expect you back tomorrow, mind. Is that a promise?'

'That's a promise.'

He left the taxi on the main road. The driver, looking at him, said, 'Will you be all right, sir?'

'Yes, I'll be all right.'

'Have you far to walk?'

'A couple of miles or so.'

'Do you think you'll manage it?'

'Oh yes, I'll manage it. If I can't walk I'll slide; the sun's forgotten to come round this way.' He indicated the frost-tipped ridges of the fields and the stiff grass.

As he left the road and walked down the bridle path he knew that the taxi driver was still watching and he thought, I must look awful, like death.

It was a few minutes after he heard the taxi start that he stopped and looked about him. The sky was lying low on the hills, the light was grey, yet let the sun appear and the sky would be pushed back and the light would be white and clear. He drew in great draughts of air. If it wasn't for the anxiety within him he'd feel like celebrating his return by leaping over the walls ahead and running across the fields. But would he ever run across the fields again? No mental excitement, no physical exertion, they said. One might as well be dead.

When he came to the copse he was out of breath and not a little fearful. What would he say to Betty? Or what would she say to him? That was more to the point. He hadn't seen her since her visit to the hospital. He'd had two letters from her since, both saying that she was too busy to get away. But that was before Christmas. He hadn't questioned her not visiting him since he had been brought North again. That was Betty, she wasn't given to sentimental sympathy, and so over the weeks her absence hadn't troubled him. Nellie had come and that was all that mattered. Only now was he telling himself that it was strange that Betty hadn't once come to visit him over the past weeks.

The change struck him immediately he left the copse. It was in the silence and the absence of any animals. The cows would be inside but you could always see sheep sprinkled over the hills yonder. The only sound that came to him was from the burn. It was running high. His step slowed as he approached the gap in the stone wall; then he was in the middle of the yard gazing about him. The place was deserted. Was he dreaming? There was no one here, nothing. His mouth opened wide, he gasped at the air, then took his gloved doubled fist and pressed it against his ribs as he warned himself to go steady. He looked first towards the cowsheds, then turned his head and looked towards the house, then again towards the cowsheds.

Now he was in the cowsheds and being unable to believe what his eyes were seeing. The stalls were empty, dry; they had been cleaned out. He turned swiftly about and just stopped himself from running by gripping the stanchion of the door, and as he leant against it for a moment the action pushed his hat on to one side and over one eye, and the detached part of his mind saw himself as a pantomime major, a drunken pantomime major, for now he staggered somewhat as he walked back into the yard.

Straightening his cap, he again looked about him, and as his eyes came to rest on the back door a strange fear assailed him as to what he might find if he opened it, and he turned away from it and went now into the barn. The bottom was swept almost clean, a few implements only lay scattered around. He raised his eyes to the upper platform. That too was bare except for some broken bales of hay.

As if in a nightmare he was walking through the alleyway, and now he was on the cinder path, at least where it had been, for now a rough stone path led down to the cottage and the burn, the work of the German prisoners he supposed. He looked over the hedge to the field where the hen crees stood. The doors were swinging open, there was not a fowl to be seen. To the right lay the pigsties. No echo of a grunt came from them.

He had to have support, so he leant back against the

wall of the byres and, his head drooping, he looked down at his feet, and the slab of stone on which he was standing disappeared and he saw his feet were deep in the cinders, and there coming along the path, was a red-headed youth, and when he stopped he grinned at him and said, 'You never thought you'd get a pip on your own, now did you, 'cos as I said you're a born loser. You lost the lass you loved, you married a whore, you even lost yourself and your bloody platoon; and now you've lost your farm. I always said you were a loser, didn't I? You've only got one more thing to lose and when that bit of shrapnel moves . . .'

He was brought from the wall as if he had been shot. His hand flashed from his side where his holster used to lie, and now it was pointing at eye level straight in front of him. He twisted round as if a hand had spun him. His mouth was wide open, he was gasping for air, his eyes were closed.

'Stop it!

'Pull up!'

He was leaning against the wall again but bent over now and about to vomit.

He stood like this for some minutes before straightening up, then, after wiping his mouth he went through the alleyway again and into the yard and walked towards the kitchen door. He put his hand on the knob and pushed but it didn't give way. Angrily now, he thrust his body against it but without effect; the door was firmly bolted on the inside. He knew that it had strong bolts but he didn't remember them ever having been used in his time.

He went to the kitchen window and peered in. His hands to each side of his face, he gazed in amazement at the bareness of it. Even the long white wooden table was no longer there.

Like someone indeed drunk, he now made his way to the front of the house, and it was the sitting-room window he first looked through. The room was as bare as it had been when it was first constructed.

He was standing now gripping the knob of the front door. He didn't expect the door to be unlocked and it wasn't. Again he was leaning for support, and now like a child he spoke aloud, one single word 'Why?' Then again, louder this time, '*Why?*'

And where was everybody? This great silence.

As a strange thought entered his mind his head fell back on his shoulders and he looked up into the sky. Was this death? Had he already died? Had his life ceased with the shock of Arthur's words? And was the farm really peopled? Was the farm still alive and it was only he who couldn't see it?

When he tore off his glove and brought his hand down sharp on to one side of the ornamental spikes that supported the foot scraper to the side of the door he knew that he was still alive.

He was walking away from the house now towards the cottages. He didn't hope to find anyone there, yet as he rounded the bend and looked up the hill he stopped in his tracks. There was smoke coming out of one chimney. Again he checked himself from running, saying, 'Take it easy. Take it easy.'

It was some minutes before his knock on the door was answered, and when it was opened there stood Arnold in his bare feet, his linings showing under an old coat. The old man's mouth opened wide, but nothing came forth, until Charlie had stepped into the room and the door was closed, and then he said, 'My God! sir, am . . . am I glad to see you! Oh my God! sir, I am, I am that at this minute.'

It was plain to Charlie that the cowman was suffering from a severe cold and he said to him immediately, 'Get . . . get back into bed, Arnold.' He pointed to the bed that was drawn up to the side of the fire, but Arnold didn't immediately get back into bed, he stared up into Charlie's face, and now, the tears spurting from his eyes, he muttered, 'God! sir, I never thought I'd live to see the day, but . . . but you're back, you're back. Sit down, sir, sit down.'

'You get back into bed, Arnold, I'll sit down.'

When Arnold had got into bed, Charlie took a seat by the side of the fire and they sat looking at each other for a moment before Charlie said, 'What's happened, Arnold? I . . . I thought the world had stopped going mad when the war finished, but down there' – he motioned towards the door – 'I can't take it in. Where is she?'

'Gone, sir. And . . . and we never expected to see you again, sir, at least' – he lowered his eyes away – 'we didn't at first. We did everything she said, you see, because it was supposed to be authorised by you.'

'The clearance of the farm?'

'Aye, sir, aye; she had a written statement. She had been down to see you in the South and . . . and when she came back she said you were in a very bad state and would never work again, I mean, not even to manage. She said, well, sir, she sort of gave us the idea that besides you being broken up in body your . . . your mind had gone, shellshock, she said.'

Charlie's head drooped on to his chest for a moment and as a shiver ran through his body he held out his hands towards the blazing fire, and Arnold went on, 'Everybody around was sorry for her, so they helped: Regan took most of the cattle, they didn't go to market, the sheep did; but the pigs and hens and the rest of the livestock, everybody around bought privately.'

'The house?'

'Oh, the house. Every stick was carted away to auction, and we, me and Mary, well, we took everything, sort of as being your wish, until, well, until she didn't talk of selling the farm itself, the land. I asked her about it and she said that would be seen to later. I know now she'd have to have gone to your solicitor, sir, and he would have wanted your word for it and deeds and things. I guessed something was wrong before she left. I smelt a rat, so did Mary, but it was all done so quickly, like lightnin', so to speak. She had got every animal off this farm within a week, and the furniture was out of the house, well, within ten days. When I asked her where she was going she said . . . she said she was going to take you to Australia as soon as you were well enough. But somehow I didn't believe her; neither did Mary. It was the way she went on like as if she wasn't right in the head.'

'Not right in the head?' It was a quiet question, but weighed with disbelief for he could never imagine anyone thinking that his level-headed little sister could do anything that would stamp her as not right in the head.

'Well, sir, one morning as Mary went in she heard a banging, and there was Miss Betty standing kicking the green-baized door, kicking it like mad she was, Mary said, like someone demented. Anyway, as I said, I smelt a rat and I went across to Mrs Chapman, her being your mother-in-law like, although I had heard rumours that you and your missis weren't . . . well, sir, hitting it off and there was a separation. But anyway, she was the only one I could go to for advice, and she said right out it was no use getting in touch with your missis, but what she did do was write to Miss Nellie, and Miss Nellie came out like a shot and she tackled Miss Betty, and there was high jinks in the house. They went at each other like two cats, Mary said. Miss Nellie threatened to bring the police, but Miss Betty said she had your written authority to sell everything, and she waved a paper at her. Also she said that she was entitled to what she had taken.'

Arnold now lifted up a cup from the floor and sipped at it before he went on, 'Miss Nellie came up here after and when I asked her if you were capable of tackling the business she said that was the point, at the moment you mustn't be disturbed. She was in a state; she sat there crying. Anyway, sir, Miss Betty

371

left the next morning an' she put a letter into me hand and said to me that when you came back, that's if you did, I was to give it you. 'Twas then I knew she had done a terrible thing to you, an' quite innocently you had given her the power to do it, but as I said to Mary you've still got the buildings and the land, you can start again.'

There followed a long silence. The room was stuffy; he wanted air, he wanted to open his mouth and draw in great draughts of air; he also wanted to open his mouth and scream as he had heard men scream so often in agony . . . Start again! He'd never be able to start again. For one thing, he hadn't the money, for if she had cleared the farm she would have cleared the bank at the same time. And even if he had the money where would he get the strength?

It was a great wonder the shrapnel hadn't moved already.

He looked at Arnold now and said, 'May I have the letter?'

'Behind the clock, sir.' Arnold nodded towards the mantelpiece, and Charlie rose to his feet and took the letter from behind the clock; then sitting down again he looked at it. Although it was sealed he knew by the crumpled envelope that it had already been steamed open, but what did that matter. Having taken the double sheet of paper out of the envelope he began to read it. The letter had no heading, it began simply:

'If the shock hasn't already killed you, you'll be

reading this. What I've taken is only my just right, nobody but you would have expected me to live in that house under another of the Chapmans because the place, both the house and the farm, are virtually mine. My father might have made it but it was I who kept it going, and after working like a black all during the war, to be told by you that I'd be taken care of was just too much. But it wasn't only that, it was the fact that you had the nerve to tell me that you intended to bring another Chapman in there. Well, see how she reacts when she knows she'll have to start and build a home from scratch . . . on nothing!

Most of the furniture in the place was what Mother bought with her own money and it should have come to me; but what happened when she died? The same as when Father died, not a penny not a stick was I left. Well, I feel no compunction in taking what I rightly feel to be mine. You'll likely be advised to take me to court. Well, you can do so if you can find me, but knowing you, you won't take that step, you'll just hide your head in the sand as always.

We never liked each other so I'm not going to end with any fond farewells, yet in a way I feel sorry for you for you were born a loser. It has always amazed me how you ever became commissioned, it was like a fluke. Well, I suppose everybody is allowed one break. That's how I see it and I'm giving it to myself, for nobody else will.

Betty.'

The letter was so characteristic of his sister, it was as if she had been sitting opposite him and talking at him.

'She's a wicked woman, sir, a hard wicked woman. There's never been a happy moment on the place since you left. What do you think you'll do, sir?'

Charlie leant back in his chair and looked up at the low smoked-dyed ceiling before he said flatly and slowly, 'I haven't the slightest idea, Arnold.'

As he finished speaking there was a sound of footsteps coming along the flags outside the cottages and Arnold said, 'That'll be Mary, she's been over to the Chapmans. Mrs Chapman is taking her on, mornings like, it helps.'

However, it wasn't Mary who opened the door without knocking but Nellie. She almost burst into the room, then held her breath for a moment as she looked across at Charlie.

Slowly now she closed the door, then came to his side and, taking his hand, said, 'Oh my dear! you had to find out some time, but I've nearly been out of my mind. Doctor Arlet's secretary phoned me. I . . . I seem to have run all the way.' She now turned her face towards Arnold and said, 'You're looking a bit better, Arnold.'

'Yes, miss, yes, I'm feeling much better.'

'Mary will be over presently; I called in home, then rode over.' The last part of her remark was addressed to Charlie and he nodded at her before getting to his feet, and now she took his arm, saying gently, 'Come on,' and looking over her shoulder towards Arnold she added, 'We'll be back. We'll be back, Arnold.'

Arnold merely nodded and watched them go out.

Neither of them spoke until they were entering the yard again and then Nellie said, 'I . . . I was afraid to tell you but I should have; it would have been better than getting a shock like this.'

He stopped and, looking down at her, asked quietly, 'Why should this happen to me, Nellie?' There was no whine in the question, it was more in the nature of a statement explaining that everything that happened to him was negative, everything.

She brought his hand tight into the fold of her arm as she answered, 'These kind of things always happen to nice people, Charlie, easygoing, kind, nice people, they never happen to the smart-Alicks, the rogues, the cheats, or the wily ones, for instance, to your father or mine. But you are different, Charlie, and—' Her lips trembled and pressed together for a moment before she continued, 'And that's why I love you, because you're so different.'

He made no reply, he just stared at her without speaking, then turned about and walked into the yard where again, looking about him, he asked, 'What am I going to do, Nellie?'

'We'll find a way; I've thought it all out.'

His head came round quickly towards her and although he didn't speak there was a look of resentment on his face. She had thought it all out, he was to be managed again, manoeuvred by another woman.

'Come in the barn and sit down,' she said softly; 'I want to talk to you.'

When they reached the barn she glanced around but there was nothing to sit on, and simultaneously it seemed their eyes lifted to the platform above on which were scattered the broken bales of hay, and she now smiled at him as she said, 'Can you risk going up into the loft with me for the second time?'

There was no answering smile on his face but he touched her cheek, then indicated that she should go up the ladder.

When a few minutes later they were sitting side by side on the straw she said quietly, 'I haven't been idle all these weeks. First thing I'd like you to know is I'm . . . I'm finished, my discharge is through.'

'Good. Good.' There was no sound of enthusiasm in his voice but she didn't seem to appear to notice for she went on, 'And I've made arrangements to sell my house. It'll bring a good price, it's got three sitting tenants and an empty flat. And added to that I have a nice little bit Aunty left me, together with what I've saved from my earnings. Now I reckon this will give us a start both outside and inside the house, and then . . .'

'Be quiet! Nellie. Don't be silly. Don't talk rot. You know I couldn't start again on your money.'

'Now! now! Charlie MacFell, don't you come the English gentleman with me.' Here was the old Nellie talking. 'What do you think you're going to do with your life? You've got to have work, some kind of work, everybody has. And you've got more than most to start with; you've got land and a farmhouse and buildings, all you need is stock, and I'm going to buy that stock whether you like it or not. *We're* going to buy that stock because what I have is yours, Charlie.' Her voice lowered now. 'You won't be able to stop me no matter what you say . . . And don't try, Charlie. Oh, please don't try.'

Slowly he turned and looked at her and, taking her hands within his, he said, 'You remember Slater?'

'Yes . . . Ginger, the one that became a sergeant and put you through it.'

'The same. Well, he told me years ago that I was a loser, and I didn't believe him, and the minute before he died he again told me I was a loser, and still I didn't believe him, but I do today because Betty has proved it.'

'Oh! Charlie. Charlie. You're not, you're not . . . you're just easygoing and quiet and . . .'

'Shut up, Nellie, and listen to me.' He shook the hands within his. 'There's some things you know about me but there's a lot you don't. I'm not easy-going and quiet. I am lazy and weak-willed and vindictive . . . Nellie, I shot Slater dead. Do you hear? I shot him when he was practically defenceless. He had a gun but he wouldn't have used it on me, he just used his tongue, and I took my revolver and at point-blank range I fired into him.'

When he felt her hands jerk within his, he said, 'Yes, I know how you feel, you're shocked, this isn't what the easy-going, soft Charlie would do, it isn't what any self-respecting officer would do, but I did it, Nellie. *I did it.*'

Her lips were trembling when she said, 'Then there

must have been a good reason, Charlie.'

'Yes, I suppose in a way there was, but as I see it now not enough reason to shoot a man dead. I should have left that to the Germans.'

'Then . . . then why did you do it?'

He still held on to her hands, while keeping his face turned away from her, and he looked down on to the floor of the barn and out into the yard, and in his mind's eye he was going through the alleyway and on to the cinder path. He saw himself standing there again watching his father draw blood from the skinny undersized red-headed boy. He saw the thin body bouncing on the cinders. He closed his eyes before turning his head once again towards her and saying, 'It all started out there on the cinder path.'

'The cinder path? You mean the road that runs down to the burn?'

'The same.'

'What has that got to do with it?'

'Everything, everything.'

Now in a quiet resigned tone he went on to tell her about young Polly and big Polly and the outcome of his father's decision to introduce him into manhood. He took her through the years of blackmail both he and Arthur suffered at the hands of Slater, then the long agony of his term under Slater, and how it was ended by being given a commission.

The only time he stumbled in the telling was when he described why he had been given a commission, and when he came to the scene in the trenches his voice faltered as he ended, 'The humiliation was too great, Nellie. I . . . I thought I had achieved something, I was a lieutenant in command of men whom I knew respected me, and then he took the ground from under my feet more surely than any shell could have done when he told me my appointment had been rigged. And what was worse, I knew that every word he said was true and that I'd known it from the beginning, but the truth was too much for me . . . The most frightening thing in life, Nellie, is to come face to face with yourself, and in that moment I couldn't bear it, and so I fired.'

'Oh! Charlie. Charlie!' Her arms were around him, her lips were covering his face, his brow, his eyes, his cheeks, and when they came direct on his mouth she held him tightly, so tightly that as they had done once before they overbalanced and fell on to the straw, and all the while she was muttering, 'Oh! Charlie. Charlie!'

'Nellie! Nellie!'

Their faces were wet, their tears were mingling.

'Oh! Nellie. Nellie!'

He had been warned, no mental excitement, no real physical exertion, if it moved to the right!

'Oh! Nellie, my love, my love.'

It would be a good way to die. Oh! Nellie, my Nellie.

He was loving a woman, really loving a woman; he was not struggling with a tigress, he was the master, the man, and he was loving a woman, his woman. 'Nellie! Nellie! *Nellie ! Oh Nellie !'*

He had climbed the mountain and the sky was still

high above him. He reached up into it and embraced the ecstasy and at the height of heights he was pierced through with pain. It came and went like the prick of a needle, but he experienced it, and he was conscious that he experienced it.

He came down from the mountain bearing her in his arms and together they lay down on the straw.

Still clinging close, they lay in the great silence of peace and fulfilment and stared at each other.

He had killed his enemy, he had loved a woman, really loved a woman for the first time in his life, and death had moved in him but had taken a turn to the left. What more could a man want to begin again?

THE END

THE HOUSE OF WOMEN
by Catherine Cookson

Emma Funnell is the matriarch of Bramble House, built for her as a wedding gift. Now, in 1968, she is in her seventies, with the avowed intent of living to be a hundred. And, as she has always done, she continues to rule the roost, for apart from herself three generations of the Funnell family live in the house – all of them women.

There is widowed daughter Victoria, increasingly a hypochondriac, granddaughter Lizzie, who bears the brunt of running the house, as well as enduring a loveless marriage to Len Hammond; and Peggy, her sixteen-year-old daughter, now trying to find the courage to drop the bombshell of her pregnancy into their midst.

This explosive situation provides the springboard for a powerful and absorbing novel that explores, over a period of fifteen years, all that fate holds in store for the dwellers in *The House of Women*, reaching its climax with a frank confrontation of a major social issue of today.

'The author's grip on the novel never flags . . . her crown rests assured'
Sunday Times

0 552 13303 5

THE RAG NYMPH
by Catherine Cookson

In the heat of a late June afternoon in 1854, abandoned by a panic-stricken mother in an all-too-obvious flight from the law, Millie Forester burst into Aggie Winkowski's life like a bolt from the blue. Aggie, who was known hereabouts as 'Raggie Aggie', for trading in rags and old clothes was her long-established business, knew well enough the dangers waiting for such a strikingly pretty girl left alone in this rough and vice-ridden quarter and could see nothing for it, other than to take her in.

But what began as a compassionate expediency led to the establishment of a new relationship that would grow and deepen, moulding Millie's destiny and giving new meaning to the life of Aggie Winkowski.

Millie Forester's advance through the coming years to the threshold of womanhood is the core of *The Rag Nymph*, as gripping and socially concerned an historical novel as Catherine Cookson has ever written. Her superb skills of narrative and characterization provide a spectrum of the good and evil of the Victorian era, frankly confronting the terrible menace of child corruption, which remains a constant issue in our own time.

0 552 13683 2

THE YEAR OF THE VIRGINS
by Catherine Cookson

It had never been the best of marriages and over recent years it had become effectively a marriage in name and outward appearance only. Yet, in the autumn of 1960, Winifred and Daniel Coulson presented an acceptable façade to the outside world, for Daniel had prospered sufficiently to allow them to live at Wearcill House, a mansion situated in the most favoured outskirts of the Tyneside town of Fellburn.

Of their children, it was Donald on whom Winifred doted to the point of obsession, and now he was to be married, Winifred's prime concern was whether Donald was entering wedlock with an unbesmirched purity of body and spirit, for amidst the strange workings of her mind much earlier conceptions of morality and the teachings of the church held sway.

There was something potentially explosive just below the surface of life at Wearcill House, but when that explosion came it was in a totally unforeseeable and devastating form, plunging the Coulsons into an excoriating series of crises out of which would come both good and evil, as well as the true significance of the year of the virgins.

'The power and mastery are astonishing'
Elizabeth Buchan, *Sunday Times*

0 552 13247 0

A SELECTION OF OTHER CATHERINE COOKSON
TITLES AVAILABLE FROM CORGI BOOKS

THE PRICES SHOWN BELOW WERE CORRECT AT THE TIME OF GOING
TO PRESS. HOWEVER TRANSWORLD PUBLISHERS RESERVE THE RIGHT
TO SHOW NEW PRICES ON COVERS WHICH MAY DIFFER FROM THOSE
PREVIOUSLY ADVERTISED IN THE TEXT OR ELSEWHERE.

☐	13576 3	THE BLACK CANDLE	£5.99
☐	12473 7	THE BLACK VELVET GOWN	£5.99
☐	14063 5	COLOUR BLIND	£4.99
☐	12476 1	THE CULTURED HANDMAIDEN	£4.99
☐	12551 2	A DINNER OF HERBS	£5.99
☐	14066 X	THE DWELLING PLACE	£4.99
☐	14068 6	FEATHERS IN THE FIRE	£4.99
☐	14069 4	FENWICK HOUSES	£4.99
☐	10450 7	THE GAMBLING MAN	£4.99
☐	13716 2	THE GARMENT	£4.99
☐	13621 2	THE GILLYVORS	£4.99
☐	14071 6	THE GLASS VIRGIN	£4.99
☐	12608 X	GOODBYE HAMILTON	£4.99
☐	12451 6	HAMILTON	£4.99
☐	12789 2	HAROLD	£4.99
☐	13300 0	THE HARROGATE SECRET	£4.99
☐	13303 5	THE HOUSE OF WOMEN	£4.99
☐	10267 9	THE INVISIBLE CORD	£4.99
☐	14090 2	THE INVITATION	£4.99
☐	14091 0	KATE HANNIGAN	£4.99
☐	14092 9	KATIE MULHOLLAND	£5.99
☐	14078 3	THE LONG CORRIDOR	£4.99
☐	13684 0	THE MALTESE ANGEL	£4.99
☐	14102 X	THE MAN WHO CRIED	£3.99
☐	14085 6	THE MENAGERIE	£4.99
☐	12524 5	THE MOTH	£4.99
☐	13302 7	MY BELOVED SON	£5.99
☐	13088 5	THE PARSON'S DAUGHTER	£5.99
☐	14073 2	PURE AS THE LILY	£4.99
☐	13683 2	THE RAG NYMPH	£4.99
☐	14075 9	THE ROUND TOWER	£4.99
☐	10541 4	THE SLOW AWAKENING	£4.99
☐	10630 5	THE TIDE OF LIFE	£5.99
☐	14076 7	THE UNBAITED TRAP	£4.99
☐	12368 4	THE WHIP	£4.99
☐	13577 1	THE WINGLESS BIRD	£5.99
☐	13247 0	THE YEAR OF THE VIRGINS	£4.99

All Transworld titles are available by post from:

Book Service By Post, PO Box 29, Douglas, Isle of Man IM99 1BQ

Credit cards accepted. Please telephone 01624 675137, fax 01624 670923 or
Internet http://www.bookpost.co.uk for details.

Please allow £0.75 per book for post and packing in UK.
Overseas customers allow £1.00 per book for post and packing.